Children's Literature
Volume 30

Founder and Senior Editor: Francelia Butler (1913–98)

Editor-in-Chief: R. H. W. Dillard

Editors: Elizabeth Lennox Keyser and Julie Pfeiffer

Editorial Assistant: Lisa J. Radcliff

Book Review Editor: Christine Doyle

Advisory Board: Janice M. Alberghene, Ruth B. Bottigheimer, Beverly Lyon Clark, Margaret Higonnet, U. C. Knoepflmacher, Alison Lurie, Roderick McGillis, Mitzi Myers, J. D. Stahl (representing the ChLA), Albert J. Solnit, M.D.

Consultants for Volume 30: Yvonne Alderman, Brian Attebery, Phyllis Bixler, Stephen Canham, Beverly Lyon Clark, Paula Connolly, Paula Feldman, Richard Flynn, Elizabeth Goodenough, Tina Hanlon, Margaret Higonnet, Nancy Huse, Kenneth Kidd, Fern Kory, Jean Marsden, James McGavran, Roderick McGillis, Claudia Mills, Claudia Nelson, Perry Nodelman, Kathy Piehl, Mavis Reimer, Barbara Rosen, David Russell, Donelle Ruwe, Sharon Scapple, Carolyn Sigler, J. D. Stahl, Morag Styles, Jan Susina, Tom Travisano, Roberta Seelinger Trites, Naomi Wood, Jack Zipes

The editors gratefully acknowledge support from Hollins University.

Volume 30

Annual of
The Modern Language Association
Division on Children's Literature
and The Children's Literature
Association

Yale University Press

New Haven and London

2002

Children's Literature

Manuscripts submitted should conform to the style in this issue. An original on non-erasable bond with a self-addressed envelope, and return postage, or submission as an e-mail attachment (MS Word) are requested. Yale University Press requires double-spacing throughout text and notes as well as unjustified margins. Writers of accepted manuscripts should be prepared to submit final versions of their essays on computer disk in Word 97 or Rich Text Format.

Editorial correspondence should be addressed to The Editors, *Children's Literature,* Hollins University, P.O. Box 9677, Roanoke, VA 24020 or to child.lit@hollins.edu

Volumes 1–7 of *Children's Literature* can be obtained directly from Susan Wandell, The Children's Literature Foundation, P.O. Box 94, Windham Center, CT 06280. Volumes 8–28 can be obtained from Yale University Press, P.O. Box 209040, New Haven, CT 06520-9040, or from Yale University Press, 23 Pond Street, Hampstead, London NW3 2PN, England.

Set in Baskerville type by Tseng Information Systems, Inc., Durham, N.C.
Printed in the United States of America by Vail-Ballou Press, Binghamton, N.Y.

Library of Congress catalog card number: 79-66588
ISBN: 0-300-09489-2 (cloth); 0-300-09490-6 (pbk.); ISSN 0092-8208

A catalogue record for this book is available from the British Library.

The paper in this book meets the guidelines for permanence and durability of the Committee on Production Guidelines for Book Longevity of the Council on Library Resources.

10   9   8   7   6   5   4   3   2   1

Contents

From the Editors

As this volume goes to press, we mark the tenth anniversary of the involvement of Hollins University in the editing of *Children's Literature* (the first volume edited at Hollins, volume 22, appeared in 1994). When Elizabeth Keyser began editing *Children's Literature,* she did so in the tradition of its founder, Francelia Butler, with an Olympia portable typewriter in a home office. Elizabeth remains grateful that the editorship forced her to exchange the typewriter for a laptop computer. Over the years, much more has changed. *Children's Literature* now has an office on the Hollins campus, and Lisa Radcliff is proving an able editorial assistant. Rather than submitting two typescripts of the manuscript to Yale University Press each year, we now submit the entire volume on two disks. Several years ago Christine Doyle took over the book review editorship from John Cech and has worked with even more autonomy than John did to make the book reviews an indispensable guide to the best children's literature criticism and scholarship. Every year *Children's Literature* receives many more books than it can possibly review just as, in the past, it has received many more submissions than it could hope to publish. In order to accommodate the increasing number of worthy submissions, *Children's Literature* began to grow. What was once a volume of less than 250 pages has, in recent years, swelled to almost 300.

This year, however, the editors have begun to share a concern raised by Carlos J. Alonso in his January 2001 *PMLA* editorial. As some of our readers may recall, Alonso, after citing a gradual decline in the number of annual submissions accompanied by a growing dependence on solicited contributions, wrote: "Could it be that once the declining number of submissions crossed a certain threshold, the number of high-quality manuscripts yielded by the process [of submission-review-selection] shrank below the level needed to sustain the journal's publication? It stands to reason that every journal must have such a minimum threshold, and it may be that *PMLA*'s slide in submission has finally reached that magic number" (11). *Children's Literature,* of course, has long relied on solicited manuscripts in the sense that the editors have encouraged submission of conference papers that seemed like superior articles in the making. But these solicited essays have, with few exceptions, undergone the same review process as the unsolicited. And we are witnessing a decline in the submission of both sorts. Thus we wish to remind our readers that *Children's Literature,* perhaps unlike its grander parent *PMLA,* is a contributor-friendly journal. It has a long tradition, established at the University of Connecticut, of helping first-time contributors and seasoned scholars edit their work so as to make it appropriate for this venue—and if it seems more appropriate for publication elsewhere, we are happy to suggest alternatives and to help place it. We know that often younger scholars wish or need to publish quickly, and publication in *Children's Literature* can sometimes take two years or more from first submission—almost as long as book publication. Remember, though, that the annual really is a book and confers some of the prestige of book publication. (Those who receive the paperback with their membership in ChLA tend to forget that it also appears in hardcover; we editors, however, are reminded by the Yale University Press editorial staff who persist in referring to the essays as "chapters"!)

That said, let us turn to the fine essays in this volume. Reading the entire manuscript is always a surprising journey, as individual essays coalesce into a whole. We were struck this year by the way the question of agency resonates through this volume. Are children the recipients of culture, rebels against it, or active contributors to it? Are they simply exploited by adults or can they in turn manipulate their elders? How do we balance the pleasure to be found in texts with their potential dangers? Although the authors whose essays appear in this volume disagree at times on the answers to these questions, they agree with Richard Flynn that our goal as adult writers/mediators of children's literature should be to affirm children and childhood.

In "Misperceived Perceptions: Perrault's Fairy Tales and English Children's Literature," Ruth Bottigheimer argues that our assumptions about Perrault's place in the history of fairy tales have to do with notions of social cohesion rather than concrete evidence. She uses the methodology of book history to disprove the commonly accepted notion that Perrault's *Tales* succeeded in England from their first publication there, a thesis that relies on and reinforces the notion of a childhood passion for fairy tales that resists adult attempts at repression. Instead, Bottigheimer's research suggests that it took a generation for Perrault's *Tales* to make headway in the market, and that John Newbery was delighted to support them only when they appeared to be profitable. The fact that later centuries were eager to believe that

Perrault's happy endings and virtuous heroes were immediately popular (claiming that children in their zeal literally shredded the evidence that would support their case) points to a perception of childhood that has become rooted in our culture. Bottigheimer argues convincingly that children did not appropriate the tales originally intended for sophisticated adults; instead, adult entrepreneurs calculated to a nicety just when parents and guardians were ready to permit children access to the pleasures of Perrault.

Ellen Butler Donovan, in her essay "Very capital reading for children': Reading as Play in Hawthorne's *A Wonder Book for Girls and Boys*," identifies one of the key moments in the creation of an ideology that links childhood and pleasure. Donovan emphasizes the historical significance of *A Wonder Book*: "it contributed to the shift in reading culture that allowed children to read with and for pleasure." *A Wonder Book* relies on the belief that children and adults share the same potential for imaginative power, that the child can and should question the authority of adults and texts. Similarly, Marah Gubar provides an example of a text that encourages children to take on power, and thus pleasure. In "Revising the Seduction Paradigm: The Case of Ewing's *The Brownies*," Gubar uses *The Brownies* to support her argument that children's literature need not oppress children and thus, Jacqueline Rose notwithstanding, is not just a possibility but a reality. Both Hawthorne and Ewing, as these critics emphasize, make their narrators characters in their texts, who engage in lively, playful, and even flirtatious interactions with their child auditors, who give as good as they get.

The next two essays, which explore the power of Gene's and Finny's relationship in John Knowles's *A Separate Peace*, provide a case in point of how the editors of *Children's Literature* work with contributors. When Eric Tribunella, then a graduate student at the University of Florida, first submitted his manuscript ("Refusing the Queer Potential: John Knowles's *A Separate Peace*"), we were excited by his sophisticated queer reading of the novel and also by its implications for the book's classroom use. During the review and decision-making process, the editors were also involved in selecting papers for the ChLA conference in Roanoke, and among the submissions was James McGavran's own queer reading of *A Separate Peace*. Remembering the dialogue between Cynthia Marshall and Bonnie Gaarden on *The Wind in the Willows* in volume 22, the editors sent Tribunella's essay to McGavran, asking if he thought their readings could be sufficiently differentiated so as to constitute a debate rather than a duplication of efforts. After considerable revision by both authors, we concluded that, despite some overlap in content, their takes on the novel were different enough to prove stimulating to our readers.

McGavran, in "Fear's Echo and Unhinged Joy: Crossing Homosocial Boundaries in *A Separate Peace*," praises the novel for exploring same-sex relationships honestly. In the friendship between Gene and Finny, McGavran sees a union that "will always remain intact," an exemplary portrayal of a same-sex relationship for teenage boys. Tribunella agrees with McGavran that Gene's and Finny's relationship is powerful, but he reads the novel not as simply reflecting the reality of a homophobic society but, at least as it has been presented in the classroom, as contributing to that homophobia. In Tribunella's reading, the novel equates same-sex desire with adolescence, a stage to be left behind. Thus Finny's death allows Gene to become a man, as masculinity is now encoded in American culture, by putting childhood and same-sex desire behind him.

Although he acknowledges the subversive potential of Knowles's novel, Tribunella fears that *A Separate Peace* will contribute to the reader's indoctrination into heterosexuality, unless this agenda is explicitly decoded, presumably by an adult. Similarly, Anita Tarr, in "The Absence of Moral Agency in Robert Cormier's *The Chocolate War*," condemns another well-known novel for tricking the young reader. According to Tarr, it is "irresponsible" of Cormier to create a fictional world where "there is no rebel hero, no moral decision making, and no resistance to antifemale rhetoric." Instead of offering an opportunity for moral education, *The Chocolate War* encourages readers to become passive observers of corruption and then makes them complicitous. Readers of *Children's Literature*, if convinced by the arguments of Donovan and Gubar, Tribunella and Tarr, are led to the curious conclusion that the nineteenth-century texts, *A Wonder Book* and *The Brownies*, offer children more autonomy, both within and outside the text, than some modern (or even postmodern) novels for young adults.

The next two essays share the assumption that children's books should empower children by encouraging their active participation as readers, thinkers, and even writers. Jackie E. Stallcup, in "Power, Fear, and Children's Picture Books," takes on the task of classifying the intersection between fear and adult-child relationships. Stallcup identifies three central issues: our desire to protect children from fear (and to reassure ourselves that we can do so), our fear of the defiant/destructive child, and our fear that children won't grow up or, in other words, become like us. Contemporary picture books no longer rely on the graphic violence of earlier books for children, but some do rely on fear to assert the importance of a powerful, protective adult in a child's life. Out of the "conflicting ideologies regarding adult-child relationships" reflected in contemporary picture books, Stallcup proposes an ideal in which children are seen as different in degree, not in kind, from adults. Picture books should help the child along the path to adulthood, not infantalize through fear or the glorification of childhood.

Richard Flynn's discussion of June Jordan, "'Affirmative Acts': Language, Childhood, and Power in June Jordan's Cross-Writing," returns to the theme of how we see the adult-child relationship, this time from the perspective of cross-writing. Jordan, in a memoir about her own childhood as well as in her writings for young people, rejects sentimental visions of children as powerless victims; instead she "delineates a poetics that combats the regressive tropes of childhood embedded deep within our culture and proposes new tropes that may well be revolutionary." By encouraging children to be poets themselves, to write in their own language, Jordan pushes past the notion of the child as active reader and asks that children insert themselves into her texts literally, not simply metaphorically.

The editors are proud of these eight substantial essays as well as of the ten book reviews, all of which attest to the health and vitality of children's literature scholarship. Elizabeth Keyser, who plans to withdraw from active editorship with this volume, leaves *Children's Literature* in the hands of Julie Pfeiffer, Chris Doyle, and the ever-helpful staff of Yale University Press. We continue to urge the members of ChLA to support its annual by submitting their work and recruiting other would-be contributors. *Children's Literature* also, as always, needs readers for what we hope will swell to a steady stream, if not a deluge, of submissions as fine as the essays in this volume.

Elizabeth Lennox Keyser and Julie Pfeiffer

Articles

Misperceived Perceptions: Perrault's Fairy Tales and English Children's Literature

Ruth B. Bottigheimer

The place of Charles Perrault's fairy tales in the development of English children's literature has been both misunderstood and overrated. This view of Perrault's role in children's literature has a history. In the libraries I've scoured for books written for and read by children in eighteenth-century England, Perrault's fairy tales have been more an absence than a presence. This observation, however, is not enough to support so fundamental a redefinition of the early history of English children's literature. What can—and does—support my argument is book history, whose perceptions and methodologies I use here.

Let me offer one example of how book history is able to correct misperceptions that have arisen from the way books are listed in published library catalogs. Catalogs take their data from title pages, but title pages can be misleading. For example, what if one publisher, after a year of dismal sales, sold his books to another publisher, who then inserted a new title page and sent the books newly titled but otherwise unchanged out into bookshops? The catalog would record two dates of publication for one printing. Book history, in contrast, would use its resources to identify the book's text and its title page and to recognize that only one printing had, in fact, taken place. This is not an imagined example; it actually happened with a 1764 printing of Perrault's tales.

Unraveling an eighteenth-century printing practice like the reissue of 1764/65 requires a methodology and a vocabulary uncommon in the study of children's literature. "Printruns," "sheets," and "fingerprints" all play a role in explicating the relative popularity of indi-

Children's Literature 30, ed. Elizabeth Lennox Keyser and Julie Pfeiffer (Yale University Press, © 2002 Hollins University).

vidual books in the eighteenth century. The argument that follows
has a slow pace, and for that I apologize. I am urging a fundamental
change in long-held views, and I want to build my case carefully and
persuasively.

With clockwork regularity literary anthologies and course textbooks
imply, suggest, or assert that eighteenth-century English children's literature was rooted in fairy tales, specifically those of Charles Perrault.
Harvey Darton, whose richly documented history of English children's
literature has provided the guiding direction for countless other accounts, wrote that Perrault's tales "have been naturalized citizens of
the British nursery" since they were translated by Robert Samber in
1729 (88). In *Classics of Children's Literature,* John Griffith and Charles
Frey put five of Perrault's tales—"Sleeping Beauty," "Little Red Riding-
hood," "Blue Beard," "Puss in Boots," and "Cinderella"—front and
center and claim that they "grew steadily in popularity" once they
were translated into English (3). Little wonder that Geoffrey Summerfield could comfortably state without further proof or elaboration that
"these tales of Perrault soon passed into England, and in Robert Samber's translation were frequently reprinted throughout the eighteenth
century" (44). Summerfield's easy acceptance of the Perrault paradigm characterizes both lay and scholarly perceptions.

The chronology of the publishing history of Perrault's tales in England would appear to substantiate such claims. Translated by Robert
Samber and published in London in 1729, those tales preceded the
1740s printings of children's books by London's Thomas Boreman,
Mary Cooper, and John Newbery by a good ten to fifteen years. But
this simple chronological sequence has made it all too easy for generations of literary historians to leap directly to the conclusion that Perrault's prior appearance represented a point of origin. Exploring late
seventeenth- and early- to mid-eighteenth-century English children's
literature presents a disturbing disjunction between scholarly claims
of Perrault's precedence and the mood evident in the literature itself.

Over the past several years I have undertaken a journey of discovery
to research libraries in the United States, Canada, and England. My
study of hundreds of books published for children between 1670 and
1770 has led, among other things, to a sense that it is necessary to
revise fundamentally the place that Perrault's fairy stories occupy in
the early history of English children's literature. The history of fairies
and fairy literature in England encourages such revision; scholarship

in such newly emerging fields as book and publishing history supports it; and most significantly, the evidence of children's literature itself requires it.[1]

The fairies of Charles Perrault's *Histories* were preceded by centuries of England's own imps and phantoms as well as by decades of Mme d'Aulnoy's supernaturals (Palmer, Palmer and Palmer, Verdier). By the time Perrault's supernatural protagonists arrived on English soil in such fairy tales as "The Fairy," "Sleeping Beauty in the Wood," and "Cinderilla" [*sic*], they represented England's third generation of fairies,[2] one which eventually overlaid both England's native fairy population (calendared by Reginald Scot) and Mme d'Aulnoy's successfully imported and disseminated fairy traditions. Perrault's tales provided the basis for the modern canon of fairy tales. That is not in doubt. But the ultimate success of Perrault's fairy tales has blinded generations of scholars to the fact that they conquered the field with near-glacial slowness. The reasons for Perrault's tardy success implicate genre and gender, while more far-reaching explanations rest on patterns of book consumption and book marketing.

Perrault's fairy tales differed fundamentally from the traditional fairy fictions of Mme d'Aulnoy. Unlike her tales, Perrault's stories generally obfuscated sex. And differing even more fundamentally from a dystopic tale like Mme d'Aulnoy's "History of Adolphus," in which Time brutally strangled the hero in the concluding paragraphs, Perrault's (rare) violence was wrought only upon the wicked. ("Red Riding Hood" is, of course, not a fairy tale but a warning tale.) Best of all for late-eighteenth-century propriety, every one of Perrault's fairy tales had a hero or heroine who was virtuous, at least in formal terms, and ended with a clearly set out moral. The morals themselves were sometimes wry, sometimes ironic, and always worldly, yet on the surface they and the fairy tales' endings regularly stressed the importance and utility of goodness. Whatever internal contradictions might on occasion disturb the smooth flow of a moral, the overt message of the majority of Perrault's tales was that happy endings crowned virtuous lives.

Mme d'Aulnoy further explored the narrative consequences of human intrusions into fairyland and of fairy entries into human life in stories like "Graciosa and Percinet," "The Fair One with Golden Locks," and "The Hobgoblin Prince." Perrault, in contrast, examined the social life of human beings, the obstacles to whose easy success were swept away either by earthly kings or by fairy magic. In his stories a fairy made roses, pearls, and diamonds fall from the mouth of a kindly but ill-treated daughter ("The Fairy"); a fairy godmother created a coach from a "pompion" ("Cinderilla"); and another fairy made the hideous Riquet appear handsome and transformed his beloved but stupid Princess into a sensible woman ("Riquet a la Houpe"). Only one of Perrault's fairy tales—"Sleeping Beauty in the Wood"—resembled Mme d'Aulnoy's stories in that a good fairy and a malevolent one pitted their magic against one another in a contest of wills that produced repercussions in the lives of the tale's human protagonists.

The date of Perrault's first translation into English, 1729, is generally cited as the moment of its initial success in England. It is easily demonstrated that Perrault's tales were translated and published in London in 1729, but many important facts in conjunction with its fallaciously claimed success have been eagerly, perhaps willfully, overlooked. To explore the question of the popularity of Perrault's tales, we need to return to the world of print as it existed in publishing centers in Paris, the Lowlands, and London at the end of the seventeenth and beginning of the eighteenth centuries.

Within a few months of the January 1697 appearance of Perrault's fairy tales in Paris, his stories had been pirated by the Amsterdam publisher Jaques [sic] Desbordes. Desbordes's book claimed to be a faithful copy of the French edition ("suivante la copie a Paris"), yet its publisher misspelled the author's name ("Perreault") even as he added Perrault's illustrious title ("de l'Academie François"). Desbordes's book sold well enough on the Continent to justify a second printing in 1700 and a third in 1708. In 1711 Estienne Roger, another Amsterdam publisher, produced a six-volume compendium of French fairy fictions and fairy tales. Volume 5, entitled *Les Chevaliers Errans par Madame la Comtesse D****, included Perrault's tales and five others by Mme D'Auneuil;[3] the sixth volume bore the title of Perrault's oeuvre, *Histoires ou Contes des Temps Passé*, and was attributed to "Perreault," but with an insouciant disregard for authorship, it contained not a single one of Perrault's tales!

Perhaps it was volume 5, *Les Chevaliers Errans*, in Estienne Roger's set of fairy tales that caught Jaques Desbordes's eye and led him to calculate that Perrault's tales could be made even more attractive by adding a traditional and lengthy fairy fiction. Whatever his reason, in 1716 Desbordes added "L'adroite Princesse ou les aventures de Finette," which had been written by Perrault's niece, Marie-Jeanne L'Héritier de Villandon. Desbordes finally spelled Perrault's name correctly and published *Histoires ou Contes du temps Passé, Avec des Moralitez. Par M. Per-*

rault. *Nouvelle Edition augmentée d'une Nouvelle, à la fin. Suivant la Copie de Paris.* His successor firm republished it in 1721 and 1729.

In 1729 Robert Samber's word-for-word translation of Perrault's tales appeared in London. It included, in the printer's fanciful typography, "THE Little red Riding-Hood," "THE BLUE-BEARD," "The FAIRY," "THE SLEEPING BEAUTY in the WOOD," "THE MASTER CAT: OR, PUSS in BOOTS," "CINDERILLA: OR, The little GLASS SLIPPER," "RIQUET A la HOUPE," and "LITTLE POUCET, AND His two BROTHERS." Samber worked from Desbordes's Dutch edition, similarly including Mlle L'Héritier's "Discreet Princess; or, the Adventures of Finetta. A Novel."[4] Mlle L'Héritier had originally addressed "L'adroite Princesse" to another French author of fairy fictions, Mme de Murat. Samber's Englishing of the book extended to the novel's dedicatee, and so on the separate title page that preceded the "novel," he addressed "The Discreet Princess" to "The Right Hon. Lady Mary Montagu," daughter of John, Duke of Montagu.

Perrault's own tales are so familiar that I needn't repeat their plots here, but Mlle L'Héritier's "Discreet Princess" has fallen from the canon and requires a brief retelling so that modern readers may understand the full reach of Samber's book as it appeared in London in 1729:

> Once upon a time there were three princesses, idle Drone-illa, prattling Babillarde, and virtuous Finetta. After their mother's death, their father feared both for his daughters' well-being and for their virtue, and so having had a fairy make a glass distaff for each of his daughters that would break if its owner acted dishonorably, he locked them all into a high tower and forbade them to receive guests. Lazy Drone-illa and prattling Babillarde were distraught at their isolation, but Finetta spent her days contentedly, reading and sewing.
>
> One day Drone-illa and Babillarde hauled up a wizened old woman who had begged entry to their tower. The "old woman" was, in fact, the crafty Prince Riche-cautelle, who easily seduced first Drone-illa and then Babillarde. The virtuous Finetta, however, repulsed his advances and defended herself with Boccaccian trickery, dropping him into a stinking sewer. To avenge his honor, Riche-cautelle had Finetta kidnapped and carried to a mountaintop, down which he proposed to roll her in a barrel studded with knives and nails. Instead, Finetta kicked *him* into the barrel and rolled him down the slope. When Finetta returned home, she

found that her two sisters had each given birth to a son born of her "marriage" night with Riche-cautelle. To conceal her sisters' shame Finetta, dressed as a man, carried the two children in boxes to the capital, and left them behind as "ointment" for the prince's wounds. Once again bested by Finetta, Riche-cautelle made his noble brother, Prince Bel-a-Voir, swear to marry Finetta and kill her on their wedding night.

Finetta, whom a fairy had warned to always be on her guard because "distrust is the mother of security" (141), substituted a straw dummy for herself in the marriage bed. From a hiding place she saw her husband stab it murderously, even though in so doing he lamented his act and declared that he intended to kill himself afterward. Finetta hindered his suicidal resolve, and they lived long and happily together.

Robert Samber claimed that the story, "though entirely fabulous . . . wrap[s] up and infold[s] most excellent morality, which is the very end, and ultimate scope and design of Fable" (140). At its conclusion, he repeated his warm approval of the novel's "great deal of good morality," for which reason, he said, it "ought to be told to little children in their very infancy, to inspire them betimes with Virtue" (201–2). A strange sort of morality, we may well conclude.

Few London parents, however, seem to have told, or read, these stories to their infants, as the following publishing history will demonstrate. Montagu and Pote, the book's publishers, took twelve years to issue a second English-language edition; a third appeared nine years after that, in 1750.

To counterbalance a century's baseless claims, it is worth carrying out a simple mathematical calculation based on reasonable numbers and rational assumptions. In the eighteenth century a print run of 1,000 books was the general maximum for the commercial market. Smaller print runs were common, but larger print runs were generally reserved for subsidized Bible printings and the like. Rational commercial practices dictated that publishers would not and did not reissue a book while stocks remained unsold on their shelves. Conversely, publishers quickly reprinted sheets when they had sold out.

Based on the commercial premises that guided publishing and republishing, we may reasonably conclude that 1,000 copies of the English-language edition of Perrault's *Histories* were sold between 1729 and 1741. That works out to about 83 books of Perrault's fairy tales sold per year over a twelve-year period (1729–41). Between 1741 and 1750 the rate of sale increased slightly to 111 books per year. Before declaring this a bestseller, however, one must remember that England's population numbered approximately seven million with large numbers of English-speakers in Wales, Scotland, and Ireland. Perrault's book in its English translation reached a very small fraction of England's population, approximately 1/3,500. When James Hodges, at the Looking Glass, facing St. Magnus Church, London-Bridge, reissued *Histories or Tales of Passed Times* in 1750, his sales of all-English Perrault tales plummeted. It took average sales of 52.6 copies a year to clear the shelves to make way for another such edition nineteen years later, in 1769!

Perrault's *Histories* had a second publishing history in England as a dual-language textbook. England had long had a market for dual-language textbooks, of which Johan Amos Comenius's *Orbis Pictus* is perhaps the most famous representative. In England his Latin-English catalog of the (principally) secular world was one of several Latin-English textbooks on the market for Latin-learning English pupils. However, with the increasing popularity of a grand European tour to crown eighteenth-century aristocratic boys' education, French displaced Latin as the language of choice in dual-language schoolbooks in England, and new French-English books like Faerno's *Fables* and Hübner's *Youth's Scripture Kalendar* found a market there.

It was to England's dual-language textbook market that England's first publishers of Perrault's tales turned in 1737 to repair their financial damage when commercial sales of the English-only edition evidently failed to cover their printing costs. They restored Perrault's French to create a dual-language book, "very proper to be read by young Children at Boarding Schools, that are to learn the *French* Tongue, as well as in private Families." Unlike the single-language English translation of Perrault's tales, the textbook flourished. If they printed 1,000 copies per print run, then the dual-language textbook sold three times as well as the English-language children's book, at a gratifying average rate of 250 copies per year, sales that justified reprinting it four years later, in 1741.

The surviving books of Perrault's tales, with their scribblings and signatures, suggest yet another consideration, gender. In the English-language and dual-language editions of Perrault's tales that I have inspected, my tally to date hints that girls more often owned English-language editions, boys French or dual-language ones. The evidence, though sparse, is tantalizing, because it corroborates the publishing history of Mme Leprince de Beaumont's girl-centered *Magasin des Enfans*, whose English translation swiftly supplanted and far outsold the French original in England.

In 1741 and after, however, sales of Perrault's dual-language *Histories* apparently slowed down, because the book was not reprinted again until 1750. In that year Montagu and Pote yielded their rights for Perrault's *Histories* to James Hodges, who supposedly printed an edition "in *French* and *English*. Price Bound 2s. 6d" (according to an advertisement in his 1750 English edition). But Hodges's 1750 dual-language edition of Perrault's *Histories* must have sold even more slowly than had the ones published by Montagu and Pote in 1735 and 1741, if indeed the dual-language edition was ever published at all. If it was not published, then the overall sales for Perrault's tales in dual-language editions fall even lower. A summary of this publishing history is listed below.

English-Language Editions

Publisher and Year	Average Sales
Montagu and Pote, 1729	83/year
Montagu and Pote, 1741	111/year
James Hodges, 1750	?
B. Collins, 1763	?

Dual-Language Editions

Publisher and Year	Average Sales
Montagu and Pote, 1737	250/year
Montagu and Pote, 1741	111/year
James Hodges, 1750	71/year
J. Melvil, 1764 (= Van Os 1765)	very few

One may well wonder why Perrault's tales lost market appeal in both their English- and dual-language editions. Because sales dipped when James Hodges took over publication, it is tempting to conclude that his books were in some way inferior. But, in fact, they differed very little from the Montagu and Pote editions in paper quality, and they had exactly the same illustrations. One explanation lies in the differing manner in which textbooks and children's books are used over time. Textbooks have a way of saturating the market because students hand their books on. That observation is consistent with the textbook's diminishing sales between 1737 and 1764. But why are sales of the English-language edition also so low? These books addressed a leisure market, in which a book was a present, something to be treasured and kept, something that one purchased anew to give as a gift. For this market, it is likely that the changing temper of the times had a powerful effect on book choice: after 1750 strong anti-French sentiment animated an English public exasperated by continuing conflicts with France.

After Perrault's fairy tales foundered as a textbook at mid-century, a publisher with access to provincial markets, J. Melvil of London and Exeter, took up Perrault's *Histories* and brought out a dual-language edition in 1764. His sales must have been poor, too, because a publisher with offices in London and The Hague, Van Os, ended up with Melvil's unillustrated, and unsold, sheets, that is, the large pieces of paper with several pages printed on each, which, when folded, produce a fascicle, or section of a book. That Melvil's 1764 sheets were reissued by Van Os in 1765 can be demonstrated by identifying the printing's "fingerprint," the letters that appear directly above a designated marker, usually A2 or A3. Van Os substituted roughly executed and reversed copies of previously published illustrations, inserted them between the pages, and provided Melvil's sheets with a new title page, *Mother Goose's Tales*, a title first given Perrault's tales by another Dutch publisher, Jean Neaulme, twenty years before. Melvil's disposal of his unsold sheets was probably an act of desperation. But what readers should note is that sales for Perrault's *Histories* were low for the English editions and steadily declined for the dual-language textbooks from 1729 to the 1760s, that is, during precisely the period in which English children's literature was beginning to assume its modern form.

James Hodges, as mentioned earlier, also brought out an English-language edition of Perrault's *Histories* in 1750. This edition should be investigated carefully because there is evidence that in 1763 B. Collins published *Mother Goose's Tales* in Salisbury, with provincial sales augmented by a Mrs. Maynard in Devizes, and with London sales managed by W. Bristow in St. Paul's Church-Yard.[5] The question to be raised here is whether Hodges's and Collins's sheets are one and the same, as were Melvil's and Van Os's (a bellwether for sluggish sales) or whether the two books represent separate print runs (and hence higher rates of sale). If Bristow's London sales were successful, then they would have set the commercial possibilities of fairy tales before the very eyes of John Newbery, a point to which I will return later.

Chapbooks are another possible place to search for tales from Perrault's *Histories*. It is far easier, however, to find assertions in histories of children's literature that Perrault's tales were widely disseminated by the chapbook trade to England's children by the mid-eighteenth century than it is to actually locate chapbook copies of those tales. It is true that Perrault's *Histoires* were common in *France's* chapbooks, the *Bibliothèque bleue*, between 1725 and 1775. But it wasn't until well after 1750 that isolated tales from Perrault's oeuvre begin to turn up in the Dicey Brothers' chapbook printing catalogs from Aldermary Church-Yard in London.[6] Gilles Duval, a French historian of English chapbooks, carefully assessed eighteenth-century chapbook content and characterized Perrault's tales as Johnny-come-latelys ("adaptées tardivement").[7] In so doing he flatly contradicted generations of assumptions and assertions about the role of Perrault's tales in the originary years of English children's literature in the first half of the eighteenth century.

Diehard defenders of the hypothesis that Perrault's tales were preeminent would probably explain the absence of Perrault's fairy tales from English chapbooks as the result of his tales having been so beloved that they were read to shreds. Book history, however, demolishes that argument: avid eighteenth-century chapbook collectors left no Perrault tales in collections that they assembled before 1750. Nor are Perrault's tales found in the records of eighteenth-century circulating libraries in child-friendly formats. Instead, as Matthew O. Grenby found, they were "designed for an adult market . . . in multi-volume editions costing several shillings."[8]

Miscellanies for children offer a final potential entry point to be investigated in an analysis of the role of Perrault's tales in the emergence of English children's literature. We don't expect to find fairy tales in such books as *Every Youth His Own Moralist* (J. Shatwell, 1771) or *Vice in Its Proper Shape* (Francis Newbery [1767]). But to modern minds there is at least the hint of a promise of fairy tales in books with titles like *A Christmass[sic]-Box for Masters and Misses* (London: Mary Boreman, 1746), *The Amusing Instructor: or, Tales and Fables in Prose and Verse* (W. Harris, 1769), *Mrs. Lovechild's Golden Present, to all the little Masters and Misses, of Europe, Asia, Africa, and America* (Francis Newbery [1770]), or Don Stephano Bunyano's *Prettiest Book for Children; Being the History of the Enchanted Castle* (J. Coote, 1770). The magic and the otherworldly characters that these books introduced, however, drew not at all on Perrault's fairies and fairy tales but on England's old heroes and giants.[9] John Newbery flirted with fairy tales in *Short Histories for the Improvement of the Mind* (1760)—not Perrault's, however, but the highly moralized ones by François Fénelon.

One other miscellany remains to be investigated, Mme Leprince de Beaumont's *Magasin des Enfans* (1756). Soon translated into English as *Magasin des Enfans, or, The Young Misses Magazine,* it retained its half-French, half-English title for decades and was published well into the nineteenth century. Alternating fairy fictions and moral tales with geography, ancient history, and Bible histories, the book valorized *history* (histoire) over *tale* (conte) in both structure and commentary. When it came to magic transformations in the service of love, Mme Leprince de Beaumont substantially revised Perrault's "Riquet a la Houpe" and then composed her own highly moralized and still popular story of female beauty and male hideosity, "Beauty and the Beast." In other words, she too rejected Perrault's oeuvre.

When John Newbery copublished B. Collins's *Pretty Book for Boys and Girls* in 1743, he associated himself with a book in which both the warning tale "Red Riding Hood" and the fairy godmother of "Cinderilla" appeared, as Elizabeth Johnson reports in her catalog description of the Ball Collection of Children's Literature at the University of Indiana. Both tales were still in the 1756 *Pretty Book,* touted as "the seventh edition," along with "Fortunatus" and "The Effect of Good Nature. A Family Tale," a retelling of Perrault's "Diamonds and Toads," a quintessentially normative narrative of good behavior rewarded.

Several questions arise in connection with the B. Collins book of 1743 and following editions. Was "the seventh edition" really a seventh edition, or was that an early example of an advertising device meant to suggest market success and therefore desirability, something that one often finds in eighteenth-century publishing? Scholarly inquiries like these make *A Pretty Book for Boys and Girls* an avenue to explore.

It is at this point that John Locke's often-cited disapproval of fairy tales becomes relevant. If we accept the evidence of the Collins provincial imprint, then we are led to the inevitable conclusion that both early and late in his publishing career Newbery's Lockean anti-fairy inclinations were directed more against England's own fairies than against French imports. The second, and equally inevitable, conclusion is that if Newbery, a canny publisher as John Buck has demonstrated, had believed before 1767 that Perrault's fairy tales would have sold well as a whole, then he would have offered them for sale. The possibility that he went in with Collins in 1743 on a book that included "Cinderilla," but that he himself didn't turn towards Perrault again until more than twenty years later suggests that he assessed England's market for such literature and concluded that Perrault was unprofitable.

What *is* verifiable is that Perrault's "Puss in Boots," the quintessential modern rags-to-riches fairy tale, appeared in a commercially successful miscellany (commercially successful by my definition means successive editions within a few years of each other) in 1767, when John Newbery included it in his gaily harum-scarum *The Fairing*.[10] Schooled as we all are to understand John Newbery as the ultimate Lockean producer of rationally based and socially useful books for children and as a publisher who doubted the suitability of fairy tales for children, we scarcely expect to find Perrauldian magic instead of Lockean literacy leading to wealth in one of Mr. Newbery's books. As an aside it is worth noting that Newbery invited one of England's own supernaturals, Queen Mab, to advertise his *Lilliputian Magazine* in 1750 (Pickering, 1981, 223), but during his entire publishing career he otherwise staved off the English imps and gnomes whom Locke had excoriated. Another London publisher, John Marshall, did the same thing. Samuel Pickering Jr. has interesting things to say in this regard. He tells us that Marshall assured buyers that his children's books were entirely divested of the prejudicial nonsense of hobgoblins, witches, and fairies.[11] The fact that Marshall eventually published Perrault's tales demonstrates that he too distinguished between England's fairy population and those in Perrault's fairy tales.

John Newbery's use of Queen Mab as a spokesperson tells us a lot about the market he addressed. Not a profound innovator, Newbery was rather an improver and popularizer of existing genres and characters, as Buck's thorough study of Newbery's literary merchandising makes clear. Consequently, his turning to Queen Mab early in his career tells us that she was a stock figure whose familiarity to his readers made her a useful advertising vehicle.

Newbery's 1767 introduction of Perrault's "Puss in Boots" into *The Fairing* was, however, a far more significant inclusion than Queen Mab, and it is legitimate to wonder why Newbery finally took this significant step. Although he had worked together with Collins over the years, he had *not* been part of the 1763 Collins-based consortium that brought Perrault's fairy tales to Mr. Bristow's shop in St. Paul's Church-Yard.

But he could hardly have missed either knowing that Mr. Bristow was selling *Mother Goose* or seeing little customers walking out of Mr. Bristow's shop with copies of the book in their hands. And so if *Mother Goose* was a commercial hit at Mr. Bristow's shop just across the way, it would have been a natural move for Mr. Newbery, who habitually added to his list from genres that were in popular demand (Buck, passim), to tap into Perrault's tales for his own books.

The year 1767 thus represents the point at which it may be asserted that Perrault's tales entered the ranks of mainstream (i.e., London produced and distributed) English children's literature. The year 1767 postdates the 1744 publication of *A Little Pretty Pocket-Book,* usually cited as the beginning of modern English children's literature, by more than twenty years. In the context of the history of children's literature as a whole, the late date (at the end of John Newbery's publishing career) at which fairy tales became a mainstream constituent in children's literature means that we need to think of the emergence of the genre as a generation-long process. It was, above all, a process that responded to market opportunities and market tastes. It can be said to have begun with Newbery's little primers and to have achieved much of its potential with Newbery's acknowledgement of Perrault.

Two years later, in 1769, Perrault's *Histories or Tales of Past Times, Told by Mother Goose with Morals* was finally both printed and published as a children's book in London. (Earlier B. Collins editions had been printed in Salisbury in the provinces and distributed, i.e., published, in London.) Gone now was the sexually problematic "Discreet Princess," which leads to the conclusion that London's middle and upper-middle classes really did not want their children to know about Prince Riche-cautelle's "pernicious pleasure" (1729 161), or about Drone-illa's immoral welcome of the knavish Riche-cautelle "for her husband . . . [with] no greater formalities than those which are the conclusion of marriage" (163), or about Riche-cautelle's caddish bedding of Drone-illa at night and Babillarde in the morning (168). Perrault's tales must have become far more attractive to middle-class English book buyers when the repellent images, affronting references, and negative examples of Mlle L'Héritier's "novel" disappeared from its pages. It is certainly noteworthy that the disappearance of Mlle L'Héritier's novel coincided exactly with an increased sales rate of Perrault's fairy tales.

By 1769, forty years after its first appearance in England, both Perrault's book and the times had changed. John Newbery had died and his heirs had taken over his publishing firm. Even at this late date, the publishers of Perrault's fairy tales were still giving signs of skittishness about the financial risk of their venture: three firms—John Newbery's successor firm Newbery and Carnan, B. Collins from Salisbury, and S. Crowder of London—carefully spread the risk by joining together in the undertaking.

Successful production of Perrault's fairy tales as a whole (rather than as individual stories) in England can be said to have begun in Salisbury in 1763 with B. Collins's *Mother Goose* and to have continued in London in 1769 with the Newbery-Carnan-Collins-Crowder team. From this point onward, Perrault's tales began their spectacular commercial ascent, blazing glory and trailing success. Whatever concerns Newbery, Carnan, Collins, and Crowder might have had about the market acceptability of Perrault's fairy tales in 1769 must have been dispelled by subsequent developments. Perrault's stories captured imaginations and markets, and chapbook editions of individual Perrault tales abounded in the late eighteenth and early nineteenth centuries.[12]

Why has Perrault's point of impact on English children's literature been misdated? One reason is that research tools available for the study of children's literature, although improving, still remain limited: reference books often repeat predecessors' views; catalog information is incomplete in such long-standard references as the pre-1956 National Union Catalog; and even the British Library's far more inclusive catalog presents another stumbling block by utilizing eighteenth-century title page practices. Meant to enhance the public's perception of a book's success, eighteenth-century publishers often misleadingly and intentionally numbered the printing of different kinds of books sequentially. With reference to the publishing history of Perrault's fairy tales in England, James Hodges called his 1750 reissue of Montagu and Pote's Samber 1729 English translation not the third edition, which would have accurately reflected the real situation, but "the fourth edition," because he counted in two dual-language schoolbook editions as second and third editions.

The nineteenth century mythologized fairy tales and saw in them expressions of nationhood, evidence of unbroken connection with the childhood of mankind, and proof of a sacred social cohesion that transcended class boundaries, with nursemaids telling children stories from time immemorial. Few nineteenth- or twentieth-century scholars have questioned this set of beliefs, and, as a consequence, what has become firmly embedded in histories of children's literature is not evidence itself but *beliefs* about evidence.

This exploration of English, French, and Englished French fairy tales in conjunction with the development of books for English children in the first three quarters of the eighteenth century leads to two fundamental revisions to the history of English children's literature.[13] First, Perrault's tales became "popular" in London's print trade only in the 1760s. Second, our old friend John Newbery did not eschew fairy tales to the end of his life. On the contrary, he introduced Perrault's magic when he saw that it sold. In both cases, market profitability took precedence over Lockean ideology in an increasingly mercantile world of publishing.

Postscript: Matthew O. Grenby of de Montfort University in England, who has recently investigated children's literature in eighteenth-century English lending libraries, has also noted a general absence of fairy tales in this period. Grenby's work will be published in a forthcoming issue of *Book History*.

Notes

1. Space does not permit me to include here my research on Mme d'Aulnoy. In brief, however, the d'Aulnoy material was first marketed to economically and socially privileged buyers, later to merchant readers, and finally to artisanal and child readers. As the collection of tales moved downmarket in social and/or economic terms, its prose was altered to address the consumers its publishers sought.

2. For a learned and lively discussion and a broad sample of seventeenth-, eighteenth-, and nineteenth-century sentiment about fairies, fairy fictions, and fairy tales, see Samuel Pickering Jr., *John Locke and Children's Books*, chap. 2. Broader access to popular publications of this period in the last twenty years has required modifying some of Pickering's conclusions.

3. "Les Chevaliers Errans," "La Princesse Zamée," "Le Prince Elmedor," "Zalmayde," and "Le Prince de Numidie."

4. Justin Schiller says that Samber worked from the 1716 Desbordes edition published in Amsterdam (Schiller, Entry no. 17), but Samber could have used the 1721 or 1729 Desbordes editions.

5. This information comes from Carpenter and Prichard, *Oxford Companion to Children's Literature*, 251, but I myself have not seen such a volume, nor do I know of any documentation of its contents, i.e., whether it included or excluded "The Discreet Princess."

6. Nicholas Tucker alludes to (undated) fairy tales' chapbook associations in "Fairy Tales and Their Early Opponents," 107–8.

7. Duval, *Littérature de colportage*, 68.

8. Matthew O. Grenby, "Children's Books in British Circulating Libraries, 1748–1848," *Book History* (forthcoming).

9. Although it is not his purpose, Andrew O'Malley describes the same result in "The Coach and Six" (2000 passim), which is devoted to book size and contents in what he terms "transitional" books of the eighteenth century. Duval, of course, treats eighteenth-century English chapbook content far more extensively.

10. "Puss in Boots" may have appeared even earlier than 1767 because the 1767 edi-

tion, according to its complete title, is a "new edition," i.e., the publisher claims that it had also appeared previously. But the complete title also claims that it has "additions," and so we can't be sure that "Puss in Boots" appeared before 1767 until we can examine an earlier edition.

11. Pickering, *John Locke and Children's Books*, 41.

12. See Schiller, "Charles Perrault and His 'Contes des Fées,'" Entry no. 36.

13. The evidence here also reveals that the popular (as opposed to textbook) emergence of Perrault's tales seems to have originated in the provinces and thus to have reversed the usual direction, from London outwards. This is, in itself, worthy of note in the history of the book.

Works Cited

Note: The fingerprint for some books has been included after basic bibliographic information.

Aulnoy, Marie Catherine Jumelle de Berneville, Comtesse d'. *The History of Adolphus, Prince of Russia; And the Princess of Happiness. By a Person of Quality. With a Collection of Songs and Love-Verses. By several Hands.* London: R. T. near Stationers-Hall, 1691.

———. [and Chevalier de Mailly]. *The Diverting Works of the Countess D'Anois, Author of the Ladies Travels to Spain. Containing I. The Memoires of her own Life. II. All her Spanish Novels and Histories. III. Her Letters. IV. Tales of the Fairies in three Parts Complete. Newly done into English.* London: Printed for John Nicholson at the Kings Arms; And John Sprint at the Bell in Little Brittain, Andrew Bell at the Cross Keys and Bible in Cornhill; and for Samuel Burows [*sic*], 1707.

Buck, John D. C. "John Newbery and Literary Merchandising, 1744–1767." Ph.D. diss., University of California, Los Angeles, 1972.

Comenius, Johann Amos. *Orbis Sensualium Pictus.* Trans. Charles Hoole (1610–67). Reproduction of 1727 (text) and 1728 (title page) London editions. Syracuse: C. W. Bardeen, 1887.

Darton, F. J. Harvey. *Children's Books in England: Five Centuries of Social Life.* 3d ed., rev. by Brian Alderson. Cambridge: Cambridge University Press, 1982.

Duval, Gilles. *Littérature de colportage et imaginire collectif en Angleterre à l'époque des Dicey (1720-v.1800).* Talence: Presses Universitaires de Bordeaux, 1991.

[Faerno, Gabriello]. *Fables in English and French verse.* Trans. Charles Perrault. London: Davis, 1741.

Griffin, John, and Charles Frey, eds. *Classics of Children's Literature.* 4th ed. Upper Saddle River, N.J.: Prentice-Hall, 1995.

Hübner, Johann. *Youth's Scripture Kalendar: or, Select sacred stories for every Sunday throughout the Year in French and English: The Former, By the Reverend I. P. Aubaret, Maitre de Langues at the Prussian Court; And the Latter, By a gentleman of Oxford, To Which is annexed a succinct Historical account, in Both Languages, of the Four Most Holy Evangelists, Matthew, Mark, Luke, and John, the Whole Calculated for the use of schools.* London: T. Caslon, 1759.

Johnson, Elizabeth L. *For Your Amusement and Instruction: The Elisabeth Ball Collection of Historical Children's Materials.* Bloomington, Ind.: Lilly Library, 1987.

Leprince de Beaumont, Marie. *Magasin des Enfans, ou dialogues entre une sage gouvernante et plusieurs de ses élèves.* London: J. Haberkorn, 1756. Rare Books Collection, University of California, Los Angeles (hereafter UCLA).

———. *Magasin des Enfans, or, The Young Misses Magazine containing Dialogues between a Governess and Several Young Ladies of Quality.* London: B. Long and T. Pridden, 1759. UCLA.

[Newbery, John?] *The Fairing: or, A Golden Toy for Children of all Sizes and Denominations.*

In which they may see all the Fun of the Fair, And at home be as happy as if they were there. Adorned with Variety of Cuts, from Original Drawings. A New Edition, with Additions. London: J. Newbery, 1767. UCLA.

Newbery, John, ed. *Short Stories for the Improvement of the Mind.* London: J. Newbery, 1760. Cotsen Collection of Children's Books, Princeton University (hereafter Cotsen).

O'Malley, Andrew. "The Coach and Six: Chapbook Residue in Late Eighteenth-Century Children's Literature." *Lion and the Unicorn* 24.1 (2000): 18–44.

Opie, Iona, and Peter Opie, eds. *The Classic Fairy Tales.* London: Oxford University Press, 1974.

Palmer, Melvin. "Mme d'Aulnoy in England." *Comparative Literature* 27.3 (summer 1975): 237–53.

Palmer, Melvin, and Nancy Palmer. "English Editions of French *Contes de Fees* Attributed to Mme d'Aulnoy." *Studies in Bibliography* 27 (1974): 227–32.

———. "The French Conte de Fée in England." *Studies in Short Fiction* 11 (winter 1974): 35–44.

Perrault, Charles (by date)

———. *Histoires ou Contes du Temps Passé. Avec des Moralitez. Par le Fils de Monsieur Perreault [sic] de l'Academie François. Suivante la Copie a Paris.* Amsterdam: [Jaques Desbordes], 1697. Cotsen.

———. *Histoires, ou Contes du temps passé. Avec des Moralitez. Par le Fils de Monsieur Perreault [sic] de l'Academie François. Suivant la Copie a Paris.* Amsterdam: [Jaques Desbordes?] 1700. Cotsen.

———. *Contes de Monsieur Perrault Avec des Moralitez.* Paris: Chez la Veuve Barbin, 1707. Cotsen.

———. *Histoires, ou Contes du tems [sic] passé. Avec des Moralitez. Par le Fils de Monsieur Perreault [sic] de l'Academie François. Suivant la Copie a Paris.* Amsterdam: Jaques Desbordes, 1708. Cotsen.

———. *Les Chevaliers Errans par Madame la Comtess D***.* Amsterdam: Estienne Roger, 1710. Houghton Library, Harvard University.

———. *Histoires, ou Contes du tems [sic] passé. Avec des Moralitez. Par M. Perrault. Nouvelle Edition augmentée d'une Nouvelle, à la fin. Suivant la Copie de Paris.* Amsterdam: Chez Jaques Desbordes, 1716. Cotsen.

———. *Histoires ou Contes du tems [sic] Passé, Avec des Moralitez. Par M. Perrault. Nouvelle Edition augmentée d'une Nouvelle, à la fin. Suivant la Copie de Paris.* Amsterdam: Chez la Veuve de Jaq. Desbordes, 1721.

———. *Histoires ou Contes du tems [sic] passé, Avec des Moralitez. Par M. Perrault. Nouvelle Edition augmentée d'une Nouvelle à la fin. Suivant la Copie de Paris.* Amsterdam: Jaques Desbordes, 1729. fingerprint A2 = _bob, A3 = _la_. Cotsen.

———. *Histories, or Tales of past Times. With Morals. By M. Perrault. Translated into English.* London: Printed for L. Pote and R. Montagu, 1729. [Morgan]

———. *Histories, or Tales of Passed Times. With Morals. Written in French by M. Perrault, And Englished by R. S. Gent. The Second Edition, Corrected. Histoires ou Contes du Tems [sic] Passe. Avec des Moralitez. Par M. Perrault. Augmentée d'une Nouvelle, viz. L'Adroite Princesse. Troisieme Edition [sic]* London: Printed for R. Montagu at the Book Ware-House, that End of Great Queen-Street, next Drury Lane, and J. Pote, at Eton, 1737. fingerprint B3 = ceefst. Cotsen.

———. *Histories, or Tales of Passed Times. With morals. Written in French by M. Perrault, And Englished by R. S. Gent. The Third Edition. Corrected. With Cuts to every Tale.* London: Printed for R. Montagu, at the Book Ware-House, that End of Great-Queen-Street, next Drury-Lane, and J. Pote, at Eton, 1741. fingerprint B2 = *iffer. Cotsen.

———. *Contes De Ma Mere L'Oye. Mother Goose's Tales.* The Hague: Jean Neaulme, 1745. Cotsen.

———. *Histories, or Tales of Passed Times. With Morals written in French by M. Perrault, And*

Englished by R.S. Gent. The Fourth Edition, Corrected. With Cuts to every Tale. London: For James Hodges, at the Looking-Glass, facing St. Magnus Church, London-Bridge, 1750. Morgan Library, New York.

———. *Contes De Ma Mere L'Oye. Ornée de neuf belles Figures de Cuivre. Sixieme Edition.* The Hague: Pierre Van Os, 1759. fingerprint A2 = ron_A3 = *t_de. Cotsen.

———. *Mother Goose's Tales.* Salisbury: B. Collins; Devizes: Mrs. Maynard; London: Mr. Bristow, 1763. See note 6, above.

———. *Tales of Passed Times by Mother Goose. With Morals. In French by M. Perrault, And Englished by R. S. Gent, To which is added a New one, viz. The Discreet Princess. The Sixth Edition, Corrected, and adorned with fine Cuts.* London: Printed for J. Melvil, Bookseller in Exeter change in the Strand, 1764. fingerprint A4 = pero. Cotsen.

———. *Mother Goose's Tales, in French and English, with Morals. Written in French by M. Perrault, and Englished by R. S. Gent. To which is added a New One, viz. The Discreet Princess. The Sixth Edition, Corrected, and adorned with fine Cuts.* Hague: Printed for Van Os and Sold by J. Pridden at the Feathers in Fleetstreet, London, 1765. fingerprint A4 = pero. Cotsen.

———. *Histories or Tales of Past Times, told by Mother Goose. With Morals. Written in French by M. Perrault, and Englished by G. M. Gent. The Fifth Edition, corrected.* Salisbury: Printed and sold by B. Collins, also by [London:] Newbery and Carnan in St. Paul's Church-Yard; and S. Crowder, in Pater-Noster-Row, [1769]. fingerprint A3 = ich_. Cotsen.

———. *Tales of Past Times, by Old Mother Goose with morals.* London: W. Osborne & T. Griffin, [ca. 1780].

Pickering, Samuel Jr. *John Locke and Children's Books in Eighteenth-Century England.* Knoxville: University of Tennessee Press, 1981.

A Pretty Book for Children, 7th ed. London: J. Newbery, J. Hodges, and B. Collins, 1756. fingerprint B3 = plig. Cotsen.

Schiller, Justin. "Charles Perrault and His 'Contes des Fées': Rare and Collectible Editions Published between 1691–1826 with Related Publications of This Genre, Being Contributions Toward a Bibliography Assembled 1977–1994 as the Personal Library of Justin G. Schiller." Kingston, N.Y., 1995. Xeroxed typescript. Cotsen.

Scot, Reginald. *The discouerie of witchcraft, Wherein the lewde dealing of witches, and witch mongers is notablie detected, the knauerie of coniurors, the impietie of inchantors, the follies of soothsaiers, the impudent falshood of cousenors, the infidelitie of atheists, the petilent practice of Pythonists, the curiosities of figure casters, the vanitie of dreamers, the beggerlie art of Alcumystrie, the abhomination of idolatrie, the horrible art of poisoning, the vertue and power of naturall magike, and all the conueniences of Legerdemaine and iuggling are deciphered, and many other things opened, which have long lien hidden, howbeit verie necessarie to be knowne. Heereunto is added a treatise vpon the nature and substance of spirits and diuills, Ec.: all latelie written by Reginald Scot Esquire.* London: William Brome, 1584.

Summerfield, Geoffrey. *Fantasy and Reason: Children's Literature in the Eighteenth Century.* Athens: University of Georgia Press, 1985.

Tucker, Nicholas. "Fairy Tales and Their Early Opponents." In Mary Hilton, Morag Styles, and Victor Watson, eds., *Opening the Nursery Door: Reading, Writing and Childhood 1600–1900.* London: Routledge, 1997. 104–16.

Verdier, Gabrielle. "Comment l'auteur des 'Fées à la mode' devint 'Mother Bunch': Métamorphoses de la Comtesse d'Aulnoy en Angleterre." *Marvels and Tales* 10.2 (1996): 285–309.

"Very capital reading for children": Reading as Play in Hawthorne's A Wonder Book for Girls and Boys

Ellen Butler Donovan

In 1837 Nathaniel Hawthorne was, once again, confronting the realities of earning his living as a writer. The funds from the Manning estate that had supported his decade-long self-imposed literary apprenticeship were drying up (Turner 90). Although he had published more than forty sketches in literary magazines and annuals, he was virtually unknown because his works had appeared anonymously. For the first time, a book, *Twice Told Tales,* would appear under his own name, but he was not sanguine that its publication would provide enough fame or fortune to support him. In a letter dated June 4, 1837, to Henry Wadsworth Longfellow he admitted that cobbling together freelance work would be necessary in order to make a living: "I see little prospect but that I must scribble for a living. But this troubles me much less than you would suppose. I can turn my pen to all sorts of drudgery, such as children's books, &c" (Turner 89). His characterization of children's books as "drudgery" was not an isolated comment of a disaffected author. In a subsequent letter to Longfellow dated March 21, 1838, he reports two offers to "perpetrate children's histories and other such iniquities," and in a letter to his friend George Hillard he characterizes "concocting school books" as well as translation work and journalism as "drudgery" (Pearce 297 and 296). As far as Hawthorne was concerned, the juvenile market was a necessary evil—it paid the bills.

Hawthorne knew the drudgery of the juvenile market. With his sister Elizabeth he had written the two-volume *Peter Parley's Universal History on the Basis of Geography* for Samuel Goodrich, a task that reduced him to a hack writer following Goodrich's specific instructions. He had contributed to the juvenile annual *Youth's Keepsake* in 1835, and he published sketches in juvenile periodicals, such as *Boys' and Girls' Magazine* and *The Child's Friend,* in the next decade but subsequently refused to contribute regularly because such sketches were "overdone" and consequently would not pay much (Pearce 301). His eventual sister-in-law, Elizabeth Peabody, was to publish his *Grandfather's Chair* series (1840–

Children's Literature 30, ed. Elizabeth Lennox Keyser and Julie Pfeiffer (Yale University Press, © 2002 Hollins University).

41) and arrange for publication of *Biographical Stories,* juvenile histories that Peabody hoped would be included in the school libraries Horace Mann was establishing in Massachusetts.

Yet a decade later, in 1851, Hawthorne willingly wrote a book for children, *A Wonder Book for Girls and Boys* (1852), and in its preface he described the task of writing the book as "one of the most agreeable, of a literary kind" (4). What had happened in the interim to change drudgery into pleasure? Probably a number of factors changed his attitude. As the father of three young children—Una and Julian, ages seven and five, respectively, and infant Rose—he probably had more sympathy for the juvenile reader than he had expressed a decade earlier as a young bachelor. But it is clear that his professional life had also taken a turn for the better, allowing him more freedom to define and execute his projects. The financial and critical success of *The Scarlet Letter* (1850), the recent completion of *The House of the Seven Gables* (1851), and a willing publisher in James T. Fields provided the stability for Hawthorne to try a project that he had been contemplating for over ten years—a book for children that might "entirely revolutionize the whole system of juvenile literature" (letter to Longfellow, March 21, 1838; quoted in Pearce 298).[1]

A Wonder Book for Girls and Boys, published by Ticknor, Reed and Fields in November 1851 but dated 1852, consists of six retellings of Greek myths, each framed by an introduction and conclusion. The frame narratives are titled to highlight the scenery of the Berkshires and the activities of the storyteller, Eustace Bright, and the children who are his auditors. *Wonder Book* has, for the most part, passed out of favor in the twentieth century, despite being continuously in print since its initial publication and being illustrated in the twentieth century by both Maxfield Parrish and Walter Crane.[2] Its coy style and sentimental tone are too saccharine for today's children, and advances in printing technology have made the large format picture book a more popular medium for myths and legends. *Wonder Book,* however, remains an important historical text because it contributed to the shift in reading culture that allowed children to read with and for pleasure. By moving the myths from the arena of scholarship and the schoolroom to the family drawing room and by encouraging a playful rather than reverential response from readers, Hawthorne encouraged reading as a pleasurable pastime activity for children.

Historians of nineteenth-century American children's literature, such as Gillian Avery and Anne Scott MacLeod, have emphasized the didactic quality of the literature. The scope and intentions of their works do not lend themselves to noting the slight variations or anomalous texts that reflect other reading practices. Studies in print culture of the period do suggest a more complicated and varied reading experience was available to mid-century readers. David D. Hall in "The Uses of Literacy in New England, 1600–1850" pinpoints a change in print culture during the decades between the 1770s and the 1850s in both England and the United States that illuminates the reading context of *Wonder Book*. Hall argues that because of changes in printing technology and a rapid increase in literacy, new literary genres, such as Samuel Goodrich's Peter Parley books, developed, and a new relationship emerged between writers and their audiences (37). Hall uses Goodrich's autobiographical writings as well as other sources to show that people approached the act of reading differently in the nineteenth century than they had previously. When books were primarily devotional and scarce, readers approached the text reverentially and with intensity. But as books became more affordable and as literacy rates rose, people's reading patterns became more voracious: "In the new age of fiction and daily journalism, people moved 'hastily' from one day's paper to the next, and from one novel to another. No book, not even the Bible, retained the aura that certain texts had once possessed" (76). This shift in reading attitudes in part explains and accounts for Hawthorne's intentions in *Wonder Book*. When readers view books as consumable rather than as precious artifacts, then readers have the freedom to consider reading as play or pastime.

Hawthorne's subject matter—the Greek myths—also had a multifaceted role in American culture in the mid-century. In *The Rise of Modern Mythology, 1680–1860,* Feldman and Richardson explain that Greek mythology was primarily the material of scholarship, though "there were also numerous handy reference books for women and schoolchildren" (505), including among a list of representative examples Samuel Goodrich's *A Book of Mythology for Youth* (1832). Explicitly designed for use in the schoolroom, Goodrich's book, like others of its kind, is "boiled out of handbooks that have been boiled out of still earlier handbooks" (505). In contrast to such tasteless and unappealing redactions of the stories into bits of information, Feldman and Richardson attribute to Hawthorne, along with Kingsley and Bulfinch, the most significant development in the popular knowledge of mythology: "These men were not students so much as retellers of myth, and they managed, apparently independently of one another, to uniformly recast Greek mythology into a genteel Victorian subject" (505–6). Although Kingsley's and Bulfinch's versions of the Greek myths are perhaps better known today, Hawthorne's *Wonder Book,* appearing in 1852, was the first of the trio to introduce the myths to children outside of the context of school.

Douglas Bush and Robert D. Richardson Jr. contribute further insights into the role of mythology in nineteenth-century America. As Richardson explains, "Most early nineteenth-century books of myth for children approached the subject rather sourly as 'heathen idolatry'" (342). In contrast, Bush, in his account of the role of mythology in nineteenth-century poetry, notes that in America Greek mythology was frequently alluded to in the work of a "swarm of small versifiers" (482–83). Hellenism (like the fairy literature that I will discuss presently) had a kind of currency in the nineteenth century: "All the ladies and gentlemen of New England possessed high ideals and a copy of Bulfinch. The more decorous Greek myths were part of the furniture of the Bostonian mind" (482). Although Greek mythology was a subject for instruction in school, Hawthorne's *Wonder Book,* appearing two years before Bulfinch's work, surely contributed to the currency of Greek mythology in the culture that Bush notes.

Hawthorne quite clearly sought to distinguish the stories in the *Wonder Book* from a dry, academic study of Greek mythology or from criticisms of "heathen idolatry." In the preface to his collection Hawthorne remarks that "in the present version they [the stories] may have lost much of their classical aspect (or, at all events, the author has not been careful to preserve it), and have perhaps assumed a Gothic or romantic guise" (9). The juxtaposition between classical and Gothic echoes other statements by Hawthorne in which he defends his romantic emphasis on sentiment and the heart over the coldness of intellect associated with classicism (McPherson 42). In addition, the emphasis suggests that readers approach the tales without the typical high seriousness of classical scholarship, thereby suggesting the child's reading experience is a suitable pastime.

Hawthorne must have assumed that such a treatment of the myths would be viewed with skepticism, for he repeatedly reminds his readers that he is not going to treat the myths with a scholarly seriousness.[3] In the "Tanglewood Porch" introduction to "The Gorgon's Head," the narrator concludes his introduction of the child auditors and the storyteller, the sophomoric Eustace Bright, by disavowing any responsibility to scholarly authorities: "incurring great obligations to Professor Anthon, he [Bright], nevertheless, disregarded all classical authorities, when ever the vagrant audacity of his imagination impelled him to do so" (9). Such a disavowal acknowledges Hawthorne's source for the myths (Anthon's work was one of the most widely published and respected scholarly treatments) but also allows his narrator complete freedom to embellish or digress from the source. In other words, unlike the school handbooks that provided information or allusions one must master to understand the literature of Western civilization, these stories were meant to be enjoyed as *stories*. Any adults who were peeking over the children's shoulders were clearly reminded that accurate transcription was not part of Hawthorne's intentions.[4]

Hawthorne's strongest statement regarding the pleasure of the tales and his disavowal of scholarly intention occurs in the "Tanglewood Fireside" introduction to "The Three Golden Apples." Mr. Pringle, the father of some of the child auditors and himself a classical scholar, requests that Bright tell a tale in his presence in order that he might "judge whether they are likely to do any mischief" (87). Hawthorne here is directly addressing the contemporary reaction to the fairy stories and other noneducational stories that were proliferating at mid-century, a phenomenon well documented by Avery, Attebery, MacLeod, and West. Bright's diffident response to Mr. Pringle's request highlights the intentions Hawthorne has for the stories: "be kind enough to remember that I am addressing myself to the imagination and sympathies of the children, not to your own" (89). Here, as elsewhere, Hawthorne refers to his audience in defense of his treatment of the tales. Consistently his appeal is to imagination rather than knowledge.

Although Hawthorne will ultimately link the imagination with the spiritual (in "The Chimera") as he does in his works for adults, throughout *Wonder Book* imagination is primarily associated with play. Hawthorne's notebooks suggest that children's imaginative play was their primary activity. He records many instances of Una and Julian role-playing activities and events, including the illness and death of his mother, without any criticism of such activity. Further, he comments, "A plaything should be suggestive to the child's imagination, but merely suggestive; and the more work it leaves the imagination to do, the better will the child be occupied and satisfied" (*American Notebooks* 428). The principle stated here, i.e., that the plaything should prompt imaginative activity, underscores Eustace Bright's argument against Mr. Pringle. Eustace's play with the myths will provide the child auditors with imaginative play in order to better occupy and satisfy them.

The connection in Hawthorne's thinking between imagination, creativity, and play is also revealed in the extant documents relating the composition of *Wonder Book*. In a letter to his publisher, James T. Fields, on April 7, 1851, Hawthorne describes the book: "It shall not be exclusively Fairy tales, but intermixed with stories of real life, and classical myths modernized and made funny, and all sorts of tom-foolery-The Child's Budget of Miscellaneous Nonsense" (Pearce 303). Later, when he writes the preface he describes as "pleasant" the task of writing the tales, "a task fit for hot weather, and one of the most agreeable, of a literary kind" (4). McPherson hypothesizes, "Since Hawthorne disliked writing during the hot weather, he must have felt that the composition of a half-dozen nursery tales would be more pleasure than work" (38). Bibliographical evidence shows that he wrote the collection over the course of just forty days in June and July of 1851, and that the writing came easily; the manuscripts show little revision.[5] Hawthorne's own composing process and his prefatory remarks about writing *Wonder Book* reinforce the book's playful quality rather than any didactic purpose.[6]

Beyond these overt statements as to his intentions, Hawthorne's use of the frame narratives encourages his readers to approach the stories with attitudes of play and pleasure rather than sober scholarship. For example, in the frames Hawthorne borrows elements of popular fairy stories prevalent in both British and American children's literature of the early part of the century. Hawthorne's models were not the tales that were based on folk material, such as those the Grimm brothers collected, but an almost forgotten body of literature that has survived only in historical surveys of children's literature. The small books portray light-hearted fantasy, "which had not a trace of moral value, nor the least touch of archness, patronage, grown-up-ness, be-good-ness" (Darton 205). The first and best known of these books, William Roscoe's *The Butterfly's Ball and the Grasshopper's Feast* (1807), was so successful as to be imitated by many other authors, including, in the United States, Lydia Huntley Sigourney.[7]

Adult audiences were also reading fairy literature. Attebery surveys the sentimental fairy verse that was published widely in popular literary periodicals during the first half of the century. According to his account, such works as Joseph Rodman Drake's "The Culprit Fay" (1835), a verse narrative describing the actions of fairies in the landscape of the Hudson River Valley, were attempts to interpret the American landscape using the conventions popular in England at the time (28–29). For the same educated, sentimental audience that was reading "The Culprit Fay" or Washington Irving's "The Legend of Sleepy Hollow," James Kirke Paulding wrote a collection of fairy stories for the Christmas trade, *A Christmas Gift from Fairy Land* (1838). In his tongue-in-cheek preface, Paulding defends the belief in the existence of fairies in the New World and articulates the ideas and values popularly associated with fairies:

> There is something intrinsically delightful in these airy creations, whether of the imagination or the senses. Their agency was of a light, pleasing, and gentle character, and unlike the old Gothic superstitions, devoid of cruelty or malignity. In their kindness they were beneficent and even in their punishments, there was nothing to inspire terror, horror, or despair. All was diminutive in Fairyland; the little beings did not, like giants, ogres, and witches, indulge unnatural appetites, or deal in bloody atrocities. They were the creations of an age of comparative simplicity and innocence, and partook in the characteristics of pastoral gentleness (ii–iii).

Paulding's preface suggests that the fairy had become a trope associated with the romantic idea of childhood as natural and innocent. Rather than call upon the complex spectrum of ideas associated with fairies that include fairies as tricksters, as inhabitants of a marvelous other world, or as explanations of the unknown and frightening, Paulding emphasizes gentleness, simplicity, innocence, lightness, smallness, and a pastoral landscape, thereby linking them to the romantic ideal of childhood.

When we turn to the frame narratives that accompany each of the mythological tales in *Wonder Book*, we find Hawthorne drawing on the same ideas that Paulding uses. Whereas Paulding's fairies are expressions of romantic childhood, Hawthorne's children are fairylike. In the naming of the characters and the descriptions of their behaviors, Hawthorne presents the child auditors and their behaviors in the context of the pastoral and innocent fairy world.

Initially, the narrator insists that he will not make the same mistake as other authors and give "the names of real persons to the characters of their books," explaining that such references get the author into "great trouble," presumably because the character can then be confused with a real person of the same name (6). Instead the narrator names the children after flowers, such as Periwinkle, Dandelion, Milkweed, or Cowslip, acknowledging that such names "might better suit a group of fairies than a company of earthly children" (6).[8] Hawthorne further characterizes the children as fairies by describing them in language conventionally associated with fairy behavior. Frequently he refers to the group of children as "little folks" (116). As the children set out to gather nuts after the telling of the first tale, the narrator uses such language as "hop, skip, and jump" and "all sorts of frisks and gambols" to characterize their movement (36). In subsequent tales, the children are associated with the natural settings. Whether nutting, sledding, or climbing a local high hill, the children are perfectly at home in the pastoral world: they spread their picnic lunch "on the stumps of trees and on mossy trunks" (38); they disappear and reappear suddenly in the snow ("And while they were wondering and staring about, up started Squash-Blossom out of a snow-bank, with the reddest face you ever saw, and looking as if a large scarlet flower had suddenly sprouted up in midwinter" [86]); they are associated with the wild flowers of meadows (116–17).

Such metaphoric connections can be used to illustrate Hawthorne's romantic view of children as beings who reside in a golden age, unencumbered with the quotidian reality of adult life (as Richard Hathaway argues in "Hawthorne and the Paradise of Children"); or to show, as Elizabeth Peck does, that such names and behaviors are remarkably nonsexist. More important, Hawthorne's strategies relieve readers from the need to see the children as didactic exempla, either for good or ill.

The idealized settings, both the Berkshire countryside and the unlocalized settings of the myths themselves, contribute to cultivation of play as a response to *Wonder Book*. The Berkshire countryside that Hawthorne creates is a real, specific locale, but it is also an idealized pastoral landscape that always offers pleasure and never threatens with danger.[9] The children in the frame narratives are always safe though they climb trees, wade brooks, and tumble into snow banks. Likewise, the myths themselves take place in settings that are idealized and unlocalized, as Richardson noted (344). Though Hawthorne mentions Greece or other geographical elements in three of the stories, he also begins four of the stories with a formulaic opening, such as "Long, long, ago" or "Once in the old, old times," creating a distant and imprecise locale familiar to readers of folk tales. The effect of these unlocalized and idealized settings is to create a safe imaginative play space, analogous to a safe physical play space. Hawthorne describes such a safe space at their home in the Berkshires: "Our metes and bounds are rather narrow; but still there is fair room for them to play under the elms, the pear-tree, and the two or three plum trees, that over-shadow our brick avenue and little grass-plot. There is air, too, as good almost as country-air, from across the North-river; and so our little people flourish in the unrestrained freedom which they enjoy within these limits" (*American Notebooks* 423). While the description does ac-knowledge the limits of the space, more interesting is that such a space allows for "unrestrained freedom." Within the limits of the covers of the book, Hawthorne creates a safe place for imaginative play, reliev-ing Eustace of any responsibility to his sources and developing in the child auditors the imaginative capacity to participate in the creation of the stories.

Key to Hawthorne's playful intentions is his remarkable invented storyteller, Eustace Bright. Eustace, a college sophomore, is a puck-ish character who is consistently described as active, playful, a larger version of the children/fairies themselves. For example, he "proved his fitness to preside over the party by outdoing all their antics and performing several new capers" (36); "he had been as active as a squir-rel or a monkey" (38); he made Christmas "merrier by his presence" (61); he invented "several new kinds of play, which kept them all in a roar of merriment till bedtime" (83); he "was as merry, as playful, as good-humored, as light of foot and of spirits, and equally a favor-ite with the little folks as he had always been" (116). Such descriptions prevent Eustace from being the typical adult figure of mid-century children's literature, sagacious, a dispenser of wisdom or truth. He is simply a larger version of the children themselves. The puckish quali-ties of Eustace reinforce the characterization of the children as fairies and heighten the playfulness that distinguishes *Wonder Book* as a book intended for pastime enjoyment rather than instruction.

Beyond the clear connections to fairy images that Hawthorne uses to develop Eustace's character, Hawthorne also undercuts Eustace's adult status in the collection. The narrator ironically describes Eustace as having reached "the venerable age of eighteen years" so that "he felt quite like a grandfather" to the children (7). He supposedly has trouble with his eyesight, which has delayed his return to college, but the narrator remarks, "I have seldom met with a pair of eyes that looked as if they could see farther or better than those of Eustace

Bright" (7), suggesting that his complaint is merely a ploy to postpone his return. Furthermore, the spectacles that Eustace has adopted are stolen from him by Huckleberry, and "as the student [Eustace] forgot to take them back, they fell off into the grass, and lay there till the next spring" (7). Such undercutting prevents readers from taking Eustace Bright seriously. In a subsequent frame narrative, the family dog accompanies the children on their expedition because he "probably felt it to be his duty not to trust the children away from their parents without some better guardian than this feather-brained Eustace Bright" (36).

Although Eustace as an adult figure is consistently undercut in the collection, the other adult, Mr. Pringle, fares worse. Hawthorne's treatment of Mr. Pringle's role goes far to suggest that Hawthorne intends for his child readers to enjoy their reading pleasure outside the influence of adult considerations or criteria.

Mr. Pringle appears only once, in a conversation with Eustace tucked deep in the collection, as part of the introductory frame to "The Three Golden Apples." The conventions of nineteenth-century children's fiction would have invested a great deal of authority in Mr. Pringle as the children's benevolent father and as a classical scholar of Greek mythology. His opinion and knowledge would have been deferred to, especially by the child characters. In other words, he should be a controlling narrative force. And though Hawthorne never subverts Mr. Pringle's role as a parent, he displaces his narrative authority by giving to Eustace convincing counterarguments to his conservative defense of classicism. Mr. Pringle complains to Eustace, "Your imagination is altogether Gothic, and will inevitably Gothicize everything that you touch. The effect is like bedaubing a marble statue with paint" (112). Disturbed by Eustace's versions of the tales, he further admonishes, "Pray let me advise you never more to meddle with a classical myth" (112). Eustace's response is based on the mutually reinforcing ideologies of literary nationalism and Romanticism established by the 1850s. Eustace insists on his right to change the legends and asserts that Mr. Pringle's appreciation of the tales is diminished because it is bound by his classicism:

> Sir, if you would only bring your mind into such a relation with these fables as is necessary in order to remodel them, you would see at once that an old Greek had no more exclusive right to them than a modern Yankee has. They are the common property of the

world, and of all time. The ancient poets remodeled them at pleasure, and held them plastic in their hands; and why should they
not be plastic in my hands as well? (112).

In other words, Eustace as storyteller is free to create rather than slav-
ishly follow the myths.[10] Conversely, Mr. Pringle does not appreciate
Eustace's play with the tales and the more comic sensibility he creates,
preferring instead the "elegance" (112) of his own scholarly treatment
which is concerned with accuracy and history. In the end, Mr. Pringle
acquiesces to Eustace without really agreeing with him. Hawthorne's
strategy undermines the authority of Mr. Pringle, thereby removing
him from the conventional role of moral guide or even as a model
of the ideal reader. This displacement, combined with the humorous
undercutting of Eustace, leaves the text open to children's imaginative
play.

Without an authoritative adult figure who might provide an interpretation or moral lesson, child readers in *Wonder Book* are freer to
respond to the stories at their own levels. This activity is encouraged,
even modeled, in the responses of two auditors, Sweet Fern and Primrose. Sweet Fern's role in *Wonder Book* is developed in "Shadow Brook,"
the concluding frame of "The Golden Touch." He is described as "a
good little boy, who was always making particular inquiries about the
precise height of giants and the littleness of fairies" (59). These questions, familiar to anyone who has read with children, satisfy the child's
particular interests but often are unrelated to what adults might consider the significant aspects of the story. Sweet Fern wants to know such
details as Marygold's weight after she was turned into gold (59), the
dimensions of Pandora's box (82), the breadth of Hercules' shoulders,
the height of the giant Atlas, even the size of the oak trees growing between Atlas's toes (111–12), and the capacity of Baucis and Philemon's
magical pitcher (138).

Such questions might be ignored as sentimental coyness or whimsy
on Hawthorne's part—the doting father portraying his own experience with his small charming children.[11] To write off such a clearly
repeated element in the stories, however, does an injustice to Hawthorne's intentions to write something that would be "very capital
reading for children" (3). He presents a view of reading that gives space
to a typical child's response rather than the clearly controlled cate-
chism of the didactic literature of the period.[12]

Eustace treats Sweet Fern's questions quite seriously, without a side glance or wink at possible adult readers. Even when he seems a little dismayed at the question, Eustace always provides the precise information Sweet Fern desires in terms accommodated to his imaginative capacity: "'O Sweet Fern, Sweet Fern!' cried the student. 'Do you think that I was there, to measure him [the giant Atlas] with a yardstick? Well, if you must know to a hair's-breadth, I suppose he might be from three to fifteen miles straight upward, and that he might have seated himself on Taconic, and had Monument Mountain for a footstool'" (111). Sweet Fern's questions continually ask Eustace to draw upon his storyteller's creativity to satisfy him. Hawthorne directs the reader's attention less toward Sweet Fern's lack of understanding than toward Eustace as storyteller. Can Eustace satisfy his auditor's imaginative needs?

Primrose is just as challenging an auditor as Sweet Fern. But instead of asking questions, she challenges Eustace or comments on his abilities as a storyteller. Clearly the oldest of the auditors, Primrose is "a bright girl of twelve, with laughing eyes" (8). She makes fun of Eustace from the moment she is introduced, and the other children, who are pleading for a story, call her "naughty" for doing so. She knows more than the other children and hence is a mild threat to Eustace's storytelling:

> "Sit down, then, every soul of you," said Eustace Bright, "and be all as still as so many mice. At the slightest interruption, whether from great naughty Primrose, little Dandelion, or any other, I shall bite the story short off between my teeth and swallow the untold part. But, in the first place, do any of you know what a Gorgon is?"
> "I do," said Primrose.
> "Then hold your tongue!" rejoined Eustace, who had rather she would have known nothing about the matter. (9)

Initially Primrose responds with skepticism to Eustace's telling of "The Gorgon's Head." She finds nothing wonderful in the one tooth the Three Gray Women share, supposing it to be a false tooth. She criticizes his portrayal of Quicksilver and his sister as "ridiculous" (35). She recognizes, however, that the story is good for something: it has passed the time and the mist has lifted so that the children can proceed with their nutting expedition. Primrose's response suggests Hawthorne's intentions for the book: the tales should be full of wonder, and they should allow the reader/auditor to pass the time pleasantly.

Hawthorne mines the conflict between Primrose and Eustace as a source of humor, reinforcing a playful tone that suggests the tales are a light-hearted pastime. After each story Primrose criticizes Eustace's storytelling ability. When he finishes his telling of the King Midas legend, "saucy" Primrose first notes that the story "was famous one thousands [*sic*] of years before Mr. Eustace Bright came into the world," before commenting ironically, "But some people have what we may call 'The Leaden Touch,' and make everything dull and heavy that they lay their fingers upon" (58). When Eustace finishes the story of Pandora's Box ("The Paradise of Children"), he asks Primrose, "Don't you think her [Pandora] the exact picture of yourself? But you would not have hesitated half so long about opening the box" (82). Primrose promptly retorts, "the first thing to pop out, after the lid was lifted, would have been Mr. Eustace Bright, in the shape of a Trouble" (82). And when Primrose calls Eustace to come tell a story before her father, Mr. Pringle, she calls his stories "nonsense" (88). (Notably, Primrose, like the other children, is silent during the discussion between Mr. Pringle and Eustace Bright on the merits of his versions of the tales.) When the children ask for a story as they rest after their climb up Bald Summit, Primrose sarcastically remarks: "Perhaps the mountain air may make you poetical, for once. And no matter how strange and wonderful the story may be, now that we are up among the clouds, we can believe anything" (143).

Hawthorne, however, also develops the relationship between Primrose and Eustace to emphasize wonder. At the end of "The Chimera," the story Eustace tells on Bald Summit, Primrose is in tears: "for she was conscious of something in the legend which the rest of them were not yet old enough to feel. Child's story as it was, the student had contrived to breathe through it the ardor, the generous hope, and the imaginative enterprise of youth" (168). Her response gratifies Eustace: "I forgive you, now, Primrose . . . for all your ridicule of myself and my stories. One tear pays for a great deal of laughter" (168). But Hawthorne refuses to allow sentiment to control the ending. Primrose recovers her wit sufficiently to remark, "it certainly does elevate your ideas, to get your head above the clouds" (168).

The banter between Eustace and Primrose at the conclusion of "The Chimera" also allows Hawthorne a self-referential wink at his readers. When the children continue their use of the Pegasus trope to signify a flight of imagination, Hawthorne, through Eustace, mentions his fellow writers living in the region. Primrose adds that the neighbor, a

"silent man" with two small children, is also an author. Eustace urges
her to hush:

> "If our babble were to reach his ears, and happen not to please
> him, he has but to fling a quire or two of paper into the stove,
> and you, Primrose, and I, and Periwinkle, Sweet Fern, Squash-
> Blossom, Blue Eye, Huckleberry, Clover, Cowslip, Plaintain, Milk-
> weed, Dandelion, and Buttercup, —yes, and wise Mr. Pringle, with
> his unfavorable criticisms on my legends, and poor Mrs. Pringle,
> too, —would all turn to smoke, and go whisking up the funnel!"
> (169–70).

By the end of the conversation Eustace has completely broken the
frame narrative, insisting that he will write out his stories (171), which
will be published by Fields and illustrated by Billings (who provided
the illustrations for the first edition). Thus, the readers are included in
the play of the exchange, for they need only be familiar with the title
page to participate in the joke. The breaking of the frame narrative
also emphasizes that the book as a whole is a playful construct, con-
flating Hawthorne with the youthful and spritely Eustace Bright and
the book as pleasurable a pastime as the stories Eustace tells.

When we turn to the specific legends and myths in *Wonder Book*, we
can see that Hawthorne presents the stories without the heroic grandeur that often accompanies the tales. In fact, one of the most serious
criticisms of *Wonder Book* is that the versions Eustace Bright tells lack
power. Attebery complains that they lack "the original grandeur and
mystery" (63). Arbuthnot trenchantly remarks, "He told an entrancing
story, but he lost almost completely the dignity of the gods, and sometimes he even lost the dignity of the story. . . . On the whole no one has
taken such devastating liberties with mythology as Hawthorne except
Walt Disney" (295).[13] Richardson, too, sees Hawthorne's retellings as
transforming myths into fairy tales. He notes that Hawthorne "generally avoided creation myths, Homeric stories and stories from Greek
tragedy" (344). Instead he chose stories that hinge on magic or transformation and then domesticates them: "Greece is never mentioned
and it all could be happening in the Berkshires. . . . Hawthorne con-
verts heroes and heroines into children and ordinary people. Gods become mysterious strangers or eccentric adults" (344). Unlike Arbuthnot and Attebery, however, Richardson looks to Bruno Bettelheim's
work to defend Hawthorne's choice of the fairy tale genre as appropriate for children. Richardson argues that "Fairy Tales as clearly dis-

tinguished from myths have an important function for children," primarily in identity formation (346). Quoting Bettelheim, Richardson states, "Unlike myth, 'fairy tales intimate that rewarding, good life is within one's reach despite adversity—but only if one does not shy away from the hazardous struggles without which one can never achieve true identity'" (346). Richardson's comments respond directly to the criticisms quoted above. By narrowing the range or scope of the stories, by transforming power and awe into magic, wonder, and delight, Hawthorne places the stories within the intellectual and emotional range of children who have neither the experience nor the intellectual ability to grasp the full implications of the myths. The safety that Hawthorne creates make these stories suitable for children's imaginative play.

Like Richardson, Baym makes explicit the ways that *A Wonder Book* reflects Hawthorne's "perceptions of audience needs and tastes" (35): "Stripped of all their real strangeness, they [the tales] display instead a kind of fanciful whimsy. They are divested of their emotional ferocity and their archaic moral and religious significances and references, and are turned instead to the function of whiling away the empty hours of children whose parents are well off" (39). According to Baym, Hawthorne turns the stories of Hercules, Bellerophon, and Perseus into "adventure stories pure and simple," while the stories of Pandora, King Midas, and Baucis and Philemon are developed as "domestic stories, stressing simplified familial relationships" (38). Baym, who brushes aside this success of Hawthorne's vision and execution to address his more ambivalent experience in the subsequent collection, *Tanglewood Tales,* concludes that the stories "exhibit a conventional socializing didacticism, inculcating feminine and masculine virtues appropriate to the places assigned to the sexes in society" (39). While I agree that Hawthorne is not breaking new ground in these stories in terms of gender assumptions, I would like to address the ways in which Hawthorne's execution of the stories does provide a creative and imaginative experience rather than another instance of cultivating conventional social behavior in children.

As Baym has argued, the domesticity of the tales precludes some of the thematic content we often associate with the myths—the mythopoetic elements that attempt to describe the role of human beings in the universe. Such treatment lessens the tragic and heroic, making the characters of the tales more common and their exploits, while wondrous, less cosmically significant. For example, instead of focusing on the isolated hero, the tales emphasize familial relationships. In "The Miraculous Pitcher," the focus of the story is on the relationship between Baucis and Philemon and their hospitality to strangers. Similarly, in "The Golden Touch" Bright includes a daughter for King Midas, Marygold, who turns to gold when her father kisses her. It is her transformation, rather than King Midas's recognition that he will be unable to eat his own food, that convinces Midas that other things have more value than gold. In "The Paradise of Children," the narrator goes to great lengths to explain how children can live happily and well without their fathers and mothers (66). Even in "The Gorgon's Head," a tale Baym classifies as an adventure story, Perseus's relationship with his mother is a motif. Repeatedly, even at moments of great danger, such as when Perseus is being pursued by the two remaining Gorgons, Bright reminds readers that Perseus has a mother: "Had Perseus looked them in the face, or had he fallen into their clutches, his poor mother would never have kissed her boy again" (31). Instead of emphasizing the heroic adventure, the narrative emphasizes the maternal loss that will occur if Perseus fails. Further, this loss would be the responsibility of the child Perseus, rather than the mother. Hence, Hawthorne is not only emphasizing familial bonds but constructing them in ways that place the child at the center of family life. The child's agency within the various stories forecasts the auditors' and readers' agency in the frame narratives.

Besides emphasizing familial relationships, Eustace always includes details of furnishings and meals, the stuff of domestic life. His most famous invention, the New England breakfast that King Midas hopes to enjoy, stops the progress of the narrative to focus on domestic details:

> What was usually a king's breakfast in the days of Midas, I really do not know, and cannot stop now to investigate. To the best of my belief, however, on this particular morning, the breakfast consisted of hot cakes, some nice little brook trout, roasted potatoes, fresh boiled eggs, and coffee, for King Midas himself, and a bowl of bread and milk for his daughter Marygold. At all events, this is a breakfast fit to set before a king; and whether he had it or not, King Midas could not have had a better (48).

The details of domestic life are also a major portion of "The Paradise of Children," the retelling of the Pandora story: the fruit Epimetheus eats, the games the children play, the elaborate description of the box—all contribute to an essentially domestic scene. In "The Three

Golden Apples," the narrator devotes one-third of the tale to a very minor incident—a group of nymphs feed and entertain Hercules before they send him on his way to the Old One who can tell him how to reach the Garden of the Hesperides. Bright develops this incident to review some of Hercules' past exploits, but that information shares the space equally with the description of the food the nymphs offer Hercules or of the flower wreaths they make and fling over his head and shoulders. Further, Bright tells the version of the story in which Hercules holds up the sky while Atlas retrieves the apples. By doing so, he avoids portraying a battle scene between Hercules and the dragons guarding the apples, and the comic exchange that allows Hercules to trick Atlas into taking the sky back onto his shoulders maintains the comic tone of the collection.

Coinciding with this domestic emphasis is a mitigation of the monstrous. As just noted, Bright presents a version of Hercules' adventures that allows him to avoid describing another monster. The Gray Women in "The Gorgon's Head" are comical rather than awesome or horrifying while the Gorgons are described as "an awful, gigantic kind of insect,—immense, golden-winged beetles, or dragon-flies, or things of that sort,—at once ugly and beautiful" (28). The metaphorical connection with insects familiarizes the monsters, making them understandable to children, even though the actual metaphor is inconsistent with previous descriptions of them. Such familiarity brings the legends into the narrower scope and understanding of children.[14]

Beyond the domestic situations that Hawthorne seems to find safe and comforting for children and thus suitable for imaginative play, Hawthorne creates in the tales a moral universe which is so familiar to his readers that he need not explicitly develop moral lessons in conjunction with or as explications of the tales. This moral universe is a romantic one, emphasizing the primacy of human relations, the benefits and beauty of the natural world, hope, and imagination. The stories become a site of shared values between the readers, the auditors, the narrator, and ultimately the author. Significantly, the values that are emphasized in the stories involve an enlargement of imaginative horizons rather than the discipline of impulse. In "The Miraculous Pitcher," Baucis and Philemon's empathetic understanding of the difficulties of travelers is highlighted while the other villagers' harassment of travelers is summarized. King Midas learns to appreciate the things of the heart rather than his material possessions. At the conclusion of "The Paradise of Children," Eustace rhapsodizes: "But then that lovely and lightsome little figure of Hope! What in the world could we do without her? Hope spiritualizes the earth; Hope makes it always new; and, even in the earth's best and brightest aspect, Hope shows it to be only the shadow of an infinite bliss hereafter" (81). No child's question prompts Eustace to make these comments. He is caught up in his own story and unself-consciously utters this spontaneous paean to Hope. Nor do his auditors question him after the tale is told. Instead the frame narrative emphasizes the mundane rather than the spiritual, thereby suggesting that Hawthorne felt that the "lesson" was sufficiently developed.

The final story in the collection, "The Chimera," is an anomaly. It lacks the light comic tone that characterizes the other tales, and the narratives that frame the tale are quieter and less rambunctious. Also, in this tale Bright (and by extension Hawthorne) has a clear theme—the role of the imagination in life. The treatment of the theme is straightforward and thoroughly developed, making it easily accessible to the child auditors and to child readers.

Bellerophon arrives at the Fountain of Pirene in hopes of bridling Pegasus. At the fountain he inquires of the magical horse and receives a range of responses: the country bumpkin doesn't believe in the existence of Pegasus, an "old, gray man" (147) has a vague memory of believing in the existence of the horse and seeing hoofprints around the fountain when he was a young man, a maiden thinks she might have seen the horse once and reports, "I heard a neigh. Oh, such a brisk and melodious neigh as that was! My very heart leaped with delight at the sound. But it startled me, nevertheless; so that I ran home without filling my pitcher" (148). Only a small boy can confidently report that he often sees the winged horse reflected in the water of the pool. As one might expect, Bellerophon trusts the boy's advice and is thereby able to bridle Pegasus, tame him, and ride him in order to defeat the Chimera.

The maiden's response to hearing Pegasus's neigh anticipates the spiritual and aesthetic role of the imagination that is developed in the tale. Bright goes into great detail describing the movement and wonder of the winged horse, but primarily in order that he may develop a spiritual relationship between horse and rider that becomes an allegory for imagination's contribution to life. At the conclusion of the tale, Bright explains, "In after years, that child took higher flights upon the aerial steed than ever did Bellerophon, and achieved more honorable deeds than his friend's victory over the Chimaera.

For, gentle and tender as he was, he grew to be a mighty poet!" (167). Hawthorne continues the theme into the frame narrative, linking the flights on Pegasus to the work of the living authors—the Rev. Orville Dewey, G. P. R. James, Henry Wadsworth Longfellow, Oliver Wendell Holmes, Herman Melville, and Hawthorne himself—residing in the Berkshires.

The serious intent of the tale is obvious, and the development of the theme is characteristic of the Romantic aesthetic. Imagination is central to the Romantics and to their conception of childhood, which was gaining increasing popularity, as evidenced by the work of Drake and Paulding discussed above, and by the gradual acceptance of folk and fairy tales as children's reading material. "The Chimera," however, makes explicit the implicit intention of the entire book—a direct cultivation of the child's imagination. Just as Eustace Bright cannot command his auditors to be imaginative but must offer them convincing imaginative tales that exercise their own faculty of fantasy (thus Sweet Fern's questions and the more sophisticated Primrose's heartfelt response), so too Hawthorne cultivates the faculty of imagination in his readers, offering them tales without an explicit lesson.

True to Hawthorne's Romantic ideology and his previous practice in *Grandfather's Chair* (Goodenough 30), the cultivation of imagination in the readers is primarily a cultivation of the heart—the empathetic identification with a character's experience. For the most part, the characters in *Wonder Book* evince an aesthetic appreciation (such as Marygold, Bellerophon, and the young boy who helps him capture Pegasus). However, the story also encourages identification with a naughty character like Pandora. Much of "The Paradise of Children" is developed from Pandora's point-of-view, allowing readers to participate in her temptation and her redemption as she frees the fairy Hope.

Hawthorne's stories also cultivate a desire to see beyond quotidian reality to the possibility of wonder or magic. Contrary to the advice that children should only read the "truthful," Bright, and by extension Hawthorne, offers children a magical flying horse, a magical pitcher with a never-ending supply of milk, a man who can hold the world on his shoulders (besides other fantastic exploits), and a young man who can not only become invisible but can lop the heads off monsters.[15] Moreover the magical elements or acts allow the characters some power to improve the world. Even naughty Pandora who has unleashed "the whole family of earthly Troubles" also frees Hope to console humanity.

Hawthorne's original plan for *Wonder Book* was to "entirely revolutionize the whole system of juvenile literature" (Hawthorne to Longfellow March 21, 1838; quoted in Pearce 297). What is revolutionary about these stories is the degree of imaginative play allowed to child auditors and by extension child readers.[16] More significant than the thematic treatment of the importance of imagination as it is developed in "The Chimera" is the free play of imagination exhibited by Eustace and his listeners. Neither Eustace nor the children accept an authorized tale. In contrast to Laffrado's argument that Hawthorne has more authority than his narrator Eustace Bright (67), I would argue that Hawthorne has erased himself out of the collection. Despite Eustace's caution to the children not to attract Hawthorne's attention with their "babble" or they may all be destroyed, the effect of the moment is to emphasize that their activity goes on *without* him. This incident, as well as the plan of the entire collection, subverts the typical narrative relationship that characterized children's literature of the period. Instead of duly receiving and accepting the narrative provided by an authority, the children participate in the creative act, each according to his or her ability. Eustace remakes the received story; Primrose and Sweet Fern remake Eustace's story. This creative act implies that children have and should cultivate the same aesthetic and imaginative power as adults. And within the context of popular child-rearing practices and children's literature even at mid-century, that is a revolutionary idea.

Notes

Many thanks to my colleagues Kevin J. Donovan and Martha Hixon who provided useful comments and criticisms in their readings of the early drafts of this essay. I would also like to thank the anonymous readers of *Children's Literature* whose comments and questions prompted me to revise the argument of the essay.

1. For a thorough discussion of the development of Hawthorne's conceptions of *A Wonder Book for Girls and Boys,* see Pearce.

2. For a thorough discussion of various editions and illustrators of *A Wonder Book,* see Richardson, "Myth and Fairy Tale in Hawthorne's Stories for Children."

3. I disagree with Nina Baym who argues: "*A Wonder Book* exhibits a rare sense of harmony between Hawthorne's own view of things and the assumed view of his audience. He seems certain that his readers will share his preference for the gothic" (36).

4. Goodenough sees in *Grandfather's Chair* a similar awareness on the part of Hawthorne of the complex audience of these works—both children and parents.

5. McPherson quotes George Parsons Lathrop's analysis of the manuscripts, which states, in part, "It appears to be certain that although Hawthorne meditated long over what he intended to do and came rather slowly to the point of publication, yet when the actual task of writing was begun, it proceeded rapidly and with very little correc-

tion" (39). See also Hathaway (164) for an extended discussion of the composition of the collection.

6. Unlike so many of the authors whom MacLeod discusses in *A Moral Tale,* Hawthorne's intentions are clearly not didactic. Her comment about Hawthorne's work for children is a footnote that acknowledges Hawthorne's talent but contends that his work for children is undistinguished: "Hawthorne was the only exception [i.e., the only writer of "genius or even outstanding talent" (12)], and his few fictional works for children, while somewhat better in style than other juvenile fiction, did not differ markedly from them in other respects" (161 n. 8). And while this judgment may be true of some of Hawthorne's work (e.g., "Little Daffydowndilly"), it isn't true of *A Wonder Book.*

7. Jordan 57. For a full discussion of this phenomenon, see Jackson 208–19 and Darton 205–15.

8. Hawthorne uses the flower names to the same effect in his story for adults, "The Snow Image," published in the previous year, 1850. Laffrado's comment that the names "indicate their [the children's] mostly decorative role as listeners" (72) does not acknowledge the role the children play as model readers or how their fairylike behavior shapes readers' responses.

9. Hawthorne's own attitude toward the region was more complicated. On July 29, 1851, he complains in his notebook: "This is a horrible, horrible, most hor-ri-ible climate; one knows not, for ten minutes together, whether he is too cool or too warm; but he is always one or the other; and the constant result is a miserable disturbance of the system. I detest it! I detest it!! I de-test it!!! I hate Berkshire with my whole soul, and would joyfully see its mountains laid flat" (439). Two days later, however, he comments: "In the earlier part of the summer, I thought that the land-scape would suffer by the change from pure and rich verdure, after the pastures should turn yellow, and the fields be mowed. But I now think the change an improvement. The contrast between the faded green, and, here and there, the almost brown and dusky fields, as compared with the deep green of the woods, is very picturesque, on the hillsides" (*American Notebooks* 445).

10. In *Grandfather's Chair* Hawthorne had previously developed a narrator who thinks his stories should be "a pleasure not a task" (Goodenough 31). In *Grandfather's Chair,* however, an unnamed narrator mediates Grandfather's tales, editing them to the sensibilities of the children. In *Wonder Book* the two roles are conflated in Bright, a narrator who does not demand authority over the children's responses.

11. Pearce notes, "The children in the *Wonder Book* are projections of his ideal images of his own offspring; their talk is marked by the style and sentiments he recorded as those of his children in his notebooks" (305).

12. Laffrado's comment that the children's function in the story is "mostly decorative" and that they do not question or comment on the stories as does Laurence in *The Whole History of Grandfather's Chair* is the result of an assumption that *A Wonder Book* is the same kind of book as *The Whole History,* i.e., a book intended to be didactic rather than entertaining.

13. In later editions of *Children and Books,* Arbuthnot softens her criticism and can faintly praise the collection. In the third edition (1964) she misses the mythopoeic elements but admires the light tone: "Eustace talked down to the children; his gods lost much of their grandeur, and his heroes were often child-sized. But the stories had a delightful style, and the chatty interludes of banter between Eustace and the children provided pleasant pictures of the New England outdoor world" (45). In the sixth edition (1981), she condenses her description to a reference to the "child-sized" gods and the "delightful" style (70).

14. Hawthorne's notebooks record his children's fascination with insects and hint at his own distaste of such creatures: "Of all playthings, a living plaything is infinitely the most interesting to a child. A kitten, a horse, a spider, a toad, a caterpillar, an ant, a fly— anything that can move of its own motion—immediately has a hold on their sympathies.

40   ELLEN BUTLER DONOVAN

Both Una and Julian have been the death of many caterpillars and other insects; but if they loved them less, they would have killed fewer. The dread of creeping things appears not to be a native instinct; for these children allow caterpillars to crawl on their naked flesh, without any repugnance" (*American Notebooks* 427).

15. Hawthorne records in his notebooks Julian's imitation of Perseus during the summer months following the writing of *Wonder Book:* "He picked up a club, and began over again the old warfare with the thistles—which we called hydras, chimaeras, dragons, and Gorgons. Thus we fought our way homeward" (*American Notebooks* 445).

16. Billman argues that Hawthorne's innovation in *Wonder Book* and *Tanglewood Tales* is his choice of classical myth as the subject matter, and that such a choice makes the collections "anaomalies, not harbingers of a new direction in children's literature" (113). Granted, Hawthorne's innovations do not start a new trend. But by overlooking the narrative relationships established in the collection, Billman fails to recognize the most innovative elements of the work.

Works Cited

Arbuthnot, May Hill. *Children and Books.* Rev. ed. Chicago: Scott, Foresman, 1957.

Attebery, Brian. *The Fantasy Tradition in American Literature: From Irving to Le Guin.* Bloomington: Indiana University Press, 1980.

Avery, Gillian. *Behold the Child: American Children and Their Books, 1621–1922.* Baltimore: Johns Hopkins University Press, 1994.

Baym, Nina. "Hawthorne's Myths for Children: The Author versus His Audience." *Studies in Short Fiction* 10 (1973): 35–46.

Billman, Carol. "Nathaniel Hawthorne: 'Revolutionizer' of Children's Literature?" *Studies in American Fiction* 10 (1982): 107–14.

Bush, Douglas. *Mythology and the Romantic Tradition in English Poetry.* 1937. New York: Pageant, 1957.

Darton, F. J. Harvey. *Children's Books in England: Five Centuries of Social Life,* 2d ed. Cambridge: Cambridge University Press, 1958.

Feldman, Burton, and Robert D. Richardson, comps. *The Rise of Modern Mythology, 1680–1860.* Bloomington: Indiana University Press, 1972.

Goodenough, Elizabeth. "*Grandfather's Chair:* Hawthorne's 'Deeper History' of New England." *Lion and the Unicorn* 15 (1991): 27–42.

Hall, David D. "The Uses of Literacy in New England, 1600–1850." In *Cultures of Print: Essays in the History of the Book.* Amherst: University of Massachusetts Press, 1996. Originally published as the introduction to *Printing and Society in Early America,* ed. William L. Joyce, David D. Hall, Richard D. Brown, and John Hench (Worcester, Mass: American Antiquarian Society, 1983).

Hathaway, Richard D. "Hawthorne and the Paradise of Children." *Western Humanities Review* 15 (1961): 161–72.

Hawthorne, Nathaniel. *A Wonder Book for Girls and Boys.* Centenary Edition, vol. 7. Columbus: Ohio State University Press, 1972.

———. *American Notebooks.* Centenary Edition, vol. 8. Columbus: Ohio State University Press, 1972.

Jordan, Alice M. *From Rollo to Tom Sawyer and Other Papers.* Boston: Horn Book, 1948.

Laffrado, Laura. *Hawthorne's Literature for Children.* Athens: University of Georgia Press, 1992.

MacLeod, Anne Scott. *A Moral Tale: Children's Fiction and American Culture, 1820–1860.* Hamden, Conn.: Archon. 1975.

McPherson, Hugo. *Hawthorne as Myth-Maker: A Study in Imagination.* Toronto: University of Toronto Press, 1969.

Paulding, James Kirke. Preface. *A Gift From Fairy Land.* New York: Appleton, 1938. Micro-
   print available in American Culture Series, reel 4657. Ann Arbor: UMI, 1951–76.

Pearce, Roy Harvey. "Historical Introduction." *True Stories From History and Biography.*
   Centenary Edition, vol. 6. Columbus: Ohio State University Press, 1972.

Peck, Elizabeth. "Hawthorne's Nonsexist Narrative Framework: The Real Wonder of *A
   Wonder Book.*" *Children's Literature Association Quarterly* 10 (fall 1985): 116–19.

Richardson, Robert D., Jr. "Myth and Fairy Tale In Hawthorne's Stories for Children."
   Journal of American Culture 2 (1979): 341–46.

West, Mark I., ed. *Before Oz: Juvenile Fantasy Stories from Nineteenth-Century America.* Hamden, Conn.: Archon, 1989.

Revising the Seduction Paradigm: The Case of Ewing's The Brownies

Marah Gubar

Children's literature has persuasively been described as a means of seduction, a solicitation by which the adult writer draws in and defines the child reader.[1] Given the anxiety that has traditionally hovered around the connection between childhood and sexuality, it is perhaps unsurprising that in this critical story seduction almost invariably gets equated with abuse. Following the lead of Jacqueline Rose, who repeatedly relies on the paradigm of abuse in her seminal work *The Case of Peter Pan*, Karín Lesnik-Oberstein twice encourages readers of her study *Children's Literature* to take "the problems of professionals dealing with child abuse and neglect as an emblem to be kept in mind in this discussion" (18, 164).[2] Even James Kincaid, who centers his analysis of texts for and about children on pedophilia precisely in order to *deconstruct* our culture's reliance on a "melodrama of monsters and innocents," ultimately focuses on how actual children are "assaulted," "sacrific[ed]," and "abuse[d]" as a result of how we—that is to say, adults—conceptualize childhood (5–6, 10). Interested in highlighting how the adult writer's desire for and investment in the figure of the child shapes children's literature, these critics tend to treat use and abuse as interchangeable activities; thus, Rose argues that "the child is used (and abused) to represent the whole problem of what sexuality is . . . and to hold that problem at bay" (4).[3]

But this conflation of terms denies the productive, reciprocal possibilities of use, even as it effaces the pleasurable aspects of seduction. Certainly, adults have the power to exploit children for their own purposes, but children can also exploit parents, loved ones, and especially texts in order to develop into creative individuals. If we conceptualize the text as a "potential space" that can be colonized not only by adult writers but also by child readers, we can reinvest seduction with its original charge; closer to flirtation than abuse, seduction is about attraction, not abduction.[4] This is not to deny the aggressive aspects of the act of seduction, but merely to restore a more flexible continuum;

Children's Literature 30, ed. Elizabeth Lennox Keyser and Julie Pfeiffer (Yale University Press, © 2002 Hollins University).

like flirtation, seduction can be invasive, threatening, and unwelcome, but it can also be flattering, titillating, and extremely pleasurable for both parties. Given that our subject here is *reading*—not actual sexual relationships—it seems crucial to keep the possibility for mutual pleasure open, even as we acknowledge the skewed power dynamic that complicates the adult writer-child reader relationship.[5]

Taking the trouble to tread this line becomes even more important when we consider how explicitly and ingeniously many texts aimed at children attend to this very issue. Even stories produced during the period famous for creating and promoting the "cult of the child" prove remarkably willing to acknowledge the aggressive aspects of romancing the child, and consequently to explore strategies for facilitating noncoercive cooperation between adults and children, between storytellers and story receivers. In her popular tale *The Brownies* (1865), for example, Juliana Horatia Ewing (1841–85) employs a plethora of individualized narrators who essentially function as a string of suitors, flattering, cajoling, and ultimately seducing the child into acting in accordance with adult desires.[6] Using multiple frame narratives, Ewing highlights the presence of this chain of storytellers, thereby acknowledging adult authorship of and investment in tales told to children. Directly addressing "the question of who is talking to whom, and why" —the key issue that Rose claims children's fiction consistently ignores —Ewing makes explicit her project of importuning and even manipulating the child (2).

Nevertheless, in the drama of seduction that Ewing depicts, the prescriptive power that adult scripts wield over children is mitigated by the force of revision, a mode of active appropriation that Ewing suggests is available to adults and children alike. The overarching frame narrative of *The Brownies* presents the relationship between a rector's children and their neighbor, a friendly doctor who successfully practices Ewing's own teasing tactics, charming children into gratified (and gratifying) submission. Like other adult storytellers in Ewing's tales, he does not simply flirt with children, he flirts with texts, appropriating and improvising on the work of other authors. By successfully engaging in this kind of productive exploitation, characters like the Doctor not only duplicate a key element of Ewing's own creative process, they serve as role models for child readers, inviting them to refuse to accept "The End" as the last word(s). A kind of collaboration, revision calls for two players, neither of whom functions merely as a passive receiver. Demonstrating by example how this process can make room for participation in otherwise prescriptive texts, *The Brownies* finds Ewing borrowing and revamping material gleaned from sources ranging from Ovid to George MacDonald. No narrative, this playful attitude implies, can be so didactic that it leaves no room for resistance; once readers recognize that they can play with texts, texts cannot abuse readers.

From the start of her story, Ewing represents revision as a strategy open to readers of all ages, since the children and the Doctor take turns improvising on the Brothers Grimm fable "The Elves and the Shoemaker," the text that most obviously serves as the basis for *The Brownies.* Complaining about the chores he and his siblings must perform, Deordie—one of the Rector's children—fantasizes about how wonderful it would be if "some little Elves" like those featured in his favorite Grimm story suddenly took over these household duties (6). Taking his cue from Deordie's musings, the Doctor gathers the youngsters together and tells them the interpolated tale of "The Brownies," in which some (other) lazy children long for the very same thing, until they find out that the legendary house fairies of former times— here rechristened Brownies—were actually children, performing their good deeds in secret. In this case, revision produces a text that is *more* didactic than its original incarnation; like Ewing herself, the Doctor transforms a fairy tale into a moral tale, and his ministrations prove prescriptive, in that his child listeners follow the good example set by Tommy and Johnnie, the newly reformed heroes of his story. For example, after hearing about how these boys change from indolent idlers into industrious helpers, Tiny weeds the Doctor's garden and vows to hem her father's pocket handkerchiefs.

The Brownies proper thus emerges as a doubly didactic narrative; not only does it incite children to help out with the housework, it also trains them in the art of listening and responding to moral tales. When Tiny and Deordie mold themselves to match the fictional children dreamed up by the Doctor, they unmask the fantasy of compliance that drives the narrative: namely, that *The Brownies* will woo actual child readers into acquiescence just as satisfactorily as "The Brownies" does their fictional counterparts. Yet even as Ewing acknowledges the beguiling power of narrative, its hypnotic capacity to seduce children into acting in accordance with adult desire, she also subverts the idea that compliance necessarily entails passive indoctrination, that didactic texts demand or enforce complete submission from child readers (or listeners). To begin with, the very act of depicting in detail how the Doctor uses fiction to influence and control children encourages Ewing's own audience to become more conscious of the pressure exerted by texts. The doubling of the title "The Brownies" underscores the metafictional quality of the story; rather than furtively attempting to inculcate a moral lesson, *The Brownies* dramatizes the scene of instruction, drawing attention to the relationship that links pedagogue to pupil, adult author to child auditor. Closely observing the Doctor as he engages in "the process of story-making," the Rector's children model the kind of alert, active reception that the story advocates; by inviting its audience to recognize that narratives are sometimes designed to manipulate their target audience, *The Brownies* encourages readers to question, resist, or *knowingly and deliberately* succumb to the stealthy machinations of storytellers (58).

Then, too, the content of the Doctor's moral lesson is undercut by the process by which he generates it; by relying on revision to produce his parable, the Doctor implicitly undermines the idea that indoctrination via narrative can ever be certain or complete. After all, if you can turn a fairy tale into a moral tale, you can conceivably convert it back again (or into something else altogether). The children in the story clearly absorb this message, as well as the more obvious one about helping out with housework; when the Doctor concludes his story, his auditors refuse to accept his ending as final, treating it instead as an opportunity for conversation and improvisation. "'That's not the end, is it?'" demands one of the boys, and when the Doctor admits that it is, Deordie coaxes him to "'make a little more end . . . to tell us what became of them all'" (57–58). Even after the Doctor composes an explanatory epilogue, his audience keeps pressing him to elaborate further on the fate of various characters: "'And [what] about the Owl?' clamoured the children" (59). When he finally declines to continue adding to the story, the children take over the task themselves; first, Deordie extemporizes on the possibility that "'there might be more and more ends,'" and then the whole group races home "to give joint versions of the fairy tale, first to the parents in the drawing-room, and then to nurse in the nursery" (61, 64).

This final scene foregrounds Ewing's conscientious habit of acknowledging the domineering power of narrative while simultaneously encouraging readers to eschew the role of passive victim. For rather than disavowing the prescriptive potential of stories, this finale effectively unmasks the Doctor as a master of indoctrination who manipulates the children into absorbing and echoing back the material he presents to them. Yet by depicting narrative as endlessly amendable, *The Brownies* implies that the meaning or moral of any given fiction is ultimately mutable; stories are subject to interruptions and extensions that may alter even the most embedded message. Indeed, Ewing portrays "story-making" as a profoundly collaborative process; eager to dislodge narrative's power as a unilateral, monologic force, she repeatedly characterizes the relationship between storyteller and story receiver(s) as potentially dialogic. In the frame narrative, for example, Deordie improvises on Grimm, then the Doctor revises Deordie's story, and finally Deordie begins the process of altering the Doctor's story. Tommy and Johnnie take an even more active role in determining the content of the tale their grandmother tells them in the interpolated tale of "The Brownies"; while the Rector's children chime in only at the beginning and the end of the Doctor's narrative, these boys interrupt their grandmother's efforts to entertain them with constant questions and criticism, eventually taking over the telling of the tale themselves.

This extended encounter provides ample evidence of Ewing's desire to present the production of narrative as a joint endeavor, a process that children can participate in rather than simply endure. Modeling the proactive stance Ewing wants to encourage, Tommy orchestrates the whole event with a string of commands: "'Tell us a tale, Granny. . . . Come, Johnnie, and sit against me. Now then!'" (19). The boys then stymie their grandmother's efforts to tell them a romantic tale or a ghost story: "'Oh! not ghosts!' Tommy broke in; 'we've had so many'" (19). But the siblings do not simply veto the various options proposed by Granny; they also keep teasing their reluctant relative to tell them "a fairy story," until she finally agrees to relate the history of the family Brownie. Then, rather than subsiding into compliant silence, the boys pepper their narrator with questions: "'What was he like, Granny?'" "'What did he do?'" "'[W]hy did he go?'" (21–22). When their grandmother slips a romantic anecdote from her own past into the story, the boys once again prove themselves active, critical listeners; Tommy exclaims, "'How stupid!'" while Johnnie steers her back on track by urging, "'Tell us more about Brownie, please'" (24).

But the most obvious example of the children's ability to assume control over the content of the tale (and the circumstances under which it is told) comes when they usurp the role of narrator for themselves. Fantasizing about the Brownie's return, the two boys take turns filling in the details:

"Oh! I wish ours would come back!" cried both boys in chorus.
"He'd—
"tidy the room," said Johnnie;
"fetch the turf," said Tommy;
"pick up the chips," said Johnnie;
"sort your scraps," said Tommy;
"and do everything. Oh! I wish he hadn't gone away." (24)

Even as the conversational format of such "story-making" reveals Ewing's desire to represent narrative as dialogic, the specific content of this passage also attests to the possibility of mutual participation: since the boys here give voice to Deordie's fantasy of palming off his chores on a fairy visitor, this passage demonstrates that the ideas and desires of a child—albeit a fictional one—can influence the course of an adult-constructed narrative. This exchange also prefigures a later scene in which Tommy, hoping to win the Brownie back, visits the Old Owl and asks her for advice. Like Granny, this aged female character recounts *her* version of the story of the Brownies; and once again, storyteller and story receiver engage in a long conversation, punctuated by questions and commands broached by both participants. Meanwhile, by having one character after another recast the legend of helpful household elves, Ewing reproduces such colloquy at the structural level; the multiple variations on this theme coexist in conversation with each other, illustrating the possibility that even those involved in echoing a particular story have the capacity to remake or creatively revise it.

To put this point another way, Ewing's decision to break up the narrative by inserting interpolated stories told by a diverse array of narrators itself attests to her interest in conceptualizing the production of narrative as a collaborative process. The omniscient narrator who opens the story never remains in control for long; a chorus of supporting voices chime in, including another omniscient narrator who tells "The Story of a Grave-Stone," the Doctor, Granny, and the Old Owl. Just as the animated interjections of child auditors in *The Brownies* encourage child readers to adopt a more active approach to stories, the contrasting styles of these storytellers jar their audience into adopting a less passive stance, since framing devices and tonal shifts alike invite readers to sit up and take notice of the constructedness of texts, reminding them that narratives issue from specific sources. For example, the pious sentimentality of the "The Story of a Grave-Stone"—"Ah! These grave-stones . . . GOD only knows how heavily they press upon the souls that are left behind"—contrasts sharply with the casual chattiness of the sections that precede and follow it (10). Intrusions of this sort not only prod readers to puzzle over who exactly is speaking, they also attest to Ewing's desire to represent narrative as a force whose flow can be interrupted, rechanneled, or diverted.

Right from the start of *The Brownies*, Ewing characterizes such intercourse—between authors and auditors, texts and readers, children and adults—as distinctly erotic. Describing how he was shut up in the back nursery for borrowing and losing his nurse's scissors, Deordie identifies fiction as a source of intimate titillation while reminding readers that even the most didactic gesture can be arousing (rather than repressive). He explains: "'I'd got "Grimm" inside one of my knickerbockers, so when she locked the door, I sat down to read. And I read the story of the Shoemaker and the little Elves who came and did his work for him before he got up; and I thought it would be so jolly if we had some little Elves to do things instead of us'" (6). His fancy tickled by the Grimm inside his knickerbockers, Deordie enjoys the pleasures of retooling fairy-tale material even more than the Doctor does, as indicated by the masturbatory moment when the boy fantasizes that his friend's story might go "on and on"; speculating on how this pleasure might be prolonged, "Deordie rocked himself among the geraniums, in the luxurious imagining of an endless fairy tale" (62). The notion of a never-ending story, like the decision to depict narrative as dialogic, blurs the line between producer and receiver; playing with texts, Ewing suggests, can prove pleasurable for both children and adults. Entertainment of this kind, she implies, is emphatically *not* about consummation, the complete and conclusive seduction of one party by another; rather, she envisions this process as a playful, eroticized exchange, a mutually gratifying flirtation between two active agents.

Of course, Ewing's characterization of narrative as an interactive joint production, highly pleasurable for both parties, could itself be viewed as a sly attempt to ensnare young readers; a cynic might argue that indoctrination works best when the weaker party can be seduced into believing that they have input, control, and power, that they are participants in—rather than victims of—the educational process. There is no need to defend Ewing's narrative against this claim, however, because the main project of *The Brownies* is precisely to keep this question in play. By portraying adult narrators as a string of suitors, whose erotic overtures run the gamut from harmless flirtation to frightening molestation, Ewing continually invites us to wonder whether such solicitations should be viewed as mutually fulfilling encounters between two willing partners or coercive acts of aggression involving an assailant and a victim. Her most evenhanded treatment of the narrator as flirt emerges early on in her characterization of the Doctor and the disembodied chronicler of "The Story of a Grave-Stone." She then champions children's own powers of persuasion in her portrayal of Granny, but promotes a much darker vision of the author-auditor relationship in her characterization of the Old Owl.

The ultimate embodiment of narrator as swain, the Doctor enjoys unlimited physical access to his child friends; virtually the first thing we learn about this talented storyteller is that he "came into th[eir] garden whenever he pleased" (1). Ewing emphasizes that his youth "was many years past," yet with Tiny in particular he behaves more like an ardent lover than an avuncular friend. For example, as the story opens, he "throw[s] himself on the grass" at her feet, inquiring as to the cause of her tears (2). Then when Tiny asks him if he ever cries, the Doctor reacts more like a startled swain than the mature man in mourning that he turns out to be; he "absolutely blushe[s]" like a schoolboy and embarks on a series of coy questions beginning with "'What do you think?'" (8). Soon afterwards, "The Story of a Grave-Stone" reinforces the idea that the Doctor's interest in the children is erotically charged, strongly suggesting that his small friends function as replacements for a lost love object. After the death of his beloved wife, we discover, the Doctor began giving "tea parties to other people's children"; and the narrator underlines this association of child with lover by describing how the Doctor casts himself "face downwards" at the foot of his wife's tombstone, an act that recalls his prostration at Tiny's feet in the story's first scene (10–11).

But the Doctor's most conspicuous method of flirting with children involves playing with language. When Tiny explains that she and her siblings have gotten into trouble for their careless and untidy habits— "'forgetting, and not putting away, and leaving out, and borrowing, and breaking'"—the Doctor responds with jokes, stories, and puns, winning his small friend's smiles with amusing word play (2). For example, reacting to Tiny's lament, in reference to her missing puzzles, that "'North America and Europe are gone too,'" the Doctor "start[s] up in affected horror," exclaiming,

"Europe gone, did you say? Bless me! What will become of us!"

"Don't!" said the young lady, kicking petulantly with her dan-
gling feet, and trying not to laugh. "You know I mean the puzzles;
and if they were yours, you wouldn't like it." (4)

When Deordie arrives on the scene, he reassures his sister that many
of the lost items have been recovered, including the rocking-horse's
nose, which "'has turned up in the nursery oven'" (5). Again, the Doctor chooses to amuse rather than chide the children, insisting, "'The
rocking-horse's nose couldn't turn up, it was purest Grecian, modelled
from the Elgin Marbles. Perhaps it was the heat that did it though'" (5).
Entertaining exchanges of this sort, which amuse both parties, contribute to Ewing's depiction of the adult author-child auditor relationship as conversational and conducive to mutual, reciprocal pleasure.

But when the Doctor shifts from playing with language to toying
with texts, the skewed balance of power between wooer and wooed
suddenly clicks into sharper focus. Unlike the children's mother and
nurse, who nag and punish their small charges to no effect, the Doctor successfully manipulates the children by taking advantage of their
fondness for fiction. When Deordie expresses his wish that some elves
would magically appear, the Doctor casually remarks, "'That's what
Tommy Trout said'" (6). Tantalized by this reference to a nursery
rhyme character, the children beg their friend to tell them more; Tiny
exclaims, "It's the good boy who pulled the cat out of the [well]: 'Who
pulled her out? / Little Tommy Trout.' Is it the same Tommy Trout,
Doctor?" (7). In response, the Doctor promises, "'If you will get that
handkerchief done, and take it to your mother with a kiss, and not keep
me waiting, I'll have you all to tea, and tell you the story of Tommy
Trout'" (7). An exposé of the way in which adults use narrative as both
a reward and an incentive for certain kinds of behavior, this comment
crystallizes the technique of the narrative tease; intrigued by the Doctor's pledge, Tiny quickly finishes her sewing while Deordie tries to
make himself useful by braiding his sister's hair.

Even before the Doctor's story is told, in other words, Ewing characterizes it as *bait*, an alluring enticement aimed at altering the behavior of its audience. At the same time, the Doctor-as-narrator emerges
as a consummate tease, an expert at the flirtatious move of flaunting
and then withdrawing a promised pleasure.[7] When Ewing herself inter-
venes as an omniscient, disembodied narrator, she too practices the
technique of the narrative tease, doling out her tale in tantalizingly

tiny tidbits. As the children race off to get permission to visit him, the Doctor laughs at their sunny conception of adult life as an eternal holiday from all chores; but soon, "the smile died away, and tears came into his eyes," a reaction that causes Ewing to inquire, "What could this 'awfully jolly' doctor be thinking of to make him cry? He was thinking of a grave-stone in the churchyard close by, and of a story connected with this grave-stone which was known to everybody in the place who was old enough to remember it" (9). After eliciting the reader's interest in this mysterious tale of grown-up life—known only to those "old enough to remember it"—the narrator teasingly refuses to relate it, remarking, "This story has nothing to do with the present story, so it ought not to be told" (9). Soon afterwards, however, she relents, noting, "And yet it has to do with the doctor, and is very short, so it shall be put in after all" (9). Prodding her audience to notice that they are at the mercy of a fickle narrator's whims, Ewing suggests that one party— the adult author—wields almost complete control over the production and dispensation of narrative aimed at children.

At the same time, however, her decision to characterize teasing and flirting as the defining gesture of such "story-making" implies that this process can be understood as a dynamic and interactive one. "The Story of a Grave-Stone" illustrates how carefully Ewing treads this line, simultaneously stressing the adult's power over the child *and* championing the possibility for mutual engagement and participation. Like Ewing and the Doctor, the narrator of this tale flaunts her ability to frustrate her listeners' desires and expectations; after whetting our curiosity with her intriguing title, she declines to dispense any specific information about the cause of the Doctor's grief, never actually revealing *who* has died.[8] Later in *The Brownies,* we learn more about the Doctor's past, but this ostensible explanation of his character winds up with the pointedly inconclusive conclusion,

> As to the grave-stone story, whatever it was to him at the end of twenty years, it was a great convenience to his friends; for when he said anything they didn't agree with, or did anything they couldn't understand, or didn't say or do what was expected of him, what could be easier or more conclusive than to shake one's head and say:
> "The fact is, our doctor has been a little odd, *ever since—*!" (11)

The promised revelation never comes; the meaning of this story is flirtatiously withheld, once again demonstrating the narrator's dominion over what gets told when. At the same time, however, this concluding dash spurs readers to take an active part in the production of narrative, to fill in the blanks for themselves. Like the white space that separates each interpolated tale from the main body of *The Brownies,* this gap in the text literally *makes room* for audience participation, inviting readers and listeners to interrupt and take over the telling of the story for themselves. Not coincidentally, a strikingly similar incident occurs at the end of the Doctor's tale; as his narrative draws to a close, the Doctor "pause[s]," and it is this little break that enables the Rector's children to chime in with their questions and suggestions (58). All of these short silences serve to stimulate reader response, and identify *The Brownies* as what French theorist Roland Barthes calls a "writerly" text. Arguing that readers derive pleasure from places where the text can be perforated—"the seam, the cut, the deflation, the *dissolve*"— Barthes claims that we are drawn to texts that we can imagine ourselves rewriting, that prompt us to become producers as well as consumers of narrative (*Pleasure of the Text* 7, *S/Z* 4). Like all writerly texts, *The Brownies* incites readers to act as collaborators in the production of meaning; privileging open-endedness and omission over closure and completion, Ewing characterizes stories as starting points, raw material that begs its audience to commandeer and creatively augment it.

Thus, even as this opening section reveals how effectively narrative can tease people into line, it also celebrates (and exposes) the power people have to tease narratives into new forms. As I noted earlier, the Doctor models the art of recycling in his version of "The Brownies"; not only does he revise Deordie's fantasy—and, by extension, the Grimm fable—he also appropriates his main character from a nursery rhyme. Furthermore, even as her surrogate narrator revamps other authors' material, Ewing herself employs the strategy of revision in constructing this charming character: the Doctor is unmistakably modeled on Uncle David, the featured male authority figure in Catherine Sinclair's popular children's novel *Holiday House* (1839).[9] Like Ewing's widowed raconteur, Sinclair's avuncular bachelor makes a practice of teasing and telling tales to his two young friends, Harry and Laura; when they misbehave, he sets himself apart from their vicious nurse and "faint weak" grandmother by resorting not to punishments or lectures but to riddles and "funny stor[ies]" (21, 95). For example, when the children confess to breaking a table, Uncle David cheerfully inquires, "'Why are your ears like a bell-rope, Harry? because they

seem made to be pulled'" (67). He then compares the boy to "Meddle-
some Matty in the nursery rhymes," just as the Doctor likens Deordie
to Tommy Trout.

But the most striking link between the two men emerges when we
consider that each of them narrates an interpolated fairy tale that features the very same didactic message; both "The Brownies" and "Uncle
David's Nonsensical Story About Giants and Fairies" extol the virtues
of exertion and diligence, while denouncing the faults of laziness and
idleness. Heralded by historians of children's literature for ushering in
a new era of openness to fantasy and nonsense, this section of *Holiday
House* nevertheless features "a strongly moral and didactic slant," as
Gillian Avery has noted (*Nineteenth Century Children* 45). Indeed, even
the briefest summary of Uncle David's tale supports Avery's claim that
such early efforts to integrate fairy-tale material into mainstream children's literature featured "didacticism unsuccessfully masked under
a thin coating of fantasy": Sinclair's story chronicles the experiences
of "a very idle, greedy, naughty boy," Master No-Book, who foolishly
chooses to visit the fairy Do-nothing rather than the fairy Teach-all,
and as a result is almost eaten by the Giant Snap-'em-up (Avery 46, Sinclair 132). Writing twenty-six years later, Ewing is able to offer a much
more subtle blend of entertainment and instruction; but even as she
proves herself a master of the technique of using fairy-tale trappings
to sweeten the pill of a moral precept, she keeps reminding her readers of the didactic intent of her narrative, its aggressive ambition to
alter the behavior of its young audience.[10]

To begin with, the very act of drawing such strong parallels with
an extremely well-known and infinitely more preachy text encourages
readers to notice the pedagogic intentions of her own narrative. Then,
too, Ewing acknowledges her dual purpose of amusing and disciplin-
ing young people by portraying her child characters as perpetually
caught between laughter and tears. A "completely . . . miserable" Tiny
weeps as the story opens, then finds herself "trying not to laugh" at
the Doctor's exaggerated reactions to her woes (1, 4). Foreshadowing
the revelation that Brownies are actually children, the Doctor reveals
in the course of his narrative that these small beings have "very uncertain tempers, they say. Tears one minute and laughing the next" (49).
Tommy and Johnnie's capers prove this point about Brownie nature;
dancing and shrieking with glee as they inform their father that they
are the true Brownies, the two boys "com[e] to a full stop . . . feel-

ing strongly tempted to run down from laughing to crying" (56). Ultimately, all three of them give way to tears: "the father and sons fell into
each other's arms and fairly wept" (57).

Given the preponderance of these hysterical moments and the teasing tone that Ewing and the Doctor adopt when addressing their young
listeners, tickling may be the most apt metaphor for the narrative exer-
tions practiced on children by both narrators. As psychoanalyst Adam
Phillips points out, tickling is a "form of sensuous excitement" shared
by adults and children that has no climax but that renders the child
helpless in the hands of the adult (*On Kissing* 9). The line between
laughter and tears blurs, and pleasure trembles over into pain; like
tickling, Ewing's version of the moral tale is at once amusing and aggressive, an act that puts its subject's reactions just out of his or her
own control. Even as such manipulation provides enjoyment, it finally
places its victim in a rather uncomfortable position, as the child protagonists of the Doctor's tale find out. Tickled by the Old Owl's "fluffy
face" and amused by her stories and riddles, Tommy enjoys an exciting
nighttime adventure in which he tries to find out what "the Old Owl
knows" (23). The unappetizing aspect of the information she eventually provides—that children are the real Brownies—does not sink in
until the next morning, when Tommy remarks disconsolately to his
brother, "'If we mean to do anything we must get up: though, oh dear!
I should like to stay in bed'" (40). As the setting of this scene indicates, Ewing stages this encounter as a seduction; and Tommy's "morning after" revelation reminds readers that succumbing to the titillating pleasures of narrative can have unpleasant consequences—in this
case, the harsh reality of having to do all the housework.

The confrontation between Tommy and the Old Owl, which I will return to in a moment, demonstrates that narrators can take advantage
of children's interest in tall tales and word play in order to court them
into compliance. But Granny's stint as storyteller suggests that children, in their turn, can seduce storytellers into satisfying *their* desires.
As I noted earlier, Tommy and Johnnie manage to tease, coax, and
wheedle this "very old, and helpless" woman into telling them about
the Brownies, despite her superstitious fear that fairies "don't like"
being discussed (14, 20). In this case, Ewing optimistically envisions
the relationship between adult narrator and child auditors as a reciprocal one; the proactive stance the boys take—dismissing the kinds of
tales they don't like, eliciting and elaborating on the ones they do—
indicates that adult narrators are not the only ones who have power

and agency. Here, Ewing sets up story-making as the scene of mutual gratification; the boys convince Granny to satisfy their longing to hear about the Brownies, but she still manages to smuggle in her favorite topic too. And appropriately enough, given Ewing's focus on the flirtatious nature of such relationships, this preferred subject is romance; the story Granny keeps returning to is the story of adult desire. First, she tries to tell the boys the history of "Miss Surbiton's Love Letter, and her Dreadful End"; then, she detours into a lengthy account of the time "when your grandfather was courting me" (20, 23).[11]

Since both Granny and the boys ultimately manage to get their favorite type of tale told, "story-making" here emerges as a mutually entertaining exchange, a harmless flirtation in which both parties avidly pursue the subjects that give them pleasure. In contrast, Tommy's rendezvous with the Old Owl evokes the specter of molestation, the upsetting possibility that all the desire and power reside on one side of the adult-child equation. First spotted perched on a beam, "pecking and tearing and munching at some shapeless black object," this intimidating "old lady" hoarsely commands Tommy, "'Come up here! come up here! . . . Kiss my fluffy face'" (27). Terrified, Tommy hangs back and "shudder[s]" at the prospect of approaching her, "but" — the narrator tells us — "there are certain requests which one has not the option of refusing" (27–28). The courted child, this line eloquently suggests, has no real choice or agency; erotic overtures of this kind exert a coercive force. When Tommy later tries to take leave of the Owl, Ewing again stresses the possibility that unwanted adult attentions constitute an offer that the child cannot in fact refuse. In reply to the Owl's statement that she had better take him home, Tommy politely points out that he knows the way; but the Owl insists,

> "I didn't say *shew* you the way, I said *take* you—carry you," said the Owl. "Lean against me."
> "I'd rather not, thank you," said Tommy.
> "Lean against me," screamed the Owl. "Oohoo! how obstinate boys are to be sure!"
> Tommy crept up, very unwillingly.
> "Lean your full weight, and shut your eyes," said the Owl. (38)

Like the commanded kiss that envelops Tommy in "unfathomable feathers and fluffyness," this compulsory hug is described in terms of drowning: "Down—feathers—fluff—[Tommy] sank and sank, could feel nothing solid, jumped up with a start to save himself, opened his eyes, and found that he was [home in bed], with Johnnie sleeping by his side" (28, 39). While the conclusion of this sentence might be said to defuse the threatening aspect of the Owl's embrace by equating it with the comforts of home, the aggressive nature of this clinch emerges quite clearly when we compare it to a similar encounter with an owl in George MacDonald's *Adela Cathcart* (1864), another text that Ewing explicitly echoes. MacDonald's narrative features yet another avuncular bachelor who narrates interpolated stories for the benefit of a young audience. One such story, "The Giant's Heart," includes the following description: "The owl spread out his silent, soft, sly wings, and lighting between Tricksey-Wee and Buffy-Bob, nearly smothered them, closing up one under each wing. It was like being buried in a down bed" (325). Expanding on this image of a soft yet suffocating caress, "The Giant's Heart" dilates on the disturbing idea that adult benevolence can actually endanger the well-being of children. Thus, the giant's wife explains to Tricksey-Wee that her husband "'is so fond of [children] that he eats them up,'" while the story itself, kindly intended as a special treat for its child audience, proves so violent and upsetting that the youngsters afterwards denounce it as "horrid," "silly," and too frightening to repeat to other children (319, 337).

As in the case of *Holiday House*, then, this intertextual reference alerts readers to the aggressive aspect of stories aimed at children; like MacDonald, Ewing explores the possibility that narrative can constitute an unwanted attention that adults impose upon their young friends. In the figure of the Old Owl, the final and most frightening embodiment of the narrator as swain, Ewing again conflates sexual and textual advances, suggesting that stories themselves can be viewed as "requests which one has not the option of refusing" (28). Like the Doctor, the Owl draws in her child audience by playing with words and encouraging participation; but in this case, Ewing intimates, no real collaboration takes place. Reciprocity stands revealed as a sham when the Owl, instead of straightforwardly informing Tommy that he and his brother are the only candidates for the unappealing position of Brownie, turns this disappointing news into a riddle that requires Tommy to fill in the blanks for himself. After Tommy begs her to "'tell me where to find the Brownies, and how to get one to come and live with us,'" she advises him to visit a nearby lake by moonlight and turn himself around three times, chanting, "Twist me, and turn me, and show me the Elf— / I looked in the water and saw—" (30). "'When you have got so far,'" she explains, "'look in the water, and at the same moment you will see the Brownie, and think of a word that will fill up the couplet, and rhyme with the first line'" (30).

The format of this instruction ingeniously echoes the devious operation of the moral tale generally; since only one answer ("myself") correctly completes the riddle, the Old Owl offers Tommy only the illusion of agency, choice, and participation, while in fact maintaining total control over the outcome and content of her literary game. Unlike the dash that concludes "The Story of a Grave-Stone," in other words, the one employed by the Owl does not really make room for dialogue or improvisation. Instead, this rhyme functions like the "requested" kiss, revealing that seemingly optional, open invitations may actually be prescriptive orders, commands masquerading as conversation. Thus Ewing anticipates Alan Richardson's argument that adult-child interactions in moral tales are "dialogic only in form" since there is "no possibility that a truth might arise through dialogue that the parents did not already have in mind" (147).[12] Intent on acknowledging the possibility that the child cannot help but parrot back the message that the adult author intends him to, Ewing features an echo as a key character in this scene. After twirling himself around and reciting the rhyme, Tommy tries out various final words—"Belf! Celf! Delf! Felf!"—and concludes,

> "What rubbish! There can't be a word to fit it. And then to look for a Brownie, and see nothing but myself!"
> "Myself," said the Echo.
> "Will you be quiet?" said Tommy. "If you would tell one the word there would be some sense in your interference; but to roar 'Myself!' at one, which neither rhymes nor runs—it does rhyme, though, as it happens," he added; "and how very odd! It runs too." (32)

By having the Echo provide the answer, Ewing suggests that Tommy's input is completely circumscribed; although he believes that he gets (to choose) the last word, that word has in fact been selected for him. Just like the other commands that the Owl "screams" at Tommy, the correct answer to this puzzle is "roared" out at him (38, 32).

Nevertheless, even though the right word is almost impossible to miss or misconstrue, Tommy *does* resist this reading of the riddle; unwilling to accept "myself" as the last word, he marches back to the Owl and demands more information, a proactive choice that parallels Tiny and Deordie's ultimate refusal to accept the Doctor's choice of ending

for "The Brownies." Defying the intimidating Owl, Tommy continues
to insist " 'I'm not a Brownie' " for an impressively long time, counter-
ing her explanations with a string of objections, including " 'You know
I'm not a Brownie,' " " 'But I couldn't do work like a Brownie,' " and
" 'But I don't think I should like it' " (33–34). Furthermore, even as
Tommy models the art of resistant reading, his chat with the Echo reveals that *she* is not compelled to behave in a completely compliant
fashion either. Musing about the fact that "myself" rhymes, Tommy
wonders,

> "What can it mean? The Old Owl knows, as Granny would say;
> so I shall go back and ask her."
> "Ask her!" said the echo.
> "Didn't I say I should?" said Tommy. "How exasperating you
> are! It is very strange. *Myself* certainly does rhyme, and I wonder
> I did not think of it long ago."
> "Go," said the echo. (32)

Even the Echo cannot hold herself to the stringent demands of mind-
less repetition, altering the number of syllables she chooses to bounce
back; and when a mere echo cannot restrain herself from practicing selectivity, how can we expect a child reader or listener to absorb
uncritically even the most explicitly didactic message? Coupled with
Tommy's determined dimness, Ewing's presentation of this independent Echo suggests that the reception of texts can never be fully determined or circumscribed.

For as this scene demonstrates, even the act of echoing someone
else's words can constitute a conversation, since Tommy and the Echo
do manage to engage in a dialogue with each other. Moreover, *The
Brownies* does not simply portray echoing as a limited but viable kind of
communication; it characterizes this mode of response as the primary
activity of authorship. By featuring multiple retellings of the same
legend, by showing narrators revamping the efforts of other narrators,
and by rewriting other authors' material herself, Ewing identifies echoing as a potentially creative act. This redefinition of repetition enables
her to associate children with artists rather than depicting them as
mere passive victims of the cunning artistry of others. For example, I
have argued that Tommy's encounter with the Echo underscores the
constrained nature of his response. But since this scene itself constitutes a retelling of Ovid's story of Echo and Narcissus, as related in

the *Metamorphoses*, it also demonstrates that freedom can be found in restriction, originality in imitation, creativity in compliance.

In other words, Ewing does not deny that texts exert a great deal of influence; but she does imply that they can inspire responses that their authors did not necessarily plot out in advance. Just as Deordie's confinement in the back nursery does not prevent his fantasies from flourishing, the disciplinary intent of stories like *The Brownies* does not prevent them from being playfully recycled or reinterpreted. Indeed, the instability of Ewing's own didactic message emerges most clearly when we recognize that nestled at the center of the Doctor's paean to selflessness lies the most famous image of complete self-absorption ever penned, that of Narcissus admiring his own image in a reflecting pool. The very rhyme that ostensibly points Tommy toward sacrificing his own pleasures and desires for the benefit of others leads him to become more wrapped up in "myself," suggesting that Brownie-hood proves alluring because it affirms rather than eliminates childish self-importance. That is to say, choosing to become a Brownie does not simply constitute compliance with adult wishes; Ewing suggests that adopting this vocation satisfies certain desires or appetites of the child's as well. After all, being a Brownie makes you a crucial member, even the savior, of your own household; the Old Owl points out that such figures are "apt to be greatly beloved," while Ewing stresses that behaving like a Brownie earns children more displays of overt affection from parents, and—in Tommy's case, anyway—a sharp new outfit (36).

Of course, such perks could be regarded as the rewards of compliance, benefits granted to those who fall into line with the overarching, adult-directed project of the narrative: namely, the reformation of the child. It is crucial to note, however, that the image of the child that *The Brownies* constructs and urges actual children to identify with is above all that of an active, creative reader, capable of resisting or revising the moral of any given text. Tiny and Deordie's response to the Doctor's story illustrates this point; both children embrace a very different message than the injunction to "Help out with the housework." Thus, Deordie never mentions how (or whether) he plans to better his behavior in this regard; but his "luxurious imagining of an endless fairy tale" clearly demonstrates that he has mastered the art of extemporizing on stories scripted by adults (62). Similarly, Tiny's coquettish reaction reveals that she has interpreted the Doctor's tale less as paean to domestic industry than as an extended lesson in the art of flirtation. After the Doctor winds up his story, Tiny promises to behave like a good Brownie, whereupon her friend invites her to "'Kiss my fluffy face!'":

> "The owl is too high up," said Tiny, tossing her head.
>
> The Doctor lifted her four feet or so, obtained his kiss, and set her down again.
>
> "You're not fluffy at all," said she in a tone of the utmost contempt; "you're tickly and bristly. Puss is more fluffy, and Father is scrubby and scratchy, because he shaves."
>
> "And which of the three styles do you prefer?" said the Doctor.
>
> "Not tickly and bristly," said Tiny with firmness; and she strutted up the walk for a pace or two, and then turned around to laugh over her shoulder. (63–64)

If the narrator functions as a swain, this passage suggests, his primary goal is to woo his child friends into becoming fabulous flirts themselves, to teach them to talk back, to countertease their teasers. Indeed, Ewing's own desire to conceptualize "story-making" as an erotically charged exchange manifests itself most explicitly in this scene. Casting her child characters as able and willing partners in sexual/textual play, she insists that they are as adept as adults at resisting conclusiveness in favor of ongoing titillation. Having been teased by the Doctor, Deordie and company show that they can cajole him into prolonging his story; similarly, Tiny demonstrates that she knows how to incite and extend a conversation with her friendly neighbor by employing various flirtatious tactics such as faux contempt, strutting, and head tossing. As in the scene featuring Granny Trout, Ewing characterizes the adult author-child auditor relationship as interactive and mutually gratifying. To this end, she actively discourages the assumption that Tiny is passively submitting to the Doctor's desires rather than acting on her own; describing how Tiny "tyrannize[s]" over "her victim," Ewing represents her child heroine as a knowing, active agent, a skilled manipulator in her own right (63–64). In keeping with this vision of shared power and reciprocated interest, the final scene of the story finds Tiny sneaking into the Doctor's yard to weed his sweet peas; in a reversal of the opening scene, she now finds satisfaction in her ability to gain access to *his* garden.

Still, it is hard not to cringe at the pedophilic overtones of the second "Kiss my fluffy face" scene. Indeed, by having the Doctor employ the Old Owl's phrase to lure Tiny into his arms, Ewing invites us to suspect that his overtures have exerted a coercive force, that he has trained Tiny to behave in a way that satisfies his private desires. The genius of *The Brownies* lies precisely in its extended entertainment of this ambiguity; appropriately, Ewing refuses to commit to one particular position, flirting first with the idea that the child operates as an active partner in pleasure, and then with the notion that she (or he) may be a hapless victim of manipulation. The content of Tiny's and the Doctor's conversation actually illustrates Ewing's interest in keeping this uncertainty alive; like the various embodiments of the narrator as swain, this discussion of different "styles"—"fluffy," "tickly and bristly," and "scrubby and scratchy"—brings home the point that interactions between adult authors and child auditors can run the gamut from fun to frightening, from pleasurable to painful. By keeping this wide range of relations in play, Ewing demonstrates that it is possible to acknowledge the adult's power and primacy in the storytelling process without categorizing this relationship as a *necessarily* abusive one.

"After having learned what theory has to tell us about the nature of childhood and the nature of literature," Perry Nodelman has recently pointed out, "we can logically conclude only that literature in each and all of its forms and manifestations is very, very bad for children" (4). In "Fear of Children's Literature: What's Left (or Right) After Theory," Nodelman ponders the implications of his own adherence to a paradigm that characterizes texts aimed at children as manipulative and oppressive, one that inevitably leads its followers "to fear the entire project of children's literature, its very existence" (9). Seeking a solution to this quandary in the very theory "which has helped me to perceive and understand this problem," Nodelman suggests that adults encourage children to become critical readers, to recognize that representations "*are* representations" rather than simply "accept them as the way things naturally and obviously are" (12). Made aware of the ways in which texts work to impose a certain kind of identity on them, he argues, children will be able to "weigh and consider the implications of the subject positions texts offer" (12).

In essence, Nodelman urges concerned adults to focus less on the vulnerability of children, and more on the vulnerability of texts, a strategy endorsed and enabled by stories like *The Brownies*. Encouraging her young readers to view stories as starting points rather than marching orders, Ewing champions the pleasures and possibilities of revision, reminding her audience that the authority of narrative is far from absolute. Her own choice of fairy-tale material attests to her deep desire to motivate children to play an active role in the production of narrative, for as Maria Tatar has pointed out, the Brothers Grimm tales "are part of an oral tradition that was constantly subject to revision by tellers and listeners alike" (282). In a comment which neatly sums up the project of Ewing's narrative, Tatar concludes that "these texts can serve as opportunities for creating new stories—for cooperative and collaborative performances of meaning enacted by adult *and* child" (282).

Indeed, Ewing chooses "The Elves and the Shoemaker" as her urtext not only in order to take advantage of the inherently interactive aspect of the genre, but also because the plot of this tale revolves around an actual collaboration between little people and larger ones; each day, the shoemaker cuts out the material for his wares, and each night the elves sneak in and sew the pieces together.[13] Elaborating on this theme, *The Brownies* likewise portrays its young and old characters as partners in craft; both children and adults wield scissors, needle, and thread, and their shared talent for clipping and stitching material of various kinds symbolizes their collective ability to cut and refashion narratives. *The Brownies* opens with Tiny sewing in the garden; similarly, the first scene of "The Brownies" features Granny knitting, and Ewing posits a link between literary and literal piecework by explaining that Granny's advanced age allows her to engage in only two activities, recounting stories and stitching together "hearth-rugs out of the bits and scraps of cloth that were shred in the tailoring" (14). Tommy and Johnnie's father, the tailor, likewise practices the art of transforming old remnants into new forms; and when Tommy helps his father remake an old suit into a new outfit for himself, his delight illustrates the pleasures available to children who learn to tailor stories to suit their own needs and desires.

To many, the idea that children can actively participate in the production of narrative will seem overly optimistic, but focusing on the weakness and vulnerability of young people surely gives rise to a graver risk: that of reinstating the old image of the child as innocent, artless, and powerless, a blank being empty of individuality and agency. Perhaps the best course would be to stake out a position somewhere in between these two extremes, to accept Ewing's and Nodelman's challenge "to both be aware of the dangers inherent in texts and still celebrate their ability to please" and inspire children (Nodelman, "The Urge to Sameness" 42). To tread this fine line, however, we must resist the tendency to automatically equate seduction with abuse, a habit that

---

has proven tenacious in its hold over recent children's literature criticism.[14] For the inflexibility of this stance not only precludes the possibility that child readers can play with and derive pleasure from texts, it also prevents us from recognizing that many classic children's texts address the very issues that have concerned critics of the genre since the publication of *The Case of Peter Pan*. Far from ignoring the problematic nature of the adult author-child reader relationship, as Rose and others have argued, authors like Ewing, Lewis Carroll, R. L. Stevenson, and E. Nesbit acknowledge the aggressive, prescriptive aspects of their chosen genre, while still striving to envision—and thus, to make possible—a more flexible relationship between text and child. Their nuanced treatment of this problem provides us with a better model than a rhetoric that requires us to embark on a crusade to "save the children" from the dangers of children's literature.

Notes

Many thanks to Peter Betjemann, Lorna Brittan, Don Gray, Susan Gubar, U. C. Knoepflmacher, Mitzi Myers, Jeff Nunokawa, Jessica Richard, and Kieran Setiya for their aid and encouragement. I also owe an enormous debt to the editors and anonymous readers at *Children's Literature* for their insightful comments and criticism.

1. In *The Case of Peter Pan*, Jacqueline Rose describes all children's literature as a form of seduction that "aims, unashamedly, to take the child *in*"; she focuses on "the adult's intention to get at the child," conceptualizing children's literature "as something of a soliciting, a chase, or even a seduction" (2). Lured into identifying with an adult-constructed image of childhood, she argues, child readers mold themselves to match the vision of the child presented in the text, a vision geared to satisfy adult needs and desires.

2. Lesnik-Oberstein's book takes as its primary subject children's literature criticism, rather than children's literature per se; however, her use of abuse is pertinent here because she, like Rose, moves directly from the claim that it is "impossible to gauge" how children respond to texts to the suggestion that we ought to focus on the needs and desires of adults (Rose 9). Whereas Rose concentrates primarily on the adult author's investment in the figure of the child, Lesnik-Oberstein examines how critics of children's literature construct "the child" for their own purposes. In both cases, however, the conviction that the child should be considered "unknowable" leads to the adoption of abuse as a governing paradigm for the discussion that follows.

3. Tellingly, when Rose added a new introductory essay to *The Case of Peter Pan* in 1992, she focused extensively on the "crisis of child sexual abuse in the 1980s," suggesting that contemporary readers might "need to approach *Peter Pan* from the angle of this level of disturbance" (xvii).

4. British child psychoanalyst D. W. Winnicott (1896–1971) coined the term "potential space" to refer to the intermediate area between internal and external reality, where play and aesthetic experience take place. As Murray M. Schwartz has argued, locating literature in this "inclusive realm" allows us to take account both of the instructions and meanings texts issue, and the individuality of our own response to them (60).

5. In promoting the possibility of pleasure, this essay aims to continue the dialogue begun by Perry Nodelman's article "Pleasure and Genre: Speculations on the Characteristics of Children's Fiction," which appeared in vol. 28 of *Children's Literature*.

6. *The Brownies* garnered instant acclaim when it appeared in Charlotte Yonge's magazine the *Monthly Packet* in 1865. Thirty years after Ewing's death, the story was used as the basis for the junior branch of the Girl Guide movement; and it was frequently reprinted and even rewritten by other publishers and writers, selling well into the 1950s. For further background on Ewing, see Avery, Gatty, Knoepflmacher, Laski, and Maxwell.

7. In his essay "Flirtation," Georg Simmel describes this type of oscillation between "consent and refusal" as "the formula of all flirtation"; expert flirts, he argues, continuously alternate between "accommodation and denial," "concession and withdrawal" (134–35, 137). Adam Phillips also elaborates on this view in *On Flirtation*.

8. As she draws *The Brownies* to a close, Ewing finally drops a hint that enables her readers to guess the identity of the dead party; gazing at the tombstone, the Doctor exclaims, "Good-night, Marcia . . . Good-night, my darling!" (65).

9. I am indebted to an anonymous reader from *Children's Literature* who suggested that I explore this link.

10. In charting this progression, I do not mean to adhere uncritically to what Mitzi Myers describes as the "Whiggish historical model of progress from quotidian instruction toward the escapist delight of fairy tale and fantasy," a paradigm embraced by children's literature historians such as F. J. Harvey Darton and Roger Lancelyn Green (97–98). Clearly ambivalent about including fantastic material in her narrative, Sinclair never manages to find a consistent tone, shifting violently back and forth between frivolity and seriousness. But this is not to say that all early authors of children's literature had this problem. Indeed, Myers mounts a convincing argument that Maria Edgeworth's children's stories often "elud[e] the binary opposition of moral tale and fairy tale," and *The Brownies* might be said to continue this tradition (98).

11. Unsure whether she should accept or reject her swain's proposal, Granny is told by her mother to ask the Old Owl for advice; embarking on this quest "at moon-rise," she runs into her suitor, who kisses her and settles the question. Not only does this story set up the link between visiting the Old Owl and getting seduced, it also reinforces the association of giving in to such solicitations with the precarious state of being caught between laughter and tears; right before she succumbs to her future husband's kiss, Granny tells the boys, she "burst out crying" (23).

12. Richardson makes this argument in reference to Maria Edgeworth's moral tales, in *Literature, Education, and Romanticism: Reading as Social Practice, 1780–1832.*

13. Like the sexualized interplay between adults and children in *The Brownies*, the nighttime collaboration featured in "The Elves and the Shoemaker" carries a distinctly erotic charge; enthusiastic voyeurs, the shoemaker and his wife hide themselves behind a curtain and avidly ogle the "two little naked dwarfs" as they stitch away at the shoes (143). Although this fable at first seems to chronicle a case of intrusive, one-way desire, it turns into a story about reciprocal pleasure when the shoemaker and his wife decide to "deligh[t]" the elves—and forego their own fun—by constructing clothes for their small visitors (143). Thus, when Ewing broaches the question of whether titillating encounters between little people and larger ones constitute molestation or mutually gratifying play, she does not depart from the Grimms' tale so much as magnify an underlying theme.

14. Jack Zipes's new book *Sticks and Stones: The Troublesome Success of Children's Literature from Slovenly Peter to Harry Potter* (2001) provides a perfect example of the continuing allure—and the ultimate limitations—of this approach. In his introduction, Zipes proposes to stake out a middle ground between those who view children as helpless victims of cultural artifacts like texts and television shows, and those who see them as resilient, creative agents, capable of retooling such materials in imaginative ways. Ultimately, however, Zipes's reliance on Rose's work leads him to take the violated child as his emblem and guide, and thus to align himself—however unintentionally—with the former group. Chronicling the recent history of children's literature criticism, for ex-

ample, Zipes intersperses excerpts from a recent *New Yorker* article about a girl gang member, Mindy Turner, in order to foreground the issue of "neglected, abandoned, and abused" children (26). Moreover, he argues that we must remodel our discipline around the icon of the victimized child; he concludes this chapter by asserting that "we shall not be able to develop our criticism further if Mindy Turner is not linked to us and what we do to and with children's literature" (37).

Works Cited

Avery, Gillian. *Nineteenth Century Children: Heroes and Heroines in English Children's Stories 1780–1900*. With the assistance of Angela Bull. London: Hodder and Stoughton, 1965.

———. *Mrs. Ewing*. New York: H. Z. Walck, 1964.

Barthes, Roland. *The Pleasure of the Text*. Trans. Richard Miller. New York: Hill and Wang, 1975.

———. *S/Z: An Essay*. Trans. Richard Miller. New York: Hill and Wang, 1974.

Ewing, Juliana Horatia. "The Brownies." In *The Brownies and Other Tales*. Illus. George Cruikshank. London: Bell & Baldy, 1871. 1–67.

Gatty, Horatia K. F. *Juliana Horatia Ewing and Her Books*. London: Society for Promoting Christian Knowledge, 1887.

Grimm, M. M. "The Elves and the Shoemaker." In *German Popular Stories*, vol. 1. Trans. Edward Taylor. London: C. Baldwyn, 1823. 140–43.

Kincaid, James R. *Child-Loving: The Erotic Child and Victorian Culture*. New York: Routledge, 1992.

Knoepflmacher, U. C. *Ventures into Childland: Victorians, Fairy Tales, and Femininity*. Chicago: University of Chicago Press, 1998.

Laski, Marghanita. *Mrs. Ewing, Mrs. Molesworth and Mrs. Hodgson Burnett*. London: Arthur Barker, 1950.

Lesnik-Oberstein, Karín. *Children's Literature: Criticism and the Fictional Child*. Oxford: Clarendon Press, 1994.

MacDonald, George. *Adela Cathcart*. Whitethorn, Calif.: Johannesen, 1994.

Maxwell, Christabel. *Mrs. Gatty and Mrs. Ewing*. London: Constable, 1949.

Myers, Mitzi. "Romancing the Moral Tale: Maria Edgeworth and the Problematics of Pedagogy." In *Romanticism and Children's Literature in Nineteenth-Century England*. Ed. James Holt McGavran, Jr. Athens: University of Georgia Press, 1991. 96–127.

Nodelman, Perry. "Fear of Children's Literature: What's Left (or Right) After Theory?" In *Reflections of Change: Children's Literature Since 1945*. Ed. Sandra L. Beckett. Westport, Conn.: Greenwood Press, 1997. 3–14.

———. "Pleasure and Genre: Speculations on the Characteristics of Children's Fiction." *Children's Literature* 28 (2000): 1–14.

———. "The Urge to Sameness." *Children's Literature* 28 (2000): 38–43.

Phillips, Adam. *On Flirtation: Psychoanalytic Essays on the Uncommitted Life*. Cambridge: Harvard University Press, 1994.

———. *On Kissing, Tickling, and Being Bored: Psychoanalytic Essays on the Unexamined Life*. Cambridge: Harvard University Press, 1993.

Richardson, Alan. *Literature, Education, and Romanticism: Reading as Social Practice, 1780–1832*. Cambridge: Cambridge University Press, 1994.

Rose, Jacqueline. *The Case of Peter Pan or the Impossibility of Children's Fiction*. Rev. ed. Philadelphia: University of Pennsylvania Press, 1992.

Schwartz, Murray C. "Where Is Literature?" In *Transitional Objects and Potential Spaces: Literary Uses of D. W. Winnicott*. Ed. Peter L. Rudnytsky. New York: Columbia University Press, 1993. 50–62.

Simmel, Georg. "Flirtation." In *Georg Simmel: On Women, Sexuality, and Love.* Trans. Guy Oakes. New Haven: Yale University Press, 1984. 133–52.

Sinclair, Catherine. *Holiday House: A Series of Tales.* New York: Robert Carter, 1839.

Tatar, Maria. "Is Anybody Out There Listening?: Fairy Tales and the Voice of the Child." In *Infant Tongues: The Voice of the Child in Literature.* Ed. Elizabeth Goodenough, Mark A. Haberle, and Naomi Sokoloff. Detroit: Wayne State University Press, 1994. 275–83.

Zipes, Jack. *Sticks and Stones: The Troublesome Success of Children's Literature from Slovenly Peter to Harry Potter.* New York: Routledge, 2001.

Fear's Echo and Unhinged Joy: Crossing Homosocial Boundaries in A Separate Peace

James Holt McGavran

At the beginning of John Knowles's great novel of male adolescence, *A Separate Peace,* narrator Gene Forrester revisits Devon, the New Hampshire boys' boarding school where fifteen years earlier, during World War II, his best friend Phineas had died. He is overcome first with memories of fear, "like stale air in an unopened room, . . . the well known fear which had surrounded and filled those days" (1). He continues: "I felt fear's echo, and along with that I felt the unhinged, uncontrollable joy which had been its accompaniment and opposite face, joy which had broken out sometimes in those days like Northern Lights across black sky" (2). By focusing on Gene's joy as well as his fear, I believe we can find a new way of looking at Gene and his friendship with Finny.

What did Gene fear at Devon? Unlike Finny and most of the other students, he comes from a less elitist part of the country than New England (apparently West Virginia, Knowles's home state) but affects, with indifferent success, the speech and attitude of an aristocrat from "three states south of . . . [his] own" (148). At one point, when Gene says "I don't guess I did," Finny responds, "stop talking like a Georgia cracker" (112–13). But Gene is not socially disadvantaged at Devon by competition with blue-blood preppies from Boston or New York; not only is he the class brain and a more than passable athlete, but conservative student leader Brinker Hadley wants Gene to be his best friend—and so does emotionally disturbed Leper Lepellier.

Nor do I uncritically accept the idea, though there is much textual and critical support for it, that self-divided, willful, guilt-haunted Gene finds jealousy and fear to be integral parts of his friendship with Finny, whereas beautiful, totally integrated, guileless Finny, portrayed symbolically as both a Greek god (Mengeling) and a Christlike sacrificial savior and victim (Bryant, *War Within* 86), lives on an altogether higher plane of moral and emotional purity and love.[1] Granted, Gene says he always hated jumping with Finny into the river from the high

Children's Literature 30, ed. Elizabeth Lennox Keyser and Julie Pfeiffer (Yale University Press), © 2002 Hollins University).

67

branch of a tree but felt compelled by Finny to do it (25–26). And granted, he feels jealous shock as well as admiration when Finny breaks a school swimming record but magnanimously refuses to let Gene publicize it: he comments first to Finny, almost Judas-like, "You're too good to be true" (36), and then to himself more than half-confessionally, "there were few relationships among us at Devon not based on rivalry" (37). And the central action of the book, where Gene's jostling of their tree branch causes Finny to fall and break his leg, seems causally though unintentionally connected to Gene's almost disappointed recognition that Finny had not been plotting to ruin his academic performance at the school but simply hadn't realized that his brainy friend needed to study before taking tests (50). Nevertheless, as Paul Witherington has observed, writing on the ambiguities and complexities of Knowles's novel, "Finny is no more of a spiritually pure being than Gene is a spiritually depraved being" (Karson 81). A closer look at the text will show that the boys trade roles as upholders and subverters of both their own relationship and the codes of society. Finny, for all of his innocent beauty and grace, also experiences inner fears and conflicts, and just as often Gene feels entirely at peace both within himself and with regard to Finny. As Gene recognizes, the fear and joy are experienced mutually, shared.

Unlike Witherington, who argues that as he matures Gene distances himself from Finny (Karson 88), I would locate the key to understanding this exchange of roles and feelings in the growing recognition on Gene's part throughout the novel, as both boy and man, that he wants not only to love Finny but to *be* Finny, to *become* part of his friend body and soul, and in Finny's acceptance and encouragement of this merging of identities both before and after the crippling fall that ends his athletic career and fatally endangers his life. Like a reciprocal Jungian integration of shadow selves, this union, highlighted when Gene wears Finny's pink shirt, reaches its zenith at the symbolically important Winter Carnival—Bostonian Finny's necessarily frosty version of a Mardi Gras celebration—where Gene, now clearly Finny's alter ego, is crowned Carnival king in a Bakhtinian exchange of roles.[2] Finny has always been a breaker of rules—game rules, school rules, the rules of a society at war that say that no one should be having fun now. But Gene's desire to break the boundaries of their separate human identities is finally still more radical. I don't think Finny's death is Gene's fault, but this desire to absorb his friend completely seems to require either Finny's actual death, which of course occurs, or the death of all difference between them, which I will argue also occurs.

We can better understand the difficult dynamic of these crossed boundaries of identity if we analyze *A Separate Peace* not only in Jungian terms of integrated shadows or in Bakhtinian terms of temporarily liberating role-exchanges but in the context of gender theory. The translation of Michel Foucault's *History of Sexuality* in the late 1970s introduced English-speaking readers to his parallel ideas that gender, desire, and sexual preference are inherently unstable and fluid and that it is the various discourses of a predominantly heterosexual society that, by policing alternative sexualities, make gender roles seem fixed and unchangeable (see Berger, Wallis, and Watson, eds., Introduction, 5–6). Beginning with the publication of *Gender Trouble* (1990) and continuing with *Bodies That Matter* (1993), Judith Butler extended these concepts by arguing that our understanding not just of gender but of sex itself, traditionally thought of as biologically fixed, results instead from a variety of performative strategies.

Foucault's emphasis on the policing of alternative sexualities had been taken up earlier in Eve Kosofsky Sedgwick's pathbreaking work on what she calls male homosocial desire. Sedgwick's theorizing about men's relationships in patriarchal societies, recorded in *Between Men* (1985) and *Epistemology of the Closet* (1990), is based on the cultural paradox that while boys and men are expected to study, play, work, and fight together—both in competition and cooperation—they are absolutely forbidden to engage in sexual relations with each other. Thus the flip side of male homosocial bonding is homophobia, an irrational loathing of homosexuality, and what Sedgwick calls homosexual panic, the terrible fear that sets in whenever a man even unconsciously feels attracted to another male, feels the other may be attracted to him, or thinks that anyone else may suspect them of sexual feelings for each other (*Between Men* 1–5, 88–89). In other words, such traditional patriarchal societies as those of the white English-speaking world—and most certainly that of the elite boys' boarding school—almost set up boys and young men to fall in love with each other and yet threaten them with social ostracism and mental and physical abuse if they express their feelings openly. Sedgwick says tellingly, "For a man to be a man's man is separated only by an invisible, carefully blurred, always-already-crossed line from being 'interested in men'" (*Between Men* 89).

A Catch-22 situation for adolescent boys, this double bind, more than his embarrassment at his not-quite-Southern origins or any alleged satanic jealousy of Finny's superior body or soul, explains the combined memories of fear and joy that Gene discovers upon returning to Devon, especially when we recall Foucault's and Butler's insistence on the natural fluidity of desire and the performative and thus unstable aspect of gender roles. This paradox also explains why, for his part, Finny seems always to be reaching beyond the rules of school, games, and a society at war to carve out a "separate peace" for himself and Gene. It explains why the other boys at Devon, led by Brinker and supported by Leper, are so eager to put Finny and Gene on trial after the carnival: the real though unspoken motivation for that ultimately fatal event is not justice or truth—to find out who made Finny fall or to force him to accept his disability, as Brinker claims (152)—but the other boys' combined homophobic fear and jealous curiosity at the closeness of his relationship with Gene and what the two of them might have been able to get away with. Finally, it explains why Gene asserts at the end of his narrative that he neither mourns nor has lost Finny, particularly if we reference another essay by Butler, "Melancholy Gender/Refused Identification" (*Constructing Masculinity* 21–36). In this remarkable piece Butler uses some of Freud's ideas on mourning and ego-formation from *The Ego and the Id* to argue that homophobia often forces the would-be same-sex lover symbolically to reject the unacceptable love-object and yet simultaneously to bear him/her, neither possessed nor mourned, within the societally constituted, and thus outwardly heterosexual, self.[3]

I do not mean to imply by any of this that either Gene or Finny can be simply and reductively construed as gay; indeed labeling is only negatively related to what this gratifyingly deep book is about. I have a hunch, however, that had Finny lived longer, or had the Carnival mood not been interrupted by Leper's telegram, either boy might have seen the patriarchal proscription on homosexual activity as just another rule to be broken; one might have suggested such an experiment to the other; and the other might have accepted. But I do not suggest that we read *A Separate Peace* as even a failed coming-out story. While there are some hints, as I will show later, that Gene has had homosexual experience since Finny's death, Knowles leaves open the question of Gene's adult sexual orientation, I believe intentionally and partly for historical reasons. Knowles was recreating a World War II-era experience in the late 1950s, a decade before the Stonewall uprisings of 1969 commonly used to date the start of the late-twentieth-century gay liberation movement and a time when both the now-current vocabulary of liberation and the editorial will to publish such stories were lacking. But I hazard a guess that Knowles had a second reason for his silence regarding Gene's subsequent orientation: according to the current general understanding, "coming out" refers to a one-time, one-way move from the safe side of Sedgwick's always-already-crossed line to the other whereas, as Sedgwick herself and others argue, and as Knowles's text seems to support, gender roles and sexual identity are in reality far more fluid and contingent. Many young men and women experiment with same-sex intimacy, especially in adolescence, but later become committed partners in heterosexual relationships; and of course, for some the reverse can also be true. In what follows I will look first at some of Gene's and Finny's expressions of love for each other, then at Gene's growing sense of identification with Finny and Finny's reciprocating responses, and finally at three moments in the novel—their clandestine overnight trip to the beach, their last conversation before Finny's death, and Gene's final summation of his friendship—where the homoerotic tide seems to flow the highest.

As the time of the novel shifts to the past, Gene begins to remember Finny's physical presence, and he remembers this in great detail. First it is his voice: "'What I like best about this tree,' he said in that voice of his, the equivalent in sound of a hypnotist's eyes, 'what I like is that it's such a cinch!' He opened his green eyes wider and gave us his maniac look, and only the smirk on his wide mouth with its droll, slightly protruding upper lip reassured us that he wasn't completely goofy" (6). Then it is his athletic body: "We just looked quietly back at him, and so he began taking off his clothes, stripping down to his underpants. For such an extraordinary athlete . . . he was not spectacularly built. He was my height—five feet eight and a half inches. . . . He weighed a hundred and fifty pounds, a galling ten pounds more than I did, which flowed from his legs to torso around shoulders to arms and full strong neck in an uninterrupted, unemphatic unity of strength" (8). Gene comes back again and again, as the narrative progresses, to these or similar details of Finny's physical appearance. He realizes that Finny's beauty lies less in his actual shape or dimensions— "he was not spectacularly built"—than in the way he inhabits his body, the energy that flows through him in a "unity of strength." This energy, which Gene later, at the Winter Carnival, calls Finny's "choreography of peace" (128), informs nearly everything Finny does: "He could also shine at many other things, with people for instance, the others in our dormitory, the faculty; in fact, if you stopped to think about it, Finny could shine with everyone, he attracted everyone he met. I was glad of that too. Naturally. He was my roommate and my best friend" (32). It seems Gene both is and is not jealous of his friend's attractiveness: there is pain as well as joy in that stand-alone "Naturally."

Later, during the period when he wrongly suspects Finny of wanting to subvert his studying and spoil his grades, he still burns with love for him, and years later, recalling this time when fear and joy clashed, the grown-up Gene cannot help writing a passionately poetic litany of love:

> Sometimes I found it hard to remember his treachery, sometimes I discovered myself thoughtlessly slipping back into affection for him again. It was hard to remember when one summer day after another broke with a cool effulgence over us, and there was a breath of widening life in the morning air—something hard to describe—an oxygen intoxicant, a shining northern paganism, some odor, some feeling so hopelessly promising that I would fall back in my bed on guard against it. It was hard to remember in the heady and sensual clarity of these mornings; I forgot whom I hated and who hated me. I wanted to break out crying from stabs of hopeless joy, or intolerable promise, or because these mornings were too full of beauty for me, because I knew of too much hate to be contained in a world like this. (47)

More of a realist than Finny—on the surface at least—Gene knows this joy cannot last; what he knows about both nature and human society tells him that each day. Later, when Finny returns to Devon on crutches, Gene feels his life once again turning to joy in the midst of fear: "For the war was no longer eroding the peaceful summertime stillness I had prized so much at Devon, and although the playing fields were crusted under a foot of congealed snow and the river was now a hard gray-white lane of ice between gaunt trees, peace had come back to Devon for me" (101). Peace—inner peace, at least—and Finny are inseparable for Gene.

Gene's love for Finny clearly is reciprocated. After their first jump from the tree into the river, when Leper and some other boys refuse to try it, " 'It's you, pal,' Finny said to me at last, 'just you and me.' He and I started back across the fields, preceding the others like two seigneurs" (10). They wrestle with each other, partly for the fun of it, partly for the excitement of the physical contact, partly to be deliberately late for dinner. Finny always wins these skirmishes, until Gene sneak-attacks: "I threw my hip against his, catching him by surprise, and he was instantly down, definitely pleased. This was why he liked me so much. When I jumped on top of him, my knees on his chest, he couldn't ask for anything better. We struggled in some equality for a while, and then when we were sure we were too late for dinner, we broke off" (11). Caught by surprise? Finny's obvious delight at having Gene on top of him suggests that this was his goal all along. Much later, calling long distance from his home near Boston, Finny is relieved to hear that Gene has not chosen another roommate (75–76). Back at Devon, Finny watches with keen interest as Gene undresses after a grueling day of shoveling snow in a nearby railroad yard, criticizing all of his clothes but the stinking, sweaty undershirt next to his skin: "'There. You should have worn that all day, just that. That has real taste. The rest of your outfit was just gilding that lily of a sweat shirt'" (96). But Gene has a stronger (because not veiled in irony) proof of Finny's love the next morning, when Finny hears that Gene has told Brinker he will enlist and enter the war: "'Enlist!' cried Finny. . . . His large and clear eyes turned with an odd expression on me. I had never seen such a look in them before. After looking at me closely he said, 'You're going to enlist?'" (99). Gene realizes the full significance of Finny's response and immediately gives up all thought of joining the war:

> Phineas was shocked at the idea of my leaving. In some way he needed me. He needed me. I was the least trustworthy person he had ever met. I knew that; he knew or should know that too. I had even told him. But there was no mistaking the shield of remoteness in his face and voice. He wanted me around. The war then passed away from me, and dreams of enlistment and escape and a clean start lost their meaning for me. . . . I have never since forgotten the dazed look on Finny's face when he thought that on the first day of his return to Devon I was going to desert him. I didn't know why he had chosen me, why it was only to me that he could show the most humbling sides of his handicap. I didn't care. (100–101)

Gene no longer cares about the war, but Brinker does, and he will have his revenge at being jilted by Gene later, in the mock-trial that leads to Finny's death.

Gene's desire to become part of Finny, implicit in some of the passages already quoted, becomes explicit soon after Finny's fall, sometimes with clear homoerotic implications. Dressing for dinner one night, Gene has an odd but irresistible temptation to try on Finny's clothes, most notably his bright pink shirt: "But when I looked in the mirror it was no remote aristocrat I had become, no character out of daydreams. I was Phineas, Phineas to the life. I even had his humorous expression in my face, his sharp, optimistic awareness. . . . I would never stumble through the confusions of my own character again" (54). This identification gains in significance if we remember that earlier, when Finny first showed him the shirt, Gene had exclaimed, "Pink! It makes you look like a fairy!" and Finny had mildly replied, "I wonder what would happen if I looked like a fairy to everyone" (17).[4]

Later, when the crew manager Cliff Quackenbush calls Gene a "maimed son of a bitch" (71), Gene reacts immediately and violently: "I hit him hard across the face. I didn't know why for an instant; it was almost as though I were maimed. Then the realization that there was someone who was flashed over me" (71). Shortly thereafter, when Gene tells him on the telephone that he is "too busy for sports," Finny groans melodramatically for some time and finally says: "'Listen, pal, if *I* can't play sports, *you're* going to play them for me,' and I lost part of myself to him then, and a soaring sense of freedom revealed that this must have been my purpose from the first: to become a part of Phineas" (77). This is Gene's clearest, most explicit statement of his desire to merge permanently with his friend.

Gene later describes the rank air of the Devon gym in oddly nostalgic detail and ends with a surprisingly intimate comparison: "sweat predominated, but it was richly mingled with smells of paraffin and singed rubber, of soaked wool and liniment, and for those who could interpret it, of exhaustion, lost hope and triumph and bodies battling against each other. I thought it anything but a bad smell. It was preeminently the smell of the human body after it had been used to the limit, such a smell as has meaning and poignance for any athlete, just as it has for any lover" (105). Gene never speaks of his postwar, post-Finny personal life. That very silence, coupled with this association of male sweat and lovemaking, opens the possibility that he has at least experimented with homosexual activity because of the desire that Finny first awoke in him. But Knowles does not make this explicit, presumably for the reasons mentioned earlier.

After Gene accedes to Finny's demand to play sports for him, a number of things happen rather quickly. First, Gene replies "not exactly" when Finny says the gym is the "same same old place" (106). He further recalls: "He made no pretense of not understanding me. After a pause he said, 'You're going to be the big star now,' in an optimistic tone, and then added with some embarrassment, 'You can fill any gaps or anything'" (106). Then Finny does three things: he starts Gene doing chin-ups; he tells him his fantasy that there isn't any war; and when Gene quizzes him as to why he alone knows there is no war, Finny lays himself open to Gene in a way he never has before: "The momentum of the argument abruptly broke from his control. His face froze. 'Because I've suffered,' he burst out" (108). This is the beginning of Finny's training Gene to become a star athlete and Gene's tutoring Finny in his studies (111), and it leads to Gene's miraculous self-discovery when he gets a second wind and, though he does not say it, for a moment feels like Finny: "I lost myself, oppressed mind along with aching body; all entanglements were shed, I broke into the clear" (112). Shortly afterward, Gene comments: "He drew me increasingly away from . . . all other friends, into a world inhabited by just himself and me, where there was no war at all, just Phineas and me alone among all the other people in the world, training for the Olympics of 1944" (119).

But before those never-to-be-held Olympics, Finny has another brain-child which he does bring off: the Winter Carnival. Although many arrangements are made, much hard cider is drunk, and several of their friends participate, there are two focal points of the carnival, and they involve Finny and Gene, respectively. The first is Finny's one-legged dance on top of the Prize Table: "Under the influence not I know of the hardest cider but of his own inner joy at life for a moment as it should be, as it was meant to be in his nature, Phineas recaptured that magic gift for existing primarily in space, one foot conceding briefly to gravity its rights before spinning him off again into the air. It was his wildest demonstration of himself, of himself in the kind of world he loved; it was his choreography of peace" (128). The second is Gene's weird, Finny-directed solo decathlon: "it wasn't cider which made me in this moment champion of everything he ordered, to run as though I were the abstraction of speed, to walk the half-circle of statues on my hands, to balance on my head on top of the icebox on top of the Prize Table . . . to accept at the end of it amid a clatter of applause . . . a wreath made from the evergreen trees which Phineas placed on my head" (128). By giving Gene all his athletic expertise, Finny gets back for a moment his own more-than-athletic grace and then happily sees Gene all but outdo him in goofiness, in "Finny-ness." The Jungian/Bakhtinian switching of identities could only be more complete if we knew that Finny started to make A's on all his tests— but sadly, there is not time for that to happen. The pent-up jealousies and suspicions of Brinker and Leper lead to the trial, with its Lenten atmosphere of accusation and doom, and thus to Finny's death.

A high point of their Edenic summer, shortly before Finny's wounding, is the forbidden bicycle trip to the beach that Finny proposes to Gene, perhaps the most overtly homoerotic sequence in the novel. Gene is aware that Finny "did everything he could think of for me" (39): he entertains Gene on the way by telling stories and jokes, doing bicycle gymnastics, and singing; after they get there and Gene gets tumbled in a wave, Finny plays in the surf for an hour, but all for Gene's amusement. Later, after eating hot dogs, they stroll along the beach and are keenly aware of each other's youthful beauty:

> Finny and I went along the Boardwalk in our sneakers and white slacks, Finny in a light blue polo shirt and I in a T-shirt. I noticed that people were looking fixedly at him, so I took a look myself to see why. His skin radiated a reddish copper glow of tan, his brown hair had been a little bleached by the sun, and I noticed that the tan made his eyes shine with a cool blue-green fire.
>
> "Everybody's staring at you," he suddenly said to me. "It's because of that movie-star tan you picked up this afternoon . . . showing off again." (39)

Gene's very next comment, spoken to himself after this declaration from Finny, sounds almost Sunday-schoolish: "Enough broken rules were enough that night" (39). Gene says this ostensibly with regard to drinking beer—each boy has only one glass—but it is also as if he knows he has had a proposition from Finny and is simply too frightened to accept. Then, before they go to sleep under the stars, Finny repeats his love song to Gene:

> The last words of Finny's usual nighttime monologue were, "I hope you're having a pretty good time here. I know I kind of dragged you away at the point of a gun, but after all you can't come to the shore with just anybody and you can't come by yourself, and at this teen-age period in life the proper person is your best pal." He hesitated and then added, "which is what you are," and there was silence on his dune. (40)

Again Gene isolates himself from the totally open intimacy Finny expresses, but this time he can't entirely refuse to understand it:

> It was a courageous thing to say. Exposing a sincere emotion nakedly like that at the Devon School was the next thing to suicide. I should have told him then that he was my best friend also and rounded off what he had said. I started to; I nearly did. But something held me back. Perhaps I was stopped by that level of feeling, deeper than thought, which contains the truth. (40)

What can that deep, truthful level of feeling be but that the boys, far more than "best friends," are in love with each other? And what can stop the sexual expression of such love but what Sedgwick calls homosexual panic?

The same forces are at work in their last conversation before Finny dies. Both boys are crying as Finny finally confronts Gene's having made him fall out of the tree and Gene confronts their mutual love and desire:

> "Then that was it. Something just seized you. It wasn't anything you really felt against me, it wasn't some kind of hate you've felt all along. It wasn't anything personal."
>
> "No, I don't know how to show you, how can I show you, Finny? Tell me how to show you. It was just some ignorance inside me, some crazy thing inside me, something blind, that's all it was."
>
> He was nodding his head, his jaw tightening and his eyes closed on the tears. "I believe you. It's okay because I understand and I believe you. You've already shown me and I believe you." (183)

Gene's agonized, desperate "Tell me how to show you" provides, in what turns out to be the last hours of Finny's life, his affirmative answer to Finny's naked emotions of love and desire expressed during their night on the beach. But now it is Finny's turn to demur; it is not clear whether his reply, "You've already shown me," should be read as a renewal of his own homosexual panic—here expressed in the magnanimous implication that their love is bigger than sex—or simply as an indicator of his extreme physical weakness.

Later that day he dies, leaving readers with many unanswered questions. If Finny had not thus absolved Gene before his death and Gene had not offered himself to Finny, could Gene have even gone on living for fifteen years, let alone return to Devon saying, as he does at the beginning of the novel (2), that he has finally escaped his boyhood fear?

But if Finny had lived and they had expressed their love physically, would even closer bonding have resulted, or would homophobia have reasserted itself in bitter division? Gene's comment on his grief, or rather the lack of it, strongly buttresses Butler's application of Freud's ideas on inner mourning to the repression of same-sex desire and the establishment of an outwardly heterosexual adult identity: "I did not cry then or ever about Finny. I did not cry even when I stood watching him being lowered into his family's strait-laced burial ground outside of Boston. I could not escape a feeling that this was my own funeral, and you do not cry in that case" (186). Of course these same words simultaneously confirm that Gene's union with Finny is complete and will always remain intact.

Trying to summarize Finny's continuing presence in his life at the end of the book, Gene writes a eulogy that underlines the fluidity and potential subversiveness of Finny's character—and thus, he seems to realize, of his own: "During the time I was with him, Phineas created an atmosphere in which I continued now to live, a way of sizing up the world with erratic and entirely personal reservations, letting its rocklike facts sift through and be accepted only a little at a time, only as much as he could assimilate without a sense of chaos and loss" (194). Still, Gene says that Phineas alone escaped the hostility of the world: "He possessed an extra vigor, a heightened confidence in himself, a serene capacity for affection which saved him" (194–95). The tone here and even the vocabulary are remarkably close to the benediction that Nick Carraway pronounces upon Jay Gatsby at the beginning of F. Scott Fitzgerald's famous novel of the 1920s: "If personality is an unbroken series of successful gestures, then there was something gorgeous about him, some heightened sensitivity to the promises of life, as if he were related to one of those intricate machines that register earthquakes ten thousand miles away" (Fitzgerald 2). Or compare the final words spoken by Henry, the narrator of David Guy's novel of adolescence *Second Brother,* about his best friend Sam, with whom he did share one homosexual experience: "My memory of Sam Golden is a talisman for me. I pick it up and hold it and it brings me luck. . . . When I think of how to live my life, not the things I want to do but the way I want to do them, I think of him. . . . I am glad I knew him. I am glad he lived" (Guy 264). Like Henry with Sam, like Nick with Gatsby, Gene is glad he knew Finny, glad he lived; there was something gorgeous about him. And, since Finny's "serene capacity for affection," coupled with his "choreography of peace" (128), now resides inside

Gene, it saves him too, perhaps not from some continuing sense of loss, but from his feelings of guilt and fear.

Given the continuing strength of homophobia and homosexual panic in Western society, such a saving can still seem almost providential; but it has been almost half a century since Leslie Fiedler noted the paradox that our homophobic society somehow keeps a soft spot in its heart for texts like *The Adventures of Huckleberry Finn* that inscribe homoeroticism and compulsory heterosexuality side by side ("Come Back to the Raft Ag'in, Huck Honey!" 3–6). In another essay ("Wordsworth, Lost Boys, and Romantic Hom[e]ophobia") I have argued that some well-known and often-taught books for teenage boys let them down because the writers, probably affected by societal homophobia themselves, fail to explore same-sex relationships thoroughly and honestly. *A Separate Peace* is an exception: like *Huckleberry Finn,* Knowles's inscription of the love of Gene and Finny sets forth a brilliant and teachable example of the clash between the fluidity of gender and the restraints of homophobic discourse as it is played out on the adolescent male body.

Notes

1. While I have no quarrel with his use of *alter-ego* to describe Finny's and Gene's friendship, I will implicitly refute, in what follows, Gordon E. Slethaug's main argument that Gene is Finny's evil twin, driven almost to the end by competition or rivalry (265) and Hallman Bryant's analysis of Gene's development in Judeo-Christian terms of fall and recovery (*War Within,* see chapter headings pp. 41, 69, 103). Finally, I cannot even begin to see Finny as the proto-Nazi villain of the novel as Joseph E. Devine has argued.
2. For a summary of Mikhail Bakhtin's ideas about Carnival and its potential for liberating role-exchanges, see Bristol 348–53.
3. Georges-Michel Sarotte precedes me in recognizing the homosexual theme in *A Separate Peace;* however, since I see Gene's and Finny's love as not only mutual but finally very positive—the fear yielding to the joy—I cannot agree with Sarotte's much more negative assessment of Gene's motives and actions as an example of "the mutilation of the American virile ideal" (295), or with his assertion that "their friendship changes into hatred out of fear of its changing into love" (45).
4. For the history of this shirt, first sold by Brooks Brothers in the early 1940s, see Bryant's "Phineas's Pink Shirt."

Works Cited

Berger, Maurice, Brian Wallis, and Simon Watson, eds. *Constructing Masculinity.* New York: Routledge, 1995.
Bristol, Michael D. "'Funeral Bak'd-Meats': Carnival and the Carnivalesque in *Hamlet.*" In *Hamlet,* ed. Wofford, 348–67.
Bryant, Hallman Bell. "Phineas's Pink Shirt in John Knowles' *A Separate Peace.*" *Notes on Contemporary Literature* 14 (1984): 5–6.

————. "A Separate Peace": The War Within. Boston: Twayne, 1990.

Butler, Judith. Bodies That Matter: On the Discursive Limits of "Sex." New York: Routledge, 1993.

————. Gender Trouble: Feminism and the Subversion of Identity. New York: Routledge, 1990.

————. "Melancholy Gender/Refused Identification." In Constructing Masculinity, ed. Berger, Wallis, and Watson, 21–36.

Devine, Joseph E. "The Truth about A Separate Peace." English Journal 58 (1969): 519–20; rpt. in Readings, ed. Karson, 122–24.

Fiedler, Leslie. "Come Back to the Raft Ag'in, Huck Honey!" In A Fiedler Reader. New York: Stein and Day, 1977. 3–12.

Fitzgerald, F. Scott. The Great Gatsby. New York: Scribner, 1925.

Foucault, Michel. The History of Sexuality; An Introduction, vol. 1. Trans. Robert Hurley. New York: Vintage, 1990.

Guy, David. Second Brother. New York: New American Library, 1985.

Karson, Jill, ed. Readings on "A Separate Peace," San Diego: Greenhaven, 1999.

Knowles, John. A Separate Peace. New York: Bantam, 1966.

McGavran, James Holt. "Wordsworth, Lost Boys, and Romantic Hom[e]ophobia." In Literature and the Child: Romantic Continuations, Postmodern Contestations, ed. James Holt McGavran. Iowa City: University of Iowa Press, 1999. 130–52.

Mengeling, Marvin E. "A Separate Peace: Meaning and Myth." English Journal 58 (1969): 1322–29.

Sarotte, Georges-Michel. Like a Brother, Like a Lover: Male Homosexuality in the American Novel and Theater from Herman Melville to James Baldwin. Garden City: Doubleday Anchor, 1978.

Sedgwick, Eve Kosofsky. Between Men: English Literature and Male Homosocial Desire. New York: Columbia University Press, 1985.

————. Epistemology of the Closet. Berkeley: University of California Press, 1990.

Slethaug, Gordon E. "The Play of the Double in A Separate Peace." Canadian Review of American Studies 15 (1984): 259–70.

Witherington, Paul. "A Separate Peace: A Study in Structural Ambiguity." English Journal 54 (1965), 795–800; rpt. in Readings, ed. Karson, 79–88.

Wofford, Susanne L., ed. Hamlet. Boston: Bedford/St. Martin's, 1994.

Refusing the Queer Potential: John Knowles's A Separate Peace

Eric L. Tribunella

John Knowles's *A Separate Peace* (1959) follows in the tradition of the school story, a genre supposedly established a century earlier by Thomas Hughes's *Tom Brown's School Days* (1857).[1] According to Beverly Lyon Clark, school stories are "so marked by gender that it becomes vital to address questions of both the instability and potency of gender in the school story" (11). Clark recognizes that while schooling, and hence stories about schooling, are implicated in various social hierarchies, they also allow "some possibility of subversion, some possibility for giving one perspective on the marginal, on class, gender, race, ethnicity, sexuality." School is, she suggests, "a site for working out contrary impulses" (8). Kathy Piehl argues for consideration of *A Separate Peace* as school story in her comparison of the novel with Hughes's own children's literature classic, and it is suggested elsewhere that one of the "ideal" types of contemporary adolescent fiction focuses on the burgeoning of one's sexuality, frequently in the school setting (Roxburgh 249). Given both the importance of gender and sexuality to the school story, a genre to which *A Separate Peace* seems clearly to belong, and the persistent use of this novel in the secondary-school classroom, an understanding of how it reinforces or potentially resists social hierarchies is crucial to deciphering its pedagogical function.

The social significance of novels taught in school is manifested by the contention that surrounds many of them.[2] *A Separate Peace* has not escaped controversy. It has been the object of attempted censorship in several cases throughout the United States brought by parents who for various reasons have found its content objectionable (see Foerstel 1994, Sova 1998). Parents, who before the late nineteenth century "were ready to accept the most ardent degree of affection between boys [in school stories] if it involved no physical expression (except a chaste deathbed kiss)," eventually came to be horrified by the mere possibility of same-sex genitality (Quigly 126). The availability of *A Separate Peace* to a queer reading was understood by the parents of

Children's Literature 30, ed. Elizabeth Lennox Keyser and Julie Pfeiffer (Yale University Press, © 2002 Hollins University).

a Vernon-Verona-Sherrill (New York) School District student who in 1980 contested the use of the novel because of its "underlying theme" of homosexuality. They claimed that the book actually encouraged homosexuality. As a result, it was removed from classroom use (Sova 213).[3]

Although educators have touted the novel as a useful tool for imparting patriotic and ethical values, teaching *A Separate Peace* involves a potentially troubling application vis-à-vis same-sex desire. To the extent that *A Separate Peace* reinforces hegemonic mechanisms of marginalization, such as homophobia and heterosexism, its usefulness for imparting "democratic ideals" cannot be understood without examining how these mechanisms and their effects in fact constitute those ideals. The book does, however, present possibilities for readings that resist such a use, as the complaint of the plaintiffs in the 1980 case attests.

In a 1983 edition of the *Connecticut English Journal* devoted to rationales for commonly challenged books used in the classroom, Diane Shugert writes that these rationales set out to explain how *A Separate Peace* "relates to the democratic ideal of the educated citizen, prepared to make her own decision" (2). Richard Hargraves, author of a course outline entitled *Values,* suggests that a system of values "should encompass recognized universal but functional ethical codes and modes which provide a basis for conduct in contemporary, American society" (4). *A Separate Peace* figures as one of the primary texts in this curriculum, which seeks to foster a personal value system including positive self-images, the ability to differentiate between tolerance and intolerance, a sense of the centrality of freedom and personal independence, and the importance of truth and reconciliation. W. Michael Reed proposes that *A Separate Peace* "offers adolescents some important perspective upon the nature of human experience" (102). In Reed's view, students should value *A Separate Peace* because of its insights concerning methods by which adolescents interact with one another. Other apologists cite the novel for its "universal" lessons about moral development and the human ideal.

I would argue, however, that the rhetoric of ethics, values, and patriotism in which rationales for this book are steeped masks its more insidious use as a tract for inscribing the "appropriate" gender and sexuality in adolescent males. These rationales, written in part as a response to attempts to censor the novel's use, represent reaffirmations of its potential to inspire normative development. Gene's "maturation" throughout the novel represents his movement away from an effete intellectualism and "adolescent" homoerotic relationship. His "moral" progression involves abandoning the queer possibility and accepting a hegemonic and necessarily heterosexual masculinity that adolescent readers of the novel are tacitly encouraged to emulate and valorize. The novel has been recruited as representative of universal adolescence in part because of its heterosexist developmental narrative, which does not simply reflect adolescent experience but contributes to the discourse compelling that experience. The themes of *A Separate Peace* do indeed represent American cultural values, including, quite significantly, heterosexuality and masculinity in men.

The novel is framed by the narration of Gene, who returns to Devon School fifteen years later to reminisce about his coming of age. By beginning and concluding the novel with the insights of an adult Gene, Knowles preestablishes the inevitable culmination of the story's movement—Gene as a man. The reader is allowed to glimpse who Gene will become, and the story told as a flashback provides the map of the course Gene follows. Hence, the process of gendering the boy to "be a man" lies at the heart of *A Separate Peace,* and the conflicts and actions it details serve to further this process as its central project.

Finny's and Gene's relationship is characterized by a subtle homoeroticism in which Gene eroticizes Finny's innocence, purity, and skill, and Finny eroticizes the companionship provided by Gene. With World War II serving throughout the novel as the backdrop against which the "peace" of Devon is contrasted, the boys initially engage in the ritual of taking off their clothes and jumping from a tall tree into the river below as practice for the possibility of having to jump from a sinking ship in battle. Jumping from the tree acquires special significance for Finny and Gene; it serves as a sign of loyalty and as an act that cements their bond and stands in for sexual play.

To describe their relationship this way is not to cite a germinal or inchoate homosexuality or to suggest that either Finny or Gene has simply failed consciously to admit an essential homosexual status. It is, however, to note, as Eve Sedgwick does, "that what goes on at football games, in fraternities, at the Bohemian Grove, and at climactic moments in war novels can look, with only a slight shift of optic, quite startlingly 'homosexual.'" It is not, she continues, "most importantly an expression of the psychic origin of these institutions in a repressed or sublimated homosexual genitality. Instead, it is the coming into visibility of the normally implicit coercive double bind" (*Between Men* 89). The "coercive double bind" of which Sedgwick writes is the simultaneous *prescription* of intimate male homosocial bonds and *proscription* of homosexuality (see *Between Men* 88–89 and *Epistemology* 185–86): "Because the paths of male entitlement, especially in the nineteenth century, required certain intense male bonds that were not readily distinguishable from the most reprobated bonds, an endemic and ineradicable state of what I am calling male homosexual panic became the normal condition of male heterosexual entitlement" (*Epistemology* 185). The boys' very presence at a school like Devon not only underscores their access to a specifically classed and gendered entitlement, but the school itself also serves as a space in which to prepare them for claiming that entitlement. It is a space in which this double bind is particularly highlighted since boys will make their earliest connections to other boys here, as well as perhaps their first sexual explorations. In order to make visible fully this double bind, it is necessary to shift the optic whereby the homoeroticism of the boys' relationship comes into view: "For a man to be a man's man is separated only by an invisible, carefully blurred, always-already-crossed line from being 'interested in men'" (*Between Men* 89).[4]

Finny demonstrates his interest in sharing intimate moments with Gene when he encourages him to skip class and spend a day at the beach. Finny reveals in his characteristically honest way that Gene is the "proper" person with whom to share such moments as they settle down to sleep on the sand. Gene considers such a naked emotional expression to be next to suicide at Devon, and he remains unable to reciprocate Finny's admission. Gene does, however, notice Finny's physical attractiveness even if he must project this sentiment onto the anonymous passersby: "I noticed that people were looking fixedly at him, so I took a look myself to see why. His skin radiated a reddish copper glow of tan, his brown hair had been a little bleached by the sun, and I noticed that the tan made his eyes shine with a cool blue-green fire" (39). Gene notices Finny's appearance, though Finny is the first to say about Gene, "Everybody's staring at you. It's because of that movie star tan you picked up this afternoon . . . showing off again" (39). While Gene reciprocates Finny's feelings, he cannot bring himself to admit them as Finny does. Gene's self-preserving silence allows him to resist both the possibility and the threat of consummating his platonic friendship with Finny, whereas Finny's willingness to expose his emotional vulnerabilities predicts his eventual expulsion from a context that forbids such expressions.

Gene allays the confusions that result from his affection for Finny and the tumult of emotions such forbidden feelings arouse in him by first causing the accident that forces Finny's disappearance from Devon and then incorporating Finny into himself. Following their trip to the beach, the night they spend alone there, and Finny's intimate expression of his fondness for Gene, Gene finds himself growing increasingly suspicious of Finny and attributes this reaction to the possibility that Finny plans to sabotage his grades. Finny and Gene later return to the tree where, after undressing, Finny suggests that they jump together hand-in-hand (163), an act that could substitute for a strictly forbidden sexual act between the boys. They climb the tree and prepare to jump, but in a moment of panic, Gene jounces the limb and sends Finny crashing to the ground, thereby setting a series of events in motion that culminates in Finny's death. His realization that Finny's intentions are not dishonest after all, coupled with Finny's suggestion that they take the jump together, ignites the moment of homosexual panic. Gene responds to Finny's advances with an act of violent separation. Finny's attempt to take Gene's hand triggers the need in Gene to conform to the heterosexual imperative that forecloses the possibility of same-sex desire by forcibly detaching himself from Finny.

Judith Butler suggests considering gender as a kind of melancholy, the unfinished process of grieving a loss that cannot be acknowledged. The lost object is incorporated and preserved in the ego as a constitutive identification in order to defer suffering the loss. She proposes that this melancholic identification is central to the process by which a subject's gender is constructed. She quotes from Freud's *The Ego and the Id:* "an object which was lost has been set up again inside the ego — that is, that an object-cathexis has been replaced by an identification . . . when it happens that a person has given up a sexual object, there quite often ensues an alteration of his ego which can only be described as setting up of the object inside the ego" ("Gender" 22). The internalization of the object offers an alternative means of possessing the object without violating the codes that prohibit and prevent its external possession. The act of jouncing the limb, which causes Finny to fall, represents a literal acting out of Gene's rejection of Finny as an object of desire. The injuries Finny incurs ensure his separation from Gene and the loss of the prohibited homosexual attachment. Gene's refusal, however, to acknowledge the loss translates into the installation of Finny, the barred object of desire, as part of Gene's ego. The loss is refused and Finny is preserved by this process of internalization, which involves Gene's accessibility to penetration by Finny in such a way that avoids the repercussions of a genital contact: "I decided to put on his clothes. . . . When I looked in the mirror it was not a remote aristocrat I had become, no character out of daydreams. I was Phineas, Phineas to the life. I even had his humorous expression on my face, his sharp, optimistic awareness. I had no idea why this gave me such intense relief, but it seemed, standing there in Finny's triumphant shirt, that I would never stumble through the confusion of my own character again" (54). When Finny does return temporarily to Devon, he attempts to aid Gene in completing the transformation. Since Finny had been a star athlete prior to the fall, he sets about attempting to train Gene to take his place and actualize the element of himself that Gene internalizes. Gene initiates the process whereby he establishes the idea of Finny at the core of a reconstituted self and, in this instance of initiative, already demonstrates a quality originally belonging only to Finny. As Gene approaches his goal, Finny gradually fades until his death coincides with Gene's ultimate success.

In Butler's view, masculinity and femininity are accomplishments that emerge in tandem with the achievement of heterosexuality ("Gender" 24). Gene's homosexual panic might then be ascribed not only to the prohibition of homo-desire but also to the related fear of being feminine or feminized. His rejection of the external possession of Finny represents not only a rejection of the homosexual attachment but also his desire to achieve a heterosexually defined masculinity by which he can bring himself into accordance with the ideal of the proper man. The "I never loved him, I never lost him" uttered by a man forms the core of his tenuous heterosexuality and hence his masculinity ("Gender" 27). Moreover, renunciation does not abolish the desire but establishes the desire as the fuel for its perpetual renunciation. If masculinity is achieved through a heterosexuality predicated on the renunciation of the homosexual attachment, then homo-desire serves as the necessary possibility that allows for its renunciation: "The act of renouncing homosexuality thus paradoxically strengthens homosexuality, but it strengthens homosexuality precisely *as* the power of renunciation. Renunciation becomes the aim and vehicle of satisfaction. And it is, we might conjecture, precisely the fear of setting loose homosexuality from this circuit of renunciation that so terrifies the guardians of masculinity in the U.S. military. For what would masculinity 'be' were it not for this aggressive circuit of renunciation from which it is wrought?" ("Gender" 31). A heterosexual man thus becomes the man he "never" loved and "never" grieved, and his masculinity is

founded upon the refusal to acknowledge this love and its incorporation as an identification within his ego ("Gender" 34). Gene becomes a
man through his repudiation of the consummation of his relationship
with Finny—"holding hands in a jump."

By killing Finny, Gene assumes his own place in this "aggressive circuit of renunciation." Following Finny's first departure from Devon
School and Gene's incorporation of the loss as an identification within
his own ego, Gene determines along with Brinker to enlist in the war
effort and, in doing so, the masculine environs of the military and
battlefield. The war propels the boys forward, away from their adolescent shelter and toward the final phase of their initiation into manhood. The return of Finny forestalls Gene's entrance into the war, and
the reemergence of the queer possibility effectively suspends Gene's
enlistment and the verification of his masculinity. The threat posed
by Finny becomes evident. His presence, in fact, his continued existence, defers indefinitely Gene's "ascension" to a proper manhood.
Finny must therefore die to prevent any further return and to allow
Gene to claim finally his masculinity and complete the gendering process that is ongoing throughout *A Separate Peace.*

Mark Simpson has described the buddy war film as a compilation
of lessons about masculinity and how to take one's place in patriarchy (214). Simpson's analysis of such films can be used to examine Knowles's novel, since the lingering war provides the context for
Finny's and Gene's homoerotic friendship. Simpson describes the intimate relationship between same-sex desire and death established in
the war film as the necessary condition for any expression of homo-
desire:

> In war films of the buddy type the deadliness of war is not glossed
> over. But it is portrayed not in the death of the enemy, who are
> often faceless or even unseen, but in the death of the comrades
> and buddies. Classically, the moment when the buddy lies dead or
> dying is the moment when the full force of the love the boys/men
> feel for one another can be shown. And, for all the efforts of the
> conscientious film maker, the deadliness is thus attached not as
> much to war as to the queer romance of it all. (214)

Paul Fussell similarly suggests that the connection between war and
love assumes a distinctly homoerotic form on the battlefield: "Given
this association between war and sex, and given the deprivation and
loneliness and alienation characteristic of the soldier's experience—

given, that is, his need for affection in a largely womanless world—
we will not be surprised to find both the actuality and the recall of
front-line experience replete with what we can call the homoerotic"
(272). Fussell even makes the direct connection between the homoerotic desires of English officers during the Great War and their experiences at English public schools: "It was largely members of the
upper and upper-middle classes who were prepared by public-school
training to experience such crushes, who 'hailed with relief,' as J. B.
Priestley remembers, 'a wholly masculine way of life uncomplicated
by Woman'" (273). Fussell reports finding in soldiers' recollections of
frontline experiences "especially in the attitude of young officers to
their men . . . something more like the 'idealistic,' passionate but non-
physical 'crushes' which most of the officers had experienced at public
school" (272).

According to Simpson and Fussell, the battlefield is a place in which
queer love can be expressed, albeit in a sublimated form, because it
occurs alongside and in the context of death. Gene allows himself to
admit his tender feelings for Finny only as Finny lies broken on the
marble steps following Gene's trial. Seeing another student wrap a
blanket around Finny, Gene recalls, "I would have liked very much to
have done that myself; it would have meant a lot to me" (170). That
Gene's expression of tenderness fails to find a more explicit articula-
tion attests to that very impossibility. Simpson writes, "But pain and
death are not just a price that has to be paid—it is as if the caress, the
kiss, the embrace *were the fatal blow* itself" (214). If the jounced tree
limb is read as the act that ultimately kills Finny, then it is Finny's attempt to grab Gene's hand and to jump with him—this symbolic moment of touch—that incites the homosexual panic in Gene. According to Simpson, the cathartic deadly climax satisfies the audience and
allows for the homoerotic impulse of the characters while reinscrib-
ing a heterosexual economy that calls for the unattainability of the
queer attachment. The desire is expressed for only an instant, and even
then it is a love that is never truly acknowledged. Its full actualization
is staved off by death. In *A Separate Peace,* the possibility of consummation is canceled by Finny's death, ensuring that their "boyish love"
remains eternal and unsullied by the transgression of a compulsory
heterosexuality. Simpson writes: "They live by love, but one of them,
the most 'sensitive' and the 'queerest', must die to save the others and
the world from the practice of it, also to demonstrate the 'proper' way
it should be sublimated: 'Greater love hath no man than this, that a

man lay down his life for his friends'" (227). Finny is, surely, the queerest of the Devon boys.

Gene's participation in the war effort is fueled by this disavowed loss of the homosexual attachment, and if Gene's development is taken to represent a collectively experienced process by which boys are made men, then it might be said that the war itself is predicated on the ungrieved loss of homosexual attachment. On the battlefield, men can place themselves in positions to be killed by the enemy such that death comes from without, and mourning one's comrades in war can stand in for mourning the homosexual attachment that was lost. The trauma of war as a purely masculine pursuit serves as a pretext for the grief that cannot be experienced at home during peacetime. One can love one's comrades and grieve their loss with the displaced love and loss "never" felt for the original same-sex object. Any resistance to the imperative that demands such an oppressive masculinity formed on the disavowal of homo-desire can be directed towards the enemy, and any guilt suffered over one's own compliance can be transformed into a hatred of this enemy. War might be described as the only appropriate place for experiencing this grief, and the possibility of eliminating *this* motivation for war (as it certainly is not the only motivation) presents a useful rationale for refusing the loss of homosexual attachment and for changing the conditions that initially demand its loss.

The context of Devon School during wartime conflates the school and the battlefield. Seeking to act out the war, Finny invents the game of Blitzball in which the boy with the ball must run from one side of the field to the other without being tackled. At any point in the game, the player holding the ball could pass it on to another player who would then become the object of attack for the other boys. One *must* pass the ball according to Finny, who invents a game with no teams. Each player is simultaneously an adversary and an ally, so these terms effectively have no meaning in the context of Blitzball in which players fluidly shift between roles never fixed in relation to other players. One can never identify allies or enemies in Blitzball, making it a queer game resisting the fixity of identities.[5] Rather than enforcing the strict dichotomization of sides, Finny rejects this fundamental attribute of competition, thereby creating a space from which to expose it as not inevitable. Finny also adopts this resistant tactic during a snowball fight when he again begins switching sides so that "loyalties became hopelessly entangled" (146). A classmate follows suit, leading Gene to describe him as a eunuch (146).

Finny repeatedly produces the central symbols of the novel. He initiates the practice of jumping from the tree, a practice that acquires
significance as a site for both the sealing of Finny's friendship with
Gene and their separation. During Finny's temporary return to Devon following his injury he begins training Gene for the Olympics in
which he himself had wished to participate. Despite the impossibility
of such a goal, Finny's encouragement persists in maintaining it as a
realistic possibility in their minds, again demonstrating his authority
over the boys' fantasies. Finny also determines the symbolic value of
the pink shirt, which he dons as an emblem ostensibly to demonstrate
his pride in the Allied victories over Central Europe. Gene expresses
concern that Finny's pink shirt might cause others to "mistake" him
for a "fairy," a concern to which Finny responds "mildly, . . . I wonder
what would happen if I looked like a fairy to everyone" (17). Finny's
lack of concern is itself queer in the homosocial context of a boys'
school where, by the 1940s, such a label might incur a significant cost
to one's social status, if not physical safety. The pink shirt, moreover,
proves central to Gene's attempt to become Finny. Wearing the shirt
completes Gene's incorporation of Finny into his own self following
Finny's first absence from Devon. That Finny originates each of these
symbols signifies a phallic authority ultimately claimed by Gene as the
story's narrator.

    In contrast to Gene, his schoolmate Leper fails to undergo the same
process by which Gene achieves manhood. Leper is—as one might
predict from his name—an outsider, never fully participating in the
boys' society, never playing their games, preferring instead to wan-
der alone in the woods. He finally leaves Devon to enlist, "escapes"
from the army, and returns to school to testify in Gene's mock trial.
In this allegory of gender construction, Leper represents the boy who
neither refuses the loss of homosexual attachment nor consummates
a potential union. He therefore never incorporates the possible object of desire within his ego, thereby proving malformed and dysfunc-
tional as a result of his failure to adhere to the normative developmental trajectory followed by Gene. When Finny first jumps from the tree
Leper refuses to join in the ritual with the other boys. In response to
Finny's insistence on Leper's participation, Gene recalls that "Leper
closed his mouth as though forever. He didn't argue or refuse. He
didn't back away. He became inanimate" (9). Leper simply watches
and so bears witness to the symbolic attachment created as an unreal-
ized possibility between Finny and Gene. At the crucial moment when

Gene jounces the limb and sends Finny crashing to the ground in a violent moment of homosexual panic—the refusal of the queer possibility—Leper stands by as the only witness to the event, silently observing the mechanisms by which Gene undertakes to assume his masculinity and authorized position in patriarchy. Although the other boys work clearing snow from the railroad yard to permit trains carrying new military recruits to pass, Leper abstains from this contribution to the war effort, choosing instead to keep his distance and explore the forest trails. Ultimately Leper enlists in the army only to suffer a mental breakdown and go "psycho."

At the climax of the novel when the boys try Gene for maiming Finny, Leper arrives to present the damning evidence, his testimony that Gene deliberately caused Finny's accident. Faced with this evidence, Finny flees from the truth and finally dies at the end of the sequence of events put in motion by Gene. In the context of the trial, Leper occupies the place of the critic, the one who reads through the allegory and exposes the underlying mechanisms motivating Gene's violent act. Leper stands as a figure that warns the reader to avoid reading too closely or looking too intently to uncover the reason for Gene's violence. The processes of achieving heterosexuality and masculinity cannot be completed properly in the witness if he becomes too aware of their workings. The figure of Leper functions in the story to present the potential risk of insanity to the student who might be drawn to the position of the critic. The student should not be a witness who observes directly these mechanisms of gender construction since insanity looms as a possible punishment.[6]

In his report of a panel discussion held to discuss literary criticism and the teaching of *A Separate Peace,* Jack Lundy quotes panelist Betty Nelick as saying that the novel is concerned with "Gene's slow and painful dying to the world of adolescence into the world of manhood, through the outward pressures of a world at war and the inward pressure of the realization of fear and evil within himself" (114). Diane Shugert claims that books like *A Separate Peace* are taught because "the book's point of view bears upon democratic and American values," which *A Separate Peace* quite clearly accomplishes through its valorization of Gene's coming-of-age, his rejection of a possible homosexual attachment, and his ascension to proper manhood at the cost of the death of his all-too-queer best friend (4). The failure of many of these critics to acknowledge explicitly the sexual politics of the novel represents the success of Leper's warning against precisely this attention. *A*

Separate Peace thus serves the education of the American ideal well—a heterosexual and "properly" gendered ideal.

The popular characterization of same-sex desire as a confusing adolescent experience at a stage that must be successfully negotiated in order to achieve a more "adult" heterosexuality lends descriptive validity to Butler's formulation in which the homosexual attachment is lost and incorporated. But this psychosocial process by which heterosexuality is achieved need not be understood as either inevitable or innate, but rather it may be understood as produced. The widespread belief that youth might experience same-sex desire during an early developmental stage that they are expected to outgrow functions as a self-fulfilling prophecy at the cultural level. Adolescents learn that they must restrict their potential object-choices by learning to understand other-sex desire as appropriate and expected, while learning to interpret any indications of same-sex desire as the product of rampant hormones, inexperience, or confusion. *A Separate Peace* encourages the understanding of this lesson. The process of gender construction allegorized in *A Separate Peace* does not fully precede the use of such texts as propagandistic media. Rather such texts might be said to collectively contribute to the discourse that materializes the phenomena they describe. When teachers take texts to be "realistic" and present them as such, they unwittingly popularize this discourse, a discourse that is generative rather than simply representational. Such texts are thought to document a psychosocial process; however, the process might instead be understood as the collective effect of those texts, an effect ensured through the perpetual repetition of their use and the insistence on their realism. The contribution of *A Separate Peace* to the procedure by which same-sex desire is constructed as adolescent positions the book at a crucial site of cultural production, that of the "adult" heterosexual and the "ideal" democratic citizen.

The lingering question still posed by students, however, is "Why must Finny die?" (Wacht 7). If the question is motivated by a desire to see Finny live, then it marks a potential impetus for the student to produce a resistant reading of the text. The question, "Why does Finny have to die?" could represent the student's desire to see the homosexual attachment completed, or at least not entirely foreclosed before the possibility of consummation is realized. Finny must die precisely because he refuses to reject the possibility of loving Gene. Even when Gene attempts to confess his guilt, Finny struggles to deny Gene's need to push him away: "it was like I had all the time in world. I thought

I could reach out and get hold of you." But Gene responds by flinch-
ing violently away from him: "To drag me down too!" (57). Even here
when Finny speaks of his previous desire to grab hold of Gene, Gene
can only recall such a wish as the desire to drag him down and prevent
him from attaining a heterosexually defined manhood. Finny must die
so that Gene can become a proper man, yet as Butler writes, "There is
no necessary reason for identification to oppose desire, or for desire
to be fueled by repudiation" ("Gender" 35).

Knowles's text, if exposed as a coercive tract for propagating normative constructions of gender, might be employed to interact with adolescents' impulse for transgression. The excessive warning away from
an overly perceptive reading symbolized by a psychotic Leper might
serve to provoke a desire to reveal what one is warned against revealing. The very prohibition used to enforce Gene's conformity might be
eroticized in such a way that its very transgression becomes desirable.
In this sense, the warning away might potentiate the desirability of the
forbidden object and serve the function of drawing one closer to it.
The inverted prohibition, one that attracts the subject to the prohibited object, could function to destabilize the force of the prohibition
so that it ultimately loses its effect to either warn away or entice. Finny
would not have to die if Gene rejected a "proper" and fixed identification. Had he refused the need to bring about and disavow this loss,
Gene might have avoided foreclosing the queer potential.

Notes

I would like to thank Kenneth Kidd and Maya Dodd for their careful readings and
thoughtful comments.

1. In *Regendering the School Story* Beverly Lyon Clark seeks to debunk the notion that
Tom Brown was the first school story, while still crediting it as having influenced hundreds
of subsequent school stories, popular culture, and mainstream literature for adults (11).

2. The uncertain status of John Knowles's *A Separate Peace* as children's, or adolescent, literature reflects the instability of these terms. First published in 1959, *A Separate
Peace* predates S. E. Hinton's *The Outsiders*, which many cite as initiating the genre. Initial
reviews in the *New Yorker, New Statesman, Saturday Review,* and *Time* made no reference to
the book as being specifically for young adults, and its review in the *Horn Book Magazine,*
a publication concerned with literature for children and young people, appeared in a
section intended to highlight current adult books of interest to high school students.
A Separate Peace has, however, arguably entered the popular imagination as particularly well suited for young adults. In a 1992 article that considers adolescent novels written before 1967, *A Separate Peace* is favorably noted as one read and enjoyed by adolescents and teachers of adolescents ("Still Good Reading" 87). The frequent use of *A
Separate Peace* in high school English classrooms might contribute to the perception that
it belongs in the young adult category. As it continues to be taught, more adults will recall their first experience with the novel as having taken place in school. The fact that

its protagonists are themselves adolescents certainly compounds the perception that it is *for* adolescent readers.

3. The novel has also been challenged for containing "unsuitable language" and "negative attitudes" and for encouraging undesirable behavior, such as skipping class, breaking school rules, and trespassing (Foerstel 181, Sova 214). In spite of this occasional opposition, *A Separate Peace* has been regularly taught in high school English classrooms since the early sixties. An early apology for its use applauded it as recommending itself immediately to high school instruction (Crabbe 111). Its popular use has been accompanied by a series of rationales that attempt to justify this use specifically in the wake of such cases as the one in New York.

4. The school story as same-sex love story is a possibility explored by Isabel Quigly. The readiness with which these stories lend themselves to such readings supports Sedgwick's contention and represents a tradition that provides the context for such an approach to *A Separate Peace*. In two of the three school stories Quigly describes as typical of the school love story, one of the boys dies. In all three, one of the boys is enormously handsome and athletic while the other is rather plain, slightly too scholastic, and perhaps a bit too nervous as well. *A Separate Peace* is thus easily placed in this tradition.

While working on this essay I came across a free New York City gay magazine, *HX*, in which a dance club advertisement depicted a number of sexual situations involving cartoon men in a library. Several books, having been pulled from the shelves, lie strewn on the floor. The texts are ones commonly known to be available to "homoerotic" readings: *Leaves of Grass, Moby Dick, Billy Budd, Lord of the Flies,* and *A Separate Peace*. What this ad demonstrates is the widespread recognition that *A Separate Peace* is in fact available for such a reading. A popular gay audience, at least, does not need such a reading to be pointed out to it. It is not my aim to say merely that the possibility of reading the text this way exists. Rather, given this possibility, I am interested in how teachers have written about the text's use, in the processes that seem to underlie this homoeroticism, and in what else the text might be saying about these things.

5. The term "queer" of course cannot—and should not—be reduced to some simplistic notion of fluidity. A number of scholars have taken up the possible implications of the term—not so much its "meaning," which must remain contingent if it is to be put to use in contesting normative regimes. See, e,g., Butler's "Critically Queer" in *Bodies That Matter;* Doty's *Making Things Perfectly Queer: Interpreting Mass Culture,* xv; Sedgwick's "Queer Performativity" in *GLQ;* Michael Warner's introduction to *Fear of a Queer Planet;* de Lauretis's "Queer Theory: Lesbian and Gay Studies: An Introduction" in *differences.*

6. It is also the case that Finny might not have fled had Leper not arrived to present his testimony. Perhaps this could be read as a warning that the critic's own words might be used to further the process being critiqued, for Leper's testimony was appropriated and used by Brinker, a student political leader representing conservative thought at the school.

Works Cited

Balliett, Whitney. "Review of *A Separate Peace.*" *New Yorker* 36.159 (April 2, 1960): 340.

Butler, Judith. *Bodies That Matter: On the Discursive Limits of Sex.* New York: Routledge, 1993.

———. "Gender Melancholy/Refused Identification." In *Constructing Masculinity.* Ed. Maurice Berger, Brian Wallis, and Simon Watson. New York: Routledge, 1995.

Clark, Beverly Lyon. *Regendering the School Story: Sassy Sissies and Tattling Tomboys.* New York: Garland Publishing, 1996.

Crabbe, John K. "On the Playing Fields of Devon." *English Journal* 52 (1963): 109–11.

de Lauretis, Teresa. "Queer Theory: Lesbian and Gay Studies: An Introduction." *differences* 3 (summer 1991): iii–xviii.

Doty, Alexander. *Making Things Perfectly Queer: Interpreting Mass Culture.* Minneapolis: University of Minnesota Press, 1993.

Foerstel, Herbert N. *Banned in the U.S.A.: A Reference Guide to Book Censorship in Schools and Public Libraries.* Westport, Conn.: Greenwood Press, 1994.

Fussell, Paul. *The Great War and Modern Memory.* New York: Oxford University Press, 1975.

Hargraves, Richard. B. *Values: Language Arts.* Miami, Fl.: Dade County Public Schools, 1971.

Hicks, Granville. "Review of *A Separate Peace.*" *Saturday Review* 43.14 (March 5, 1960): 800.

Knowles, John. *A Separate Peace.* New York: Bantam, 1959.

Lundy, Jack T. "Literary Criticism and the Teaching of the Novel." *University of Kansas Bulletin of Education* 21.3 (1967): 112–15.

Piehl, Kathy. "Gene Forrester and Tom Brown: *A Separate Peace* as School Story." *Children's Literature in Education* 14.2 (summer 1983): 67–74.

Quigly, Isabel. *The Heirs of Tom Brown: The English School Story.* Oxford: Oxford University Press, 1984.

Reed, W. Michael. "*A Separate Peace:* A Novel Worth Teaching." *Virginia English Bulletin* 36.2 (1986): 95–105.

"Review of *A Separate Peace.*" *Time* 75.96 (April 4, 1960): 550.

Richardson, Maurice. "Review of *A Separate Peace.*" *New Statesman* 57.618 (May 2, 1959): 210.

Roxburgh, Steve. "The Novel of Crisis: Contemporary Adolescent Fiction." *Children's Literature* 7 (1978): 248–54.

Sarotte, Georges-Michel. *Like a Brother, Like a Lover: Male Homosexuality in the American Novel and Theater from Herman Melville to James Baldwin.* Trans. Richard Miller. Garden City: Anchor Press/Doubleday, 1978.

Scoggin, M. C. "Review of *A Separate Peace.*" *Horn Book Magazine* 36.421 (October 1960): 200.

Sedgwick, Eve Kosofsky. *Between Men: English Literature and Male Homosocial Desire.* New York: Columbia University Press, 1985.

———. *Epistemology of the Closet.* Berkeley: University of California Press, 1990.

———. "Queer Performativity: Henry James's The Art of the Novel." *GLQ: A Journal of Lesbian and Gay Studies* 1.1 (spring 1993): 1–16.

Shugert, Diane P. "About Rationales." *Connecticut English Journal* 15.1 (1983): 1–4.

Simpson, Mark. "Don't Die on Me, Buddy: Homoeroticism and Masochism in War Movies." In *Male Impersonators: Men Performing Masculinity.* Ed. Mark Simpson. New York: Routledge, 1994. 212–28.

"Still Good Reading: Adolescent Novels Written before 1967." *English Journal* 81.4 (April 1992): 87–90.

Sova, Dawn B. *Banned Books: Literature Suppressed on Social Grounds.* New York: Facts on File, 1998.

Wacht, Francine G. "The Adolescent in Literature." Paper presented at the annual meeting of the Teachers of English, San Diego. November 1975.

Warner, Michael. Introduction. In *Fear of a Queer Planet: Queer Politics and Social Theory.* Ed. Michael Warner. Minneapolis: University of Minnesota Press, 1993.

The Absence of Moral Agency in Robert Cormier's
The Chocolate War

C. Anita Tarr

Since the publication of *The Chocolate War* (1974), Robert Cormier has earned praise for breaking taboos and for introducing tragedy to young adult literature.[1] On the basis of *I Am the Cheese* (1977) and *Fade* (1988), he has also positioned himself as a postmodern novelist. Patricia Head claims that Cormier's *Fade* "educates his readers, not by presenting a schematic view of their world, but by revealing its constructed nature." Furthermore, "the liberating qualities of Cormier's narrative forms . . . apply in one way or another to most of Cormier's novels" (32). Frank Myszor adds that Cormier "foster[s] the autonomy of his readers. He achieves this moral goal by structuring the novel so as to require an 'interrogative' style of reading" (88). Assuredly, the postmodern elements in *Fade* are also present as early as *The Chocolate War*.[2] *The Chocolate War* is a complex novel, obviously rich for academic perusal, as testified by the numerous papers devoted to it. The depressing story and unusual narrative structure work together to create a fictional universe that is already disturbed, and disturbing.

The common reading of *The Chocolate War* is that because Jerry refuses to sell the chocolates, even after his Vigils assignment is over, he is a hero, a rebel against the corrupt world of Trinity—that is, Brother Leon, Archie, and Emile. This is the way that many of us would *like* Jerry to be, a Braveheart screaming "freedom" even as he is tortured, the individual fighting against the system. A close reading of the novel, however, shows us that there are simply not enough narrative cues to support this. In fact, I offer an opposite interpretation: Cormier presents only the *illusion* of moral decision making and the *illusion* of a rebel hero. Jerry is no moral agent and his refusal to sell chocolates is *not* the result of a moral dilemma.

Specifically, there are two problems with the interpretation of Jerry as rebel hero fighting against a corrupt system: (1) even if Jerry is a rebel, he is only one of many rebels at Trinity, for rebellion itself is status quo; and, besides, Jerry actually has no idea whom he is fight-

Children's Literature 30, ed. Elizabeth Lennox Keyser and Julie Pfeiffer (Yale University Press, © 2002 Hollins University).

ing or what he is fighting for; and (2) the basic "system" at Trinity is not just terrorizing to Jerry but is totally antifemale, and absolutely no one challenges it, not even Jerry. Thus, rather than giving autonomy to readers, as Myszor suggests, Cormier forces on them basically one view, one that disallows any counterview to the moral vacuousness of the characters and their misogyny.

A "moral agent" is defined by James Rachels in his *The Elements of Moral Philosophy* as "someone who is concerned impartially with the interests of everyone affected by what he or she does; who carefully sifts facts and examines their implications; who accepts principles of conduct only after scrutinizing them to make sure they are sound; who is willing to 'listen to reason' even when it means that his or her earlier convictions may have to be revised; and who, finally is willing to act on the results of this deliberation" (13–14). Jerry, in contrast, is clueless as to how his actions will affect others; he does not seem to deliberate on his actions; he does not listen to others' warnings; and, finally, as Perry Nodelman speculates, "Jerry's heroic action, his way of disturbing the universe, is a negative decision not to act, rather than a positive decision to do something" ("Paranoia" 30).

The strained efforts by critics to posit *The Chocolate War* as a groundbreaking young adult novel for not glossing over the hostile realities of life, and by teachers to cast Jerry as a rebel hero, result in a tunnel vision that refuses to see the novel's misogyny. The characters' insistence on treating females as sexual objects, and on fearing and despising women, is a correlative issue to Jerry's refusal to sell the chocolate, but it *should* be of primary concern to all of us. One could argue, in fact, that the misogyny is the most important ethical issue of the entire novel.[3] In *The Chocolate War*, there is no rebel hero, no moral decision making, and no resistance to antifemale rhetoric.

Lack of Moral Agency: Narrative Structure

The narrative structure of *The Chocolate War* is intimately connected with the lack of moral agency. This lack can be demonstrated by examining the operative word for *The Chocolate War*, "screw," which functions as more than a euphemism for "fuck" and is uttered frequently by the narrator and characters. The entire novel hinges on the dialogue between loose and tight, unscrewed and screwed, illusion and reality, anarchy and despotism, chaos and order. Myszor has written that Cormier's *After the First Death* is "a series of binary oppositions," with Cormier stressing "the ambiguity of these oppositions" (77–78). Similarly, in *The Chocolate War* Cormier employs binary opposites as a structural motif; however, it is Cormier's *failure* to create tension between these binaries—not moral dilemmas, but the *lack* of them—that causes problems in reading the book. At different times in the novel, being unscrewed is as bad or as good as being screwed tight. There is no ambivalence as to which is better—it doesn't matter, for both conditions are equally miserable. It's not that Cormier refuses to privilege one over the other, but that he offers no balance between them or negotiation. He commits himself to neither, and to nothing in between. There is simply no available option, no possible choice for his characters (or for readers) to make. Resistance to binary opposites is a hallmark of postmodernism, to be sure, but making them interchangeable is erroneous and denies readers any chance of making a judgment vicariously, and thus any chance of realizing any moral agency. There is only paralysis.

The binaries of "screwed" and "unscrewed" are best displayed in what I consider the emblematic chapter of *The Chocolate War*, chapter 11, after Goober has been intimidated into the Vigils' assignment of unscrewing all the desks and chairs in Brother Eugene's classroom. The result of Goober's work, which is aided by Obie and other Vigils (the result of cooperation), gets to the crux of Cormier's desperate paranoia.[4] The chairs in Brother Eugene's room serve as a representation of each person's fragile constructed reality: the chairs teeter, threatening to crash at the slightest touch. They look like chairs but are not really, because no one can sit in them. The chairs are simply constructed by our minds and waver on the edge of nonreality. Similarly, Brother Eugene comes unglued, unscrewed, when he sees his world destroyed before his eyes; his screwed-together world is now screwed-up. He is weak, having placed his faith in what he could see, and is destroyed along with his world. Cormier is suggesting that each of us constructs our own reality, which can fall apart at any time. The real world is chaotic; the order we impose upon it is an illusion. The real world consists of a fight to determine whose reality will be shared by the most people, but Cormier never implies that one reality is better than another. In other words, good = evil, screwed = unscrewed.

Just as the Vigils play a cruel trick on the vulnerable Brother Eugene, Cormier plays a trick on readers, one he sets up in the first chapter. When Jerry is trying out for the position of quarterback, he is pummeled by the other football players, but he always gets back up.

He is tough (and because he is tough Archie singles him out for an assignment). No matter how many times he is beaten, Jerry gets back up. At the end of the tryout, the coach says, "You'd make a better end" (9). Jerry interprets this remark to mean that he has failed at making quarterback, but the coach will try him in a new position, as a tight "end." This is Cormier's joke: the first chapter shows Jerry being beaten but always getting back up, hopeful. This is the proper "end" for the novel. The actual end of the novel shows Jerry being beaten but not getting back up. He stays down, defeated. Cormier unscrews conventional narrative structure; he creates and then deflates the expectation that Jerry will rise one last time in his lonely defiance. Jerry is not victorious. Only Cormier is. In *The Chocolate War,* Cormier collapses conventional narrative structure to make readers see it is a fragile construction that was held together by our minds.

Lack of Moral Agency: The Illusion of Rebellion

It is just an illusion created by Cormier that Jerry is a rebel against an unjust system. Admittedly, Cormier invites this reading of Jerry as rebel hero and, in an interview given long after the publication of the novel, has even shaken his finger at readers to warn them that the only way to defeat evil is through cooperation (DeLuca and Natov 116–20). Critics have often repeated this statement as the obvious theme of the novel. But I believe Cormier's statement is disingenuous. If the novel truly exemplifies the idea that cooperation is necessary to fight evil, then why does he have the hippies congregate outside the school, to no purpose? And why do the football players all gang up against Jerry so that he will fail as quarterback? And why does the whole school, including Jerry but minus Goober, cooperate to present the disastrous boxing match between Jerry and Emile, when Jerry is finally defeated? The only hint that Cormier allows that he is reaching for cooperation as a solution occurs when Brother Leon condemns the whole class for his intimidation of Bailey. He condemns the students for allowing it to happen. We should note, however, that it takes only one boy, anonymous at that, who says, "Aw, let the kid alone" (38), to make Leon stop. It doesn't require that the whole class resist Leon, just one boy. This scene, while helping Leon to transfer the blame to the whole class, foreshadows Jerry's lone voice refusing to sell the chocolates, and also foreshadows the likelihood that Jerry's refusal to sell the chocolates will result in a victory for him—an expectation that Cormier ultimately destroys. Rather than cooperation being touted as the way to resist evil, it's more accurate to say that, in *The Chocolate War,* cooperation among a group—attained by whatever means—is effective only in *spreading* corruption. There's not a single example in the book that illustrates how cooperation is effective in fighting it.

Even if we label Jerry a rebel for his refusal to sell chocolates, his is not the only rebellion, but just one of many. In fact, the Vigils themselves operate as symbols of rebellion against the school's administration. The Vigils appear to be termites eating away at the core of the school's traditions and authority. But the truth is that the Vigils are needed simply to maintain the school's illusion of order. The entire structure of authority is built upon the existence of the Vigils. Obviously the Trinity Brothers have winked at the Vigils because, as Archie is aware, they "served a purpose. Without The Vigils, Trinity might have been torn apart like other schools had been, by demonstrations, protests, all that crap" (25). The Brothers do not want anarchy, for that would mean total extinction of the school, total loss of control. The Brothers realize how precarious their own control is and therefore sanction the Vigils as a release of pent-up energies, allowing the boys to let off steam without destroying the foundations of the Brothers' authority. Thus the Vigils as a representation of a threat against authority is also an illusion. And the Brothers' dominance is an illusion. The world of Trinity is fragile, threatening, like Brother Eugene's chair, to fall apart. The appearance of order is simply a mask for anarchy, which is itself an illusion.

Rather than rebellious, Jerry is, like the Vigils, the epitome of convention. Jerry is called "square" by the hippies at the bus stop because he looks like a preppie and is thus akin to the establishment that the hippies are rebelling against, the establishment responsible for such acts as the Vietnam War and Watergate. (The hippies, though, are presented as useless; even banding together in a passive show of rebellion is ineffective.) But Jerry is square because, despite his seeming rebellion against the school's chocolate sale, he is tightly screwed together; he doesn't see how fragile his reality is and thus doesn't see the evil at Trinity. One of Cormier's tenets seems to be that innocence or ignorance is no excuse; not knowing about evil just makes it easier for evil to triumph. In Cormier's world, there is no one to blame except Red Riding Hood herself for being eaten by the wolf; she should have known better than let herself be seduced by him. But also in Cormier's world, even if she is aware of the danger, she'll be eaten anyway. She's screwed either way. Just like Jerry, the only thing she can count on is being a victim.

Jerry is a conformist to the very end. He makes no attempt to defy tradition: his art project is "copying a two-story house" because he is no good at "free art," preferring "formal or geometric designs" (141). Even at the end of the novel, while standing in the boxing ring facing Emile, Jerry "planted himself, like a tree" (181). His world is still screwed tight; he still believes that he and he alone is right and virtuous. He is defeated because he abides by the rules, even when the rules are formulated by blood-hungry spectators. The boxing ring finally is a world in which anything goes; the rules of boxing are flouted. Jerry cannot fathom this, but Emile can and thus destroys Jerry. The boxing match is representative of mob rule, for the spectators have cooperated enough to make sure the event happens. There are boundaries, but they are flexible; there are no squared angles (though squared, it is a boxing "ring").[5]

Jerry follows the rules, no matter who constructs them. Archie, though, constructs his own rules: "That's what Archie did—built the house nobody could anticipate a need for, except himself, a house that was invisible to everyone else" (29). Archie is the real nonconformist. As Assigner, Archie has to be creative; his position depends upon his thinking up new roles for Vigil recruits to perform. He assures Obie that thinking up assignments is "artistic . . . an art" (16). He often feels "used up, empty," even while he is aware that he, too, is playing a role that depends upon the other boys sharing in the perception that he is in control of their lives; they have to cooperate with his view. As Yoshida Junko has noted, the Vigils are panoptic in their surveillance and control over all the boys at Trinity (111). And the boys are willing participants in this power relationship. Archie is not square; he is loose, flexible. He keeps all the boys in line by manipulating them, recreating and revising their realities to fit his own. To convince Emile to participate in a showdown against Jerry, Archie says that "guys like Renault are your enemy, not guys like me. They're the squares, Emile, they're the ones who screw it up for us, who blow the whistle, who make the rules" (173). Of course he is manipulating Emile, for Jerry doesn't make the rules; he simply follows them, plays the game.

Archie is the true artist, one who defies convention and creates improbable worlds that others can believe in. He constructs his own reality so convincingly, and manipulates others to share in it so well, that he appears to dominate everyone in the novel as well as the reader.

His created world is a fictional world, as all worlds are, but, as he says to himself, "I am Archie. My wish becomes command" (174). Or, more tellingly, recognizing himself as the "*arch*itect" of the boxing match, Archie revels in how "He had successfully conned Renault and Leon and The Vigils and the whole damn school. I can con anybody. I am Archie" (170, emphasis mine). Archie is, in fact, the character who functions most like Cormier does as a writer. As do all writers, Cormier creates new worlds and manipulates his readers to share in those worlds. But Cormier sees all readers as victims, just waiting to play his game. He has to be flexible, adjusting the fiction to forestall the incredulity that might make readers simply toss the book away. At the last page, Cormier can then spit in the reader's face and say, see, I made you do it; I made you read it; I made you believe me. And aren't you a chump for all that.

Archie's mistake, as he is himself aware, is accepting Brother Leon's alliance to sell the chocolates. This alliance makes him conform to the wishes of authority figures (even though, ironically, he is himself an authority figure). The purpose of the Vigils is always to loosen the tightly screwed world of the authorities, to spread disrespect and the illusion of rebellion in order to dissipate the possibility of anarchy. But by allying himself with Brother Leon, Archie makes the Vigils an official part of the school structure, and therefore no outlet remains for unofficial rebellion. Brother Leon overlooks the boxing showdown between Jerry and Emile and allows it to continue and is no doubt pleased by the outcome. The boxing match, the Vigils, Emile's cruelty—all have become the school itself, and mob action is the only possible result. But once the Vigils and the Brothers are equal, once the Vigils are simply enacting the wishes of the Brothers, then the illusion of the Brothers' control falls apart. Brother Jerome, rather than being a force for good by turning off the lights and stopping the fight, is simply re-establishing the status quo. He will not report Brother Leon or Archie, and the school will survive with all its cruelties intact. Jerry's supposed defiant act is meaningless; it doesn't change anything.

Most of the boys display rebellious tendencies, even apart from the Vigils' own sanctioned pose as anti-authority rebels. Archie, Emile, Goober, and other minor characters are all rebels in different ways. Benson, a minor character who is mentioned only once, is indicative of all the boys at Trinity who are described by Cormier as being rebels: Benson, who congratulates Jerry for not selling chocolates, is known for "his complete disregard of the rules" (96). And Emile, described as an animal, probably a sociopath, has complete disregard for the school's policies or for human decency. He "didn't play by the rules" (40). Unlike Jerry, who does not understand how the world works until he is beaten by Emile in the boxing ring, Emile is able to intimidate and terrorize others because he realized at an early age how fragile the world is. He had a "revelation" in which he gained the "knowledge," the "truth," that no one wants to cause trouble, or to stand out of the crowd, or to be humiliated (41). He is a thief, but it is his harassing of teachers, the authority figures, who are as intimidated by him as are the other boys, that has made his reputation. He, too, though, seems to be sanctioned by the school, for all his acts of rebellion, which are committed in the open, are winked at, just as the existence of the Vigils is. These small acts of rebellion serve only to maintain the status quo.

When discussing the character of rebel hero, we should recall Milton's *Paradise Lost* to find the literary prototype for such a figure. In this epic, Satan is the most attractive character; his wailing against unjust treatment by God is affecting. In *The Chocolate War*, not only do we see that God's school of Trinity is corrupt, but we are not even sure who Satan is: Archie, or Jerry. Satan represents disorder and chaos and advocates lascivious behavior. His minions in hell are a reflection of the angels in heaven, or, more precisely, a parody of heaven, and he is a charismatic leader to his fiends. Many readers think of Archie as evil, and in some ways he does reflect Milton's Satan, for he, too, wants to sow seeds of chaos, to disrupt order. Milton's Satan in Western European literary history became remolded into the Byronic hero, the tortured soul, found later in Emily Brontë's Heathcliff. Thus Archie, who calls himself a "silent hero" (176), has a long provenance as a character who is bad to the bone and is presumably appealing, especially to women. Cormier fleshes out his portrait of Archie as satanic hero in his *Beyond the Chocolate War* by detailing the intense sexual attraction Archie has for women. His "favorite of all the girls at Miss Jerome's" is Jill Morton, "pretty and popular and intelligent" but with a "weakness for Archie," who makes her "compliant" to his sexual appetite (143–46).

It is thus easy to make Archie a satanic hero as a rebel against the system. (Or he is Prometheus defying the authority of Zeus?) Even though that system is God's, represented by Brother Leon, it is corrupt. Nevertheless, there is still Jerry. For many readers, he, too, is *the* rebel hero, but actually he is not so much different from Archie. Unlike Archie, Jerry has no attraction for women, but he does aspire to sow seeds of chaos in the system of Trinity. Furthermore, one of Milton's most persistent metaphors for Satan is the pine tree; he will not bend but stands alone in his intelligence and passion. It should again be noted that during the fight with Emile Janza, Jerry "planted himself, like a tree" (181). Using *Paradise Lost,* we see that Cormier is following literary tradition in drawing a portrait of a rebel who is appealing in his badness. The difference is that in *Paradise Lost,* in spite of Satan's pull on our sympathies, we still know that Satan is pitiful and God is good. Even if we place Archie as Satan and Jerry as Christ, who can also be seen as a revolutionary because he disrupted the conventional order of Judaism, we still have a problem. It's not so much that Satan wins but that Christ does not rise again, and even if he did, it wouldn't make a difference. Both Archie and Jerry offer the illusion of being rebels, and it doesn't really matter which one wins.

Misogyny

Besides rebellion, the boys at Trinity all have one thing in common: their objectification of women. If Jerry really is a hero, then I would think he would challenge the prevailing misogyny of the novel; but he doesn't. No one does. Yoshida has recently credited Cormier with being "daring enough to portray the all-male world as bleak, to find fault with traditional gender roles, and to depict his protagonist, Jerry, as seeking a new male identity" (106). Trinity is certainly bleak, but to suggest Cormier was being ironic in his presentation of gender is surprising. One would have to be a very sophisticated reader to play with this idea, and its argument also rides on the sequel *Beyond the Chocolate War.* I believe that instead of positing a journey to new male identity, Cormier is presenting, in his warped view, what is. What is, is not up to him to change. In *The Chocolate War,* sex *is* the single male. The tragedy of this novel is that not one male is ever given the chance to have a fulfilling relationship with a woman (or even with another man, for that matter). Having sex is a lonely act, perpetrated by oneself on oneself. Even in *Beyond the Chocolate War,* Jerry is planning to become a priest — in order to fight the good fight, he says, but as a priest he will still be denied a mutual sexual relationship. Cormier's ideology regarding sex is, frankly, appalling.[6]

The Chocolate War is undeniably misogynist. All women, not just dead women, are objectified. The end of the first chapter, when Jerry has been pummeled by the other football players, sets the tone for Cormier's treatment of women:

> As Jerry took another deep breath, a pain appeared, distant, small
> —a radar signal of distress. . . . The bleep grew larger, localized
> now, between his ribs on the right side. He thought of his mother
> and how drugged she was at the end, not recognizing anyone,
> neither Jerry nor his father. The exhilaration of the moment vanished and he sought it in vain, like seeking ecstasy's memory an
> instant after jacking off and encountering only shame and guilt.
>
> Nausea began to spread through his stomach, warm and oozy
> and evil. (9–10)

That Jerry is suffering from unresolved Oedipal feelings is clear. Cormier connects Jerry's pain in his rib (reminiscent of the birth of Eve) with the memory of his dying mother as well as with masturbation; he thus seems to be suffering from shame because of his sexual desire for his mother. I am not objecting to this portrayal of his mother; this feeling is probably not that rare in an adolescent boy's subconscious. The depiction of Jerry's mother as sexual object, however, is set, and, more important, so is her description as weak, as woman. She is never given any life in Jerry's memories but is always an object, either objectified sexually or as "a *thing* suddenly, cold and pale" in the coffin (48). The only information Cormier offers about Jerry's mother is that she had been born in a "small Canadian town" (49) and "she'd loved her home so much, always had some project underway, wallpapering, painting, refinishing furniture" (49). Cormier implies that her death left a gaping hole in Jerry's and his father's lives, one that Mrs. Hunter, the housekeeper, cannot fill, yet because of the lack of information about her, it is impossible to imagine Jerry's mother as taking up any space in their lives at all. Sylvia Iskander's statement that Cormier "carefully develops . . . the positive aspects of Jerry's home life, which was warm and loving before his mother's death and which can be so again when Mr. Renault recovers from his grief over his wife's death" (12) is insupportable. Cormier provides a brief sketch of Jerry's mother, expecting readers to fill in with their own stereotyped details. Furthermore, there is no indication that Jerry's father was ever any more active; he has, apparently, always been resigned to being a pharmacist rather than a doctor. A doctor, after all, writes the prescription order; the pharmacist just fills it.

Although other mothers in the novels are alive, they are seen as nuisances. Their voices are silent or are ignored. This portrayal, too, is probably realistic, as adolescent boys sometimes cruelly reject their mothers so that they can better break the bonds and identify with their fathers. The problem is that there is no mother or any other female to counteract this negative image. Thus the only ideology regarding the role of women in society, whether implicit or explicit, is one of objectification. While Kevin is talking on the phone, his mother is "making sounds at him. Kevin had learned long ago to translate whatever she was saying into gibberish. She could talk her head off now and the words reached his ears without meaning" (102). He perceives "her mouth moving and sounds coming out, and he sighed, tuning her out, like shutting off the sound on television while the picture remained" (104). The picture that remains is the image of his mother, but with no voice. She, too, is object.

One last mother is not the mother of a Trinity boy—not yet, that is. While trying to sell the notorious chocolates, Paul Consalvo knocks at the door of a clearly harassed woman who is at home with two children. The house "smell[s] of pee" (73), thus associating a mother with dirtiness, with body fluids, and with the home. Her children are "howling" for her, so at this point she is needed as a source of nourishment. When she is no longer needed, when she instead is the needy one, she will be ignored. When Paul returns to his own home, he "couldn't wait to get out of the house. 'Where're you going all the time?' his mother asked as he fled the place" (73–74).

It is important to note that the chocolates, which give the story its title, are unsold Mother's Day chocolates—stripped of their ribbons and sold for twice their original price. These "boxes" of chocolates are not even eaten by women, though they very well represent women (a woman's box). The only characters whom we see eating the chocolates are the boys at Trinity. Thus the boys are still receiving food from their mothers, though it is no longer nourishing, only candy.

The scene of the harassed mother is significant enough, but Cormier adds weight to it by placing it just after one of the novel's most disturbing scenes involving a female: Tubs Casper and his girlfriend Rita. As the only girlfriend in the novel, Rita represents all girls who are potential girlfriends. His mother would disapprove of her, but his mother, we are told, is never home, "always driving around" (71)—we can easily speculate what she is doing away from home. Rita appears to be a prostitute trainee, using Tubs to buy her sexual favors. He is selling chocolates for fast money, planning to repay the school later, so he can buy Rita an expensive bracelet for her birthday. If he gives her the bracelet, he will be rewarded: "she'd probably let him get under her sweater" (73). Deep in his heart Tubs knows he is being used by Rita. He is "forty pounds overweight, which his father never let him forget" (72) and assumes no good-looking girl like Rita would give him a chance if it were not for the money. Even though she is only fourteen years old, in typical Cormier fashion, Rita is completely aware of her power of seduction, which gives her the illusion of control:

> She walked along the sidewalk with him, her breast brushing his arm, setting him on fire. The first time she rubbed against him he thought it was an accident and he pulled away, apologetic, leaving a space between them. Then she brushed against him again— that was the night he'd bought her the earrings—and he knew it wasn't an accident. . . . Him—with this beautiful girl's breast pushed against him, not beautiful the way his mother thought a girl was beautiful but beautiful in a ripe wild way, faded blue jeans hugging her hips, those beautiful breasts bouncing under her jersey. (72)

This portrayal of Rita suggests that women are complicit in the sexual game. Rita is not innocent nor is she ignorant. If she is treated as object, it is because she wants to be treated as an object, albeit a desired one. Cormier asks us to sympathize with Tubs, who is being indoctrinated into male-female relationships in this way: in order to get a woman, you buy her, and you do that by selling your own mother, that is, Mother's Day candy.

Although Rita is the only girlfriend mentioned in the novel, other boys in the novel are also thinking about girls. Jerry fantasizes about a girl he sees several times at a bus stop, Ellen Barrett. He finally gathers enough courage to call her, but of course she has no idea who he is. As Jerry thinks, it's no wonder she doesn't remember him: "A fellow didn't call up a girl on the evidence of a smile and introduce himself this way. She probably smiled at a hundred guys a day" (129), implying that her favors are passed around indiscriminately. She calls Jerry a "pervert" and is both demure and annoyed. Jerry persists in trying to explain—until she says the word "crap." This one word "destroy[s] all illusion . . . like meeting a lovely girl and having her smile reveal rotten teeth" (129). Cormier's metaphor is very fitting for Jerry's dream girl, the untainted, innocent girl he longs to see. Girls are just another example of the innate corruptness of life; all might look shiny on the surface, but that is only an illusion.

An equally disturbing scene occurs later between two Trinity boys, Harry Anderson and Richy Rondell, who appear only once in the novel. In this scene, the word "screwed" takes on both slang and sexual connotations, for the girls are screwed—victimized, cheated—simply because they are female, but they are also screwed sexually—raped. Howie is president of the junior class, a boxer, football player, and honor student. He is at the pinnacle of Trinity success. All we learn about Richy, however, is that he constantly has his hand down his pants, "grabbing shamelessly, something he couldn't resist whenever he got excited, about a girl or anything else" (105). The entire time that Howie is talking to him about Jerry not selling chocolates, Richy is observing a girl who has stopped to examine some newspapers. The words Cormier uses are telling: Richy is described as "devouring" the girl and her friends "with wistful eyes"; he "gazed at her with wistful lust," "feasted himself on her rounded jeans," and when she walks away, he begins "looking for another girl to enjoy" (104, 106). The verbs used refer to eating as an obvious metaphor for sex. Because Richy's inner thoughts about the girl are juxtaposed with Howie's comments about the chocolates and how Jerry is no longer selling them, this scene becomes a powerful one; the girl becomes "eye candy." Perhaps the worst comment comes from Howie, who, in the midst of his preoccupation with the chocolates, also sees the girl. "But it didn't break his train of thought. Watching girls and devouring them with your eyes—*rape by eyeball*—was something you did automatically" (104, emphasis mine, though none is needed).

With this one scene, *The Chocolate War* becomes the poster child for the damaging, pervasive effects of the male gaze. Male readers participate in the male gaze; female readers become passive acceptors of the male gaze; all readers become voyeurs. This attitude is never challenged through the novel but is instead compounded by the many boys' voices saying the same thing. I find it difficult to believe that Cormier, after carefully choosing the words to dramatize these two boys' callous lust, is sensitive enough to portray Jerry as a boy searching for a new definition of male, as Yoshida suggests. Instead, Cormier consistently describes the adolescent male as posturing before other males, tuning out females while objectifying them. In his *Pleasures of Children's Literature*, Perry Nodelman suggests that the all-male atmosphere of *The Chocolate War* is homosocial. Borrowing from Eve Kosofsky Sedgwick, he defines homosocial desire: relationships with other men are what "matter to them, first, through exchanging women with other men, and second, by making clear that their desire is homosocial and not homosexual: for homosociality traditionally requires homophobia as a condition for its acceptability" (*Pleasures* 125–26). Thus books like *The Chocolate War* that keep such matters "hidden in the closet" actually "help to teach the homophobia that allows homosociality" (126). The worst damage Emile can do to Jerry is call him a homosexual, "The worst thing in the world—to be called queer" (153). It stands to reason that Jerry agrees to fight Emile in the boxing ring not because he is standing on principle about the chocolates, but because he is trying to prove his manhood. Thus Jerry's so-called fight against evil degenerates into a well-worn script of male competition.

The homophobia of *The Chocolate War* becomes obvious in *Beyond the Chocolate War*. Brother Leon, who is seen by many readers as not just manipulative and power hungry, but downright evil, is portrayed as a stereotype of the male homosexual. In a student burlesque of the faculty, a boy "minced across the stage, speaking in a prissy voice, wielding an oversized baseball bat the way Leon used his teacher's pointer, as a weapon" (246)—as a phallic weapon, we would add, like Captain Hook's hook. Leon is limp-wristed and walks with "short mincing steps" (41). Every student at Trinity, and every reader, hates Brother Leon. It becomes clear in this sequel that Cormier indoctrinates readers with hatred against Leon because Leon is homosexual. Brother Leon is evil; Brother Leon is homosexual; therefore, homosexuality is evil. In her *Disturbing the Universe: Power and Repression in Adolescent Literature,* Roberta Seelinger Trites claims that "Archie and Brother Leon are enmeshed in a homoerotic triangle: first the chocolate sale, then Jerry Renault serve as the object of exchange between the two men" (37). Like Nodelman, she believes that in *The Chocolate War* homophobia is insidious: "the reader is meant to despise these two males [Leon and Archie] who are so corrupt that they have reached the ostensible pinnacle of debauchery, homosexuality" (38).

I would, again, assert that Jerry conveys no moral commitment. His "decision" to not sell the chocolates is based on several emotions involving sexuality; the desire to be a nonconformist is not one of them. Cormier seems to be dramatizing in not very subtle ways how the adolescent boy's turmoil of incestuous desire for his mother is displaced by society's legitimizing of the objectification of women. If there is a motivation for Jerry's refusal to sell chocolates, other than rebellion, it seems to be a reaction to his helplessness at his mother's death. When she died, he could do nothing, not even vent his anger and pain. He could not save her, and "his anger was so deep and sharp in him that it drove out sorrow. He wanted to bellow at the world, cry out against her death, topple buildings, split the earth open, tear down trees. And he did nothing" (48). Jerry is still angry, though his father's reserved behavior has clued him to keep the anger inside. The Vigils assign him to refuse to sell chocolates as part of their initiation, and Jerry complies. It is not until Jerry announces that, even though the Vigils' assignment to refuse the chocolates is over, he still will not sell them, that his anger is finally released, for he is not defying the authority of just Brother Leon, but of the Vigils as well: "Cities fell. Earth opened. Planets tilted. Stars plummeted" (89). Since his mother's death, Jerry has felt impotent, and his saying no to selling the chocolates might be a refusal to sell out his mother's memory (the Mother's Day candy), but it is just as likely an effort to screw, become potent, make the earth move. Not selling the chocolates may be Jerry's way of disturbing the universe, but this particular universe is the one that allows mothers to die with no one seeming to care, no one demonstrating emotional upheaval. That he also affects Trinity's infrastructure is just a byproduct. At last, Jerry's anger and pain are given the attention he craves from his father, or from anyone. The physical pain inflicted by the boxing match is symbolic of his inner pain. And the hurt he feels is masochistic comfort, punishment to ease the guilt he feels for forbidden desire for his mother and for his inability to transform her from lifeless object into a living being.

Consequences for Adolescent Readers

The Chocolate War supposedly offers a polyphony of voices, many different points of view. We are privy to the thoughts of many of the characters: Archie, Obie, Brother Leon, Jerry, Goober, just to name a few. Not only does each chapter highlight the thoughts of a particular male (never female) character, but in chapter 14, for example, no less than five characters' inner voices are heard: those of John Sulkey, Goober, Tubs Casper, Paul Consalvo, and Brian Cochran. At least in terms of the objectification of women, however, all the voices are saying the same thing. There are no competing voices, no dissent. They are all shouting with one voice, one message. Thus there is simply an *illusion* of many voices—another trick played on the reader by Cormier.

Because of the multiplicity of voices in the novel, Michael Cadden in a recently published essay asserts, "*The Chocolate War* does not ask the young adult reader to trust in the voice of a single speaker or to accept a single, unchallenged view of events" (151). But in her *Ideologies of Identity in Adolescent Fiction: The Dialogic Construction of Subjectivity*, Robyn McCallum argues convincingly the opposite view: "While the presence of thirteen focalizing characters implies that this might be a radically polyphonic novel, point of view in the novel is actually quite limited. Only the school boys focalize—the teachers and parents do not—and despite the rough divisions between groups of characters, there is a sameness about the ways that different characters view the world—the way that they all perceive women, for example" (45–46). We know that *The Chocolate War* is often taught in junior high classrooms, but it is not likely that most teachers are guiding their students to an appreciation for the many different voices in the novel. Instead, adolescent readers and their teachers are led by Cormier to assume that Jerry is playing the expected role of the rebel fighting the corrupt system. Evidence for how the novel is being used in the classroom can be seen in a new textbook edition of *The Chocolate War* that is obviously capitalizing on this popular interpretation. (Surely Cormier saw the irony of *The Chocolate War* becoming sanctioned by the educational establishment!)

In 1998 the publishers McDougal Littell released a textbook called *The Chocolate War and Related Readings*. There is no introduction and no editor is given credit, although there are small one-paragraph introductions to the readings that follow the novel. Emily Dickinson's "I took my Power in my Hand" immediately follows *The Chocolate War;* the unnamed editor states that Dickinson "considers what can happen when an individual goes against the larger world" (219), a very simple reading of this poem. "Some Opposites of Good" by Leslie Norris, a very good story about a boy's disillusionment, is prefaced by the instruction "Compare what little Mark learns in school to what Jerry learns" (220), assuming that all readers interpret both the novel and the story in exactly the same way. The next related reading is an interview with a gang member who is violent but does have his own sense of loyalty and morality; readers are invited to compare him to Archie (233), although Archie has neither loyalty nor a sense of morality. A poem by Philip Cioffari called "Breaking Bones," written from the viewpoint of the bully, "shows how tragic and permanent the effects of childhood bullying can be" (238); I would agree that a more articulate Emile could have written it, but if Emile were more articulate, he wouldn't be Emile. A short story, "White Places" by Mary Flannagan, follows, describing the cruelties inflicted on a disabled, overweight child by her sister and cousins, including burying her in a snowdrift and forgetting about her; the editor implies that this type of bullying is specific to girls (apparently physical beatings are specific to boys). The last reading, reprinted from *Seventeen,* is "Bad Company," which distills interviews with high school girls who were once in "nasty groups" and purports to "share a few traits that can help you distinguish them from a potential circle of genuine friends" (253). The advice given is to duck the problem: "if your friends are planning to egg your biology teacher's car because she flunked someone's boyfriend, and you can't find the courage to tell them how stupid they are, just say you'd rather not take part in the yolkfest. Then make a point of not being around when it happens" (258). In other words, the essay advises that Goober's behavior is the best option. That this textbook even exists indicates that *The Chocolate War* is being used in the schools to promote Jerry as a moral agent, a nonconformist fighting the unfair system and keeping true to what he knows is right.

Even if teachers, by using *The Chocolate War,* feel they are helping to raise adolescent readers' awareness of moral judgment to the point that they can distinguish between society's unfair rules and their own inner feelings of justice, the novel itself undercuts this accomplishment. As I hope I have demonstrated, the dominant reading offered by many critics and teachers of *The Chocolate War*—a reading that is used to mold adolescent readers' interpretations—is simply not supportable when we look at the text. We—and I mean not just middle and high school teachers, but college teachers as well—want adolescent readers to develop cognitively and morally. (We don't, after all, teach *The Giver* because it's supposedly great literature, but because it stimulates discussion about several ethical issues we want students to ponder.) We want them to think for themselves, not just to prepare themselves as citizens in a democracy, but to be able to live in our world where information is readily available but with very little mediation. Readers need guidance in how to judge what is presented to them, but *The Chocolate War* does not offer any.

In *The Company We Keep: An Ethics of Fiction,* Wayne Booth quotes John Updike: "Surely one of the novel's habitual aims is to articulate morality, to sharpen the reader's sense of vice and virtue" (24). In her "Finding The Way: Morality and Young Adult Literature," Carol Jones

Collins stresses "the power of narrative" (160). Indeed, young adult literature "is a rich and growing body of literature whose moral power has been too long neglected by literary critics and ethical theorists alike" (159). Borrowing from Lawrence Kohlberg and Carol Gilligan, Collins states that both justice and care are "foundation ethic[s]" of any society and should be "valued and nurtured" in young people (166). Books can be a guide to a young person's moral development. She ends her discussion by stating:

> What this all means is that books, all books, that young adults read have power. Their power rests in their ability to sway and to change the reader in so many ways, not the least of these is morally. These books can create a moral sense in the young by demonstrating what is morally right and what is morally wrong. They can raise and resolve ethical issues. The reader may not agree with each resolution, but is certainly forced to think about issues he or she may never have thought about before. (181)

Booth offers an even stronger reason for an author's power: "we are largely 'made,' 'constituted' by the figurings offered by narratives. . . . Every art of the imagination, benign or vicious, profound or trivial, can colonize the mind" (295–96, 298). In other words, books can help young readers realize their moral agency, to weigh the pros and cons and take action when necessary. But, to reiterate, Jerry Renault is not a moral agent; rather, he is the prototype of a popular kind of protagonist in young adult literature, one who is paralyzed by postmodern society's anxieties.

In *Ethics, Theory and the Novel* (1994), David Parker argues the need for a "theoretically self-aware ethical criticism" (4) that begins to fill the void created by poststructuralism's tunnel vision about ethics. Admittedly advocating a partial return to humanism, he calls for both political criticism (including feminist, Marxist, ethnic) as well as ethical criticism; neither is sufficient alone (194). Iris Murdoch also insists upon being a critic who

> approaches a literary work in an open-minded manner and is interested in *all sorts of ways:* which certainly does not exclude treating a tale as a 'window into another world', reacting to characters as if they were real people, making value judgments about them, about how their creator treats them, and so on. Here the enjoyment, or otherwise, of the critic is *like* that of the layman,

only generally (one hopes) well informed and guided by a respect
and love for literature and a liberal-minded *sense of justice.* He will
beware suitably of his own prejudices, but will not be chary of
speaking his mind. (189)

John Gardner, in his *On Moral Fiction* (1977), published just three
years after *The Chocolate War,* claims that lack of moral commitment
was typical for those writing more than a quarter-century ago: "That
helplessness, that feeling of imprisonment in [a] meaningless, dull system, was a common state of mind in the late sixties and early seventies"
(89). Gardner's book was readily dismissed by rising postmodernists
who blanched at such statements as this: "Great art celebrates life's
potential, offering a vision unmistakably and unsentimentally rooted
in love" (83). But Gardner's berating of writers of his time, such as
Joseph Heller, centers on their reliance on propaganda or their insistence on "'tell[ing] it like it is,' which normally means taking no position, simply copying down 'reality,' and throwing up one's hands" (76).
   Gardner could just as easily be writing about Cormier, who says he is
"truthful to the situation I'm writing about. . . . [Letters from readers]
say, 'You tell it like it is'" (Campbell, "Conversing" 2). Gardner laments
the penchant for the artist's "treating himself and his society as guilty
on principle. If everyone everywhere is guilty," says Gardner, "then no
models of goodness, for life or art, exist; moral art is a lie" (44). Along
these same lines, he says about Heller, the "indifferent system makes
devils of us all . . . but Heller does not care enough to search out an
answer to the real question: What are we to do?" (90). Cormier says in
a recent interview with Patricia Campbell, "I think our lives are driven
by guilt." And although he claims that the sins of omission "haunt"
him, when he tells Campbell that fifth- and sixth-graders are reading
Tenderness, and she responds by saying she is "appall[ed]. . . . [It] makes
my blood run cold," Cormier characteristically throws up his hands:
"but what am I going to do?" (2, 3).
   Cormier asks himself Gardner's question, What are we to do? And
answers, Nothing. He's just a writer. He has no control over who reads
his books or how they are interpreted. He has no clout as a famous
writer. He can't put the screws to his editor, his agent, his publisher. He
can't address audiences and write articles about his intended reader-
ship. Of course not. He's just a writer. And now, because of Cormier's
recent demise, in Booth's words, "I must leave it to each reader to practice an ethics of reading that might determine . . . which of the world's

narratives should now be banned or embraced in the lifetime project of building the character of an ethical reader" (489).

To conclude our discussion of moral agency in *The Chocolate War,* we can look at its treatment of the Holocaust, a treatment that epitomizes the ethical stance of the polyphonic one-voicedness—that is, feel guilty, do nothing. You can't change the world. Discussion of the Holocaust is included in *The Chocolate War* when Brother Leon is questioned by a student while he is intimidating Bailey. Always the slippery one, Leon turns his failed power play into a lesson for the rest of the class. He diminishes his own guilt by sharing it with all the others, who are silent witnesses to the intimidation. He tells them, "those of you who didn't enjoy yourselves allowed it to happen, allowed me to proceed. You turned this classroom into Nazi Germany for a few moments" (38). The students sitting in the class momentarily forget that this is a Hitlerite speaking these words of admonition, and they all fall prey again to his manipulation by feeling guilty. At least one critic, too, has fallen under Leon's sway: discussing Archie and Brother Leon as manipulators, Anne Scott MacLeod points out that "neither could work his will without the cooperation of others. The acquiescence of the community is essential to their power[;] . . . the source of the power . . . is, of course, the students themselves" (191). We should recall Cormier's after-the-fact defense of this novel that it is the fault of all the boys that Jerry is beaten, because they did not cooperate to defeat the trinity of evil. This is Cormier's plot, once again: we all crucified Christ; we all are responsible. All the students at Trinity and all readers persecuted Jerry, not just Emile, or Archie, or Leon. We hang our heads in despair, paralyzed with guilt.

Compare this scene to a similar one in Jane Yolen's *The Devil's Arithmetic* (1988). Yolen will have none of Cormier's easy displacement of guilt and demoralizing confusion of truly evil with good. When the main character, Hannah, feels guilty when she watches a young child she knows get "chosen" by the commandant for the gas ovens, she says, "I should have said he was my brother," feeling that she has betrayed him and thus contributed to his death. Rivka, the girl who teaches the others how to survive in the camp, reminds Hannah that this futile gesture would have resulted in her being "chosen," too; staying loyal to the child would not have saved him but would only have destroyed herself as well. Unconvinced, Hannah says, "We are all monsters . . . because we are letting it happen," an echo of Brother Leon's words. But Rivka adamantly tells Hannah, and the reader, "*We* are the victims.

. . . *They* are the monsters" (141). Yolen very clearly offers an antithesis to Cormier's crass, facile sermonizing, while at the same time maintaining the dignity and strength of those in the concentration camp— no matter how many times they are beaten, they get back up.

Although Murdoch, Booth, Parker, and especially Gardner are commenting on adult literature, their thoughts offer intriguing questions regarding children's and adolescent literature. Should this literature require intervention, if, according to Gardner, even adults require it? Should there be guidance or at least options to consider regarding moral dilemmas? If we look to Cormier, we can readily see that he refuses to offer guidance. As I have noted, he claims that readers are supposed to infer that only cooperation will defeat evil when the only examples he shows of cooperation result in the *propagation* of evil. Cormier sees himself as a helpless cog in a machine of corruption; all he can do is write what he sees, and what he sees is corruption—just the muck, not the way to get out of it. If I act, as Jerry supposedly does, I'm destroyed. If I don't act, as Goober doesn't, I'm condemned.

It's easy to condemn Goober. Cormier says Goober "had washed his hands of the school and its cruelties" (179), as if he is Pontius Pilate, unable to prevent the inevitable crucifixion, so he observes from the stands while the crowd calls for the thief Barabbas (i.e., Emile). All Goober can do is cradle the defeated Christ figure after the damage has been done, an act which Trites interprets as Goober's realization that "Jerry has died for his [Goober's] sins" (15). The irony is that, instead of condemning Archie or Brother Leon or Emile, Cormier condemns Goober, the one character who realizes what is going on and has tried to stop Jerry from perpetuating the game. Goober is the only character who indicates his disgust with what he recognizes as evil by simply refusing to participate. He is not betraying Jerry, as Cormier wants us to believe, and he is not a coward. Instead, by refusing to participate, he no longer can be victim or perpetrator; he cannot be exploited by either Brother Leon or the Vigils. Jerry, who does not recognize what is going on at the school, continues to play football and continues to play the "game" that is controlled by, ultimately, Archie. It is Goober who is the true rebel, who simply refuses to play. If you see a poker game and realize that the dealer not only is cheating but is holding a gun, you don't sit down, as Jerry did, and expect fair play. Instead, like Goober, you just don't play. In normal circumstances, you would go get the sheriff to intervene, but Cormier has fixed it so that the sheriff is already there, winking in approval at the crooked dealer.

So you don't even stick around for a drink. You get out of there and consider yourself lucky.

The Cormier Legacy

In all Cormier's novels for adolescents, I see only two characters who actually have moral agency. One is the Avenger in *We All Fall Down* (1991). This character has committed two murders, his first at the age of eleven, and has been in a state of arrested development ever since. He takes it upon himself to condemn Buddy and the other boys who trash Jane's house and are responsible for the near-rape of her sister, now in a coma. Buddy's parents are divorced; Buddy is an alcoholic trying to cope; Buddy is in love with Jane; Buddy is exploited by the leader of the gang who trash the house. Therefore, Buddy is not accountable. We readers do not condemn him. Only the Avenger does — but the Avenger is a preadolescent, too young (in mind, not body) to take on multiple points of view. Only those who are underdeveloped can pass judgment because, apparently, to do so requires an infantile mind-set. Seemingly for Cormier, one must see only in terms of black and white to be able to state that good *is* better than evil.

The other Cormier character is Kate in *After the First Death* (1979). She knows exactly what her position is and who the terrorists are and even learns of the indoctrination of the young terrorist Miro, which up to now has offered him no chance to think for himself. Kate pities Miro; nevertheless, she reminds herself that he is a monster. Kate is brave, maternal, sympathetic, and yet totally cognizant of what the terrorists are capable of. Cormier allows her to retain her moral judgment — but after all, she is a hostage on a bus with small children, two of whom die; the ambiguities in the novel apply less to the young people (Kate, Miro, and Ben) and more to Ben's father, whose unquestioning patriotism is equal to the terrorists'. Kate's only problem is that she forgets momentarily that she cannot trust Miro, that he is a monster, and in that moment he kills her. In all of Cormier's novels for adolescents, Kate is the truest moral agent — and yet Cormier kills her.[7]

Cormier takes his inability or refusal to allow his characters to act morally to its point of absurdity with a more recent novel, *Tenderness* (1997). The novel begins with the thoughts of a serial killer, Eric Poole, and we learn through the progress of the novel that he is suffering from incestuous feelings for his mother and kills young women as a result. His victims are accomplices to the murder because they are gullible and stupid. The fifteen-year-old girl, Lori Cranston, who is nameless through most of the novel, wants—yes, wants—to be his next victim. Like another Rita, she is fully aware of her seductive powers over men and is self-destructive to boot. By the end of the novel, we actually sympathize with the serial killer, Eric; we want him to reform his life and accept the love Lori is giving him, which would somehow redeem him. But just as Eric acknowledges himself for what he is and stops himself from murdering Lori, she drowns anyway. The policeman, Jake Proctor, who hunts him down, is in a good position to express the moral implications of both Eric's past crimes and his innocence of this most recent one, but he allows Eric to be arrested on false charges. Whether Eric killed her or not doesn't make any difference. Eric is guilty of past murders, so that's enough. Through the tired policeman, readers are told that no one can pass judgment, and thus no one can act according to one's moral conscience.

Cormier does have one novel that actually is centered on a Holocaust survivor, *Tunes for Bears to Dance To* (1992), which is often touted as teaching a great moral lesson for young readers. In fact, in a recent interview with Cormier, Mitzi Myers refers to it as "a small gem of a book that encapsulates central moral issues in your body of work" (456); "It certainly is a story of moral growth" (458). I believe, however, that in this novel there is the same inability to follow through with a character's moral agency. Henry, who is seduced into destroying a Holocaust survivor's model of his village, which was destroyed by the Nazis, at the last moment decides not to comply. His decision is thwarted by a rodent that causes him to drop the sledgehammer on the model village anyway, demolishing it. Henry's decision is meaningless; he was helpless after all; the seducer's plan would go into effect because seemingly nature itself was complicit.

Conclusion

Clearly Cormier is a postmodern writer. He questions traditional narrative structure, his narrators (especially in *Fade*) are self-reflexive, and his use of multiple points of view reflects postmodernism's challenge to absolute truths. No one who has a sense of recent critical theory can read *The Chocolate War* without an awareness of the underlying assumptions of postmodernism; otherwise, we reduce it to the very simple theme of man vs. man, or an allegory of good vs. evil, when Cormier is by the very nature of this novel exploding the idea of there being a theme at all. Nevertheless, I reject the idea that *The Chocolate War* is such a sophisticated novel that it requires a complex critical apparatus to understand it. In many ways it is a modern study of adolescent cruelty and an expression of an outdated paranoid view that confirms the juvenile mentality that distrusts anyone over the age of thirty. Furthermore, I believe that it is at least partly an illusion that *The Chocolate War* is a postmodern novel, for the many voices conjoin to shout one message: No matter what you do, *it doesn't matter;* you're screwed.

Rather than simply label Cormier a writer of postmodern literature, which makes him into some kind of pioneer in the writing of children's literature, I would suggest that as a writer Cormier is irresponsible. Gilligan states that "adolescents are passionately interested in moral questions. Thus adolescence may be a critical time for moral education" (xvi). Education, however, requires not just exposure to evil, but guidance in how to respond to it. Perhaps it seems old-fashioned to use the presence of moral agency as a standard for evaluating young adult literature. But moral behavior is not just an issue for public school elementary teachers or pedagogical theorists. If it is productive to examine gender, racial, ethnic, and class issues, why not also moral issues, especially when ethical judgments are at the core of all these issues? To discuss moral dilemmas in young adult novels is not to invite a return to a 1950s state of mind, of imprisoning roles for women, overt bigotry, and McCarthyism. I'm not advocating a return to the comparatively simple moral codes of *Tom Brown's Schooldays* or eighteenth-century Sunday School tracts. Rather, investigating moral agency is a neglected aspect of our perception. It should never be the sole criterion, but it should always be at least one measure for evaluating a young adult novel. As Collins says, what we're talking about is reading novels that illustrate characters making choices, both good and bad, and seeing the consequences. Whether we agree with the choices is less important than whether characters actually see that they have choices, and that their actions do make a difference. They shouldn't feel that no matter what they do (or don't do), they are screwed.

Cormier offers us a literary version of the once-popular program of values clarification, in which students argued moral positions, but without teacher intervention, without guidance. As Melinda Fine describes it, a values clarification program "embodies certain premises of that socially transformative period [the 1960s and 1970s]—for example, an antiauthority ideal and the approbation of the individual's freedom from oppressive social constraints." (The 1960s and 1970s of course were the decades in which Cormier produced his first works for young adults.)[8] Although a student's position on a question might be clarified, through discussion, it could remain very subjective, for the discussion involved no "evaluation of moral content. . . . [Thus] values entirely antithetical to the public good (stealing, lying, treating others with disrespect, and so forth) might be voiced and implicitly validated" because the teacher's role was to instigate discussion, not act as a guide for moral agency (114). The inherent ideology of values clarification programs was lambasted by both the right and the left and discarded, but the idea continues to influence us through such novels as *The Chocolate War*.

Consistent with the ideology of values clarification is Cormier's narrative strategy of the camera's eye—impassively recording the thoughts and actions of characters—but he employs none of the film-maker's traditional forms of directing an audience's reactions—such as swelling of music or voice-over narration. Myszor has described Cormier's use of cinematic techniques in his novels; for example, the multiple points of view are like the "cross-cutting" techniques used in films to increase dramatic tension. Cormier himself says he is "a frustrated script writer . . . [and] write[s] cinematically" (DeLuca and Natov 116–20). Cormier is just offering pictures, telling us this is the news ("if it bleeds, it leads" is a popularly known guide for local newscasters) but without Peter Jennings' raised eyebrow.

Cormier claims that *The Chocolate War* was not intended to be read by teenagers, but he is of course aware that all of his later books have been targeted at teens. He claims that he is responsible only to a certain point—to be realistic and interesting, but after that he "can't care about what lessons they draw from the book" (qtd. in Gallo 159). If he doesn't care, and obviously his publishers don't care, then why are many of us so eager to teach his books to teenagers? If he is not concerned with how young adults interpret his writings, then why do we keep labeling them as young adult literature instead of Stephen King-like horror?

Cormier is even dishonest with himself. He doesn't care how other teens read his books, but obviously he cares how his own children read them. A scene describing Archie masturbating was cut from the final draft of *The Chocolate War* because he did not want his daughter to read it (Campbell, *Presenting* 48). Cormier creates young characters who are terrified, alone, defeated, never given the opportunity for an honest, emotional, romantic relationship; Cormier creates these nightmares as he writes in the dark of the night, while "all the time the ones [he] love[s] are asleep and safe under [his] roof" (qtd. in Campbell, *Presenting* 29). At a recent ChLA conference in Omaha, his daughter Christine assured us that Cormier was the perfect father, always there to listen to his children's problems, reassuring, generous. So why hasn't Cormier offered a kinder, gentler version of himself in his novels for young adults? Why is the world he maintained for his own biological children so much happier, so much more secure than the worlds he creates for his fictional children? It seems that all the bad stuff he tried to protect his own children from emerged in his stories, only there are no reassuring fathers in his fiction—just ones like Miro's in *After the First Death* who bases his whole strategy for defeating the terrorists on the assumption that Miro will be a coward.

Nobody prevented Cormier from writing and publishing—only his recent death has done that—and nobody is stopping anyone from reading his works. But if I want to read about an adolescent character who is facing a moral dilemma, I'll turn to Madeleine L'Engle or Monica Hughes or Peter Dickinson or Cynthia Voigt or Ursula LeGuin or Zibby Oneal or James Bennett. These authors offer real moral dilemmas with characters making decisions; some of them turn out to be good decisions, and some of them are not, but at least the characters are aware that they are making moral decisions that have far-reaching consequences. What they do, or don't do, does make a difference.

Notes

I would like to thank my colleagues at Illinois State who have always shown respect for my ideas about Cormier; the anonymous readers at *Children's Literature* for their valuable suggestions; and especially Elizabeth Keyser for her support and editorial acumen.

1. The bulk of this essay was completed before Cormier's death on November 2, 2000.

2. *Fade*, because of its questions of fiction and reality, of its doll-within-a-doll narrative plotting, is challenging to read and interesting because of that. Unfortunately, it is also voyeuristic and depraved; once again Cormier makes readers become, in essence, cops on the take. Because Cormier is a suspenseful writer, we are unwilling to stop reading, but also because we are just readers, we cannot stop and correct what we are reading about. The few characters who actually maintain their integrity (not their "innocence") are almost invisible. However, *I Am the Cheese* is fantasy, fascinating storytelling. For some of us, it feeds our suspicions and we begin to read fantasy as truth (which, in many ways, it is). For others of us, it purges our suspicions and helps us look at government policy as neither perfectly good nor evil, but just humanly bizarre. *I Am the Cheese* is first-rate storytelling, and the postmodern fragmented, multiple narratives coalesce perfectly with the fragmented vignettes of Adam's life. It is suspenseful. It is inconclusive, open-ended. Adam is an adolescent, but being a teenager in this novel is simply symbolic of every person who feels trapped, powerless to cope, just as Lewis Carroll's Alice is symbolic

of every person who feels trapped by a bureaucratic world of arbitrary rules but who mercifully escapes back into blissfully ignorant childhood. Adam's outlook is bleak, but because he doesn't die, there is still the possibility of his finding a way out of the trap. The deconstruction of Adam's life has already taken place, so what readers do is try to put the puzzle back together, along with Adam. If we don't like what the puzzle pictures when we finish, we can start all over again, willing ourselves to believe that the ending might change. We engage in self-deception, yes, but Adam pulls us into his fragile reality. As long as he keeps bicycling, he's not beaten; his bicycling is what keeps up the circus tent of his world of illusion.

3. Booth would include feminist theories as part of ethical criticism.

4. Nodelman, in fact, states that "the horrific world of *The Chocolate War* represents a distorted, paranoid vision of the ways things are" ("Paranoia" 26).

5. See Susina for a discussion of how "Cormier uses the boxing match as a critique of all that is corrupt at Trinity" (174).

6. Arthea J. S. Reed is one of Cormier's most ardent defenders, calling *The Chocolate War* "a fine work of literature." When her students say it is depressing, she "bristle[s], biting [her] tongue and reminding [her]self that [she] still [has] much to teach them, and they have much to learn." Oddly, Reed compares it to *Vision Quest*, by Terry Davis (1979), which her male students find realistic and involving, but she finds lacking in literary quality. Furthermore, she is "not particularly fond of the sexually explicit scenes" in *Vision Quest* and wishes the main character "Louden and the other teenage boys would learn to think of women as more than sex objects" (26). Like many a seventeen-year-old boy, Louden is both drawn to women's breasts and intimidated by their sexuality, and he uses crude language in his first-person narration. However, the slightly older, once-pregnant girl who moves in with him and his father and becomes Louden's lover is given a personality and supports Louden emotionally while she herself heals. The objectification of women Reed sees in *Vision Quest* is considerably less than that in *The Chocolate War*. But once again, because she sees Jerry as a rebel hero, Reed's vision is clouded and she does not see the truly distressing pictures of women in *The Chocolate War*.

7. *After the First Death* is about father-son relationships and political ideologies, but Cormier also manages to get Kate, the one adolescent female character, to feel shame and perhaps even to believe she is complicit in her own victimization and murder by the terrorists. It's not enough that Cormier gives her migraines, which mysteriously disappear after the first part of the novel. He makes her incontinent as well, a decidedly rare condition for a seventeen-year-old girl. She sees this as a weakness, her flaw, especially when her fear of the terrorists causes her to wet her pants so badly that they begin to chafe her legs. She goes to the back of the bus and removes her jeans and also her underwear, an action which the young terrorist Miro sees. She puts her jeans back on and places her underwear in her pocket. The underwear is mentioned only once afterwards, as is her incontinence, as if the underwear itself was almost causing the problem. Any intelligent girl with such a condition would be prepared by wearing, in the 1970s, a menstrual pad. I almost like *After the First Death*, as I like *I Am the Cheese*, but Cormier portrays this young woman's body as a source of betrayal and embarrassment for the female, and desire for the male.

8. Reiterating Nodelman's assertion that *The Chocolate War* is "a metaphor for the Vietnam War," Trites explains that the novel investigates "social organization and how individuals interact with that organization . . . [but] institutions are not to be trusted" (24).

Works Cited

Booth, Wayne C. *The Company We Keep: An Ethics of Fiction.* Berkeley: University of California Press, 1988.

Cadden, Michael. "The Irony of Narration in the Young Adult Novel." *Children's Literature Association Quarterly* 25.3 (2000): 146–54.

Campbell, Patricia J. "Conversing with Robert Cormier." Interview. http://www.amazon.com/exec/obidos/subst/.rt-cormier-interview/002-5432586-6379643.

———. *Presenting Robert Cormier*. Updated ed. Boston: Twayne, 1989.

The Chocolate War *and Related Readings*. Evanston, Ill.: MacDougal Littell, 1998.

Collins, Carol Jones. "Finding the Way: Morality and Young Adult Literature." In *Mosaics of Meaning: Enhancing the Intellectual Life of Young Adults Through Story*. Ed. Kay Vandegrift. Lanham, Md.: Scarecrow Press, 1996. 157–83.

Cormier, Christine. Acceptance speech for *I Am the Cheese* for the Phoenix Award. Children's Literature Association's 24th annual international conference, Omaha, June 21, 1997.

Cormier, Robert. *After the First Death*. New York: Pantheon, 1979.

———. *Beyond the Chocolate War*. New York: Alfred A. Knopf, 1985.

———. *The Chocolate War*. 1974. New York: Dell, 1986.

———. *Fade*. New York: Delacorte, 1988.

———. *I Am the Cheese*. 1977. New York: Dell, 1983.

———. *Tenderness*. New York: Delacorte, 1997.

———. *Tunes for Bears to Dance To*. New York: Delacourte, 1992.

———. *We All Fall Down*. New York: Delacorte, 1991.

Davis, Terry. *Vision Quest*. New York: Viking, 1979.

DeLuca, Geraldine, and Roni Natov. Interview. *Lion and the Unicorn* 2 (fall 1978): 109–35.

Fine, Melinda. *Habits of Mind: Struggling over Values in America's Classrooms*. San Francisco: Jossey-Bass, 1995.

Gallo, Donald R. "Reality and Responsibility: The Continuing Controversy over Robert Cormier's Books for Young Adults." In *The VOYA Reader*. Ed. Dorothy Broderick. Metuchen, N.J.: Scarecrow Press, 1990. 153–60.

Gardner, John. *On Moral Fiction*. New York: Basic Books, 1978.

Gilligan, Carol. "Prologue: Adolescent Development Reconsidered." *Mapping the Moral Domain: A Contribution of Women's Thinking to Psychological Theory and Education*. Cambridge: Harvard University Press, 1988. vii–xxxix.

Head, Patricia. "Robert Cormier and the Postmodernist Possibilities of Young Adult Fiction." *Children's Literature Association Quarterly* 21.1 (spring 1996): 28–33.

Iskander, Sylvia Patterson. "Readers, Realism, and Robert Cormier." *Children's Literature* 15 (1987): 7–18.

McCallum, Robyn. *Ideologies of Identity in Adolescent Fiction: The Dialogic Construction of Subjectivity*. New York: Garland, 1999.

MacLeod, Anne Scott. "Ice Axes: Robert Cormier and the Adolescent Novel." In *American Childhood: Essays on Children's Literature of the Nineteenth and Twentieth Centuries*. Athens: University of Georgia Press, 1994. 189–97.

Murdoch, Iris. *Metaphysics as a Guide to Morals*. London: Chatto and Windus, 1992.

Myers, Mitzi. "'No Safe Place to Run To': An Interview with Robert Cormier." *Lion and the Unicorn* 24 (2000): 445–64.

Myszor, Frank. "The See-Saw and the Bridge in Robert Cormier's *After the First Death*." *Children's Literature* 16 (1988): 77–90.

Nodelman, Perry. "Robert Cormier's *The Chocolate War*: Paranoia and Paradox." In *Stories and Society: Children's Literature in Its Social Context*. Ed. Dennis Butts. London: MacMillan, 1992. 22–36.

———. *The Pleasures of Children's Literature*. 2d ed. White Plains: Longman, 1996.

Parker, David. *Ethics, Theory and the Novel*. Cambridge: Cambridge University Press, 1994.

Rachels, James. *The Elements of Moral Philosophy*. 2d ed. New York: McGraw-Hill, 1993.

Reed, Arthea J. S. "Selecting Adolescent Literature and Avoiding Censorship." *English Journal* 81 (April 1992): 92–93.

Susina, Jan. "*The Chocolate War* and 'The Sweet Science.'" *Children's Literature in Education* 22.3 (1991): 169–77.

Trites, Roberta Seelinger. *Disturbing the Universe: Power and Repression in Adolescent Literature*. Iowa City: University of Iowa Press, 2000.

Yoshida, Junko. "The Quest for Masculinity in *The Chocolate War*: Changing Conceptions of Masculinity in the 1970s." *Children's Literature* 26 (1998): 105–22.

Power, Fear, and Children's Picture Books

Jackie E. Stallcup

One of my students in a recent children's literature course wrote a paper on Edward Gorey's *The Gashlycrumb Tinies,* an alphabet book that traces in upbeat rhythm and rhyme the gruesome deaths of twenty-six children. My student noted that its format suggests that it is a children's book: it is small, just the right size for small hands and a size that often indicates a children's book; it is short, for the supposedly short attention spans of children; it has pictures of children on every page; and, finally, it is an alphabet book, traditionally a form designed for children learning to read. But my student argued that despite these elements, *The Gashlycrumb Tinies* is an adult book because of the overt violence enacted upon children's bodies in the depictions of their deaths—deaths that in some pictures occur in the midst of ordinary daily activities. Underlying her argument were the unspoken assumptions that children would be psychologically damaged by witnessing, in print, the grisly deaths of other children and that children's books depicting violence will instill fear in their young readers and, hence, are problematic and inappropriate.

The Gashlycrumb Tinies is part of a long tradition in children's literature in which young characters meet with violent punishments and even death because they transgress social boundaries and challenge adult authority. Many eighteenth- and nineteenth-century texts were designed to frighten young readers into obedience through threatening dire punishments for disobedience. But for modern adults, books that purport to *relieve* children of their fears of everything from monsters to nightmares are preferable to the older, fear-inducing texts. Many of these modern "fear-alleviating" books are explicit attempts at bibliotherapy, designed to help children, psychologically and emotionally, by demonstrating how young characters overcome frightening situations.[1] Yet, their ideological functions are more complicated than this informal definition suggests. In fact, the varied cultural work performed by these texts reveals the many conflicting assumptions

Children's Literature 30, ed. Elizabeth Lennox Keyser and Julie Pfeiffer (Yale University Press, © 2002 Hollins University).

A is for AMY who fell down the stairs

Figure 1. Edward Gorey. Illustration from *The Gashlycrumb Tinies or, After the Outing*, copyright ©1963 and renewed 1991 by Edward Gorey, reprinted by permission of Harcourt, Inc.

adults hold regarding children. Because the overt goal of some of these modern, fear-alleviating books is to free children of fear, they appear at one level to be liberating and possibly subversive of adult power. Underlying these possibilities, however, are unspoken issues of authority and control that add layers of complexity and suggest parallels with older texts that sought to control children through implicit and explicit threats of violence.

While such threats are considered unacceptable by modern adults (as my student's reaction to *The Gashlycrumb Tinies* suggests), the goal of securing adult authority has not changed—only the means of attaining it have been inverted. Rather than invoking threats of violence to frighten children into submission, many modern picture books seek to reassure children that they have nothing to fear from imaginary dangers while at the same time demonstrating that there are very real

K is for KATE who was struck with an axe

Figure 2. Edward Gorey. Illustration from *The Gashlycrumb Tinies or, After the Outing,* copyright ©1963 and renewed 1991 by Edward Gorey, reprinted by permission of Harcourt, Inc.

dangers that only adults can defuse. Indeed, in some cases, parental control of the child's environment forms the foundation of a child's sense of security. Thus, many of these books consolidate and disseminate adult authority while diminishing the possibilities for children's empowerment and emotional growth. But this potentially oppressive pattern is not the only one offered. In some cases, fear-alleviating books offer a model in which children overcome their fear not simply through relying on adults but through developing adultlike characteristics themselves; more rarely, a book encourages the child reader to reject the adult world altogether. Alleviating children's fear, thus, is not the only goal of such texts; their subtexts reveal some of the unstated ideologies that shape our relationships with children.

There are many criteria one can use to evaluate these books to determine their literary or artistic merit. For purposes of this essay, I will focus on examining their cultural dimensions in order to isolate and illuminate the messages that they contain regarding adult-child relationships. The varying possibilities delineated in these texts reveal some of the limitations of cultural theories that represent adult-child relationships as a dichotomy characterized by power differentials. While works by theorists like Perry Nodelman and Alison Lurie are very useful in establishing how adults can be said to oppress children, such theories do not consider the broad range of ways in which adults actually interact with children or the spectrum of motivations driving such interactions. Taking a different tack in his book *Child-Loving: The Erotic Child and Victorian Culture,* James R. Kincaid deconstructs and analyzes many of the binaries that adults use to demarcate the boundary between adults and children. He notes, "If the child is not distinguished from the adult, we imagine that we are seriously threatened, threatened in such a way as to put at risk our very being, what it means to be an adult in the first place" (7). Although Kincaid proceeds to focus on issues of desire, I find the fear that he alludes to here equally fascinating. By examining our fears as they intersect with issues of childhood and by analyzing the ways in which fear is addressed in children's picture books, we can further dismantle some of the representations used to place adults and children on opposite sides of an ideological divide. Fear-alleviating books articulate a variety of models for adult-child relationships (some of which can be read as empowering for children); therefore, examining the implicit ideologies in these texts can allow us to suggest a critique of theories that portray children as inevitably subject to power wielded with veiled hostility by adults and to introduce different models for depicting the relationships between adults and children.

Adults, Children, and Fear

Modern attitudes about children and fear are firmly rooted in specific historical conceptualizations of childhood. I have shown *The Gashlycrumb Tinies* to other classes and encountered the same horrified reaction—a reaction grounded in beliefs held by many adults today. As numerous critics and historians have discussed, assumptions of purity and innocence are prevalent in modern representations of childhood.[2] As a result, we adults persist in believing that innocence is a defining aspect of childhood, and we resist giving books to children that might suggest otherwise. This attitude is also visible in the popular media, as

Charles Krauthammer's 1995 *Time* magazine essay "Hiroshima, Mon Petit" suggests. Why should we, he argues passionately, "assault [children's] innocence" and disturb their "cozy, rosy view of the world" by exposing them to such horrors as the Holocaust (80)? Such reactions suggest that we believe that fear is—or should be, in an ideal world—fundamentally alien to children, who therefore require our protection from anything that might frighten them. This attitude toward children and fear is exemplified in A. S. Neill's 1960 text *Summerhill: A Radical Approach to Child Rearing*, which delineates the child-rearing methods used at a progressive British school.[3] Neill notes: "Fear can be a terrible thing in a child's life. Fear must be entirely eliminated—fear of adults, fear of punishment, fear of disapproval, fear of God. Only hate can flourish in an atmosphere of fear" (124). Of course, Neill is discussing fear in humans in general, not just in children. But his point is that one should never use fear to enforce authority over a child: "Goodness that depends on fear of hell or fear of the policeman or fear of punishment is not goodness at all—it is simply cowardice" (129). Instead of using fear, Neill advocated allowing children the freedom to "grow in the natural way" (110), shaped by a combination of parental common sense and what he termed "self-regulation" on the part of the child (104–6). Obviously, Neill's ideas provide an extreme example that has fueled many a conservative fire, but they also are indicative of general modern attitudes about children and fear. Numerous parenting manuals currently available seek to reduce fear in children's lives, while articles on helping children cope with common childhood fears are widely disseminated in both scholarly journals and general interest magazines.[4]

In spite of the modern rejection of fear as a child-rearing tactic, control issues have long been—and remain—an essential part of adult-child relationships. As critics have suggested, from at least the mid-eighteenth century through today, adults have used children's literature as a means of transmitting ideology, repressing children, and assuring adult mastery—often through inducing fear.[5] While methods of governing children have shifted with changing perceptions of children's nature, issues of control, penetration, surveillance, and the indoctrination of the dominant ideology provide the foundation for children's literature. In his article "Second Thoughts on Socialization through Literature for Children," Jack Zipes argues that one of the major organizing features of children's books is the socialization process:

Literature for children is not children's literature by and for children in their behalf. It never was and never will be. Literature for children is script coded by adults for the information and internalization of children which must meet the approbation of adults. . . . It is the adult author's symbolically social act intended to influence and perhaps control the future destiny of culture. At heart are notions of civility and civilization. Adults who write literature for children want to cultivate raw sensibilities, to civilize unruly passions, and to reveal unsocial forces hostile to civilization (19).

Zipes's comments suggest an interesting and subtle reason for our use of fear to control children; that is, because we fear children ourselves. We fear them because they appear to be fundamentally different from us. We don't always understand them, we cannot always control them, and they sometimes do the very things that we want to do, but cannot or will not do, such as act upon antisocial impulses or act out angry or hate-filled fantasies.[6]

Adult fear of the potentially anarchic power that resides in children is embedded in many texts. Novels like *Lord of the Flies* (1954), plays like *The Bad Seed* (1955), and movies like *Village of the Damned* (1960), *Children of the Corn* (1984), and *The Good Son* (1993) all exhibit radically uncontrolled children who pose physical threats not only to specific adults in their vicinity but also to general social stability. These thrillers foreground adult fears of what would happen should children slip away from adult-centered socialization, while such characters as Bart Simpson and the children of "South Park" provide more comedic representations of children who thumb their noses at adult values. Perhaps it is not surprising that despite their focus on child characters, such works trigger heated discussions of their suitability for young viewers, often centering on the concern that Krauthammer expresses: will exposure to such characters strip real children of their veils of innocence? We should note, however, that because of real life experiences, many children's worldview is already far from "rosy" or "cozy." Hence, these discussions are just as likely to offer insight into adult fears as they are to uncover the dangers to children's innocence. Other questions lurk beneath the surface of such cultural concerns: will watching these shows or reading these books cause children to unleash the potential anarchy that resides within themselves? What will be the eventual outcome to adult systems of power? And, at the most personal level: what will my kids do to me if I let them watch these shows or read these books? That this is a genuine cultural concern is attested to by the fact that articles and books abound on the dangers posed by children who run amok.[7]

Adult fear of children may be the impetus behind a strand of child-rearing theory that stands in opposition to those who reject fear as a means of discipline. James Dobson's child-rearing manuals offer a clarion call for a return to more overt uses of fear in commanding respect from a child. He strongly cautions that he does not condone abuse, but he argues that physical punishment should be used to create fear of consequences in order to squash defiance. Dobson's examples of the moments at which spanking is appropriate suggest that his call for corporal punishment is rooted in a fear of the consequences to adults when children defy adult authority and seek to control their parents through asserting their own desires.[8] First published in 1970, *Dare to Discipline* was reissued in a revised and expanded edition in 1992 as *The New Dare to Discipline* with a headline on the cover trumpeting "more than 3,500,000 copies sold." Very few associations or formal publications still advocate corporal punishment of children, but the fact that Dobson's book has proven so popular suggests that there remains a groundswell of public support for such methods.

Our modern conflicted attitude towards children and fear, represented by these two extremes of Neill and Dobson, has a long history of debate in child-rearing manuals,[9] but before the twentieth century, authors of books for children were far less squeamish about using threats of violence to induce respect through fear of severe consequences. In fact, harsh punishments for fairly benign childhood behavior (running in the street, quarreling with siblings, sucking one's thumb) are common in children's books of the eighteenth and nineteenth centuries.[10] The fear of consequences that these books seek to inculcate in child readers mirrors the unspoken fear felt by the adult authors and illustrators: What, indeed, might happen should children run madly through the streets? Obviously, at one level, the children's lives would be endangered. But at another level, the anarchy that could spread from such unchecked children might also be dangerous for adult social order. Both aspects of "fear" permeate these texts; adult fear of children leads directly to the use of fear to control children's behavior.

My point is not that we should allow children to run amok nor that we should refrain from warning children about common dangers. Ensuring (as far as possible) children's safety is obviously a necessary and important part of our jobs as adults so that children can grow up as healthy and safe as possible. But our interactions with children also carry ideological weight along with the purely practical concerns of everyday safety. That is, there are many ways to ensure children's safety and the methods that we choose expose our assumptions about children—assumptions that often benefit adults. We can uncover these ideological implications by examining *how* we seek to keep children safe. Investigating my students' reactions to Gorey's book is instructive. Gorey depicts some of the very things that eighteenth- and nineteenth-century writers were also depicting, and, in general, he portrays the deaths of the children no more graphically than these writers. Our attitudes about children, however, have shifted dramatically and as a result, what was once considered highly suitable, even necessary, for children is no longer considered even remotely appropriate.[11]

In fact, far from attempting to frighten children into submission, many late-twentieth-century picture books overtly attempt to alleviate various forms of children's fears, appearing to empower children (on one level at least) through helping them overcome a misplaced or misdirected fear. But in some modern fear-alleviating picture books, the positive message is undercut by a fear-inducing subtext with parallels to eighteenth- and nineteenth-century texts. In *Ghost's Hour, Spook's Hour* (1987), author Eve Bunting and illustrator Donald Carrick use fear-inducing text and imagery to encourage children to turn to adults for safety and security. The book opens on a dark, frightening night as a young boy creeps out of his bed and wanders around his house, worried because the electricity is out and his parents seem to have disappeared. All the pictures in this first section are created with dark, dreary colors, and there are many shadows in which anything could be hiding. The illustrations of the boy and his dog emphasize their anxiety and fear. On one page, the dog cowers back, reluctant to leave the bedroom, while the boy, though determined (as we can see from the forward slant of his body), fights against a fear that compels him to twist his body forward as if leaning against a great force. The other pictures depict his smallness and insignificance in this huge, dark, shadowy house. The text also contributes to the frightening tone; for example, the boy perceives the dining room furniture as threatening and animal-like: "Our table seemed monstrously big. Chairs, humpbacked, clawed and crouched around it" (n. pag.).

The climax of terror occurs when the boy sees what he thinks is a ghost but is actually only his own reflection. His mirrored image functions as a symbolic representation of the dangers he himself embodies:

Figure 3. Donald Carrick. From *Ghost's Hour, Spook's Hour* by Eve Bunting. Illustration copyright © 1987 by Donald Carrick. Reprinted by permission of Clarion Books, an imprint of Houghton Mifflin Company. All rights reserved.

to the adult world, the only thing truly dangerous in this boy's house is the potential for anarchy that resides within *him*. The book thus subtly suggests that this is what he (and by extension the child reader) should fear. That point made, the following page shows his father bursting in from the next room. The doorway in which the father stands and the father himself are infused with a comforting sense of security through the warm yellow light radiating all around, while outside the doorway (where the boy is) lies in darkness. Once the boy joins his father and mother in their downstairs "nest," the whole room glows warmly with the light of the parents' candle, and they loom on either side of the boy, touching his small, now-relaxed body in order to comfort him (figure 3).

The next two pages show the boy tucked up in the couch with his parents by his side, and though the candle has been snuffed, the picture is still infused with an orange-yellow brown much warmer than the drab browns of the previous pages, emphasizing the overall message that security lies with one's parents. The first half of the book is so threatening and scary that it serves to drive this message home by offering a vision of what life would be like without the parents: lonely, frightening, and dark. The book does not merely seek to assuage fear, as a shallow reading might suggest, but to actually inculcate it first, creating a sharp contrast with the feeling of relief created when we see that the parents haven't actually abandoned the boy. This technique demonstrates one of the more subtle ways in which we adults are still using fear to control children's impulses. Certainly there is no hint that the child could run riot through the house, scaring away spooks by the very exuberance of his being. Such a depiction might strike adults as sending a dangerous message to children because it would suggest that one does not need one's parents for security and that one can run about the house at night without fear of reprisal.

This book demonstrates that despite our modern discomfort with "frightening" texts, we still are not above using fear (albeit in more subtle ways than in the past) to control children. Our slippery and inconsistent attitudes toward fear suggest that our assumptions about children are just that: assumptions, not an unchanging, substantiated core truth that must be accepted. Thus, they reveal the varying facets of our shifting ideological stances regarding the concept of "childhood." As Perry Nodelman argues in his 1992 essay "The Other: Orientalism, Colonialism, and Children's Literature," adults seek to oppress children through invoking a stable concept of childhood, unchanging and ultimately fully knowable only by adults. This "knowing" places adults into a position of mastery over children.[12] But as Nodelman suggests, if we acknowledge the changes that have taken place in our conceptions of children, we can then examine them to discern the ideological impetus behind such changes. If the idea that children need to be free—and freed—from fear is not a "truth" about childhood, but merely a modern concept, then several questions become relevant: Why do we have this concept? What does it do for us as adults? What are the implications for our relationships with children? Just as feminists have had to distinguish between apparent and actual empowerment for women, a critic who examines these modern picture books that seek to relieve children of their fears must also determine how much power—and what kind of power—is actually invested in the child reader. In some contemporary picture books, such as *Ghost's Hour, Spook's Hour,* very little power is invested in the child reader, as they either are frightened into obeying adult rules or strongly encouraged to fear their own impulses and to seek safety in a space created by adult authority. Hence these books and others like them reinforce adult control over children without offering children any kind of personal empowerment or emotional growth.

Fear, Power, and Subversive Children's Literature

If we fear children and wish to control them through fear (even despite cultural rhetoric to the contrary), then how do we interpret fear-alleviating books that do *not* contain fear-inducing subtexts? One possibility is that these books are functioning as subversive children's literature. In her 1990 book *Don't Tell the Grown-Ups*, Alison Lurie argues that while most children's literature, particularly that preferred by adults, is designed to inculcate adult values, there are what she calls the "sacred texts of childhood, whose authors had not forgotten what it was like to be a child" (x). Lurie contends that "these books, and others like them, recommended—even celebrated—daydreaming, disobedience, answering back, running away from home, and concealing one's private thoughts and feelings from unsympathetic grown-ups. They overturned adult pretensions and made fun of adult institutions, including school and family. In a word, they were subversive" (x). It would seem that a book designed to assuage fear and even empower children might fit into this description. The case is far more complicated, however, because issues of subversiveness and empowerment become slippery when we try to employ them together. The concepts do not dovetail neatly; one text might subvert adult social conventions without offering the child a modicum of empowerment while another may articulate adult values that ultimately can be read as empowering rather than oppressing children. Examples of both of these variants can be found in fear-alleviating texts.

Of all of the picture books examined here, Ed Emberley's *Go Away, Big Green Monster!* (1992) comes closest to fitting Lurie's definition of subversive children's literature. Emberley utilizes an ingenious die-cut technique to make a monster appear and then disappear piece by piece as the child turns the pages. As the monster gradually appears, each page is entirely black, with pieces cut out that reveal a colored page later in the book. Each cut out gives shape to part of the monster. For example, one page reads "scraggly purple hair" (n. pag.) and holes in the shape of scraggly hair are cut into the black page to reveal a purple page later in the book. As the reader turns the pages, more and more parts of the monster become visible. This is a spooky effect, as if the monster is peering out from a darkened room and, like the Cheshire Cat, slowly appearing. Then, after the monster is fully revealed, the text reads "But . . . YOU DON'T SCARE ME! So GO AWAY, scraggly purple hair!" (n. pag., emphasis in original) and as the reader continues through the book, the monster is deconstructed as the colored pages take over from the black pages, so that "scraggly purple hair" becomes, simply, a purple page. The immediate effect of the change from black to colored pages is one of relief and cheerfulness, which is heightened, page by page, as the monster's parts disappear.

Adults are entirely absent from the text; there is no one besides the monster and the reader. The first few times a child encounters this book, a parent or other adult might read it aloud, but the sentences are simple and closely tied to the illustrations so that children should quickly be able to read it themselves. The language of the text *is* important at the level of subversion: the comment midway through the book "you don't scare me" clearly represents the child's voice, and all of the sentences following this comment are in the imperative mood, a powerful tool as any parent can attest—one that brooks no protest. This also creates a sense of the book as a "script," telling the reader what to say to the monster on each page and thus tightly linking the reader with the voice of the text. Thus, the children reading the book seize power over the monster and retain that power both through the voice and through engineering the monster's disappearance. At the end of the book, the text reads, "and DON'T COME BACK," and the last line (printed suggestively in "monster green") adds, "Until I say so." This suggests the power of the child over the monster: she can make it come or go at will; and the potential for subversiveness: she might just summon the monster back. . . . One might ask, for what purpose? This last line of *Go Away, Big Green Monster!* suggests the myriad possibilities available to the brave child who invites the forbidden and forbidding monster to come back and play.

What does this conclusion suggest about the relationship between adulthood and childhood? If a monster can be defined as something ungoverned by rules, then this linking of child and monster in play suggests an alliance resistant to adult attempts at control. In his 1992 book *Language and Ideology in Children's Fiction,* John Stephens situates certain children's texts within the form of carnivalesque, arguing: "carnival in children's literature is grounded in a playfulness which situates itself in positions of nonconformity. It expresses opposition to authoritarianism and seriousness" (121). The conclusion of *Go Away, Big Green Monster!* engages these elements by implying that instead of rejecting or vanquishing the monster, the child can summon and play with the monster at her will. The book encourages children to embrace rather than reject the "monster" that resides in all of us: the impulse to anarchy that we must control in order to fully participate in mutual interactive social relations. The equivalent impulse in *Ghost's Hour, Spook's Hour* would be for the boy to run riot through the house, romping with whatever "ghosts" he could imagine and embracing the image he glimpses in the mirror as part of himself, instead of rejecting it as alien and frightening. Stephens further argues: "play is [a] human activity liable to carry heavy ideological markings. It is the opposite of 'seriousness,' and can thus be devalued; it often signifies the innocence and happiness of childhood, and is therefore temporary and transient; it represents moments of freedom, and is (therefore) subject to adult attempts to impart order, structure and meaning to it; it is one means through which a child explores the world, and so is harnessed for educational purposes and is appropriated by adult culture" (186–87). But in *Go Away, Big Green Monster!* the lack of adult authority inside and outside of the text frees both child and monster; they can have their "moments of freedom" and exploration without being subject to such adult interference in their play. The child herself is in control, yet, paradoxically, that control is aimed at unleashing a potentially subversive impulse to playfulness that is linked to the scariness and indeterminacy of the monster. The fact that this time of play remains always in the future and under the control of the child suggests a sense of indeterminacy regarding the child's potential growth into maturity: she can play or not play—she chooses the path. Thus, this book is subversive and liberating in the sense of allowing the child to escape or repudiate (if only briefly and through fantasy) the bonds imposed by adults on children, on children's play, and on the very heart of "childhood"—which is, in part, the refusal to "act like an adult" by curbing one's impulses.[13]

But, for the child reader, "liberating" does not necessarily equate with "empowering." While *Go Away, Big Green Monster!* creates a subversive space for the child to resist adult control, it does not force or even encourage her to reject the ultimately subordinate role of "child at play." Thus, although this role is subversive of many adult values and concerns (particularly that of self-control), it maintains and even strengthens a division between adults and children that (as Nodelman argues) is disempowering for children. Henry Jenkins points out in his introduction to *The Children's Culture Reader* (1998) that "embracing a politics of appropriation and resistance runs the risk of romanticizing child's play as the seeds of cultural revolution" (30). In other words, one cannot simply valorize subversiveness; doing so is merely another form of romanticizing and oppressing children. Hence, while *Go Away, Big Green Monster!* offers a model of resistance to adult power, it does not necessarily offer empowerment to the child reader. Because the anarchic play celebrated by the book remains childlike, we must look to other fear-alleviating books to explore how they might empower children within our culture.

Peer Group Power?

Picture books that suggest turning to one's peer group for reassurance rather than to parents or other adults might subvert certain adult conceptions about children as well as offer readers visions of a world in which they do not have to depend upon adults. In *Franklin and the Thunderstorm* (1998), written by Paulette Bourgeois and illustrated by Brenda Clark, Franklin (a turtle) is afraid of thunderstorms but his friends help him to overcome his phobia. Instead of trying to invoke fear in the children reading the book (as *Ghost's Hour, Spook's Hour* does), the author and illustrator do not make either the pictures or the text scary. Even on the darkest page, Franklin's colorful attire offers cheerfulness and comfort, and although Franklin is frightened of the storm, his friends are excited by it, imagining funny explanations for the thunder and lightning. So the book is not engaged in frightening the child further and even appears to suggest that one can turn to one's peer group for support instead of turning to adults: his friends' stories make Franklin literally come out of his shell and finally laugh about the storm.

The adult world, however, permeates the background of the book, providing a secure space for the children. When the children decide to run to the tree house instead of inside Fox's home as the storm breaks, Fox's mother appears and makes them come into the house. The implication is that they are not safe within their own "child" space outside the boundaries of the home; they are only safe within the adult space, where Fox's mother can light candles and bring them food and drink. She creates warmth and security, signified here (as in *Ghost's Hour, Spook's Hour*) with a warm yellow glow (figure 4).

Figure 4. Brenda Clark. Illustration from *Franklin and the Thunderstorm* by Paulette Bourgeois and Brenda Clark, used by permission of Kids Can Press Ltd. Illustration copyright © Brenda Clark Illustrator Inc., 1998.

The book does note that there are real dangers associated with storms, and it links those dangers (the tree being struck by lightning) with the children's wish to be in their own space. Despite the emphasis on children helping one another to soothe their fears, it is the adult world that provides the safe matrix within which the children can do this. This reinforces adult dominance by suggesting to children that they put themselves in danger when they chose to step outside the boundaries set by adults.

Again, I am not suggesting that we allow children to place themselves at risk; it is part of our job as adults to protect children from hazards that they have not yet learned to respect. Children are not born with the knowledge that playing in a tree house during an electrical storm can be deadly, and neither the characters nor real children should engage in such a dangerous activity. But is it possible to convey such important information without simply subjecting children to adult authority? Letty Cottin Pogrebin wrestles with this problem in her 1983 book, *Family Politics: Love and Power on an Intimate Frontier.* After discussing sharing responsibility with children, she notes:

> But, someone is sure to say, families cannot allow three-year-olds to refuse to wear seat belts, four-year-olds to decide the menu, or eight-year-olds to spend money at will. Surely parents' greater maturity and the wisdom born of experience entitles adults to exercise authority over children. Yes, of course. Giving children reasonable rules of safety and consideration, guidance, support, and protection, and establishing moral and intellectual standards are the fundamental responsibilities of parenthood. That is what a loving parent or caregiver *does.* But *how* the job is done is the question. (102, emphasis in original)

Similarly, I am not arguing that adults should let children engage in dangerous activities in order not to oppress them; this could obviously result in parental neglect or worse. But not all picture books address such issues in the same way, and the varying methods reveal underlying agendas. Picture books, like other media, contain embedded messages, as Stephens notes: "every book has an implicit ideology . . . usually in the form of assumed social structures and habits of thought." He further argues that a book with underlying (rather than overt) socializing agendas "can be the more powerful vehicle for an ideology because implicit, and therefore invisible, ideological positions are invested with legitimacy that things are simply 'so'" (9).[14]

On a practical level then, in *Franklin and the Thunderstorm,* one can admire the goal of ridding children of fear and admit that it would be dangerous for Franklin and his friends to play in a tree house during a lightning storm. But the way this decision is made and disseminated is grounded implicitly in a particular, hierarchized view of adult-child relationships. As Jacqueline Rose points out in *The Case of Peter Pan* (1984), the child characters in children's literature are not real children but are a means for the adult to try to "secure the child who is outside the book, the one who does not come so easily within its grasp" (2). In *Franklin and the Thunderstorm,* the text does not merely communicate safety practices to young readers but also imbues them with a particular perspective on the proper roles of adults and children. Because that perspective is embedded in the text and pictures implicitly, the reader is encouraged to simply accept a hierarchical view of the adult-child relationship. The text could disseminate the same basic safety message in numerous ways without adhering so tightly to this implicit ideology. The other children know about storms, judging by their comments elsewhere in the text. Therefore, one of Franklin's friends could deliver the information about the danger of playing in the tree house as the youngsters quickly return to safety. I am not suggesting that this change would create an improved or preferable plot in any literary sense. Instead, my scenario demonstrates that the same basic safety information can be presented in a way that suggests a very different cultural agenda. In this scenario, the children would have a voice and would be participating in decisions rather than simply being subject to them. Hence, they would be developing a sense of growing autonomy and maturity. In *Franklin and the Thunderstorm,* the way that the information is offered sets up the adult in the role of benevolent protector and thus reinforces adult power and control. To have children who know about storms pass along the information without the intervention of an adult would allow them to start taking responsibility for themselves, and this is not quite what the author and illustrator of this book seem to want to achieve, preferring to infantilize the children and reinforce adult power.

In other words, to paraphrase Pogrebin, it is not so much the decision that is made, but *how* it is made and who gets to make it that matter. The relationships between adults and children depicted in *Ghost's Hour, Spook's Hour* and *Franklin and the Thunderstorm* are not designed to empower children by aiding them in developing adult characteristics. Instead the child characters (and, by extension, the readers) are encouraged to reject and even fear their own autonomy and to depend upon adults for comfort, security, and decision making. Hence, they are discouraged from unleashing their subversive impulse to "play" (as *Go Away, Big Green Monster!* encourages them to do) and also are deprived of the opportunity to develop maturity, initiative, and independence by coping with frightening situations on their own. The characters and readers are encouraged to remain childlike in their continuing reliance on adult authority to provide safety and security. Therefore, these books are neither empowering nor subversive but instead reinscribe traditional lines demarcating adult power and authority.

Becoming an Adult

If children's safety and security depends upon rejecting the very core of themselves (as implied in *Ghost's Hour*), then they cannot grow in independence or even in partnership with the adult figures in their lives. This is a fundamentally unrealistic mode of viewing the world; the cure for childhood, of course, is adulthood, and the fact that children do become adults thoroughly complicates the discussion. Although Nodelman's conception of the adult-child relationship is valuable because it reveals how we consciously or unconsciously oppress children, his argument depends upon a problematic analogy comparing children with adult colonized subjects, using Edward Said's concept of "Orientalism" as a springboard for analyzing how we interact with children. But unlike colonizers and colonized subjects, children and adults are, in fact, fundamentally different in important ways. Very young children require someone at least marginally older to help them survive; as well, crucial cultural skills must be acquired within a social context from those who have already mastered them. Equating children with colonized subjects means defining adult power as essentially negative and oppressive. This fails to take into account myriad adult agendas that stretch across the spectrum of adult-child interactions. Defining adults as oppressors leaves no room for the acts of love and nurture that children absolutely must obtain in order to become fully empowered in our social system.

Nodelman acknowledges that children must become adults and that this is a point at which his ideas diverge from Said's, but he does not explore how children can become fully functioning members of society without adult intervention, and he suggests at the end of his essay that even helping children to understand the strategies that adults use to oppress them is yet another form of colonization (34). But this conflation of "help" and "colonize" makes it difficult to see how adults are to socialize children—what options remain? This is a fundamental dislocation between Said's theory of Orientalism and Nodelman's application of Orientalism to relationships between adults and children. Initial socialization into a cultural group cannot be conflated with pressing a new social order onto subjects who are already embedded in a culture. Adult colonized subjects are already part of a social system, and colonization disrupts that system in an attempt to replace it with what the colonizers perceive as a better one. Children who remain unsocialized are not in an equivalent position. Studies of feral children, such as Kaspar Hauser, Genie, and the Wild Boy of Aveyron, suggest that if socialization is neglected, then children are not liberated from adult society but are disempowered by their inability to participate in normal social relationships.[15]

Children need to and will become adults. As A. S. Neill argues in the 1992 edition of *Summerhill School,* "No one really wants to remain a child. The desire for power urges children on" (52) and Beverly Cleary concurs, noting that "to grow up is the ambition of normal children" (562). In this context, Homi Bhabha's concept of mimicry helps to differentiate the colonizer-colonized relationship from that of adults and children. Bhabha argues "the authority of that mode of colonial discourse that I have called mimicry is . . . stricken by an indeterminacy: mimicry emerges as the representation of a difference that is itself a process of disavowal" (126). Hence, within the context of colonization, the value of the "mimic man" in defining the dominant culture lies in the difference that must never be erased: "to be Anglicized," Bhabha points out, "is *emphatically* not to be English" (128, emphasis in original). The adult colonized subject approaches similarity to the colonizer but, by definition, can never become the colonizer.[16] The child, on the other hand, must ultimately fully negotiate the barrier between childhood and adulthood. To do anything less implies a failure of control on the part of adults, as well as the potential for an end of adulthood as we know and value it. In opposition to the mimic man who, theoretically, can never become the colonizer, the child must eventually become the adult. Hence, the stakes for adults are very different from those for colonizers in Said's and Bhabha's concept. It is to our benefit for children to become adults and it is to the benefit of children as well.[17]

A striking set of analogies created by C. S. Lewis illustrates two approaches to accounting for differences between adults and children. In *The Abolition of Man* (1943), Lewis compares two methods of education, using metaphors to illustrate their difference. The old way of education (which he prefers) "dealt with its pupils as grown birds deal with young birds when they teach them to fly: the new deals with them more as the poultry-keeper deals with young birds—making them thus or thus for purposes of which the birds know nothing" (436–37). These images point to the problem at the heart of the adult-child relationship: do we define our interactions with children as a continuum involving potential equals or as a hierarchy in which adults are empowered at the expense of children? The second approach assumes a difference of *kind* and results in a hierarchical relationship that defines adults and children as "different" and that places adults in charge while reducing children to the level of beasts. In contrast, the first approach assumes a difference merely of *degree,* with adults invested in the success of children because of defining them as "like" adults.

Lewis's analogies reveal the heart of the problem of comparing children to colonized subjects. Bhabha argues that the colonizer-colonized relationship depends upon the fact that the colonized subject can never become the colonizer. This presumes a difference in kind as the basis for the colonizing project and results in a fundamental dislocation between what is perceived as best for the two groups. But while many parents and educators would defend themselves vehemently on the grounds that they abide by the first representation, Nodelman and other theorists argue that despite this perception, our relationships with children too often partake of elements of the second. Perhaps it is fair to conclude that both representations are at work in varying levels. With this in mind, Mary Louise Pratt's work in colonial and exploration discourse suggests a more fruitful means of conceptualizing the complexities of adult-child relationships than Said's and Bhabha's theories offer. Pratt deconstructs the colonizer-colonized dichotomy in her 1992 book *Imperial Eyes: Travel Writing and Transculturation,* creating the concept of "contact zones" to explore the complex and diverse relationships between subjects of different cultures. She argues: "A 'contact' perspective emphasizes how subjects are constituted in and by their relations to each other. It treats the relations among colonizers and colonized . . . not in terms of separateness or apartheid, but in terms of copresence, interaction, interlocking understandings and practices" (7). Like Bhabha and Said, Pratt emphasizes the fundamentally conflictual nature of the colonizer-colonized relationship, noting that such cultures often function in "highly asymmetrical relations of domination and subordination" (4) and that their contact usually involves "conditions of coercion, radical inequality, and intractable conflict" (6). Pratt's concept of the contact zone, however, also allows for a wide range of possible interactive relationships between subjects. If we map this idea onto the conceptual framework surrounding adult-child relationships, we can conceive of the possibility for a spectrum of interactions between adults and children, even as we draw away from a dichotomy that insists, problematically, upon an unbridgeable gulf between adults and children. Thus, we can acknowledge and address the troubling, asymmetrical power relationships between adults and children and, at the same time, explore the possibility of sharing power with children in mutually beneficial ways.

Less oppressive representations of the relationship between adulthood and childhood are enacted in certain fear-alleviating picture books, which take a very different approach from that of *Ghost's Hour, Spook's Hour* by acknowledging the inevitability of children's growth. Far from simply relieving children's fear by encouraging them to rely on adults, these books model methods for children to overcome fears on their own by encouraging them to access adult language and behavior. These books are not subversive in the sense of rejecting or critiquing the adult world; instead, they encourage the child to become self-empowered through developing adult-order initiative. In his 1995 text *Five Ugly Monsters,* Tedd Arnold parodies the familiar rhyme of the five little monkeys to reveal how a young boy overcomes his fear of the monsters who jump on his bed. Each time the monsters appear (in decreasing increments), the boy calls the doctor and then holds out the phone while the doctor shouts (with increasing irritation and anger), "No more monsters jumping on the bed." The monsters scurry away each time. Despite a few scary illustrations, this book is not designed to frighten children into submission as *Ghost's Hour, Spook's Hour* seems to be. The opening endpapers and the first page are a bit threatening: the boy is in bed, surrounded by eyeballs that peer at him from hiding places. The tension this creates is heightened abruptly on the next page, when five of the monsters erupt from hiding and encircle the terrified boy. But the tension is diffused on the next page as he leaps safely out of bed while the monsters, now uninterested in him, jump playfully on the bed, looking so silly that one cannot be scared of them. They have soft rounded curves, chubby cheeks, no teeth and seem designed to alleviate fear rather than induce it. There is a lesson here, but Arnold does not scare the reader into learning it.

In the boy's reaction, we can see that he has absorbed one concept already: racing to the phone, he turns immediately to the adult world to solve his problem. Just as in *Ghost's Hour, Spook's Hour,* the adult world is symbolically coded as comforting by the invitingly glowing lamp by the telephone that connects him, via an umbilical-like cord, to the doctor. But the boy now needs to develop a more mature method for dealing with his fears in order to model such behavior for the readers. We see a gradual, mirrored transformation in the boy and the doctor. The boy's terror is slowly transformed to cockiness as each time the doctor makes the monsters go away. Simultaneously, the doctor

Figure 5. Tedd Arnold. From *Five Ugly Monsters* by Tedd Arnold. Published by Cartwheel Books, a division of Scholastic Inc. Copyright © 1995 by Tedd Arnold. All rights reserved. Used by permission of Scholastic.

grows increasingly annoyed at the interruptions to his sleep. The climatic moment comes when the doctor, in a fury, throws his phone out the window, breaking the connection with the boy—a separation symbolically enacted by the severing of the phone cord. The next page displays the moment of crisis. The doctor is comfortably asleep, totally unconcerned with the boy's plight, while the boy is shocked and dismayed (figure 5). But the boy negotiates the next step successfully: he assumes the voice of authority for himself. With a determined look on his face, he hangs up the phone as the text notes, "then I said," and on the following page his words are printed in a large banner across the top of a two-page spread: "No more monsters jumping on the bed!" The terrified monsters flee for good and the closing endpapers show the boy quite happily asleep with nary a monster in sight.

Here is a boy who has learned that he doesn't need adults to banish his fears after all—potentially a very empowering message for the boy and the readers, encouraging them to assume responsibility for themselves. Still, we must note that in finding his courage, the boy echoes the voice of the adult. He develops a sense of security by participating in the adult realm, but the goal of the book is to encourage the child to assimilate through merely mimicking adult language. This mimicry on the part of the boy returns us, problematically, to the issue of colonization. Frantz Fanon discusses the oppressive uses of language in *Black Skin, White Masks,* arguing: "Every colonized people . . . finds itself face to face with the language of the civilizing nation; that is, with the culture of the mother country. The colonized is elevated above his jungle status in proportion to his adoption of the mother country's cultural standards" (18). In other words, according to Fanon, a colonized subject is elevated in the eyes of the oppressor by his adoption of the language of the dominant culture and by his ability to assimilate into this culture. But he goes on to argue that regardless of this mastery of language, the colonized can never be seen as anything but Other. Assimilation can only be attempted, never fully achieved, and is accompanied by high psychological and cultural costs. Fanon notes that "the fact that the newly returned Negro adopts a language different from that of the group into which he was born is evidence of a dislocation, a separation" (25).

Again, this is where a comparison between adult colonized subjects and children breaks down: language can be used to hail colonized subjects into place, while adoption of the dominant language implies a separation from their original identities. But this separation, so problematic for colonized subjects, is of essential importance to children. Retaining their own language would be an imprisonment in the childhood state, just as colonized subjects are imprisoned by their original language. Unlike colonized subjects, children *must* learn to utilize the language of the dominant group because they must eventually, systematically, imperceptibly become one with it. Thus, the boy in *Five Ugly Monsters* is empowered in the sense that he is moving toward maturity by taking the initiative and driving the monsters out of his room. However, he has no words of his own to express independence, and thus he remains dependent upon adults to offer him the words needed to secure his safety and well-being. As Roderick McGillis notes in "Postcolonialism, Children, and Their Literature" (1997), the "older generation might encourage children to speak, but it does so by expecting them to speak its words, to pass on its wisdom, to perpetuate its vision of the world" (10). In *Five Ugly Monsters,* the monsters, with their anarchic silliness and their propensity for the forbidden, also symbolize that which is dangerously childlike in the boy. One might argue that it is subversive for the boy to take charge of his nightmares and send them away himself without the doctor. But the repetitive plot structure strongly suggests that the doctor is modeling appropriate adult behavior, and the climax of the book comes not when the boy rejects this — for he doesn't — but when he embraces it with all of his being; when he validates the power of the adult world by infusing himself with it; when, in short, he begins to become "one of us."

In other fear-alleviating books, child characters move even further along the path to maturity, independence, and adulthood. They may be imitating adult behavior, but they do so in order to set aside disempowering elements of childhood as they shoulder the burden of responsibility for themselves and others. Frances in Maggie Smith's *There's a Witch Under the Stairs* (1991), for example, is empowered by assuming the mantle of adulthood. A mean and scary witch lives under her cellar stairs, and, one day, Frances is forced to go down the stairs and face the witch by herself. For security, she takes her stuffed elephant, Ellie, with her but inadvertently drops Ellie right under the stairs where the witch resides. Ellie's plight compels Frances to gather her courage and confront the witch. She goes to the cellar, equipped with weaponry and armor, only to find that the witch has disappeared, leaving Ellie behind. In the final picture, the witch trudges off with her belongings, presumably to find another cellar to inhabit.

Frances's empowerment is a transformation that develops over a two-page spread of illustrations. As she races around gathering up clothing and tools, her worried and fearful expression gradually changes to one of determination and anger. On the next page, we are introduced to the new and improved Frances, decked out in a witch-hunting outfit gathered from both the adult world and her own. She has her stuffed snake and her Halloween mask, but she also has her father's tie and her mother's colander, as well as a broom and flashlight (figure 6).

Through her outfit and her protective attitude toward Ellie, Frances emulates adults, shouldering their roles as she dons their external trappings. Other aspects of both text and illustration also subtly emphasize this shift in Frances. Early in her quest to banish the witch, she makes a special "witch's brew" out in her sandbox. It has "everything in it. Nine gum balls. Two bottles of slime. One cup of dust" (n. pag.). Coded as child's play by the outdoor location, the sandbox, and the ridiculous ingredients, this method of dispelling the witch is ineffective, suggesting that Frances will be powerless as long as she continues to remain a child. After she has vanquished the witch, we see her inside the house getting ready for a celebration of the witch's departure. She is in the kitchen wearing a dress instead of play clothes and the recipe ingredients are those found in a real cake; that is, she is participating in the adult world, taking on an adult task, using adult ingredients. In the background, the witch is disappearing behind a hill with her witch's pot, her broom and her knapsack full of belongings. In these

Figure 6. Maggie Smith. From *There's a Witch Under the Stairs* by Maggie Smith. Copyright © 1991 by Maggie Smith. Used by permission of HarperCollins Publishers.

illustrations, the witch is the symbol of the anarchy that is implicit in the very idea of childhood, which must be subdued if we are to fully accept adult tasks and responsibilities. In fact, if we read the witch as symbolic of the dangerous propensities of childhood, then the message of this book (just as in *Ghost's Hour, Spook's Hour*) is that children should be frightened of this potential within themselves. In this book, however, Frances is encouraged not to turn to adults for safety, but to actually take on adult roles.[18] Conquering and routing these impulses is cause, as we see here, for celebration.

The Boy and the Cloth of Dreams (1994), written by Jenny Koralek and illustrated by James Mayhew, moves the child reader even further along the road to independence and self-reliance. A young boy has long been protected as he sleeps by a "cloth of dreams" sewn for him by his grandmother, but when the cloth tears, nightmares enter his sleep and he must find a way to repair the cloth in order to end the nightmares. The cloth represents the adult protection that surrounds the boy when he is very young, whereas the new hole suggests that he is beginning to realize that adults cannot protect him from everything. He is now ready to move to the next step: sharing responsibility for his well-being with an adult. His grandmother is willing to fix the cloth of dreams for him but insists that he must collect the materials. When he forces himself to overcome his fears, he is able to gather the materials needed and, hence, become engaged in the production of the protective cloth and, by extension, in the production of authority.

In the illustrations, the boy must make a "dark crossing" to reach the light-filled safety of his grandmother's room, but his quest does not end with his dash for the security of adult space. Instead, his grandmother sends him back out: he must leave her behind on his quest for maturity. On the page that illustrates this movement, his grandmother stands enveloped in light at the bottom of the staircase the boy is climbing. Although he cannot see the light from his position on the stairs, the reader can view both the child and his grandmother and be reassured that he is anchored by the adult figure even as he moves upward and away from her (figure 7).

This is far more empowering than *Ghost's Hour, Spook's Hour,* in which the boy simply seeks the security of his parents and is content to go no further. It also emphasizes a partnership between adult and child, in contrast to *Five Ugly Monsters* and *There's a Witch Under the Stairs,* both of which depict adults as forcing children to take the next step by abandoning them or showing little concern for their fear and their plight. In *The Boy and the Cloth of Dreams,* the boy and his grandmother collaborate in his growth: he can face and conquer his fear, knowing that his grandmother "would not let harm come to him" (n. pag.). Using the materials that he supplies, the grandmother fixes the cloth of dreams and tells him that he has "forged his own courage." Then, instead of going back to bed with the newly woven cloth of dreams, the boy runs out into the light of the "new day" to swing "higher than he ever had before." Maturing in partnership with his grandmother makes the boy feel not only secure but also newly authoritative and free. Firmly striding down the road to adulthood, the boy is not going to arrive there by simply relying on or imitating adults, but by discovering his own ways to confront and alleviate his fears.

Figure 7. James Mayhew. From *The Boy and the Cloth of Dreams* by Jenny Koralek. Text copyright © 1994 Jenny Koralek; illustrations copyright © James Mayhew. Reproduced by permission of the publisher Candlewick Press, Inc., Cambridge, Mass., on behalf of Walker Books Ltd., London.

Conclusion

Stephens argues that in "both society and literature, it appears that the individual strives for autonomous selfhood, and it is usual for narratives in children's literature to represent this striving as having a positive outcome" (57). This schema, however, often is problematized in books that seek to alleviate fear in children's lives. Because we have not fully worked through our own fears and ambivalence regarding childhood, at least three conflicting issues become tangled in these books: first, our desire to comfort and protect children (mingled with our need to reassure ourselves of our ability to do so);[19] second, our deep-rooted fear of children's potential to be defiant and destructive; and, third, our need for children to become acceptably socialized adults. Hence these books become sites where conflicting ideologies regarding adult-child relationships become visible.

Not all books created to combat fear are equal; in spite of their surface similarities, they perform different kinds of cultural work depending on their embedded assumptions regarding the relationship between adults and children. To return to Lewis's analogy, books like *Ghost's Hour, Spook's Hour* and *Franklin and the Thunderstorm* presuppose a "difference in kind" as they encourage children to seek safety through passively accepting or actively seeking the authority of their elders. As such, these books are emblematic of the oppressiveness that Nodelman explores. *Go Away, Big Green Monster!* also assumes a "difference in kind," even though it is a far more playful book than the other two. Although its subversive linking of the child with the monster is potentially liberating, it also reinscribes the line between adult and child rather than erasing it because it encourages the child to remain in the playfully anarchic state of childhood.

Finally, while *Five Ugly Monsters, There's a Witch Under the Stairs,* and *The Boy and the Cloth of Dreams* do not challenge adult values in Lurie's sense of subversive children's literature, neither do they oppress children in quite the way that Nodelman argues children's literature does in general. Instead they depict the possibilities (at varying levels) of a powerful alliance between adults and children rather than a hierarchized struggle for authority. In her 1988 essay "The Philosopher's Child," Judith Hughes suggests what such an alliance might entail: "Growing up, maturing, emerging into autonomy is the process of the child taking from the adult more and more of the responsibility for those actions which she does knowingly. Respect for the dignity and freedom of the child consists in the recognition that the burden of responsibility shifts from the adult to the child as she herself demands it" (87). Grounded in an assumption of a difference in degree between adulthood and childhood rather than a difference in kind, these books explore the myriad possibilities for children's growth as they travel along the road that connects childhood with adulthood. In addition to delineating for child readers specific methods for dealing with their fears, they simultaneously demonstrate how children can develop into independent beings who take initiative and responsibility for themselves.

Notes

1. This idea corresponds with Bruno Bettelheim's argument in *The Uses of Enchantment* that traditional fairy tales are psychologically therapeutic, and it also suggests the overtly didactic content of many fear-of-the-dark books. For more information on bibliotherapy, see Brown; Clegg; Haldeman; Hynes; Mikulas et al.; Morris; Riggs; Rubin; Sarafino; Stasio.

2. See, e.g., Aries 100–127; Cable 107–19; Calvert 67–80; Coveney 29–90; Giroux; Greven; Hardyment 77, 201; Hays 22–50; Hazard; Jenkins, ed. 2–37; Lurie 1–15; MacLeod 143–56; Margolis 30; Nodelman; Rose 1–65; Schorsch 151–69; Spigel; Stone 255–60; and Zipes.

3. I am referencing the 1960 edition of Neill's book, but his work has also been reissued in a more recent edition (1992) that encapsulates the earlier text and appends other pieces of his writing. The fact that his work has been reissued suggests that his ideas remain part of the cultural dialogue regarding child-rearing, while discussions of the implications of his work continue among scholars. See, e.g., Darling, "A. S. Neill on Democratic Authority," and "Summerhill: From Neill to the Nineties"; Hart; and Small.

4. See, e.g., Merritt; Mikulas et al.; Robinson; Sarafino; Stasio. The entire spring 1996 issue of the journal *Educational Horizons* is devoted to exploring children's fears in various educational contexts.

5. See, e.g., Hazard; Jackson; Kramnick; Lurie 1–15; and Nodelman.

6. In the revised edition of *Summerhill School* (1992), Neill argues that any gulf that exists between adults and children is created by adult fear: "If a gulf is there it is not made by music or other tastes: it arises from the inability of the old to understand the young. And it arises largely through fear, fear that the young will stray, fear that they are not studying enough, fear that they will not succeed in life. We can disapprove of some of the things the young do, but we must not disapprove of the young themselves" (245).

7. Mike Males delineates and debunks such widespread misconceptions about dangerous youths in *The Scapegoat Generation* (1996), *Framing Youth: 10 Myths About the Next Generation* (1999), and magazine and newspaper articles.

8. See, e.g., his story about "Sandy," a "defiant three-year-old" who had become a "tyrant and a dictator" (*New Dare to Discipline* 4). In fact, Dobson reserves spanking specifically for "willful defiance"—the moments when the child is most strongly and openly resisting the authority of an adult (*Strong-Willed Child* 37).

9. See, e.g., such child-rearing manuals and conduct books as the following (listed in chronological order): Wollstonecraft (1787 and 1788); Jennings (1808) 163; Child (1831) 31–38; Abbott (1834) 108; Goodrich (1839) 31; Mann and Peabody (1870) 120–21, 147; Chavasse (1873) 104; Ballin (1902) 263–65; Kirkpatrick (1911) 99–104; Read (1916) 148, 213, 218. For more information on historical intersections of fear and childhood, see Badinter 30–39; Greven; Hardyment 85–86, 184, 247; Hays 22–50; Hazard; Stearns and Haggerty; and Thurer 158–67.

10. See, e.g., Arnold *Pictures* 9, 12, 20; Hoffman; and Watts 28.

11. Of course, there are modern books that blatantly use fear as a method of social control—one only has to think of Trina Schart Hyman's *Little Red Riding Hood*, for example, or of *The House that Crack Built* written by Clark Taylor and illustrated by Jan

Thompson Dicks. But books like these often generate public outrage and censorship, and many of them do little more than expose our own fears of children. There are also many "descendants" of Heinrich Hoffman's *Struwwelpeter:* modern stories in which children exhibit a variety of socially unacceptable behavior and are eventually cured through experiencing the consequences of such behavior. The consequences, however, are not nearly as extreme as those depicted in *Struwwelpeter.* See Betty MacDonald's popular *Mrs. Piggle-Wiggle* series for good examples of this type of text.

12. See also Darling "A. S. Neill on Democratic Authority"; Jenkins, ed. 2–37; McGillis; Rose 1–41; and Stephens 158.

13. For further theoretical discussions of children's play, see the essays on "child's play" in Jenkins, ed. 297–453.

14. For further discussion of implicit ideologies, see also Apple; Benson; Myers; Sutherland; and Zipes.

15. For a recent fictional speculation about how a child might be socialized into something other than human society, see Karen Hesse's 1996 young adult novel *The Music of Dolphins.* Mila, raised by dolphins, is unable ultimately to join human society, but from her dolphin family she does acquire language and the ability to think complexly. Mila is one of many fictional children who are socialized by other animal species, the most famous of whom are Tarzan and Mowgli. Still, these are not wild children in the same sense as Genie and Kaspar—they have been socialized by others outside of themselves who are presumably older and "wiser." For more information on feral children, see Candland; Lane; Maclean; and Shattuck.

16. This is a broad definition of the relationship that does not account for certain possible complexities, such as cases in which people who have been colonized by a specific group, in time, gain some measure of independence and go on to colonize a third group. The overall colonialist project, however, is grounded, according to Bhabha, in definitions that depend upon the theoretical opposition of colonizer-colonized and the inability of either party to merge or change places with the other.

17. For further discussion, see Cummins 72; and Hughes.

18. In a discussion of Maurice Sendak's *Where the Wild Things Are,* Lyn Ellen Lacy notes that the book "assuages childhood's fears and pains by labeling as universal the inner monster we all have known, a monster that must be controlled if we are to survive emotionally" (109). Lacy is arguing that the recognition that everyone—adults and children—contains these anarchic impulses is comforting to children, but the closing part of her sentence suggests that these impulses remain within us, though under control. In *Witch,* the illustrations specifically suggest that our "monsters" must be expelled, not merely controlled. This emphasizes the differences between adults and children rather than their similarities (as Lacy's conception suggests). That is, in *Witch,* we see that adults are children who have vanquished their anarchic impulses, whereas in her discussion of *Wild Things,* Lacy suggests that adults still have these impulses but have learned to contain and control them.

19. It is for this reason that *The Gashlycrumb Tinies* is such a disturbing and subversive text for modern adults. In addition to playing with assumptions about appropriate and inappropriate themes for children by marrying death and destruction with an alphabet book format, it also reminds adults that we cannot, in fact, keep children safe; even within the middle-class household myriad dangers lurk.

Works Cited

Abbott, John S. C. *The Mother at Home; or The Principles of Maternal Duty Familiarily Illustrated.* 1834. Family in America. New York: Arno Press and *The New York Times,* 1972.

Apple, Michael. *Ideology and Curriculum.* London: Routledge & Kegan Paul, 1979.

Aries, Philippe. *Centuries of Childhood: A Social History of Family Life.* Trans. Robert Baldick. New York: Alfred A. Knopf, 1962.

Arnold, Arnold. *Pictures and Stories from Forgotten Children's Books.* New York: Dover, 1969.

Arnold, Tedd. *Five Ugly Monsters.* New York: Scholastic, 1995.

Badinter, Elisabeth. *Mother Love: Myth and Reality.* New York: Macmillan, 1981.

Ballin, Ada. *From Cradle to School, a Book for Mothers.* London: Constable, 1902.

Benson, Linda. "The Hidden Curriculum and the Child's New Discourse: Beverly Cleary's *Ramona Goes to School.*" *Children's Literature in Education* 30.1 (1999): 9–29.

Bettelheim, Bruno. *The Uses of Enchantment: The Meaning and Importance of Fairy Tales.* New York: Random House, 1977.

Bhabha, Homi. "Of Mimicry and Man: The Ambivalence of Colonial Discourse." *October* 28 (spring 1984): 125–33.

Bourgeois, Paulette. *Franklin and the Thunderstorm.* New York: Scholastic, 1998.

Brown, Eleanor Frances. *Bibliotherapy and Its Widening Applications.* Metuchen, N.J.: Scarecrow Press, 1975.

Bunting, Eve. *Ghost's Hour, Spook's Hour.* New York: Clarion Books, 1987.

Cable, Mary. *The Little Darlings: A History of Child Rearing in America.* New York: Charles Scribner's Sons, 1975.

Calvert, Karin. "Children in the House: The Material Culture of Early Childhood." In Jenkins, ed., *Children's Culture Reader,* 67–80.

Candland, Douglas Keith. *Feral Children and Clever Animals: Reflections on Human Nature.* New York: Oxford University Press, 1993.

Chavasse, Pye Henry. *Advice to a Wife on the Management of her Own Health and on the Treatment of Some of the Complaints Incidental to Pregnancy, Labour, and Suckling with an Introductory Chapter Especially Addressed to a Young Wife.* And *Advice to a Mother on the Management of her Children and on the Treatment on the Moment of Some of Their More Pressing Illnesses and Accidents.* London: J. and A. Churchill, 1877.

Child, Lydia Maria. *The Mother's Book.* 1831. Bedford, Mass.: Applewood Books, 1992.

Cleary, Beverly. "The Laughter of Children." *Horn Book Magazine.* 58.5 (October 1982): 555–64.

Clegg, Luther B. "Using Children's Literature to Help Children Cope with Fear." *Educational Horizons* 74.3 (spring 1996): 134–38.

Coveney, Peter. *The Image of Childhood. The Individual and Society: A Study of the Theme in English Literature.* Baltimore: Penguin Books, 1967.

Cummins, June. "The Resisting Monkey: 'Curious George,' Slave Captivity Narratives, and the Postcolonial Condition." *Ariel: A Review of International English Literature* 28.1 (January 1997): 69–83.

Darling, John. "A. S. Neill on Democratic Authority: A Lesson from Summerhill?" *Oxford Review of Education* 18.1 (1992): 45–58.

———. "Summerhill: From Neill to the Nineties." *Educational Forum* 58.3 (spring 1994): 244–51.

Dobson, James. *The New Dare to Discipline.* Wheaton, Ill.: Tyndale House, 1992.

———. *The Strong-Willed Child: Birth Through Adolescence.* Wheaton, Ill.: Tyndale House. 1985.

Emberley, Ed. *Go Away, Big Green Monster!* Boston: Little, Brown, 1992.

Fanon, Frantz. *Black Skin, White Masks.* Trans. Charles Lam Markmann. New York: Grove Weidenfeld, 1967 (1952).

Giroux, Henry A. "Stealing Innocence: The Politics of Child Beauty Pageants." In Jenkins, ed., *Children's Culture Reader,* 265–82.

Goodrich, Samuel. *Fireside Education.* London: William Smith, 1839.

Gorey, Edward. *The Gashlycrumb Tinies.* New York: Harcourt Brace, 1991 (1963).

Greven, Philip J., Jr. *The Protestant Temperament: Patterns of Child-Rearing, Religious Experience, and the Self in Early America.* New York: Alfred A. Knopf, 1977.

———. *Spare the Child: The Religious Roots of Punishment and the Psychological Impact of Physical Abuse*. New York: Alfred A. Knopf, 1991.

Haldeman, Edward G. *Bibliotherapy*. Washington: University Press of America, 1977.

Hardyment, Christina. *Dream Babies: Three Centuries of Good Advice on Child Care*. New York: Harper & Row, 1983.

Hart, Harold H., pub. *Summerhill: For and Against*. New York: Hart Publishing Company, 1970.

Hays, Sharon. *The Cultural Contradictions of Motherhood*. New Haven: Yale University Press, 1996.

Hazard, Paul. *Books, Children and Men*. Trans. Marguerite Mitchell. Boston: Horn Book, 1972.

Hesse, Karen. *The Music of Dolphins*. New York: Scholastic, 1996.

Hoffman, Heinrich. *Struwwelpeter: Merry Stories and Funny Pictures*. New York: Grolier Society, n.d.

Hughes, Judith. "The Philosopher's Child." In *Feminist Perspectives in Philosophy*. Eds. Morwenna Griffiths and Margaret Whitford. Bloomington: Indiana University Press, 1988. 72–89.

Hyman, Trina Schart. *Little Red Riding Hood*. New York: Holiday House, 1983.

Hynes, Arleen McCarty, and Mary Hynes-Berry. *Bibliotherapy the Interactive Process: A Handbook*. Boulder: Westview Press, 1986.

Jackson, Mary V. *Engines of Instruction, Mischief, and Magic: Children's Literature in England from Its Beginnings to 1839*. Lincoln: University of Nebraska Press, 1989.

Jenkins, Henry, ed. *The Children's Culture Reader*. New York: New York University Press, 1998.

Jennings, Samuel K. *The Married Lady's Companion, or Poor Man's Friend*. 1808. Medicine & Society in America. New York: Arno Press and *The New York Times*, 1972.

Kincaid, James R. *Child-Loving: The Erotic Child and Victorian Culture*. New York: Routledge, 1992.

Kirkpatrick, Edwin A. *Fundamentals of Child Study: A Discussion of Instincts and Other Factors in Human Development with Practical Applications*. New York: Macmillan, 1911.

Koralek, Jenny. *The Boy and the Cloth of Dreams*. Cambridge, Mass.: Candlewick Press, 1994.

Kramnick, Isaac. "Children's Literature and Bourgeois Ideology: Observations on Culture and Industrial Capitalism in the Later Eighteenth Century." *Studies in Eighteenth-Century Culture* 12 (1983): 11–44.

Krauthammer, Charles. "Hiroshima, Mon Petit." *Time* 145 (March 27, 1995): 80.

Lacy, Lyn Ellen. *Art and Design in Children's Picture Books: An Analysis of Caldecott Award-Winning Illustrations*. Chicago: American Library Association, 1986.

Lane, Harlan. *The Wild Boy of Aveyron*. Cambridge: Harvard University Press, 1976.

Lewis, C. S. *The Abolition of Man: Reflections on Education with Special Reference to the Teaching of English in the Upper Form Schools*. *The Essential C. S. Lewis*. Ed. Lyle W. Dorsett. New York: MacMillan, 1988. 427–58.

Lurie, Alison. *Don't Tell The Grown-Ups: Subversive Children's Literature*. Boston: Little, Brown, 1990.

MacDonald, Betty. *Mrs. Piggle-Wiggle's Magic*. Philadelphia: J. B. Lippincott, 1949.

Maclean, Charles. *The Wolf Children*. New York: Farrar, Straus and Giroux, 1978.

MacLeod, Anne Scott. *American Childhood: Essays on Children's Literature of the Nineteenth and Twentieth Centuries*. Athens: University of Georgia Press, 1994.

Males, Mike A. *Framing Youth: 10 Myths about the Next Generation*. Monroe, Maine: Common Courage Press, 1999.

———. *The Scapegoat Generation: America's War on Adolescents*. Monroe, Maine: Common Courage Press, 1996.

Mann, Mary Tyler (Mrs. Horace Mann), and Elizabeth Peabody. *Moral Culture of Infancy and Kindergarten Guide.* 3d ed. New York: J. W. Schemerhorn & Co., 1870.

Margolis, Maxine. *Mothers and Such: Views of American Women and Why They Changed.* Berkeley: University of California Press, 1984.

McGillis, Roderick. "Postcolonialism, Children, and Their Literature." *Ariel: A Review of International English Literature* 28.1 (January 1997): 7–15.

Merritt, Jon E. "Reducing a Child's Nighttime Fears." *Elementary School Guidance & Counseling* 25.4 (April 1991): 291–95.

Mikulas, William, et al. "Behavioral Bibliotherapy and Games for Treating Fear of the Dark." *Child and Family Behavior Therapy* 7.3 (fall 1985): 1–7.

Morris, Richard J., and Thomas R. Kratochwill. *Treating Children's Fears and Phobias: A Behavioral Approach.* New York: Pergamon Press, 1983.

Myers, Mitzi. "Socializing Rosamond: Educational Ideology and Fictional Form." *Children's Literature Association Quarterly* 14.2 (summer 1989): 52–58.

Neill, A. S. *Summerhill: A Radical Approach to Child Rearing.* New York: Hart Publishing, 1960.

———. *Summerhill School: A New View of Childhood.* Ed. Albert Lamb. New York: St. Martin's Press, 1992.

Nodelman, Perry. "The Other: Orientalism, Colonialism, and Children's Literature." *Children's Literature Association Quarterly* 17 (spring 1992): 29–35.

Pogrebin, Letty Cottin. *Family Politics: Love and Power on an Intimate Frontier.* New York: McGraw-Hill, 1983.

Pratt, Mary Louise. *Imperial Eyes: Travel Writing and Transculturation.* London: Routledge, 1992.

Read, Mary L. *The Mothercraft Manual.* Boston: Little, Brown, 1916.

Riggs, Corinne W., comp. *Bibliotherapy: An Annotated Bibliography.* Newark, Del.: International Reading Association, 1971.

Robinson, Sandra. "Monsters, Big Monsters, and Really Big Monsters: The Self-Reported Fears of Three-, Four-, and Five-Year-Old Children." *Dimensions of Early Childhood* 22.1 (fall 1993): 23–35.

Rose, Jacqueline. *The Case of Peter Pan or the Impossibility of Children's Fiction.* Philadelphia: University of Pennsylvania Press, 1992.

Rubin, Rhea Joyce. *Using Bibliotherapy: A Guide to Theory and Practice.* Phoenix, Ariz.: Oryx Press, 1978.

Sarafino, Edward. *The Fears of Childhood: A Guide to Recognizing and Reducing Fearful States in Children.* New York: Human Sciences Press, 1986.

Schorsch, Anita. *Images of Childhood: An Illustrated Social History.* Pittstown, N.J.: Main Street Press, 1985.

Sendak, Maurice. *Where the Wild Things Are.* New York: HarperCollins, 1963.

Shattuck, Roger. *The Forbidden Experiment: The Story of the Wild Boy of Aveyron.* New York: Farrar, Straus and Giroux, 1980.

Small, Robin. Review of *The New Summerhill,* by A. S. Neill. *Australian Journal of Education* 38.1 (April 1994): 99–100.

Smith, Maggie. *There's a Witch Under the Stairs.* New York: Lothrop, Lee & Shepard Books, 1991.

Spigel, Lynn. "Seducing the Innocent: Childhood and Television in Postwar America." In Jenkins, ed., *Children's Culture Reader,* 110–35.

Stasio, Marilyn. "What's a Good Scare?" *Parade Magazine* 26 (July 1998): 4–5.

Stearns, Peter N. and Timothy Haggerty. "The Role of Fear: Transitions in American Emotional Standards for Children, 1850–1950." *American Historical Review* 96.1 (February 1991): 63–94.

Stephens, John. *Language and Ideology in Children's Fiction.* New York: Longman Publishing, 1992.

Stone, Lawrence. *Family, Sex and Marriage in England 1500–1800*. Abr. Ed. New York: Harper & Row, 1979.

Sutherland, Robert D. "Hidden Persuaders: Political Ideologies in Literature for Children." *Children's Literature in Education* 16.3 (1985): 143–57.

Taylor, Clark. *The House That Crack Built*. San Francisco: Chronicle Books, 1992.

Thurer, Shari L. *The Myths of Motherhood: How Culture Reinvents the Good Mother*. Boston: Houghton Mifflin, 1994.

Watts, Isaac. *Watt's Divine Songs for the Use of Children*. New Haven: Sidney's Press, 1818.

Wollstonecraft, Mary. *Original Stories from Real Life: with Conversations Calculated to Regulate the Affections and Form the Mind to Truth and Goodness*. London: Joseph Johnson, 1788.

———. *Thoughts on the Education of Daughters: with Reflections on Female Conduct, in the more Important Duties of Life*. London: Joseph Johnson, 1787.

Zipes, Jack. "Second Thoughts on Socialization through Literature for Children." *Lion and the Unicorn* 5 (1981): 19–32.

"Affirmative Acts": Language, Childhood, and Power in June Jordan's Cross-Writing

Richard Flynn

In a famous essay reprinted in *What is Found There,* Adrienne Rich meditates on the meaning of "The Hermit's Scream"—"'Love should be put into action!'"—in Elizabeth Bishop's poem "Chemin de Fer," and more particularly about the way poetry might serve as "a carrier of sparks" in a culture given over to "the language of therapy groups, of twelve-step programs, of bleached speech" (56–57).[1] Among the poems she discusses in the essay is June Jordan's "For Michael Angelo Thompson" (1973) about a thirteen-year-old boy, hit by a city bus, who died after being refused treatment at a Brooklyn hospital. In her discussion, Rich confesses that for a long time, "Race came between me and full reading of the poem: I wanted to believe the poet was elegiac, not furious":

> "Peace" is not the issue here, but the violent structures of urban class and racial power. The poem is a skin—luminous and resonant—stretched across a repetitive history of Black children's deaths in the cities, in a country that offers them neither hope nor respite. (67–68)

Learning to read Jordan's "For Michael Angelo Thompson" as "furious" rather than "elegaic" is tantamount to understanding "the difference between poetry and rhetoric," a phrase that is central to Audre Lorde's "Power," another poem Rich discusses in the essay (67–68). The univocal perspective of the "confession," Rich implies, is merely rhetoric, while "the double-edge, double-voicedness" she finds in "Michael Angelo Thompson" is poetry (67). From her first book, *Who Look at Me* (1969), a poem initially intended for children (and only later for adults), to her striking recent memoir *Soldier: A Poet's Childhood* (2000) Jordan has insisted on a poetics that interrogates private notions of childhood through activist, public positions.

Such a stance is unusual in contemporary poetry, and more unusual still in the now commonplace genre of the childhood memoir. Subverting the popular trope of the "traumatic childhood" Jordan insists

Children's Literature 30, ed. Elizabeth Lennox Keyser and Julie Pfeiffer (Yale University Press, © 2002 Hollins University).

in *Soldier* on "June's" agency, eschewing the pathos present in such works as Frank McCourt's *Angela's Ashes,* Tobias Wolff's *This Boy's Life,* or even Maya Angelou's *I Know Why the Caged Bird Sings.* As Patricia Pace argues, in her provocative article "All Our Lost Children: Trauma and Testimony in the Performance of Childhood," "the traumatized child" has become "a powerful locus of cultural anxiety" in contemporary memoirs (238). Using Mary Karr's *The Liar's Club* as her primary example, Pace shows that we are, perhaps, too adept at reading such accounts of childhood trauma. Just as the insights of so-called confessional poetry once seemed fresh but are now exhausted, "our experience with memoirs and other confessional texts" about childhood are by now so familiar that our "imaginative reconstructions" obscure the material circumstances of actual, rather than remembered, children. Furthermore, the power of a contemporary view of childhood "activated by sentimentality"—the "designation of the child to the private realm"—obscures the ways in which the child participates in our social, historical, and economic matrices (Pace 237–38).

By locating childhood victimization in the private sphere of a particular family, writers' testimony about that victimization tends to re-inscribe fictions of innocence violated rather than revealing the ways in which childhood and children are interpellated by the social. To testify against a broader ideology (in place since at least the eighteenth century) that views children contradictorily and often simultaneously as "little innocents and the limbs of Satan" (to use Fred Inglis's terms [70]) violates Romantic notions of authenticity and disturbs the Romantic and post-Romantic fiction that childhood is at once innocent and endangered.[2]

Jordan's approach to the memoir shares with other innovative works like Lyn Hejinian's *My Life* the view that "a child is a real person, very lively" (Hejinian 79). In other words, identity, including child identity (beyond that which is merely given), is complex. For the child, identity is formed from being in the world and negotiating that world, just as it is for adults. Rejecting the discourse of victimization as reductive, Jordan is also aware that such discourse ultimately serves to reinforce children's powerlessness. In a review of *Soldier* in the *Atlanta Journal-Constitution,* Valerie Boyd asserts that the book's "primary flaw" is that the writing resembles "a child's storybook rather than an adult's memoir of childhood." While praising Jordan for "refresh[ing] the form" of "the overused, much-maligned genre of memoir," she nevertheless criticizes the book's "creative, not-always-linear structure." But it is just this "poetic" quality—what Boyd praises as "the simple, direct language of a little girl"—that gives *Soldier* its power and distinguishes it from childhood memoirs that depict the child as victim rather than as agent. Jordan's consciously Joycean strategy of attempting to represent the child's perspective (the book was originally announced for publication as "Portrait of the Poet as a Little Black Girl") grows out of a lifelong commitment to experimenting with child language, and particularly with exploring the use of Black English as part of a powerful and longstanding commitment to teaching and promoting children's voices and children's poetry. In light of this career-long commitment, it should come as no surprise that Jordan distinguishes herself among contemporary poets with a decidedly unsentimental view of the child as a soldier-poet who wrests power over a literally paternal language.

Much of *Soldier* focuses on June's relationship with her father, Granville, who forced her to memorize poetry, raised her as a "boy soldier," and helped create the poet she is today. Granville, a Jamaican immigrant who had taught himself to read and write as an adult, was, Jordan writes, "loquacious, argumentative, and visionary" (*Soldier* 5). He also beat his daughter. But in a *New York Times* interview about *Soldier,* Jordan rejects the adjective "abusive" to characterize Granville. Although she doesn't excuse the beatings, she recognizes the cultural baggage that such an adjective carries and thus rejects simplistic explanations, as she has throughout her political and poetic career. Was her father abusive?[3] Jordan remarks, "Anyone can come up with an adjective, a pejorative. . . . I had committed myself to writing [*Soldier*] in the consciousness of a child, which meant making no judgments. I hope in a way this is very good news: I'm O.K. One can reasonably say some pretty dire things about my folks, but I love my father. I'm here to say, I'm here; I'm O.K." (qtd. in Lee).

In their introduction to a special issue of *Children's Literature,* Mitzi Myers and U. C. Knoepflmacher advance the useful term "cross-writing," a term that accurately describes Jordan's poetic project. "A dialogic mix of older and younger voices [that] occurs in texts too often read as univocal," cross-writing implies the "interplay and cross-fertilization rather than a hostile internal cross fire" (vii) that may be found in works intended for both children and adults and is often particularly pronounced in writers who address younger and older audiences with equal care and respect. Myers and Knoepflmacher see cross-writing as a way to "dissolve the binaries and contraries our culture has rigidified and fixed" (viii) and as a kind of versatile "critical Swiss Army knife" that will open the way to "children's cultural studies" (xv).

If June Jordan's success as a cross-writer lies first in her exploration of adult and child concerns dialogically (in writing for both adults and children), it is also articulated in her conscious theorizing about actual children in relation to historical and material concerns. This view has its origin in her early work with actual children, work that enriches her later focus on her own remembered childhood. Jordan's earliest publications either feature child writers whom she taught during the late sixties and early seventies or they are published as books for young people. Her early work and the circumstances of its publication demonstrate how much child-adult cross-writing is inflected by historical and material forces. Jordan's creative writing, political essays, and teaching are a model for the kind of Swiss Army knife called for by Myers and Knoepflmacher, and they remind us that children's cultural studies should concern itself with actual children as well as with literature and culture.

In order to appreciate *Soldier's* fresh take on the genre of childhood memoir, one must turn to Jordan's career-long engagement as a child advocate and an understanding of her cross-fertilizing and testing of generic boundaries. Jordan's first volume of poetry for adults, *Some Changes* (1971), was published in Dutton's short-lived Black Poets Series, edited by Julius Lester; but it was preceded by three books of poetry either marketed for children— *Who Look at Me* (Crowell, 1969)[4] — or featuring children's writing— *soulscript: Afro-American Poetry* (1970), part of Doubleday's Zenith series dedicated to "minority cultures," and, with Terri Bush, *The Voice of the Children* (Holt, Rinehart, 1970), an anthology of poetry by the children who had participated in their writing workshops in East Harlem and Brooklyn. In the preface to the *soulscript* anthology, Jordan gives a contemporary account of an "Afro-American poetry" of "witness" that "until recently" had "suffered an alien censorship" (xviii). She opens the anthology with a selection of poems by children ages twelve to eighteen,[5] an unusual strategy that comes from a deep conviction that the "springs of poetry"—"reaction, memory, and dream" are available to children ("a four-year-old flows among them as fully as any adult" [xvi]) and out of a belief in the promise of social change: "when American classrooms change from confrontation to communion, black poetry will happen in the schools as well" (xvi). This optimism, unfortunately, has not been borne out today, when less African-American children's literature is being published than in the 1970s, when poetry has been further marginalized in American classrooms, and when the classrooms themselves have become symbols of violence and neglect. As Jordan herself has recently noted: "our children are compelled to attend school—day after day—in buildings that are not only disgraceful to see, but hazardous to occupy . . . and useless as far as what they impart" (Gilbert 3–4).

Nevertheless, Jordan's early optimism and refusal to underestimate children served to foster respect for children's voices as well as to instruct children in the rigors of craft and give them good poetic models in order to enable them to write "real poetry." In her provocative study *The Child as Poet: Myth or Reality?* noted children's poetry authority Myra Cohn Livingston praises Jordan as a "creative teacher" who exemplifies a "new mythology" that rejects prepackaged notions of childhood in order to foster meaningful children's writing (268–72). From Jordan's pioneer membership in the Teachers and Writers Collaborative (beginning in 1967) to her present position as professor at Berkeley where she has taught a course in "the Politics of Childhood" and established the very successful Poetry for the People program, Jordan has demonstrated a rare understanding of both children's poetry and the poetics and politics of childhood. On both theoretical and pragmatic levels, this engagement with childhood (or, more accurately speaking, childhoods) has been fruitfully complicated by Jordan's own sense of multiple "identities" (little girl, soldier-boy, daughter, mother, African American, bisexual, activist, teacher) and her investment in different kinds of language and literary genres (Black English, standard English, poetry, fiction, essays, plays, journalism, memoir, literature for children, adolescents, adults).

Indeed, Jordan's poetical and political interventions into childhoods actual and remembered involve the skillful negotiation of these various languages, genres, and identities. Jordan has thought deeply about children both as an audience for her writing and as writers themselves. While attuned to children's real suffering, she resists the ways in which the child (and particularly the "disadvantaged" child) is reified as an object of pity, preferring to emphasize children's agency by helping them to become writing subjects.

Jordan's response to the criticism of one of her child poets' work is illustrative here. In 1968 she was taken to task by Zelda Wirtshafter, the director of the Teachers and Writers Collaborative, for allowing her student Deborah Burkett to write a poem called "Travel" modeled on Robert Louis Stevenson's poem of the same title from *A Child's Gar-*

den of Verses. The memo that occasioned Jordan's impassioned response has been "lost in the holes of time," according to Philip Lopate (*Journal* 113), but presumably it criticized Jordan for "foisting" Stevenson on the young black poet, rather than encouraging her to write in her own voice. Jordan's letter of reply of February 12, 1968, both insists on the importance of poetic craft for the young poet and criticizes the subtle racism in seeing black or poor children primarily as victims:

> Contrary to your remarks, a poet does not write poetry according to the way he talks. Poetry is a distinctively precise and exacting use of words—whether the poet is Langston Hughes or Bobby Burns.
>
> One should take care to discover racist ideas that are perhaps less obvious than others. For example, one might ask: Will I accept that a black child can write "creatively" and "honestly" and yet not write about incest, filth, violence, and degradations of every sort? Back of the assumption, and there is an assumption, that an honest and creative piece of writing by a black child will be ungrammatical, misspelled, and lurid titillation for his white teacher, is another idea. That black people are only the products of racist, white America and that, therefore, we can be and we can express only what racist white America has forced us to experience, namely: mutilation, despisal, ignorance and horror.
>
> Fortunately, however, we have somehow survived. We have somehow and sometimes survived the systematic degradation of America. And therefore there really are black children who dream, and who love, and who undertake to master such "white" things as poetry. There really are black children who are children as well as victims. (qtd. in Lopate, *Journal* 146)[6]

Already cognizant of what she would call in her essay about Phillis Wheatley "The Difficult Miracle of Black Poetry," Jordan does not here advocate a capitulation to "the official language of the powerful" (*On Call* 36). But recognizing something of herself in Deborah Burkett, an "exceptional child" and a "clearly gifted writer," Jordan is loathe to discourage a child who "has been learning the streets and . . . learning in school and in the library" (Lopate, *Journal* 146). While Philip Lopate observes that Jordan's "training as a poet and the insistence on literary quality" sometimes conflicted with her "broad political and social goals," such as her early advocacy of Black English, it would be more accurate to say Jordan's commitment to "literary quality" reflects an equally strong commitment to a literary/linguistic theory that is inseparable from the political realm. As Jacqueline Vaught Brogan points out, "in addition to her deep and obvious involvement with contemporary African American writers, Jordan is deeply involved with literary/linguistic history" (203).[7]

Jordan's first book, *Who Look at Me* (1969), is a sophisticated poem about race and representation set in conversation with twenty-seven paintings by both black and white artists. Published as a children's book in 1969 and dedicated to her son Christopher, then eleven years old, the poem has been reprinted at the beginning of both of Jordan's volumes of selected poems. Though the poem works in its "text-only" version, it was initially composed in conjunction with the paintings that were selected by her editor, Milton Meltzer,[8] and like all good picture books, it depends on the conversation between text and illustration to achieve its full impact. The title serves as a Black English refrain, a call followed by responses, a litany of the ways in which African Americans are represented or rather are not represented in white culture:[9]

> Who look at me?
>
> Who see the children
> on their street the torn down door the wall
> complete an early losing
>   games of ball
> the search to find
> a fatherhood a mothering of mind
> a multimillion multicolored mirror
> of an honest humankind. (24)

This poetry (reminiscent of the early work of Gwendolyn Brooks) uses multiple address (black and white children; black and white adults; north and south), so that there is no subject position from which one can evade the speaker's command to:

> look close
> and see me black man mouth
> for breathing (North and South)
> A MAN (25)

This page of verse is followed by four portraits of black men: African-American artist John Wilson's *Self Portrait* (in color), Alice Neel's *Taxi Driver*, Symeon Shimin's *Boy* (black and white but reproduced in color on the front dust jacket) and Thomas Eakin's portrait of Henry O. Tanner (the first "Negro artist to be elected to the National Academy of Design" [96]). Following the portraits is a blank page, recto, and centered, verso, on page 31, a single line of verse: "I am black alive and looking back at you" so that looking close (demanded by the text and skillful layout) is answered by the text and portraits looking back at the reader in affirmation and accusation both. The poem continues as a succession of children "stranded in a hungerland / of great prosperity" are shown "reckless to succeed" but confined by a "solid alabaster space / inscribed keep off keep out don't touch / and Wait Some More for Half as Much" (36). "No doubt," says the speaker, "the jail is white where I am born / but black will bail me out," and the poem proceeds to journey back to the "complicated past" of the Middle Passage, the Amistad Revolt, the slave market, the Underground Railroad, the "lynchlength rope":

> so little safety
> almost nowhere like the place
> that childhood plans
> in a pounding happy space   (60)

By insisting that African American history is "complicated," the poem and accompanying visual texts resist and subvert an Anglo-American version of history that defines the African American as an "absence" — a definition practiced even in the liberal discourse surrounding the civil rights movement. And black childhood, as the preceding passage suggests, was defined in sixties journalism and documentary photography as the absence of "normal" childhood. This trope of absence, popularized in photographs documenting the civil rights movement in such magazines as *Life, Look,* and *Newsweek* is both evoked and criticized by the poem:

> Who see starvation at the table
> lines of men no work to do
> my mother ironing a shirt?
>
> Who see a frozen midnight
> of the winter and the hallway cold
> to kill you like the dirt
>
> where kids buy soda pop
> in shoeshine parlors
> barber shops so they can hear
> some laughing   (23–24)

Significantly, this portion of the poem is not accompanied by images because the poet does not wish to reinforce the reified magazine images she wishes to disrupt. The most striking and effective disruption of the stereotypical view of African Americans and African-American children as victims or as absences occurs near the end of the poem in a double-page spread. The text:

> Although the world
> forgets me
> I will say yes
> AND NO   (84)

is opposite Romare Bearden's montage *Mysteries* (1964), a work that art historian Lee Glazer demonstrates is Bearden's response to the "well-known" journalistic "stereotype" of the "old, unpainted" southern shack (figure 8). In the work, argues Glazer, Bearden "confronts the received belief that black life and culture are unknowable and ultimately unrepresentable except as an absence" (423). Glazer describes Bearden's treatment of the figures and his "emphasis on faces, especially the eyes," as "a strategic use of direct confrontation" in which "the exchange of gazes . . . challenges the expected relationship between viewer and viewed" (423).

But *Mysteries* also disrupts the boundaries between child and adult, and this disruption is magnified when it is placed in the context of Jordan's children's book. The figure in the center of the collage evokes the child as object of pathos (a face with large eyes on top of a diminutive body), but that pathos is disrupted by the spectral, almost translucent quality of the image, as well as by a second face peering out from behind her. Furthermore, though the image looks childlike, we can't be certain she is a child, just as the other figures appear to be composed of fragments of both children and adults, faces within faces. The indeterminacy of the figures allows them to resist the very stereotypes evoked by the "shack" in which they are placed, just as Bearden's manipulation of the gaze disrupts the viewer's potential for sentimentalizing condescension. Like Jordan's text, Bearden's collage explores the complexity of simultaneous presence and absence, of "yes / AND NO" (84).

Turning the page, that "NO" is reinforced:

> NO
> to a carnival run by freaks
> who take a life

Figure 8. Romare Bearden. From *Mysteries* by Romare Bearden. Copyright © Romare Bearden Foundation/Licensed by VAGA, New York, NY.

             and tie it terrible
             behind my back   (86)

Composed at about the same time as Jordan's angry letter to Zelda Wirtshafter, *Who Look at Me* uses poetic language in relation to visual images as a way of making many of the same points. Bearden's collage interrogates "racist ideas that are perhaps less obvious than others": liberal stereotypes that perpetuate a view of African Americans as less than human. Jordan's poetry emphasizes the way that Bearden's *Mysteries* appropriates the tropes of exoticism and freakishness historically forced on African Americans and turns them against the viewer. It tells us that those who perpetuate the fragmented and fragmenting images of African Americans as exotic freaks are themselves the real freaks; the collaboration between text and image in *Who Look at Me* becomes a way of seeking liberation from their carnival.

Insofar as it is a children's book, *Who Look at Me* reflects Jordan's understanding that child identities, even more than adult identities, are constructed by language as it is being learned. For any child, the power conferred by language mastery is not so much appropriated as it is wrested from those in authority (adults), and the material and emotional circumstances surrounding their attempt at language mastery are largely beyond children's control. For the African-American child, as Jordan points out in her 1972 essay "White English/Black English: The Politics of Translation," such disparities of power are even more pronounced: *"White power uses white English as a calculated, political display of power to control and eliminate the powerless"* (Jordan's italics; *Civil* 65). To demonstrate this point she contrasts a passage from *Romeo and Juliet* with a passage from her adolescent novel in Black English *His Own Where* neither of which "ain no kind of standard English":

> Both excerpts come from love stories about white and Black teenagers, respectively. But the Elizabethan, nonstandard English of *Romeo and Juliet* has been adjudged, by the powerful, as something students should tackle and absorb. By contrast, the Black, nonstandard language of my novel, *His Own Where,* has been adjudged, by the powerful, as substandard and even injurious to young readers. (*Civil* 71–72)

His Own Where, which was widely and favorably reviewed, nominated for the National Book Award, and named an ALA Best Book for Young Adults, nevertheless elicited criticism like the following 1980 "curriculum unit" from the Yale New Haven Teachers' Institute currently available on the World Wide Web:

> This book, even though the content would interest students, lacks many of the elements of a good novel. Therefore, the book will be used to illustrate how not to write. During the reading of *His Own Where,* you will find opportune time to teach sequence in writing, descriptive narrative writing, character development, and story line. Since it is written in Black English, it also affords an excellent exercise in translating paragraphs into proper grammar.
> [Exercise] 1. Choose one of the many poorly written sentences to show correct verb tense, double negatives, possessives, etc.
> ex: "Angela mother explain how Angela run out on her because she wouldn't hardly leave." (Petuch)

Although the novel's use of modernist techniques of narration, such as flashback and dream sequence, is also criticized as "deficient" by this teacher, it is the "unappropriateness" [*sic*] of Black English that is her primary target. This curriculum unit illustrates Jordan's claim that "the Black child is punished for mastery of his non-standard, Black English; . . . [that] America [has] decided that non-standard is sub-standard, and even dangerous, and must be eradicated" (*Civil* 65). And as the media reaction to the Oakland School Board Ebonics con-troversy demonstrates, even curricula that adopt a positive attitude toward Black English primarily in order to foster proficiency in stan-dard English are deemed substandard and "unappropriate."[10]

In a 1998 essay, "Affirmative Acts: Language, Information, and Power," in which she criticizes the dismantling of affirmative action and bilingual education in California, Jordan recalls the reaction to *His Own Where* shortly after its 1970 publication. She expresses surprise that her writing the novel in Black English became controversial while the controversial subject matter of the novel was ignored:

> As part of my story, I advocated sex education and the availability of free condoms in the sixteen-year-old hero's high school. And I presented the two young lovers, Buddy and his fourteen-year-old Angela as calmly and romantically planning to "make a baby" together.
> I thought I'd get some flak about the baby.
> I never expected what happened, instead: The book was banned in several cities and Black parents organized against it/me on the grounds that *His Own Where* would lead Black children into educational disaster. Black English was perceived to be the trigger to failure, not the public schools where shockingly high drop-out rates and shockingly low verbal aptitude scores held, as the norm, for these kids. (*Affirmative* 245–46)

Oddly enough, several favorable contemporary reviews pointed out the difficulty of the language in the novel. Christopher Lehmann-Haupt wrote in the *New York Times*, "The prose takes some getting used to" (67), and the anonymous reviewer for the *Center for Children's Books Bulletin* suggested that the "tell-it-like-it-is book in black talk, a poem in prose" was perhaps too sophisticated for all but the "special reader" (58). Although Jordan says that she chose to write *His Own Where* in Black English in order "to interest teenagers in reading it" so they could learn the "activist principles in urban design,"[11] it is most com-pelling for its linguistic power. Its use of the "home language" of black children is attractive to young readers, and the care and attention required to read it underscore the ways in which we both inhabit and are inhabited by language.[12] It is through language, the novel's refrain tells us, that the young protagonists and readers learn that "you be different from the dead" (*His Own Where* 1, 87). Jordan depicts material and political circumstances that conspire to deny life to the schools, the neighborhoods, the families in the African-American community. Buddy and Angela attempt to create a life for themselves (and to create a new life) by claiming their "own where" in the cemetery, an attempt that attests to the children's hopefulness and resiliency. They are able to construct a life "different from the dead" by asserting their right to speak and dream in a language that, far from being deficient, is complex and poetic. That language is also, like Buddy's and Angela's dwelling in the cemetery, makeshift—constructed of necessity as a means of survival.

In some ways, those objecting to the novel's Black English got it right in that they identified where the novel was truly subversive. By 1970 sensationalist subject matter had become practically de rigueur in the relatively new young adult genre. Jordan's demonstration that Black English is as much a vehicle for conveying the complex and the poetic as "so-called Standard English" (*Affirmative* 246) is ultimately far more radical than her depiction of two teenagers "planning to 'make a baby.'"

Another Jordan book for young people published in 1972 is, as Suzanne Rahn points out, "even more radically experimental in form and language than *His Own Where*" (251). In *Dry Victories,* Jordan presents a dialogue entirely in Black English between two young boys, Kenny and Jerome, as they compare the failures of Reconstruction to the failures of the civil rights movement. Their conversation is interspersed with documentary photographs and news clippings and framed by twin versions of the Declaration of Independence in positive and negative reproductions. There is also a frame within a frame: Jordan's preface written in Black English ("We taking the facts up front because the front is where we're at" [viii]) and an author's note at the back, written at the behest of the publisher, in "standard" English with Black English interpolations:

The Publisher is worried. He wants me to write something, besides this book. Call it An Afterword. This whole book is an "afterword." It is written *after* the Civil War, *after* the Reconstruction Era, *after* the Civil Rights Era, *after* the assassination of Malcolm X, the

Kennedys, Dr. King, little girls in a Birmingham Sunday School,
and *after* the assassination of countless hopes and acts of faith.
    The Publisher is worried, but I'm not. I'm angry and you should
be too. Then we can do something about this after-mess of after-
math, following on so much tragedy. (75)

"History," Jordan concludes, "don't stop to let nobody out of it." The
truth as Jordan sees it can't be rendered in "no kind of Standard English."[13]

Soldier builds on this experiment with nonstandard discourses, not
by employing Black English but by attempting to find a language
whereby the adult can render the child's perspective with greater im-
mediacy. By depicting the child as both incipient artist and incipient
fighter, Jordan hopes to lend that fictional child agency: to be a soldier,
she implies, is to refuse to be victim. Jordan's work for adults, as much
as her work for children, provides the necessary preparation for finding the poetic voice for *Soldier* that can come close to accurately representing the child's experience. *Soldier* could not have been written
without the insights developed in early poems, such as "Gettin Down
to Get Over" (1972), "Ah Momma" (1975), "Poem for Granville Ivan-
hoe Jordan" (1974), and the fascinating prose poem "Fragments from
a Parable" (written from 1958 to 1973). In this work, Jordan focuses
on understanding the circumstances under which her parents, both
of them West Indian immigrants, attempted to construct new lives as
Americans and provide opportunities for her, their only daughter, and
also on "wrestl[ing] my own language out of an enemy language" (Carroll 145). In the memoir, Jordan attempts to write "with the consciousness of a child, without the filter of adult perceptions and judgments,"
but that child's consciousness exists in dialogic (or perhaps dialectic)
relationship to the adult poet and activist, one who understands that
"childhood is the first, inescapable political situation each of us has to
negotiate" (qtd. in Lee). Poetic language is particularly suited to this
material, and Jordan's "prose" memoir regularly slides into verse. In
fact, she asserts, "The whole thing should be a poem," but she "was
afraid if it was poetry, people wouldn't read it" (qtd. in Lee).
    Although Jordan does not excuse her father's erratic violence, she
seems to have come to terms with it in various poems and essays and,
most recently, in *Soldier*. Addressing the Northwest Regional Conference of the Child Welfare League in 1978, she explains, "it would not
have helped me, it would not have rescued me, to know that one rea-

son my father beat me to the extent of occasional scar tissue was because he himself felt beaten and he himself felt bullied and despised
by strangers more powerful than he would ever be" (*Civil* 134). The
complexity of her father's role in the family dynamic in relation to the
outside world is explored in her fine "Poem About My Rights" (1980):

> and according to the *Times* this week
> back in 1966 the C.I.A. decided that they had this problem
> and the problem was a man named Nkrumah so they
> killed him and before that it was Patrice Lumumba
> and before that it was my father on the campus
> of my Ivy League school and my father afraid
> to walk into the cafeteria because he said he
> was wrong the wrong age the wrong skin the wrong
> gender identity and he was paying my tuition and
> before that
> it was my father saying I was wrong saying that
> I should have been a boy because he wanted one/a
> boy and that I should have been lighter skinned and
> that I should have had straighter hair and that
> I should not be so boy crazy but instead I should
> just be one/a boy . . .   (*Naming* 103; *Passion* 87–88)

The father ironically feels displaced in his own gender identity at the
Barnard cafeteria, and "before that" he has visited his feeling that he
is "wrong" upon the speaker. He recognizes, if only intuitively, that
the masculine identity that has been his only route to power is ineffec-
tual in this female-dominated, white bastion of privilege. First person
and masculine pronouns—"he" and "one/a boy"—dominate this part
of the poem, but, like the father, they are out of place, are "wrong."
Only in the conclusion of the poem will the speaker ultimately insist

> I am not wrong: Wrong is not my name
> My name is my own my own my own
> and I can't tell you who the hell set things up like this
> but I can tell you that from now on my resistance
> my simple and daily and nightly self-determination
> may very well cost you your life   (*Naming* 104; *Passion* 89)

Explaining in *Soldier* that behind her father's determination was his
conviction "that a Negro parent had to produce a child who could be-

come a virtual whiteman and therefore possess dignity and power," Jordan concludes that, for Granville Jordan, "Probably it seemed easier to change me than to change the meaning and complexion of power" (18). "Poem About My Rights," on the other hand, *does* try to change the meaning and complexion of power by refusing consent. The speaker refuses to capitulate to society's definition of her as "the history" and "the meaning of rape / . . . the problem everyone seeks to / eliminate by forced / penetration" as she connects the sanctity of her body with

> the sanctity
> of each and every desire
> that I know from my personal and idiosyncratic
> and indisputably single and singular heart.
> (*Naming* 104; *Passion* 88–89).

Understanding her mother's role in family politics and the wider political sphere was far more difficult and painful. Jordan's mother, Mildred, committed suicide in 1966 after a debilitating stroke, but it was not until 1981, in an essay called "Many Rivers to Cross" that Jordan could write explicitly about her death (*On Call* 19–26). Even so, one senses the poet's continuing difficulty in coming to terms with her mother's legacy. As recently as 1994, in an interview with Peter Erickson, Jordan is able to discuss at length her father's legacy, that he gave her "a keen sense of my intellectual aptitude." But when Erickson asks, "What was the most important thing you received from your mother?" Jordan replies, "Oh dear. I don't know how to answer that." Nevertheless, since the late sixties, Jordan has written poetry in which she tries to understand and honor "The Spirit of Mildred Jordan" (1971, *Naming* 13–14; *Things* 26–27). Indeed, it seems the very difficulty of understanding her mother leads Jordan to write some of her most important poetry, such as "Gettin Down to Get Over," in which she interrogates tropes of black womanhood—from "bitch" to "Queen"—juxtaposing the sexist epithets:

> MOMMA MOMMA
> *Black* Momma
> *Black* bitch
> *Black* pussy
> piecea tail
> *nice* piecea ass   (*Naming* 67; *Things* 28)

with white rhetoric that described the black family as a "tangle of pathology." In her 1969 poem "Memo to Daniel Pretty Moynihan" Jordan, a single mother, had already declared, "Don't you liberate me / from my female black pathology" (*Things* 117).[14] In "Gettin Down" she is even more specific about the ways in which "black female pathology" is constructed by the intersection of sexist and racist rhetoric:

> Black Woman
> Black
> Female Head of Household
> Black Matriarchal Matriarchy
> Black Statistical
> Lowlife Lowlevel Lowdown
> Lowdown and up
> to be Low-down
> Black Statistical
> Low Factor
> Factotem
> Factitious Fictitious
> Figment Figuring in Lowdown Lyin
> Annual Reports   (*Naming* 68; *Things* 28)

Jordan here signifies on the kind of language contained in the 1963 Moynihan Report: bureaucratic language such as "Black / Female head of household" that is essentially a kinder and gentler way of implying "Lowlevel Lowlife Lowdown." Statistics, interpreted correctly, should indicate a call for political action, for social justice, but the "facts" that appear in "Lowdown Lyin / Annual Reports" become "Factitious Fictitious" as the "Black Matriarchal Matriarchy" is blamed for social problems whose root cause is a continuing history of racial and gender discrimination. Those "facts" become a "Factotem" (a portmanteau pun indicating a worship of "facts" and statistics that are ultimately designed to keep the black woman in the servile position of "factotum"). In contrast with this rhetoric, the speaker appeals directly to the mother in the poem's conclusion:

> Teach me how to t.c.b./to make do
> and be
> like you
> teach me to survive my
> momma

> teach me how to hold a new life
> momma
> help me
> turn the face of history
> *to your face.*   (*Naming* 75–76; *Things* 37)

In order to grow up, the little soldier of the memoir must learn to reject the objectifying discourse that would blame a mother like Mildred Jordan for the "breakdown" of the black family while ignoring the strength, sacrifice, and success of such women despite the great odds against them. In another poem, Jordan promises her mother that she will transform "the rhythms of your sacrifice, the ritual of your bowed head" into "an angry, an absolute determination that I would one day, prove myself to be, in fact your daughter" ("Ah Momma," *Naming* 15; *Things* 38–39; *Civil* 101–2).

As Jordan asserts in "Thinking About My Poetry," "I have moved from an infantile reception of the universe, as given, into a progressively political self-assertion that is now reaching beyond the limitations of a victim mentality" (*Civil* 129). Paradoxically, however, this rejection involves understanding the ways "an infantile reception of the universe" contributed to Jordan's becoming a poet. She may have had trouble answering Peter Erickson's question about her mother in the 1994 interview, but she begins to answer the question in *Soldier*. Although Granville Jordan looms large as a presence in *Soldier* and the book is dedicated to him, Mildred Jordan's influence is just as important, despite her tendency to "more or less hide inside her 'little room,' where she would probably begin to pray" (xviii).

In fact, Jordan identifies her love of poetry as originating in relation to her mother, from those earliest experiences in which language is embodied: "Pretty soon my body had absorbed the language of all the Mother Goose nursery rhymes, and my mother's dramatization of the rhythms of these words filled me with regular feelings of agreeable intoxication" (*Soldier* 9). Jordan's pleasure in the rhythms of her mother's nursery rhymes and the rhythms of Bible stories, "the magical language and its repetition that left you feeling united and taken care of," is the bedrock upon which she constructs her later oppositional poetics, a poetics that arises from her resistance to her father's required reading. Forced to memorize and recite her father's "canon" through "compulsory reading assignments and next-day examinations" (45) that included Poe, Shakespeare, and Dunbar, as well

as "The Ugly Duckling," *Rebecca of Sunnybrook Farm,* Zane Grey, and
Sinclair Lewis, the rhythms and music that Jordan learned from her
mother's nursery rhymes and Bible stories enabled her to perform
"passages from memory, on demand," even when she didn't understand the meaning of what she was reciting, which "tended to placate,
if not entirely satisfy, my father" (49). At an early age Jordan learned
to question her father's canon, preferring the popular works of Zane
Grey to the "serious" works of Sinclair Lewis, and even more tellingly,
characterizing her first Broadway show, *The Member of the Wedding,* as
"this play about a white girl and her Negro 'Mammy' looking after her"
whose most striking moment occurs when "the girl uses this huge knife
to slice at something on her foot" (259–60). Jordan taught herself to
become a "resisting reader," the kind of child reader who questions
as well as appreciates literature, as her reaction to her first storybook
demonstrates:

> Why did the Ugly Duckling lose its mother?
> How could a duck turn into a swan?
> Why would that be a happy ending for a duck?
> The Ugly Duckling was depicted as a black baby duck.
> The swan was white.
> How did the black baby duck turn white?
> Why was that a happy ending?
>
> I thought I understood that story,
> and I didn't believe it,
> and I kept reading it to myself,
> over and over.
>
> I never wanted and I never got a Shirley Temple doll.
> (*Soldier* 23)

But as "June" comes to see herself at the center of her parents' arguments, Jordan writes, "My father' voice got loud":

> My mother didn't say much, but she never said, "All right."
> She was fighting.
> They were fighting.
> They were fighting with each other.
> I had become the difference between them. (15–16)

In part 6, "More About My Father and My Mother: Fighting," her parents' argument centers on Mildred's insistence that her husband, who

is arranging for June to attend a white boarding school where "she will rub elbows with the best: the sons of bankers, the sons of Captains of Industry," recognize that "June is not a Rockefeller boy. She have to become a Black woman!" Her father replies: " 'She will learn herself how to hold his own. She will come out the school a veritable prince. Among men." This argument rises to such a pitch, that her father slaps her "mother's face / from one side to the other" after which the child "tumbles down the stairs" to recite the ending of Kipling's "If": "And— which is more— / You'll be a Man, my son!" After Granville goes out to buy ice cream as a reward for the recitation, June pulls close to her mother, lays the Bible "across my mother's knees," and together ("you repeat it after me") they recite the Beatitudes.

Thus we see the origins of Jordan's adult verse, which combines rhythm and musicality with a critical and interrogating language. The recognition that even the most seemingly innocent uses of language are embedded in the social and the political, a recognition she first encountered as a child, inspires Jordan to tap into the "place of rage" with the subtle music of her mature poetry, that, nevertheless, is frequently attentive to the child's perceptions. Adult work, then, is incorporated in the childhood memoir, such as the first three sections of her major poem, "War and Memory," the final six pages of part 3 of *Soldier.* The sections of "War and Memory" not reprinted, however, that concern adult experience make explicit that the child "warrior growing up" bears an important relation to the adult poet's quest:

> and I
> thought I was a warrior growing up
> and I
> buried my father with all of the ceremony all of the music
>   I could piece together
> and I
> lust for justice
> and I
> make that quest arthritic/pigeon-toed/however
> and I
> invent the mother of courage I require not to quit
>   (*Naming* 210–11)

Jordan's recognition that she must pay attention to the "mother of courage" and the mother of invention, as much as the father's instruction, is an insight that translates into a richer portrait of the child's perspective in *Soldier*. Furthermore, inventing the "mother of courage" allows Jordan to discover her poetic form, her craft, learned first in her body, in early childhood from her mother's music and rhythms. Jordan calls this form "vertical rhythm," which, she explains, will "propel a listener or reader from one word to the next or one line to the next without possible escape" (qtd. in Muller 38).[15] The reader is required "not to quit."

Likewise, three separate accounts of a horrifying incident of police brutality remembered from childhood provide a stunning example of the powerful uses of cross-writing in showing the way that both adult and child perceptions may inform each other dialogically and intertextually. Jordan recalls the brutal disfigurement of her childhood friend, Jeffrey Underwood, when she was nine or ten, in an interview in Pratibha Parmar's 1991 film *A Place of Rage:*

> There was one boy, for example, named Jeffrey Underwood, who was really cute, and I liked him a lot. And the police went up on the roof after Jeffrey, and just beat him mercilessly. I mean everybody knew Jeffrey and his family—his parents were friends with my parents, and so on—this was really shocking. And it permanently disfigured him—in what was later explained as a kind of case of mistaken identity. And to see this boy that I idolized—who belonged to us, in the sense of our block and all of us—disfigured by these strangers who came in with all this force, and license to use that force, was really terrifying. And also it—it hardened me. I would say, early on. In a kind of place of rage, actually.

"Poem from Taped Testimony in the Tradition of Bernhard Goetz" is a poem Marilyn Hacker describes as "an ironically issue-oriented dramatic monologue." "Jordan's speaker," Hacker writes, "breathlessly appropriates to a black perspective the reasoning Goetz used to justify arming himself and firing on black youths in a New York City subway" (135). The irony Hacker identifies is complex in that not only does Jordan point out the faulty logic of accepting Goetz's testimony and his claim, "This was not I repeat this was not a racial thing" (*Naming* 153), but that she continues to insist that we reject such logic, even after we discover the speaker of the poem is a black woman who offers far more compelling background stories than those of Goetz. Patricia Williams performs a similar analysis of Goetz's testimony in *The Alchemy of Race and Rights* (72–79), which corroborates Jordan's poetic performance, albeit somewhat less compellingly. One of the stories

that makes "Poem from Taped Testimony" so effective is the story of
Jeffrey Underwood, which appears as section 4:

> then the policeman beat Jeffrey
> unconscious and he/the
> policeman who was one of them he kicked
> Jeffrey's teeth out and I never wanted to see
> Jeffrey anymore but I kept seeing
> these policemen and I remember how
> my cousin who was older than I was I remember how
> she whispered to me, "That's what they
> do to you"   (*Naming* 155)

In *Soldier*, the child is spending an idyllic summer at a YWCA summer
camp, and her version of the Jeffrey Underwood story is perhaps the
most moving version:

> I felt so clean! I felt so safe!
> I felt myself far away from Valerie [Jordan's older cousin with
> whom she lived] and her beautiful, tall boyfriend, Jeffrey Under-
> wood, when the cops busted up his face and kicked out his teeth
> because they were cops and they were white people and Jeffrey
> lived on our block and he hadn't done anything besides that be-
> sides live on our block because he belonged there on our block
> and then the cops chased him to the roof and they caught him
> and they messed everything up and nothing was the same after
> that: Nothing. (*Soldier* 234–35)

The passage from *Soldier* certainly gains resonance placed next to
the 1991 interview and the 1989 dramatic monologue, but the representation of the child's perspective is, in itself, striking. The "really
terrifying" story that Jordan says "hardened" her is presented in the
rush of a run-on sentence, but also in the context of the voice of the
child soldier established in the 233 pages preceding it. It is not so
much the "hardening" that impresses the reader as the way Jordan
manages to tap into "a place of rage" as the child herself seems to
have experienced it. And that place of rage is made productive. Like
"Poem from Taped Testimony," the memoir rejects victim mentality,
refuses to participate in the logic of Bernhard Goetz. The poet's min-
ing of childhood experience makes possible the deep ironies—"the
double-edge, double-voicedness" that Rich identifies, or a Du Boisian

"double-consciousness" (45)—employed in the poem for adults. And the sophisticated perspective in the poem for adults makes possible a way for the poet to represent a child's perspective, without sentimentality, in the memoir.

"Nothing was ever the same after that: Nothing," says the narrator of *Soldier.* The memoir itself ends with the young Jordan getting on the train to go to the Northfield School wondering whether, like Jackie Robinson, she would be a "first" (248). Her father tells her, "Okay! Little Soldier! G'wan! G'wan! / You gwine make me proud!" (261). It is, the section title tells us, "The Only Last Chapter of My Childhood," implying both the importance of this particular childhood for this particular child and the necessity of growing up. As the memoir's epigraph from Mark 5:42 suggests, Jordan is thereafter reborn like the "damsel" who arose "straightway," "for she was of the age of twelve years." "And they were astonished with a great astonishment," continues the passage from Mark; for Jordan, the astonishment involves "putting love into action."

Like the action of mentoring young poets in her Poetry for the People program at Berkeley or in teaching a class called "The Politics of Childhood," rechanneling "the pain of so much of the [students'] testimony" about their own childhoods into helping them form "a new organization advocating children's rights" (qtd. in Muller 5), adult-child cross-writing, then, has not only aesthetic but also practical value. A focus on children and childhood can either produce superficial, debilitating nostalgia and victim-consciousness, or it can produce an occasion for love put into action where real adult-child dialogue takes place. As in her stunning memoir, Jordan's writing, for children, for adults, and across what are ultimately artificial adult-child boundaries, recognizes the limits of the confessional and rejects the "bleached speech" of a therapeutic culture in favor of living language. By crossing genres, by recognizing the relationship between history and politics and the personal, and by promoting discovery rather than foreclosure, Jordan delineates a poetics that combats the regressive tropes of childhood embedded deep within our culture and proposes new tropes that may well be revolutionary.

Notes

This essay is dedicated in loving memory of my wife, Professor Patricia Pace (September 22, 1952 to November 17, 2000), my ardent companion in the fields of scholarship, as well as in the fields of love. This is the last essay of mine to have been enriched by her critical scrutiny and loving encouragement. Thanks also to Professor Aldon Nielsen for making suggestions about an earlier draft.

1. In a striking uncollected essay, "Writing and Teaching" (1969), Jordan discusses the writing of her Upward Bound students ("mainly Black teenagers from economically impoverished backgrounds" [481]). Inspired by *Life* magazine photographs of starvation in Biafra, the students wrote "asking for action." "Quite apart from the political effectiveness of their campaign, which was no worse than our adult effectiveness," writes Jordan, "the students' writing leaped into an eloquent fluency that had never even been hinted at in their earlier work" (481). "Everything we read and everything we wrote," Jordan concludes, "quite literally, translated into action: it became part of our hopeful, conscious lives" (482). In a 1994 interview, Jordan says, "I make observations in my writing that will lead to action. I make suggestions for action" (Carroll 149).

2. For a discussion of the legacy of Romantic views of the child for contemporary poetry, see my "'Infant Sight': Romanticism, Childhood and Postmodern Poetry."

3. Jordan uses the adjective herself in the "After Identity" interview: "Because he had raised me in a lot of ways as a boy, it seemed perfectly natural to resist him when he was being abusive. At least at the time it was very unusual for a little girl to resist her father's beatings. It just never occurred to me not to do that, because he had taught me, don't let anybody pick on you" (Erickson, "After Identity" 135).

4. One may attribute the publication of Jordan's first volume of poetry, *Who Look at Me,* as a children's book at least in part to particular economic and historical circumstances that created a climate for black children's literature in the late sixties and early seventies (the same climate that facilitated the publication of children's literature by other major African-American poets such as Lucille Clifton). The surge in the publication of African-American writing for children by mainstream publishers during this period was largely a response to the Black Power or New Black Arts movement, as Dianne Johnson notes, in which "'black children's literature' gained weight and recognition within the publishing world, to a level which it has not enjoyed since" and in which that movement "was often exploited for its marketing value" (77). In her 1974 article "Black Children's Books: An Overview," Judy Richardson notes another impetus for the surge in African-American children's books—the passage of the Elementary and Secondary Education Act of 1965, which provided financial incentives to organizations to meet the needs of low-income, "educationally deprived children." According to Richardson, "Suddenly the [publishing] industry geared up to meet the challenge— be 'relevant' and try to get as much money as you can before it runs out" (389–90). Richardson then predicted that, although the publication of high-quality "black children's books [was] at an all-time high" many publishers were abandoning the market as a passing fad, and that recession and drastic Federal cutbacks threatened the "so-far upward trend" (399–400). According to Johnson, by 1990, "deplorably, less Black children's literature [was] being published than was published in the 1970s" (12). See also Suzanne Rahn, "The Changing Language of Black Child Characters in American Children's Books," which contains a discussion of Jordan's use of Black English in *His Own Where* and *Dry Victories.*

5. The young poets published in *soulscript* had been Jordan's students. Among them were Julia Alvarez and Gayl Jones.

6. This letter and other entries are also reprinted as "The Voice of the Children" in *Civil Wars* (29–38). The fullest selection of Jordan's teaching journals, however, is in Lopate's *Journal of a Living Experiment.*

7. In her 1980 manifesto, "For the Sake of a People's Poetry: Walt Whitman and the Rest of Us," Jordan proclaims her allegiance to the "New World poetry" of "Walt Whitman, Pablo Neruda, Agostinho Neto, Gabriela Mistral, Langston Hughes, Margaret Walker, and Edward Brathwaite," dismissing unapologetically, the Anglo-American traditional poets "Emily Dickinson, Ezra Pound, T. S. Eliot, Wallace Stevens, Robert Lowell,

or Elizabeth Bishop. If we are nothing to them," she proclaims, "they are nothing to us! Or, as Whitman exclaimed: 'I exist as I am, that is enough.'" However, Adrienne Rich has discussed Jordan's work in conjunction with Bishop's in "The Hermit's Scream" (*What Is Found* 54–71) and Brogan ("From Warrior" 198–209) has pointed out the common ground between Bishop's "Roosters" and Jordan's "Problems of Translation: Problems of Language" (*Living Room* 37–41) and "In the Waiting Room" and "War and Memory" (*Naming* 204–11). Brogan has also discussed the influence of Bishop and Stevens on Jordan and Rich ("Planets" 255–78).

8. According to Peter Erickson's *Dictionary of Literary Biography* entry on Jordan, the project was originally intended for Langston Hughes before his death in 1967 (page 149–50).

9. The "African-derived . . . call-response" form, as Geneva Smitherman points out, as practiced in African-American churches, occurs not only between the preacher and the congregation, but also among members of the congregation itself. It is "a basic organizing principle of Black American culture generally" derived from "the traditional African world view" that "does not dichotomize life into sacred and secular realms, you can find call-responses both in the church and on the street" (104). See also Smitherman, "Word from the Hood," esp. 208–10.

10. For a lively and cogent defense of the Oakland Ebonics Resolution, see Perry and Delpit, esp. part 4, 143–86.

11. Jordan was working at the time as an urban planner. With R. Buckminster Fuller, she had designed a plan for "the architectural redesign of Harlem" and on Fuller's recommendation she was awarded the 1970 Prix de Rome in Environmental Design largely on the strength of the novel that depicts its protagonist Buddy redesigning the apartment he shares with his father who is dying in the hospital after being hit by a car. See *Civil Wars* 23–28; 59–62.

12. *His Own Where* also reflects Jordan's experience teaching the children in her workshop: "my first novel, *His Own Where*, which was written entirely in Black English, was based upon two 'regulars' of our workshop, and, of course, upon my own, personal life as a child growing up in Bedford-Stuyvesant" (*Civil* 128–29).

13. While Jordan has continued to write children's books on occasion, her later books, such as *New Life, New Room* (1975) and *Kimako's Story* (1983), are neither as interesting as the earlier works nor as centrally related to her larger poetic project.

14. The phrase "tangle of pathology" appears in Daniel Patrick Moynihan's controversial 1963 report *The Negro Family: The Case for National Action.*

15. Jordan explains vertical rhythm in detail in Muller, 38–42.

Works Cited

Brogan, Jacqueline Vaught. "From Warrior to Womanist: The Development of June Jordan's Poetry." In *Speaking the Other Self: American Women Writers.* Ed. Jeanne Campbell Reesman. Athens: University of Georgia Press, 1997. 198–209.

———. "Planets on the Table: From Wallace Stevens and Elizabeth Bishop to Adrienne Rich and June Jordan." *Wallace Stevens Journal* 19.2 (fall 1995): 255–78.

Boyd, Valerie. "'Soldier' Enlists Child's Memories." *Atlanta Journal and Constitution.* May 7, 2000. (Lexis-Nexis)

Carroll, Rebecca. *I Know What the Red Clay Looks Like: The Voice and Vision of Black Women Writers.* New York: Carol Southern Books, 1994.

Du Bois, W. E. B. *The Souls of Black Folk.* With a new introduction by Randall Kenan. New York: Signet Classic, 1995.

Erickson, Peter. "After Identity: A Conversation with June Jordan and Peter Erickson." *Transition* 63 (1994): 132–49.

————. "June Jordan 1936–" *Dictionary of Literary Biography* 38 (1985): 146–62.

————. "State of the Union." *Transition* 59 (1993): 104–9.

Gilbert, Derrick I. M. (a.k.a. D-Knowledge), ed. *Catch the Fire!!! A Cross-Generational Anthology of Contemporary African-American Poetry.* New York: Riverhead, 1998.

Glazer, Lee Stephens. "Signifying Identity: Art and Race in Romare Bearden's Projections." *Art Bulletin* 76 (1994): 411–26.

Hacker, Marilyn. "Provoking Engagement." Essay-review of *Naming Our Destiny,* by June Jordan. *The Nation* 250.4 (29 January 1990): 135–39.

Hejinian, Lyn. *My Life.* Los Angeles: Sun & Moon, 1991.

Inglis, Fred. *The Promise of Happiness: Value and Meaning in Children's Fiction.* Cambridge: Cambridge University Press, 1981.

Johnson, Diane. *Telling Tales: The Pedagogy and Promise of African American Literature for Youth.* New York: Greenwood, 1990.

Jordan, June. *Affirmative Acts: Political Essays.* New York: Anchor/Doubleday, 1998.

————. *Civil Wars.* Boston: Beacon, 1981.

————. *Dry Victories.* New York: Holt, Rinehart and Winston, 1972.

————. *His Own Where.* New York: Thomas Y. Crowell, 1971.

————. *Naming Our Destiny: New And Selected Poems.* New York: Thunder's Mouth, 1989.

————. *On Call.* Boston: South End, 1985.

————. *Passion: New Poems, 1977–1980.* Boston: Beacon, 1980.

————. *Soldier: A Poet's Childhood.* New York: Basic Civitas, 2000.

————. *Some Changes.* New York: E. P. Dutton, 1971.

————. *Technical Difficulties: African-American Notes on the State of the Union.* New York: Pantheon, 1992.

————. *Things That I Do in the Dark: Selected Poetry.* Boston: Beacon, 1981. Rpt. of 1st ed. New York: Random House, 1977.

————. *Who Look at Me. Illustrated with Twenty-Seven Paintings.* New York: Thomas Y. Crowell, 1969.

————. "Writing and Teaching." *Partisan Review* 36 (1969): 478–82.

Jordan, June, ed. *soulscript: Afro-American Poetry.* New York: Zenith/Doubleday, 1970.

Jordan, June, and Terri Bush, eds. *The Voice of the Children.* New York: Holt, Rinehart, 1970.

Lee, Felicia R. "A Feminist Survivor with the Eyes of a Child." *New York Times.* July 4, 2000, page E1. (Lexis-Nexis)

Lehmann-Haupt, Christopher. "A Children's Reading List." *New York Times.* December 16, 1971, page 67.

Livingston, Myra Cohn. *The Child as Poet: Myth or Reality?* Boston: Horn Book, 1984.

Lopate, Philip, ed. *Journal of a Living Experiment: A Documentary History of the First Ten Years of the Teachers and Writers Collaborative.* New York: Teachers and Writers, 1979.

Mostern, Kenneth. *Autobiography and Black Identity Politics: Racialization in Twentieth-Century America.* Cambridge: Cambridge University Press, 1999.

Muller, Lauren, and the Poetry for the People Collective, eds. *June Jordan's Poetry for the People: A Revolutionary Blueprint.* New York: Routledge, 1995.

Myers, Mitzi, and U. C. Knoepflmacher. "'Cross-Writing' and the Reconceptualizing of Children's Literary Studies." *Children's Literature* 25 (Special Issue on Cross-Writing Child and Adult) (1997): vii–xvii.

Pace, Patricia. "All Our Lost Children: Trauma and Testimony in the Performance of Childhood." *Text and Performance Quarterly* 18 (1998): 233–47.

Perry, Theresa, and Lisa Delpit, eds. *The Real Ebonics Debate: Power, Language, and the Education of African-American Children.* Boston: Beacon, 1998.

Petuch, Carol Ann. "I Hate to Read! An Assortment of Young Adult Literature." Yale New Haven Teachers Institute Curriculum Unit 80.01.06 <http://www.yale.edu/ynhti/curriculum/units/1980/1/80.01.06.x.html>

A Place of Rage. Dir. Pratibha Parmar. With Angela Davis, June Jordan, Alice Walker, and Trinh T. Minh-ha. Women Make Movies, 1991. 52 min.

Rahn, Suzanne. "The Changing Language of Black Child Characters in American Children's Books." In *Infant Tongues: The Voice of the Child in Literature.* Ed. Elizabeth Goodenough, Mark A. Heberle, and Naomi Sokoloff. Detroit: Wayne State University Press, 1994. 225–58.

Review of *His Own Where,* by June Jordan. *Center for Children's Books Bulletin* 25 (December 1971): 58.

Rich, Adrienne. *What Is Found There: Notebooks on Poetry and Politics.* New York: Norton, 1993.

Richardson, Judy. "Black Children's Books: An Overview." *Journal of Negro Education* 43 (1974): 380–400.

Smitherman, Geneva. *Talkin and Testifyin: The Language of Black America.* Boston: Houghton Mifflin, 1977.

———. "Word from the Hood: The Lexicon of African-American Vernacular English." In *African-American English: Structure, History, and Use.* Ed. Salikoko S. Mufwene et al. London: Routledge, 1998. 203–25.

Williams, Patricia J. *The Alchemy of Race and Rights.* Cambridge: Harvard University Press, 1991.

Reviews

Alcott Reading: An American Response to the Writings of Charlotte Brontë

Christopher A. Fahy

Louisa May Alcott and Charlotte Brontë: Transatlantic Translations, by Christine Doyle. Knoxville: University of Tennessee Press, 2000

Near the end of her book, *Louisa May Alcott and Charlotte Brontë: Transatlantic Translations,* Christine Doyle reiterates her desire for a more literary approach to Alcott, one that apprehends the significance of Alcott's reading and authorial models and does not exclusively focus on either "feminist" or "cultural contexts" (168). Doyle's approach highlights Alcott's role as a working professional simultaneously concerned with the "adoption" of Brontëan themes, characters, and plots, and their creative "adaptation" (xxiii). Her employment of comparison and contrast also illuminates Alcott's quintessentially *American* character. Spiritually akin to Brontë, Alcott is a peculiarly New World relation who has absorbed the optimism and social progressiveness of her Transcendentalist milieu.

Overall, Doyle asserts that Charlotte Brontë was a lifelong influence on Louisa May Alcott, that the younger woman, raised in a family much like the Brontës, was preoccupied with many of the same issues. Borrowing freely and fairly literally from Brontë's plots and characterizations early in her career, Alcott's adaptations became increasingly subtle as she gained confidence in her craft. Both writers examined the struggles of independent young women who attempted to combine love and work despite the presence of overbearing men and societal prejudice. Alcott, however, is more sanguine regarding her protagonists' eventual success: where Brontë at her most optimistic

Children's Literature 30, ed. Elizabeth Lennox Keyser and Julie Pfeiffer (Yale University Press, © 2002 Hollins University).

sees a socially isolated Jane Eyre sustaining a Rochester who remains her "master," Alcott foresees her women engaging in egalitarian marriages, choosing from a wider range of careers, and actively changing society. In this respect, Alcott, in contrast to a more fatalistic Brontë, displays a thoroughly American belief in individual action's efficacy.

Doyle divides her study into five chapters: two deal with Brontë's "overt" influence on Alcott through both the latter's knowledge of their similar upbringings and her employment of Brontëan plots and characters; three deal with the Englishwoman's more "subtle" impact on the themes of spirituality, familial and societal association, and self and work (xxii). In chapter 1, Doyle chronicles the parallels in the two authors' biographies, similarities that include living with eccentric, moralistic fathers and talented siblings, the death of siblings, engagement in home theatricals, backgrounds as teachers and governesses, the support of their families through writing and the disparagement of that occupation by the wider culture, a preoccupation with "inspiration," and experience publishing anonymously. At the same time, whereas Brontë's mother died young, Abba Alcott cultivated a family environment that was less self-enclosed, more open to engaging in and serving the community. Even though Alcott vacillated more in her ambition to be a serious artist than her predecessor, the American environment generally provided more opportunities for gifted female authors, and Alcott was less discouraged about the possibilities for advancement. Specifically developing a more general point that Robert Weisbuch makes in *Atlantic Double-Cross: American Literature and British Influences in the Age of Emerson,* Doyle perceives that Brontë and Alcott are joined by a sense of women's oppression but separated by Alcott's desire to develop her own identity as an American author (22).

In chapter 2, Doyle emphasizes how Alcott "adopts" and then "adapts" Charlotte Brontë's plots and characters (xxiii). In some of Alcott's earliest work the influence is quite transparent: both the governess and her haughty rival in *The Inheritance* and the Rochester-like antihero, illicit marriage, deception of the bride, and flight from temptation in *A Long Fatal Love Chase,* mirror elements in *Jane Eyre.* Later, *Moods* has a Byronic hero in Adam Warwick and a double marriage reminiscent of Brontë's *Shirley,* while *Work* employs orphan and governess motifs from *Jane Eyre* and theatrical themes from *Villette.* In "A Nurse's Story," Alcott fuses elements from both *Jane Eyre* and *Villette;* in *Little Women,* she gives Jo March a foreign teacher for her mate just as, in *Villette,* Brontë matches Lucy Snowe to the schoolmaster,

M. Paul. In general, as Alcott matures in her art, her adaptations of
Brontëan materials become more distinct. For example, unlike Jane
Eyre, Sylvia Yule does not marry her Rochester, Adam Warwick, and is
helped to realize that such a marriage would be undesirable because
he is too psychologically domineering. According to Doyle, Alcott's
Byronic hero must redeem himself without the aid of a redemptive
household angel. Doyle also relates how Alcott devises satirical variations on Brontëan themes in her sensation fiction: in "Behind a Mask,"
the governess motif is satirically transformed to critique snobbishness,
expose the theatrical nature of the "angel" role, and reveal the possibility of social change.

In chapter 3, Doyle compares and contrasts Brontë's and Alcott's
positions regarding the interior, spiritual life. Both women were highly
religious, depicted the clergy freely in their fiction, considered mis-
sionary work in a (mostly) positive light, and perceived women as embodiments of the merciful, "feminine" side of God. But where Brontë
attempted to combine masculine and feminine conceptions of deity in
Jane Eyre, by the time of *Shirley* and *Villette* she despairs of integration.
Characteristically, Alcott is more optimistic: for her, religion should be
"non-sectarian, active, and linked inextricably with the reform move-
ments of the day" (88). Her religion is more public; her ideal clergy-
man, as embodied in Reverend Power of *Work*, more warm; her Christ,
a true reformer. Alcott is also more tolerant. Where Brontë's work reflects negatively on Catholicism, Alcott generally refrains from stereotyping priests and displays a genuine openness to such formulations
as reincarnation in Buddhism and pantheism in Transcendentalism.

In chapter 4, Doyle examines the two authors' approach to the self
in society. Both believed in the need for family and community; both
believed in the cause of egalitarian marriage. Yet Brontë, whose heroines seem to simultaneously desire equality and a mentor, was trapped
by this contradiction and became (in her fiction, at least) increasingly
discouraged regarding the possibility of true marriage. To her mind,
lonely though a solitary woman might be, the stoic, single life was often
the best option. Alcott agreed with Brontë that marriage was not necessary for personal fulfillment but saw the single state in more positive
terms. Whereas Brontë seemed to perceive warm same-sex friendships
as a precursor of the truly significant event of marriage, Alcott saw
both those friendships and communities of women as enduring goods.
Indeed, Doyle relates that Alcott sought a new social reality, matri-
archally oriented families that included sympathetic outsiders. Plum-

field, with Jo March, husband, and children augmented by relatives and students, constituted such an alternative grouping. In identifying it, Doyle perceives Alcott striking a balance between the Transcendentalist conception of voluntary communities and traditional families, thus effecting a solution to the conflict between friendship and blood that had incapacitated her father at Fruitlands.

In chapter 5, Doyle considers how both Brontë and Alcott stressed the importance of work for the mental health, self-esteem, and happiness of women. In Brontë's society, however, becoming a governess was virtually the only occupation a poor gentlewoman could undertake, and even that occupation was considered morally suspect. The fact that women worked longer, at a greater variety of professions, and with less societal censure in America encouraged Alcott to envision a more positive future than Brontë, whose fatalism extended even to the profession of writing. For the Englishwoman, writing and motherhood were either/or contingencies; in contrast, in the March trilogy, Alcott proposes that a woman might enjoy both options.

Louisa May Alcott and Charlotte Brontë: Transatlantic Translations is, in all respects, admirable work. The biographical connections between the Brontë and Alcott families and the textual connections between *Jane Eyre* and both *Moods* and *A Long Fatal Love Chase* are particularly striking, though all the cited links are plausible. One strength of this study is that such Brontëan works as *Villette* and *Shirley* are, for the first time, systematically related to Alcott, illuminating the transatlantic influence of not only a Jane Eyre but a Lucy Snowe. This breadth, and the carefulness of the close readings done on both authors' texts, make this a valuable work.

At its best, comparison and contrast highlights aspects of its subjects that might otherwise be obscured. Here the method works exceptionally well, illuminating Alcott's role as a professional, American writer. Previous feminist criticism of Alcott has sometimes cast her as psychologically reactive, melodramatically angry, and compulsive in her need to expose women's oppression. Doyle limns Brontë's and Alcott's mutual sense of what constitutes important feminist issues, but here Alcott equally emerges as a conscious craftsperson, choosing what to adopt, what to transform. Comparing the settled, recessive British culture to the more dynamic American culture heightens the sense of Alcott's controlled energy. I've interpreted the aging Jo March's desire for the single life as reflecting Alcott's disappointment over her career; this study forces reconsideration, an understanding that while Jo (and Alcott) make compromises, their positions on work and marriage retain a sometimes startling originality.

While Doyle focuses on the literary dimensions of these authors, such a focus does not come at the expense of feminist or cultural contextualization. There are illuminating sections on the demographics of working women in Britain and America, the status of the governess and actress, the anti-Catholic movement, sensation magazines, Fruitlands, and the concept of a feminine religion. Although the principle analytic method is comparative reading of texts, that reading is always conditioned by the consideration of relevant historical backgrounds.

Rhetorically, *Louisa May Alcott and Charlotte Brontë: Transatlantic Translations* is exceptionally lucid. Doyle employs no jargon or unexplained terms and does not assume that the audience already knows all the previous criticism. Structurally, the study is also exemplary: Doyle abets clarity first by conceptually separating the two authors' affinities into categories of biography, plot and character, and themes, then by subdividing the themes section further into studies of spirit, society, and work. Consequently, while the overall thesis builds throughout and is convincing, this book may also, with profit, be read for the arguments in individual chapters.

Two of these arguments are particularly compelling. The chapter on "The Inner Life" is as good a study of Alcott's religious belief as I've seen, neatly balancing her tolerance, reforming spirit, and frequently heterodox views. I was also impressed by Doyle's insight that Alcott had developed an understanding of a new form of family, one that would be united by both blood and conviction. This is a compelling observation that should simultaneously help us forge deeper connections between Alcott and her father Bronson and correct misunderstandings of her as a defender of the domestic status quo.

While agreeing with Doyle on all of her major themes, I perceive an additional riff worth developing. Ann Douglas writes of the "taming" that Alcott women undergo (63), but I believe something might be added here regarding the "taming" of Alcott's male characters. Doyle writes of Alcott's skepticism regarding the ultimate equality of the Eyre-Rochester union and the impossibility of the angelic heroine truly reforming the Byronic hero. Yet here, too, I perceive Alcott "adapting" one of Brontë's themes for her own purpose. Gladys and Cecil, the "angels" of *A Modern Mephistopheles* and "A Marble Woman," have, for all their sincerity, also learned to act, to practice what Mary Chapman calls "deception" (172), when it serves their purposes. Cast as Galatea figures by Pygmalion-like creators, they turn the tables and mold their older "masters" with their performances. In that way, through a combination of virtue and guile (a technique perfected by Jean Muir of "Behind a Mask"), the men are "tamed" and re-formed.

Also, I wished for more clarification of the generational differences between the two women. Doyle does thoroughly explain the distinctive variations between English and American society that influenced Brontë and Alcott. And given the chronologies of the authors' careers, it is appropriate to compare mid-century Britain to America circa 1860–80. Yet, recalling Nina Baym's and Elaine Showalter's analyses of the transformations a few decades wrought in American women writers' self-perception (see *Woman's Fiction* [32, 33] and *Sister's Choice* [8–16, 67–70]), I wondered how much of the difference between Brontë's and Alcott's views could be attributed to recent cultural change. To what extent did American culture in 1840–60 mirror Britain's; would Alcott be less optimistic regarding women's prospects for love and work had she been writing earlier? Conversely, to what extent did British culture keep pace with American: would 1870–80 have been a more hospitable environment for Charlotte Brontë to envision marriage and career than the 1840s proved to be? (And what are we to make of the fact that Brontë did ultimately marry while Alcott did not?)

These are minor concerns. This is a fine book that I recommend to both Brontë and Alcott scholars and to any general reader with an interest in either. It is also a book that offers, in its way, a challenge for critics to consider Alcott from a more "literary" perspective. Here, such an examination places Alcott in an optimistic light where progressive views and artistic control are emphasized. In the concluding pages, however, Doyle also writes of Alcott's "humor" as a distinguishing "technical aspect" of her work (171). That humor (too often slighted in Alcott criticism though examined here in the analysis of "Behind a Mask") could reveal both high spirits and rage, balanced equanimity and a forced "whistling in the dark." It could provide a springboard for more formal literary explorations that, like *Transatlantic Translations,* also uncover fresh feminist and cultural ground. It is a virtue of this book's approach that it encourages just such explorations.

Works Cited

Baym, Nina. *Woman's Fiction: A Guide to Novels by and about Women in America, 1820–1870.* Ithaca: Cornell University Press, 1978.
Chapman, Mary Megan. " 'Living Pictures': Women and Tableaux Vivants in Nineteenth-Century Fiction and Culture." Ph.D. diss., Cornell University, 1993. Ann Arbor: UMI, 1993. 93030082.
Douglas, Ann. "Mysteries of Louisa May Alcott." *New York Review of Books.* September 28, 1978, 60–63.
Showalter, Elaine. *Sister's Choice.* Oxford: Clarendon Press, 1991.

Little House on a Big Quilt

Anne K. Phillips

Constructing the Little House: Gender, Culture, and Laura Ingalls Wilder, by
Ann Romines. Amherst: University of Massachusetts Press, 1997.

The paperback cover of Ann Romines's analysis of Laura Ingalls Wilder's and Rose Wilder Lane's pioneer stories features a pieced quilt block of a little house surrounded by a border predominantly composed of floral triangles and solid diamonds. The visual effect is twofold: the prints used in the house and the border suggest contentment while the angles of the border, the points in the block, and the border's effect of isolating or confining the little house imply a certain tension. This cover illustration is an apt metaphor for the contents of *Constructing the Little House.* Deftly piecing together the literary, cultural, and familial issues at work within and behind the Little House books, Romines enables readers to recognize both the harmony and the dissonance of the series.

Romines draws on extensive training in nineteenth-century American literature and culture, American women's writing, and children's literature, providing the most comprehensive, sophisticated reading of the series to date. Not only is she well versed in the Little House scholarship, but she has studied and made use of all of the relevant personal and library holdings; the notes and works cited for *Constructing the Little House* are themselves a treasure trove for scholars at all levels. She also reveals an impressive personal familiarity with the Little House books, and it is a highlight of her study that she is not afraid to acknowledge her personal investment in them. She is both critic and fan, outside observer of the Little House phenomenon and avid follower, from childhood into adulthood. Stories about being driven by her grandmother on her tenth birthday to Springfield, Missouri, to have Laura Ingalls Wilder sign her copy of *These Happy Golden Years,* or admissions that she, too, owns a Charlotte doll and has toured the Little House sites throughout the Midwest, prove to be central to much that Romines has to say about the series. Aside from the breadth

Children's Literature 30, ed. Elizabeth Lennox Keyser and Julie Pfeiffer (Yale University Press, © 2002 Hollins University).

of knowledge and intelligence that Romines brings to her study, her voice in this work is innovative and inspiring.

Constructing the Little House is organized in a fashion that is both linear (a chronological analysis of the books in the series) and circular. Within the thought-provoking discussions of race and diversity in her chapter on *Little House on the Prairie,* for instance, she also incorporates references to Laura's attraction to "half-breed" Big Jerry from *By the Shores of Silver Lake* and the minstrel scene from *Little Town on the Prairie.* In her discussion of female rituals and mother-daughter relationships relative to *The Long Winter,* Romines usefully incorporates a discussion of the history of Laura's doll, Charlotte, based on events described in *Little House in the Big Woods* and *On the Banks of Plum Creek.* The arrangement is successful: the chapters thoroughly analyze individual works, but they also demonstrate significant connections between the volumes in the series.

Following her introduction, "The Voices from the Little House," in which she sketches her personal and professional history with the Little House books, Romines provides five chapters devoted to the individual books as well as a conclusion. The first chapter, "Preempting the Patriarchs: Daughters in the House," traces the way in which Wilder and Lane tell the stories of their fathers in *Little House in the Big Woods* and *Farmer Boy.* Here, Romines focuses on the way that Wilder and Lane ostensibly tell the stories of men in their first two collaborations. Both works, however, offer a more sophisticated commentary on gender than has been previously acknowledged, not only in connection with the most prominent characters in the books but also through references to such characters as *Big Woods'* Grandma Ingalls and Cousin Charley and *Farmer Boy's* James and Alice Wilder. As Romines notes, "In many ways," *Little House in the Big Woods* "is a story about the burdens of enacting a patriarchal role" (32), and in *Farmer Boy,* Almanzo's sisters "provide much of the cultural complexity" (42). Ultimately, according to Romines, Wilder's and Lane's first two books are "the work of dutiful daughters honoring their farmer fathers; but they are also subtly iconoclastic works, dismantling patriarchal prerogatives to facilitate the emergence of wide-ranging female sensibilities" (46).

Chapter 2, "'Indians in the House': A Narrative of Acculturation," focuses on *Little House on the Prairie.* In it, according to Romines, Wilder and Lane "propose some of the hardest and most persistent questions

for an emigrant nation: questions of possible cultural interaction, cultural collision, and a potentially multicultural life" (57). Throughout
the chapter, Romines argues convincingly for the complexity of the
novel's response to such questions. Moving beyond the oft-quoted,
"The only good Indian is a dead Indian" into an analysis of such scenes
as Pa's introduction of his daughters to the abandoned Indian camp,
Romines asserts that "with all the force of his male and parental authority, Pa presents Native American life as worthy of respect and attentive reading and he includes women and their traditional domestic work (as defined by Euro-Americans) in his instructive text" (62).
Romines grounds much of her analysis of the book's racial issues in
relevant considerations of gender. Thus, Caroline Ingalls's outbursts
against Indians might be seen as "her one major outlet for anger, resistance, and defense of the values of feminine domestic culture on the
unsettled prairie" (69). The chapter usefully incorporates references
to other works on Native Americans (published and unpublished) by
Wilder and Lane, Wilder's journals, and relevant scholarship on the
settlement of the Great Plains and frontier life. This chapter is an important addition to the body of criticism generated by *Little House on the
Prairie,* the most contested volume in the series and "one of our most
disturbing and ambitious narratives about failures and experiments of
acculturation in the American West" (94).

    Chapter 3, "Getting and Spending: Materialism and the Little
House," assesses identity and consumerism in *On the Banks of Plum
Creek.* Here, Mary and Laura Ingalls receive "an education in consum-
ing: the choosing and buying of things, the spending of money" (98).
In *Little House in the Big Woods,* Mary and Laura acquiesced as Ma chose
the fabric for their dresses; in *Plum Creek,* they begin to assert their
own tastes and buying power. Tracing the patterns of desire and acquisition, from Pa's purchase on credit of machine-made house materials to Laura's first experience with a community Christmas tree,
Romines convincingly argues for the increasing significance of things.
Her analysis of the Ingalls's major domestic purchases through the
series—the cast-iron stove, a sewing machine, and a parlor organ—
traces the way these commodities elevate the family's social status as
well as the way their acquisition enables the daughters to "learn about
what girls and women can buy and do and be on the Great Plains frontier" (120). Here, Romines's attention to Mary's emerging role as pro-
ficient consumer throughout the later books provides readers with an
original perspective on this often-neglected but significant character.

Chapter 4, "The Little House That Gender Built: The Novels of Adolescence," focuses on *By the Shores of Silver Lake* and *The Long Winter*. In them, Laura must be separated from her father, who has always been her closest ally and the family member with whom she has most affinity. "As an adolescent, she must (her parents assert) live within the parameters of a socially permissible *female* story" (144). In *Silver Lake*, Laura is introduced to her boundaries: she must become a teacher because her parents—particularly her mother—expect it; she must not develop a friendship with her cousin, Lena, of whom Ma disapproves; she must assist Ma in the house because Mary is now blind and there are younger children to help care for. Despite these increasing constraints, *Silver Lake* is "the book in which Laura Ingalls most visibly recoils from identification with her mother" (155), as evidenced by her desires to watch the men build the railroad, to move farther west, to slide in the moonlight on Silver Lake's frozen surface. In contrast, in *The Long Winter*, "the dynamics of the series change. Pa's weaknesses begin to be apparent, and Laura is pushed to recognize that, as a young woman, her primary affinities must be with her mother, not her father" (163). This chapter serves as a welcome extension of previous work on the Little House series that persists in identifying Ma solely as the angel in the house or, more particularly, a china shepherdess on a shelf. Romines rightly recognizes that "as much as Pa, Ma is the conceptual architect of the Little Houses" (174).

Dealing with *Little Town on the Prairie* and *These Happy Golden Years* in chapter 5, "Laura's Plots: Ending the Little House," Romines focuses not only on the courtship of Almanzo and Laura but also on Laura's experiences as a teacher, her increasingly adult status within her family and the community, her confidence as a consumer, and "her subtle growth as a recipient and arbiter of gendered culture" (194). Incorporating theories of carnival, Romines traces the way De Smet becomes "an intensely contested site," writing that "if Laura is to have freedom and even limited mobility, the values of the Little House must prevail in the Little Town as well" (205). The chapter also acknowledges Laura's growth as a writer, an issue of relevance to considerations of Wilder's evolving literary career. Of particular interest is Romines's attention to the range of teaching models available to Laura and her developing opinions about those models. Adding to the previous chapter's analysis of Ma's increasing prominence in the series, Romines focuses here on Ma's mentoring of Laura during her tenure at the Brewster School, usefully extending Marianne Hirsch's work with the Demeter-Persephone myth to Ma's and Laura's relationship in the later books (and to Wilder's and Lane's collaboration throughout the series and their lives).

The conclusion, "The End of the Little House Books," reproduces Helen Sewell's original illustration from the last page of *These Happy Golden Years,* which many readers of the Little House books might never have seen. Working against Wilder's insistence on providing such definite closure to the series is, of course, the continuing appeal and commercialization of the Little House series. Accounting for our cultural inability to let the series end, Romines writes that Laura's life "is hard and dangerous and sometimes marginal; it is often curtailed by cultural constructions of gender and race. Nevertheless, this girl is presented as someone with her own compelling, continuing claim: a claim to a life, and a claim to a story" (256).

The back cover of *Constructing the Little House* features another quilt block, also of a cabin, this time executed in alternating dark and light solids. This block is not only pieced; it has also been quilted, and the design of the quilting is apparent even at a distance. It is appropriate that this quilt on the back cover appears in the background of a photograph of the author. In *Constructing the Little House,* Ann Romines has artfully stitched together layers of literary analysis, cultural commentary, and personal memoir, producing an artifact that is at the same time useful and aesthetically pleasing. Her smart, significant commentary on the Little House series should endure and be exhibited as the finest of Wilder studies for many years to come.

Apologizing for Scott O'Dell—Too Little, Too Late

C. Anita Tarr

Scott O'Dell: Twayne's United States Authors Series, by David L. Russell. New York: Twayne, 1999.

Scott O'Dell certainly deserves a Twayne book. A decade after his death, it is time to offer a retrospective analysis to help us reflect on O'Dell's reputation, his development as a writer, and his impact on children's literature. This Twayne book is a solid exercise in New Criticism, examining theme, characterization, plot structure, and style, but unfortunately it does not go beyond that. Russell has divided O'Dell's many works into logical groupings: adult works; *Island of the Blue Dolphins;* novels set in the Old Southwest; literary experiments; the Seven Serpents trilogy; present-day realistic novels; and the last few historical novels. All this is followed by a "critical assessment," which sums up O'Dell's alleged strong and weak points as a writer for children and young adults. Rather than offering much in-depth analysis, however, Russell is apologetic about O'Dell:

> If he [O'Dell] seemed to develop little as a writer of children's books during his career, we must not forget that he began that career fairly well at the top . . . produc[ing] a Newbery Medal winner and three Newbery Honor Award books. . . . Ultimately it will be these works on which O'Dell must and should be judged. (x)

I am not convinced that any artist should be judged only on his/her best work, least of all O'Dell. It has always disturbed me that this author of mediocre historical novels for adults was awarded accolades when he began writing for children.

Russell's first chapter provides the most surprising information: Scott O'Dell was not his true name at all; he was originally named Odell Gabriel Scott and legally changed his name after a publisher transposed the first and last name and he thought Scott O'Dell sounded more like a writer. His birthdate, too, is often incorrect: he was born in 1898 (not 1903, as often stated). While he did begin publishing newspaper articles and even a book in 1924 on popular photo-

Children's Literature 30, ed. Elizabeth Lennox Keyser and Julie Pfeiffer (Yale University Press, © 2002 Hollins University).

plays (screenplays), his career for a long time was that of a cameraman
and part-time writer. He was already in his sixties when a new career
of writing for children took hold, and he kept at it, with his second
wife's help and support, until he died in 1989. The information presented in this chapter serves as a necessary precursor to the later chapters that deal with O'Dell as a writer. Nevertheless, from Russell's viewpoint, there does not seem to be much connection between O'Dell the
cameraman and friend to Hollywood and O'Dell the children's writer.
Other critics (e.g., Leon Garfield) have said that O'Dell's novels read
like film scripts, but Russell does not develop the cinematic connection
to the writing other than that there is "an almost cinematic quality" in
O'Dell's later works, especially with his "lively action and colorful characters . . . and his aversion to both lengthy exposition and philosophical musings" (11). This seems like a missed opportunity, for O'Dell's
early fascination with film might help explain his problems with character development, a problem that Russell recognizes throughout: "As
would be true of his entire writing career, character development is
not O'Dell's strong suit" (13).

It might be a surprise to some that O'Dell was a half-hearted writer
for adults earlier in his career. Russell summarizes his three early novels and helps us see them as a kind of apprenticeship allowing for
O'Dell to work through several recurrent themes: his abhorrence of
slavery, of greed, and of the treatment of Native Americans. Russell,
however, gives scant attention to *Country of the Sun: Southern California,
An Informal History and Guide* (1957), which is particularly unfortunate
because it is here that we see the beginnings of so many of O'Dell's
later stories, including "The Lost Woman of San Nicholas"—that is,
Karana (the heroine of *Country* jumps ship because her child, not her
brother, has been left on shore). We also see the scandalous behavior
of a Spanish woman who refused to ride side-saddle, as do Carlota and
other O'Dell characters; we read of the Spanish landowners and their
customs, reused in *Carlota;* and we are given a partial telling of the
journey of Coronado, expanded later in *The King's Fifth*. Undeniably,
O'Dell's fiction written for adults is important for children's literature
critics to examine, so we can see how these full-blown treatments were
reformatted (watered down, frankly) into the plots and characters of
his children's novels.

Most readers applaud O'Dell for one book, *Island of the Blue Dolphins* (1960), because it covers three areas of concern: multicultural-
ism, gender stereotypes, and environmental awareness. No one would

dispute that Karana, as both female and Native American, displays a very progressive view toward nature. Russell, however, does not delve below the surface in his analysis of this novel. Russell praises the novel's structure, as the chapters alternate between mundane domestic affairs and adventure, and he states that *Island* "exudes a poignancy and dignity that the author was never to equal again" (36), an opinion I share. Like other reviewers, Russell employs the adjective "stoic" to describe Karana as well as other of O'Dell's Native-American characters, such as Sacajawea, even though we must assume that the Ghalas-at and Shoshone nations are different cultures. I would maintain that O'Dell basically uses the same style of writing no matter who is narrating in first person—a Native-American girl, a Spanish boy, an English woman. For some characters, the style seems stilted and unrealistic, but for others, such as Karana, it works. Russell does not consider the idea that Karana's speech appears natural simply because she *sounds* like a Hollywood Indian, using no contractions, resisting any emotional display, appearing stoic.

Similarly, Russell's analysis of *Island*'s strongest point—Karana—falls short. O'Dell claims that originally his editor wanted the main character changed to a boy, but he was appalled at the thought because the story is based on an actual occurrence ("Scott" 357). Russell states that a constant agenda of O'Dell's is providing strong female characters. Karana is praised because she knowingly breaks the tribal taboo of making weapons, and she survives on her own while creating her own moral values about animals. But are Karana's more sensitive values developed out of necessity, because she is alone and needs companionship? Because she is a woman? Because she is Native American? Does it matter? One of the hallmarks of O'Dell's writing, for both adults and children, is the focus on females who subvert their cultures' expectations. Surely some feminist criticism would have been valuable here to help guide the discussion of this very important issue.

Unfortunately, as with *Island,* Russell offers no real discussion about *Carlota* (1977) and the titular character's changing sensibilities (in chapter 4). He outlines examples of how she proves her physical strength, how she rides a horse like a boy and is treated like her father's lost son. At this point, she has taken on the role of an obedient son, and she must acquiesce to all her father's decisions. Then she rebels. Again, I would have liked more theoretical context: is it because O'Dell's heroines are physically more free that they desire more personal and moral freedom, to run their own lives, to activate their modern ideologies? At the least, O'Dell's female characters deserve more study in the future. Susan Naramore Maher's essay that labels O'Dell's stories of the Old Southwest as "counterwesterns" is oddly absent from Russell's discussion (it is only listed in the selected bibliography). His descriptions of O'Dell's novels about the Old Southwest could have benefited from Maher's analysis of how "O'Dell gave voice to the oppressed, to those who lost their lands and their cultures" (216), and how his "female narrators are significant agents in his revisionist tales" (226).

In the last chapter, "Critical Assessment," Russell lists five major roles for which we should remember O'Dell: as a consummate storyteller; as a historical novelist; as a moralist; as an environmentalist; and as a multiculturalist. All these areas that are alleged by Russell to be strengths are nonetheless problematic. Russell outlines O'Dell's basic formula for writing, which involves a character developing a moral code that is at odds with the environment around him/her. But O'Dell is "seldom elegant" or "seldom reflective" (121), and the first-person narrator, the use of which O'Dell refused to abandon, often is too limited to tell the story. O'Dell gave his characters twentieth-century attitudes, but Russell still praises the smooth inclusion of historical details. Russell could have used some of Suzanne Rahn's suggestions to help illuminate O'Dell's purposes for writing historical fiction: to preserve the past? to provide hope for the present? to both comment on and guide the present? Moralist is clearly the most fitting of descriptors. His agenda to create characters who are sensitive to others' needs is an admirable one; the problem is that often he achieves this goal at the expense of character development and credibility, even historical accuracy. Russell sees O'Dell's environmental philosophy as fairly simple—that human beings and nature should live in harmony, best exemplified by Karana. Russell himself finds the most questionable label for O'Dell is that of multiculturalist. In this section Russell devotes a few paragraphs to the criticisms of O'Dell's portraits of minority cultures, especially Hispanic and Native American. Russell recounts these criticisms briefly but does not really argue against them; instead he tries to point out that any negative portraits in O'Dell's novels are balanced by more positive ones, or, in defense of *Black Star, Bright Dawn* (1988), quoting Ellen Sallé, that Inuit children wrote him to tell him of their appreciation for his portrayal of their culture. Russell reminds us that "O'Dell was among the first children's authors to portray Native American characters with sympathy for their mistreatment at the hands of the Europeans and European Americans and with respect for their cultural beliefs and mores" (128). Russell ends this section and the book with an appeal that, since O'Dell received so many accolades, we should be satisfied with that and, I assume, be quiet.

And that is my major concern with this book. Russell, I feel, has muzzled a lot of critics, not just those who write negatively about O'Dell's talent, but even those who, basically sympathetic, could have helped place O'Dell's work in perspective, such as Maher, Rebecca Lukens, and John Townsend. Malcolm Usrey's *DLB* essay on O'Dell offers good critical analysis of almost all of the children's novels but is used only piecemeal by Russell. Granted, this is not a book intending to describe the critical reception of O'Dell—this clearly is Russell's statement only—but there are other voices that should have been heard as well. Other critics have written about O'Dell's pilfering from his earlier works and about his stereotyping, but they get little or no recognition here. When Isabel Schon calls O'Dell a "dilettante historian" who "promote[s] gross misconceptions" of pre-Columbian and Hispanic cultures (322–33), I think we should listen very carefully. When Leon Garfield laments O'Dell's unemotional, uninvolving characters, I think we should pay attention. We should continue to ask questions about O'Dell and not assume that, because he has published, because he has won awards, he is beyond reproach.

So what can Russell's book on O'Dell offer readers? He is especially good at analyzing how O'Dell's insistence on using first-person narrators often had detrimental effects on plot and character development. (O'Dell claimed first-person narration was just easier [123]). And he has offered valuable critiques of the novels' structure regarding cohesion and clarity. He has brought to light O'Dell's frequent criticisms of institutionalized Christianity, which are not at all at odds with the characters' basic humanitarian values. He has confirmed the reviewers' oft-mentioned problems with O'Dell's character motivation. And he has brought together O'Dell's strengths—especially as suspenseful storyteller, moralist, and environmentalist. All of this would be useful for a general audience, apparently Twayne's goal. But as long as O'Dell is being recommended on the basis of his awards—and he still is— I would like to see this book as a beginning, not an end, to O'Dell scholarship. It should not have the last word.

Works Cited and Consulted

Garfield, Leon. "Young Man Among the Mayans." Review of *The Captive,* by Scott O'Dell. *Washington Post/Book World.* March 9, 1980, page 7.

Maher, Susan Naramore. "Encountering Others: The Meeting of Cultures in Scott O'Dell's *Island of the Blue Dolphins* and *Sing Down the Moon.*" *Children's Literature in Education* 23.4 (1992): 215–27.

Rahn, Suzanne. "An Evolving Past: The Story of Historical Fiction and Nonfiction for Children." *Lion and the Unicorn* 15 (1991): 1–26.

Schon, Isabel. "A Master Storyteller and His Distortions of Pre-Columbian and Hispanic Cultures." *Journal of Reading* 29 (January 1986): 322–25.

"Scott O'Dell: Immortal Writer." *American Libraries* (June 1973): 356–57.

Tarr, C. Anita. "Fool's Gold: Scott O'Dell's Formulaic Vision of the Old West." *Children's Literature Association Quarterly* 17 (spring 1992): 19–24.

———. "An Unintentional System of Gaps: A Phenomenological Reading of Scott O'Dell's *Island of the Blue Dolphins.*" *Children's Literature in Education* 28 (June 1997): 61–71.

Usrey, Malcolm. "Scott O'Dell." *Dictionary of Literary Biography,* vol. 52: *American Writers for Children since 1960: Fiction.* Ed. Glenn E. Estes. Detroit: Gale Research, 1986. 278–95.

Dangerous Intersection: Feminists at Work

Karen Coats

Girls, Boys, Books, Toys: Gender in Children's Literature and Culture, edited by Beverly Lyon Clark and Margaret R. Higonnet. Baltimore: Johns Hopkins University Press, 1999.

Feminist criticism, with its insistence on disrupting and challenging hegemonic, patriarchal assignations of value, seems a natural companion to a literature that often seeks to do the same. When simpletons become kings, when pigs become minor celebrities, when geeky orphans save the world, we know we are in a utopian space, a space where the oppressive restrictions of age and gender can be successfully overcome. In fact, so many children's books feature marginalized subjects without much physical or political power overcoming their oppressors through intelligence, imagination, courage, and a facility with language that I might argue that feminism itself can trace its unconscious ideological genealogy, at least in part, to the empowered heroes and heroines of children's fantasy fiction. But that argument is not one that is often made or acknowledged, and this is why the project undertaken in *Girls, Boys, Books, Toys* is such a significant one to both feminist and children's culture scholarship. Beverly Lyon Clark and Margaret Higonnet have brought together scholars from various disciplines to work at the current intersections of feminism and children's literature and culture. Clark's introduction sketches the lines of development of both fields, and elegantly posits a range of fruitful and exciting possibilities engendered by feminist inquiries into children's texts and artifacts that seek to go beyond traditional, simplistic readings of how girls have been portrayed in children's texts, or how women's writing differs from men's. The rhetorical force of her introduction and her assertion that what follows will "illuminate the vibrant intersection between children's literature and feminist criticism and spark new questions for scholarship" (8) create high expectations for the volume.

Imagine my disappointment, then, upon finding that the first essay in the collection is one more feminist reading of a fairy tale by one of

Children's Literature 30, ed. Elizabeth Lennox Keyser and Julie Pfeiffer (Yale University Press, © 2002 Hollins University).

the venerable fathers of the field of children's literary criticism. U. C. Knoepflmacher's "Repudiating 'Sleeping Beauty'" compares and contrasts the literary retellings of the tale through male and female authors, tracing its lineage through Basile's ur-text and Perrault's sanitized, though still masculinist, retelling. It is not that this essay is not important and informative; rather, what caused my dismay is its pride of place in this particular effort. I feared that the lineage he traces for Sleeping Beauty, from masculine ur-text to feminine repudiation, was somehow the fated structure of the volume itself—resulting in a defensive rather than a creative act. Or perhaps Knoepflmacher's essay was somehow necessary as the authorizing presence for what was to follow—one more example of the totemic Freudian father circumscribing the field of feminine work and play, turning what followed into so much more phallic *jouissance* after all.

It turns out that my fears were mostly unfounded. The sixteen short, lively essays are divided into three sections—History, Theory, and Culture—but as Clark notes, these categories are not as exclusive as they might appear, and there is much overlap. For instance, Lissa Paul's reading of the poetry of Grace Nichols against that of Robert Louis Stevenson in the Theory section nonetheless brings history and culture together in its treatment of this postcolonial poet. Susan Willis's study of dinosaurs, in the Culture section, reminds us of the historical turns that the scientific and cultural study of dinosaurs has taken since feminism entered the popular imagination. Other essays fit more squarely into their designation. In the History section, for instance, Claudia Marquis' study of nineteenth-century adventure stories gives a strong feel for the imperialist drive to domesticate the exoticized other characteristic of the period. John Stephens and Robyn McCallum offer a post-Althusserian interpretation of the implied reader— who is interpellated as feminist—of adolescent fiction in the Theory section, and Lori Kenschaft's reading of *Mary Poppins* enacts the necessary, but often frustrating, deferral of ideological certitude in postmodern culture. Is *Mary Poppins* ultimately subversive or conservative; does it espouse feminist values or merely reinforce traditional "family values," understood in the narrowest sense? Yes, yes, yes, and yes.

Read individually, the offerings cannot be characterized by that ubiquitous adjective reviewers dish out when describing anthologies— uneven; none of the essays falls flat. They are all interesting, evocative pieces with more or less stand-alone value. To see the value of the work as a whole, however, I find it useful to tinker with the structure that

Clark and Higonnet have chosen and to introduce another structure that allows us to see the book's potential to retheorize the intersection of feminism and children's literature criticism. As I see it, *Girls, Boys, Books, Toys* does three vitally important things: it provides a history of mainstream feminism's relation with children's literature, it mounts a critique of certain outdated modes of feminist thinking, and it issues a call for children's literature scholars to enter the space opened by feminist criticism in order to articulate the dynamic role of children's texts in literary history.

As I noted above, Clark's introduction traces the lines of development of feminist literary theory and children's literature criticism, noting that each has at times and significantly ignored the other. This makes the introduction a valuable pull-out feature for students needing an overview of the field; in fact, I'm including it in my syllabus for a graduate course on critical theories in children's literature. Refashioning and extending some of the arguments that she made in her 1993/94 *Children's Literature Association Quarterly* essay "Fairy Godmothers or Wicked Stepmothers: The Uneasy Relationship of Feminist Theory and Children's Criticism," Clark chastises feminist thinkers for largely ignoring children's literature, and she chastises children's literature critics for largely ignoring feminism. Both Mavis Reimer and Mitzi Myers offer further insight into the historical impasses of children's literature and feminist theory, extending the scope of Clark's general appraisal. In addition, Kuznet's focused discussion of theoretical treatments of domesticity elegantly weaves together the personal and political history and progress of an idea intimately connected to children's and women's lives.

But in addition to a straightforward presentation of history, there is critique. Clark's use of quotation marks around "images of girls," the hallmark of traditional liberal feminist criticism, in her introduction suggests to me at any rate that she is wary of this hackneyed approach to children's literature study, and indeed the article cowritten by sociologists Roger Clark, Heidi Kulkin, and Liam Clancy bears out this interpretation. "The Liberal Bias in Feminist Social Science Research on Children's Books" highlights the landmark Weitzman study in 1972 of the depiction of gender in American picture books. The study became a "rallying point for feminist activism" (72) and was largely responsible for the subsequent changes in publishing practice regarding "images of girls." The authors go on to point out that the success of the Weitzman study "established a liberal-feminist paradigm for social science investigations of children's books that has been virtually un-challenged" (73) and suggest possible ways in which future study could pay more attention to issues of class, race, age, and the depiction of feminist values rather than simply looking for the egalitarian portrayal of girls.

This questioning of values is at the heart of the challenge issued by *Girls, Boys, Books, Toys*. Rather than simply looking at where girls and women fit into a masculinized, adult-centered worldview, feminist critics of children's literature and culture must begin to think about how youth culture has the ability to change that worldview. This is the main thrust of Lynne Vallone's essay, "Grrrls and Dolls: Feminism and Female Youth Culture." Vallone's exploration of the raw world of Riot Grrrl culture causes her to question her own desire for her daughter to grow up to be a feminist, "just like [her]" (197). She sets the up-beat, girl-celebrating but largely innocuous publication *New Moon: The Magazine for Girls and Their Dreams* against the abrasive, anarchic zines of the Riot Grrrl network and poses the question: How can we accom-modate the forceful presence of these angry young feminists, or better yet, how can we hear without accommodating them? For to accommo-date their voices is to undo the possibility of their revolution.

But revolution, it seems, has a long and unacknowledged history in children's literature, according to Mitzi Myers, whose voice is most powerful in insisting that feminists scholars of children's literature have a great deal of work to do in terms of rewriting literary and cul-tural history to include literature written for children. In her essay, "Child's Play as Woman's Peace Work," she takes Maria Edgeworth as her model in "taking the child's part" as she seeks a new understanding of the discourses of revolution and Romanticism. She challenges other feminist scholars to do the same: "If we really mean to redefine literary history, if we seek more than an additive canon with female ghettos, we need child's play" (38). Mavis Reimer joins Myers and Vallone in their call for a new hearing, a rereading of the children's narrative in the midst of an adult-centered feminism. This challenge seems to me to set a new and important direction for feminist scholars of children's lit-erature and culture and remains the most valuable feature of the book as a whole.

There are things that a reader will not find in this anthology, how-ever. There is, for example, no hint of queerness; curiously enough in this current moment of feminism, each essay turns on the unques-tioned, nearly essentialized binary of women versus men, boys versus girls. William Moebius's look at picture books by male and female authors and illustrators is exemplary of this binary approach; feminine agency is, for him, most evident when it succeeds in sending subversive "messages to the masculine occupants of the moment" (129). In addition, despite the fact that the volume pays attention to multinational texts, the methodology of the essays consistently showcases white, Western, mainstream liberal humanist feminism. For instance, Lynn Vallone's essay on Riot Grrrls charts the new directions feminism is taking among American and British teens but acknowledges that the audience for the Riot Grrrl message is a "narrow constituency" (205) of "'mainly white'" (Tucker and Sawyer, qtd. in Vallone 203) middle-class girls. Two essays in the collection, "Fictions of Difference: Contemporary Indian Stories for Children," by Rajeswari Sunder Rajan, and "An Arab Girl Draws Trouble," by Allen Douglas and Fedwa Malti-Douglas, hint at the need for a less universalizing understanding of feminist concerns, but their texts seem positioned as "outside, over there," as if race only matters in the kinds of feminism practiced in non-Western cultures. On the other hand, Cheryl B. Tornsey's "Comforts No More: The Underside of Quilts in Children's Literature" does the important work of acknowledging that quilting is not simply black women's art. By bringing together the writings of Alcott, the pseudonymous writings of a mill worker from Lowell, Patricia Polacco's immigrant experience, Deborah Hopkinson's narrative of a slave girl, and Faith Ringgold's tale of a girl in the 1930s, she shows a continuity in the art of quilting that follows the tendency of liberal feminist thinking to universalize women's experience, but this tendency is fortunately undercut by the specificity of cultural detail she includes in her close readings of the texts.

Class is another factor that tends to be elided in the majority of the essays. Although many of the essays mention that class will be part of their investigation, it seems that the writers do not acknowledge its vital role in shaping their own perspective. When Karen Klugman blithely asserts that her "home was populated with more than a hundred Playmobil guys and countless Lego body parts" (169), I couldn't help seeing those artifacts in terms of dollar signs and wondering about the subtext that feminism belongs to people who can afford to shop at upscale toy stores, and that what had really failed her in her efforts to protect her son from a hyper-masculinized material culture was her class status—the alienating aisle marked "Action Figures" at Toys "R" Us is for people whose class experience hasn't taught them any better. Lois Kuznets's reflection on dollhouses participates in the same upper-middle-class materialism, which is thrown into sharp relief with her invocation of homeless women who have refused or lost their places in the dollhouses of Western culture. Kuznets, however, is aware of and refreshingly self-reflexive about her place of privilege and how it affects her scholarly interests and conclusions.

Looking back over the entire volume, I can reconcile myself to the gesture of placing Knoepflmacher's piece first. It is, after all, at the beginning of the History section, and the project itself is a variant of where feminism and children's literature first intersected—with the fairy tale. But as fairy tales are only children's literature through a certain orphaned and adopted state, I would hope that this volume will inspire future feminist scholars to more and more clearly articulate the place of the *child* at the intersection of children's literature and feminist theory, as well as the place of children's literature in literary history. As Mitzi Myers states, "Children's literature has been nobody's baby long enough" (39); I'm afraid that at the end of *Girls, Boys, Books, Toys,* it may still remain only fostered to contemporary feminist theory. And yet, my favorite books are those that point out a direction and inspire me to get to work; this is one of those.

Work Cited

Rose, Jacqueline. *The Case of Peter Pan or the Impossibility of Children's Fiction.* London: Macmillan, 1984.

Daughters, Mothers, Stories

Michelle Pagni Stewart

Is It Really Mommie Dearest*? Daughter-Mother Narratives in Young Adult Fiction,* by Hilary S. Crew. Lanham, Md.: Scarecrow Press, 2000.

As a mother, a daughter and a critic interested in daughter-mother relationships in literature, I eagerly approached Hilary S. Crew's book, *Is It Really* Mommie Dearest*? Daughter-Mother Narratives in Young Adult Fiction,* looking for some new insights on a favorite subject. Clearly, Crew is well read in the genre of young adult literature as well as in studies of mother-daughter relationships. Those looking to find young adult novels about mothers and daughters to teach or read will find a plethora of sources to choose from and a brief but insightful listing of some of the larger issues that link young adult novels to adult novels in her concluding chapter. Likewise, those interested in the way adolescent theories have been translated into fiction for young adults will benefit from Crew's research. Yet overall, the potential inherent in Crew's study is not fulfilled in the book because *Is It Really* Mommie Dearest*?* seems more devoted to classifying the young adult novels than to analyzing the books and the trends that Crew has identified.

The first chapter explains the theoretical terms Crew will employ, which would be helpful to those who do not have a solid grounding in theory. I was curious to see how Crew would apply the narrative theories she was explaining to the young adult novels, but instead she merely describes the narrative structures found in the various novels. Had she discussed the discourse at work in the various novels and either analyzed trends in narrative structures or analyzed the effect of the choice of narrative structures on the mother-daughter relationships depicted in the novels or on young readers, the use of theory would have been justified, but here and throughout the study it seems extraneous.

After an interesting chapter devoted to mother-daughter relationships in fairy tales and their retellings, Crew begins to classify the various conventions and motifs used in young adult novels about mothers and daughters. She considers the imagery and language of these novels

Children's Literature 30, ed. Elizabeth Lennox Keyser and Julie Pfeiffer (Yale University Press, © 2002 Hollins University).

(chapter 3), Freud's theories as they apply to these novels (chapter 4), the way conflict is depicted in mother-daughter relationships (chapter 5), the loving bonds between mother and daughter (chapter 6), the lessons daughters derive from their mothers' stories (chapter 7), and the grandmother-mother-daughter triangle motif (chapter 8) before delving into cross-cultural and African-American instances of mother-daughter young adult novels in chapters 9 and 10, respectively. Her concluding chapter focuses on novels that celebrate rather than problematize mother-daughter bonds. Overall, the book demonstrates a wide scope of knowledge on the subject matter, and the way Crew has focused her discussion within the chapters works well.

Nevertheless, the lack of conclusions throughout the study was frustrating for this reader. Crew has started an interesting discussion, but just as she begins to come to some determination of why this all matters, she will introduce the topic for the next chapter and move on. Her knowledge of young adult literature proves to be both an advantage and a disadvantage to her with regard to conclusions. Although she has read a great deal and clearly is in a good position to identify motifs and trends at work in young adult fiction, she does not capitalize on her knowledge to take her discussion to the next level. Further, she often discusses so many novels in such a short space that the novels do not get the in-depth analytical treatment that might have been more helpful for theorizing about the novels. By discussing the novels so briefly and often jumbling the discussion of several within close proximity, the novels begin to be indistinguishable. If Crew were trying to argue that there is not enough variety in narrative strategies and in treatment of mother-daughter relationships, she would be making her case, but again, her purpose seems more descriptive than analytical.

Another concern is in her use of race. In the bulk of the book, chapters 3–8, Crew makes a point of limiting her discussion to white, North American families, but this is problematic in several ways. First of all, ethnic examples have been omitted from the larger discussion as if they do not belong with the rest of the examples. Although Crew does discuss cross-cultural and African-American novels in later chapters (more on this shortly), that ethnic novels have been segregated—ghettoized, as it is commonly known—is disconcerting. Although it is true that there may be variances in the way mother-daughter bonds are viewed in other cultures, Crew herself admits that the "hegemonic blueprint for adolescent development . . . [has] been used as an overlay for understanding adolescence in other cultures" (56). Furthermore, while Crew continuously specifies she is working only with white, North American families, several times she refers explicitly to race (for example: "The interrelationships between grandmother, mother, and adolescent daughter form a significant element of the daughter-mother narrative in different racial and cultural contexts" [169]), then defers the discussion of race until the "race" chapters. Perhaps most striking are the two references to African-American literature within these "white, North American" chapters: at one point, Crew introduces the concept of "blood mother" used in African-American literature but uses it to discuss white literature only. The other reference is in the chapter on mother-daughter conflicts, when Crew discusses physical contact; she writes: "There are scenes, however, in which physical as well as verbal confrontations take place in which mothers are depicted as slapping and pushing their daughters in anger and exasperation. The 'proverbial' or 'notorious' mother-slap is delivered to daughters in selected African American novels" (103). That she has singled out African-American texts here, without any discussion of the context of the slaps is bothersome, especially when she later glosses over a slap in Nancy Honeycutt's *Ask Me Something Easy*, a "white" novel.

When Crew does discuss cross-cultural and African-American novels, in chapters 9 and 10, she does so with sensitivity. In fact, because she discusses significantly fewer novels in each of these chapters, she deals with the novels in more depth, which makes her analysis of each novel more telling. Her explanation, in chapter 10, of why white psychological theories do not necessarily apply to African Americans is perhaps a stronger justification for excluding blacks in the chapters dealing with Freud's theories than any given in earlier chapters, although this does not justify the exclusion in the chapters on mother-daughter conflicts and bonding. And, while Crew's analysis of the various ethnic novels is interesting, neither of the chapters dealing with ethnic novels comes to any conclusions about mother-daughter narrative constructions and tendencies, which may not be a problem for readers interested in individual texts, but in the context of the book as a whole, Crew here misses yet another opportunity to make a larger statement.

Crew's study is at its most interesting when she shows how contemporary theories of mothering and adolescence get reflected in stories being written, as when she discusses novels influenced by feminism (chapter 5) and when she discusses the ideas of "loving" and "letting go" of the 1980s (chapter 6). Yet there is a tension throughout the book in that it is often unclear whether Crew is attempting to identify the problems inherent in authors using certain conventions of young adult literature dealing with mothers and daughters or whether she is merely identifying the conventions. She does at one point say we should question the often-used convention of making the protagonist's mother weak and dependent, of the "*conventional* literary practice to diminish mothers in order to present shining and independent daughters" (95). More often, however, I found myself wondering what point she was trying to make—for example, whether she saw the conventions as stereotyping the mother-daughter bond and thus something we should question; whether she saw the convention as reflecting theories of adolescence and thus asking us to question the nexus of theory and story; or whether she just wanted to make us aware of the number of young adult novels utilizing certain motifs, such as the images of flight, boundaries, and mirrors discussed in chapter 3.

The range of information provided in Crew's book demonstrates the breadth of her knowledge of young adult novels and theories of the mother-daughter relationship. In the process, she has certainly raised a number of questions about the narrative constructs that predominate in this kind of fiction. Perhaps she preferred to leave it to readers to draw their own conclusions, but given her knowledge of the subject, the book would be more effective if she had come to some conclusions. As it is, she just gives readers a starting point for making their own.

Saussure, Sex, and Socially Challenged Teens: A Polyphonic Analysis of Adolescent Fiction

Michelle H. Martin

Disturbing the Universe: Power and Repression in Adolescent Literature, by Roberta Seelinger Trites. Iowa City: University of Iowa Press, 2000.

Roberta Seelinger Trites's new critical text, *Disturbing the Universe: Power and Repression in Adolescent Literature,* arose out of Trites's dismay with the dearth of rigorous criticism in young adult (YA) literature. Firmly situated within poststructural theoretical discourse, *Disturbing the Universe* does the kind of challenging intellectual work with adolescent literature that Trites asserts is still largely missing from American teacher education programs and therefore from high school English classes. Trites makes the bold statement that postmodern theory is a particularly appropriate lens for examining YA texts because this genre "emerged from postmodern thinking" (18), and accordingly, she uses postmodern theory to scrutinize contemporary texts as recent as Francesca Lia Block's Weetzie Bat books (1989–95) and J. K. Rowling's *Harry Potter and the Prisoner of Azkaban* (1999). Taking a further step, though, she uses this postmodern lens for examining YA texts as early as Louisa May Alcott's *Little Women* (1868, 1869) and Jean Webster's *Daddy-Long-Legs* (1912). If, as Trites suggests, postmodern *thinking* evolved long before the dawn of postmodernity, then this approach is indeed appropriate. Although readers may feel as skeptical as I did about Trites's applying postmodern theory to nineteenth-century texts, she justifies her approach with the light she sheds on these early texts.

Given the breadth of YA texts—both primary and critical—that Trites discusses, *Disturbing the Universe* offers an excellent introduction to YA critical discourse for those new to teaching and studying YA literature, yet it also gives those who have long been working in this field some new analytical perspectives to consider. Despite the fact that well-written YA and multicultural YA literature have been available for several decades, many American high school administrators

Children's Literature 30, ed. Elizabeth Lennox Keyser and Julie Pfeiffer (Yale University Press, © 2002 Hollins University).

still place *Beowulf, Hamlet* and *The Scarlet Letter* on required reading lists to the exclusion of the literature composed specifically for YA readers. Inclusive in scope, Trites's multicultural and eclectic approach embraces canonical YA writers like Twain, Alcott, Hinton, and Cormier, but also others, such as Crescent Dragonwagon, Lawrence Yep, Jacqueline Woodson, Rosa Guy, Amy Tan, and Walter Dean Myers. The polyphony that abounds in *Disturbing the Universe* is, I would argue, the most impressive aspect of Trites's second critical book and the aspect that will make this text useful to a wide variety of readers.

As suggested by the "Power and Repression" in its title, *Disturbing the Universe* takes a primarily Foucauldian approach. But even in defining the terminology that she will use throughout the book, she sets up a miniature version of Burke's parlor: she takes the ways that Max Weber, Louis Althusser, Michel Foucalt, Judith Butler, Marilyn French, and Jacques Lacan use the term "power," then makes use of appropriate pieces of all of these theories to construct her own definition: "Power is a force that operates within the subject and upon the subject in adolescent literature; teenagers are repressed as well as liberated by their own power and by the power of the social forces that surround them in these books. Much of the genre is thus dedicated to depicting how potentially out-of-control adolescents can learn to exist within institutional structures" (7). In a similar fashion, Trites also problematizes and clarifies the generic terms "adolescent literature," "YA literature," *Bildungsroman* (a novel of development in which the protagonist grows into adulthood), and *Entwicklungsroman* (a novel of mere growth). If I had been the least bit unclear in the introduction about why Trites expends so much effort distinguishing between the *Bildungsroman* and *Entwicklungsroman,* I had little doubt once I read her explanation in chapter 2 of why Adam Farmer's lack of power in Robert Cormier's *I Am the Cheese* makes this book an *Entwicklungsroman:* "Access to discourse both endangers Adam and saves him from the American government . . . as long as he is caught in this dynamic, he cannot become an adult" (27). This book could therefore not possibly be a *Bildungsroman.* Despite having taught adolescent literature for the past four years, I found this clarification of generic terminology useful.

In the four main chapters of the book (2–5), Trites demonstrates how social institutions—authority, sex, and death, respectively—interact with power (or the lack thereof) in the lives of fictional adolescents as they grow toward adulthood. In chapter 2, she argues: "All YA novels depict some postmodern tension between individuals and institutions. And the tension is often depicted as residing within discursive constructs" (52). Here again, readers may question the breadth of the postmodern blanket that Trites throws over "all YA texts." Even if the "postmodern-ness" of the earlier texts is dubious, Trites does effectively illustrate this tension between individuals and institutions in a variety of nineteenth- and twentieth-century YA novels.

Choosing four "social institutions" that occur most frequently in YA texts, Trites analyzes the role of government politics, schools, religion, and "identity politics"—which she defines as "the social affiliations that members of any society construct to position people in relationship to one another" (45)—in several YA novels, situating these social institutions within Althusser's idea of the "Ideological State Apparatus." Trites insists here, as she does throughout the book, on the importance of historical contextualization. In fact, she says: "It is not enough to use novels to teach about the historical period in which they are set. These novels are themselves historical artifacts of the time period during which they were written" (31). This belief leads her to examine how explicit and implicit ideologies in a novel comment on its author's historical context as well as the historical context of the novel's setting. And as she does earlier, Trites continues to encourage multiple readings. After offering her own reading of school as a social institution in John Knowles's *A Separate Peace,* she writes, "A Freudian might argue . . . or a Bakhtinian might say" (36), emphasizing the postmodern indeterminacy of her own critical discussion of this work.

Chapter 3, subtitled "The Paradox of Authority," takes up the YA version of Jacqueline Rose's question of children's literature as an "impossibility"—as a seduction of sorts—since "'Children's fiction sets up the child as an outsider to its own process, and then aims, unashamedly, to take the child *in*'" (qtd. in Trites 83). Trites makes a parallel argument to Rose's by suggesting that "issues of authority are embedded in the narrative structure of YA novels" and by demonstrating the tension between parental authority in the lives of both fictional and real adolescents and the authorial control that YA authors hold over adolescent readers. In this chapter, Trites uses Saussurian and Lacanian analysis to illustrate the primacy of language in the adolescent struggle with authority, but she takes some linguistic creative license in her use of Lacan. She establishes three types of parental conflict that adolescents experience: actual (with live and present parents), in loco parentis (surrogate parents like the gang members in S. E. Hinton's *The Outsiders*), and—a Trites coinage—*in logo parentis* (parents like Jerusha

Abbott's benefactor in Jean Webster's *Daddy-Long-Legs* who exist only in language). This categorization of parents serves to illustrate the primacy of the parental relationship: even when young adult protagonists have no parents, they will often create them—if only linguistically—which enables them to rebel against them.

Although this chapter offers an illuminating discussion, I was surprised at the extent to which Trites relies on Freudian and neo-Freudian theories, some of which she admits are "misogynistic and homophobic" (69). Readers who are resistant to psychoanalytic criticism, such as in Trites's discussion of Virginia Hamilton's *Planet of Junior Brown* (65), will find parts of this chapter difficult to digest; readers with little or no training in psychoanalytic criticism will find it downright unintelligible. For instance, in her discussion of the Symbolic Order and the "Name-of-the-Father," Trites writes: "The crucial action for the child, then, is to somehow eliminate the threat of the symbolic father, 'thus showing that if this murder is the fruitful moment of debt through which the subject binds himself for life to the Law, the symbolic Father is, in so far as he signifies this Law, the dead Father'" (57). Moreover, readers who know Trites's feminist work, *Waking Sleeping Beauty,* might also feel some dissonance between this submergence into Freudianism and Trites's feminist agenda. But if gender—often considered a fixed part of a person's identity—can be as performative as Judith Butler claims it is, then perhaps Trites's foray into Freudianism illustrates that criticism can be just as performative as gender is. Although Trites may have felt compelled to situate her argument within psychoanalytic discourse, given its centrality within poststructural theory, I found this section of her book the least compelling, the hardest to follow, and the least true to her other work.

In contrast, the fourth chapter on sex and power was the most thought-provoking. Using both gay and straight YA fiction as examples, Trites argues that "sexuality is a source of power and pleasure for many adolescents in YA novels, yet more novelists are comfortable portraying sexuality in terms of displeasure than pleasure" (116). Most surprising is that even novels that *look* nontraditional in all sorts of ways and acknowledge the sexual power that teens possess still convey the underlying message that teen sexuality must be controlled in repressive ways and are therefore depicted in a less-than-positive light. In Francesca Lia Block's *Baby Bee-Bop,* for instance, Dirk finally does resolve the conflict he has with his father over his sexual orientation—but by this time, his father is already dead and communicating with

Dirk as a ghost, which in some ways compromises the power of Dirk's coming out. Given the prevalence of sexual issues in YA fiction, Trites's illuminating look at the dynamic interaction between power and sexuality expands the interpretive possibilities of a vast array of contemporary YA novels.

The fourth chapter, subtitled "Death and Narrative Resolution," begins with a compelling discussion of the connections between death and sex, and the difference in death's literary function in children's literature versus YA literature. In children's texts, writes Trites, death is "part of the cycle, an ongoing process of life," and the child's learning about death "seems to be a stage in the child's process of separating from the parent more than anything else" (118). Mortality in YA fiction, however, is a threat—"an experience that adolescents understand as a finality" (118). While sexuality is often considered the issue that divides children's from adolescent literature, in Trites's definition, the role of death draws a dividing line between the genres. Throughout the chapter, Trites uses Heidegger's term "Being-towards-death" to indicate fictional adolescents' awareness that they are finite beings and that death is not just a part of the life cycle but *for them*—an awareness that some YA fiction has the power to convey to teen readers, who, because of the nature of adolescence, don't acknowledge that they, too, will one day die.

The "Death, Photography and Language" section of chapter 4 provides a fascinating discussion of photography as metaphor and its relationship to the protagonist behind the camera in Lois Lowry's *A Summer to Die*, Francesca Lia Block's *Witch Baby*, and Trudy Krishner's *Spite Fences*. Trites demonstrates how YA novelists use the camera to "explore the relationship between agency, death and discourse" and thereby help the protagonist and the reader to gain a better understanding of both life and death. Trites takes ideas from Saussure and Barthes to establish the notion that photographs are one medium in which the signifier and signified are "immediately indistinguishable" from one another and uses this idea to suggest that perhaps adolescent novels "employ camera metaphors as a way to explore agency as a linguistic construct that empowers the adolescent" (125). Trites cites Barthes's suggestion that the beginning of our society's negativization of death and the beginnings of photography evolved during approximately the same historical period and then adds that not long after this time came the codification of adolescence as a distinct life stage—commenting on two connections that I had never before considered. "Both photography and developmental psychology," in other words, "confirmed the process of fixing things in time for a culture that was increasingly teleologically oriented" (136). And because photography is all about acknowledging the aging process—the "towards-death" process—Trites argues that YA characters' use of photography makes sense.

In the same way that a good environmentalist would, Trites executes a zero waste policy throughout this book. She makes excellent use of the ideas of not only poststructural theorists and widely studied children's and young adult literature critics but also of those closer to home: she cites from the publications of many of her former students as well as from those of three of her current colleagues. As I read the book, I saw fully developed ideas that I recalled as kernels of graduate seminars that I took with her. With this zero waste approach, Trites constructs a subject position for herself as an observant, skillful reflective practitioner—setting a good example for others who seek to put their research and teaching in conversation with one another. In this Roberta-styled, feminist version of Burke's parlor, polyphony reigns, and voices that would normally speak only among themselves and only from the margins play a central role in parts of the discussion.

In the last paragraph of the final chapter of *Disturbing the Universe: Power and Repression in Adolescent Literature,* Trites writes, "The important thing to me in the revolution that has occurred in the last twenty years of the study of YA literature is the degree of dialogue that informs the field" (152). Trites's ground-breaking critical text stands as a testament and a substantial contribution to this dialogue. Since this book is itself at least partially the result of a productive and positive relationship between Trites's teaching and research, it is most appropriate that *Disturbing the Universe* ends with a chapter on pedagogy. As I prepare to make pedagogical use of *Disturbing the Universe* in my own adolescent literature class, largely populated by preservice teachers, I suspect that many of them will find it challenging—not just because of the difficulty of some of the theoretical content but also because as they consider their own greater empowerment as critical readers, they will inevitably try to project this new critical consciousness into their own teaching. Given the need for both new and practicing teachers to challenge the status quo and to bring new critical perspectives into the American education system, these students are sure to ask themselves, "Do I dare?"

Worlds Enough—and Time

Michael Joseph

Maria Nikolajeva. *From Mythic To Linear: Time in Children's Literature*. Lanham, Md.: Children's Literature Association and Scarecrow Press, 2000.

From Mythic To Linear divides children's literature into three categories according to the representation of underlying temporal structure: as an irreversible, linear flow (Collapse), as recurrent, reproducible patterns (Utopia), or as something in between (Carnival). The argument proceeds through comparisons and analyses of individual texts, including such literary classics as *Peter Pan, Tom's Midnight Garden, Little Women, The Wind in the Willows,* and *Tom Sawyer,* and many titles more obscure. Indeed, Maria Nikolajeva's broad familiarity with children's texts, Swedish and Russian in particular, is her book's strongest asset, though no less impressive is her way with critical methodology, such as Jungian criticism and narratology, her intellectual engagement with published criticism, and a bold, forthright style of argument. It is with these in mind that I particularly commend *From Mythic to Linear* as a noteworthy event.

Beginning with the mythic, Nikolajeva discusses texts that portray childhood utopia, or Arcadia—a timeless idyll, or a "cyclical time"— in which the characters dwell in a serene, pastoral setting unaffected by the passing world. Intrepidly crossing genre boundaries, she treats diverse kinds of material, including pastoral and domestic fiction, animal stories, toy stories, and social utopias. The underlying temporal structures of these works are fundamentally the same, she argues, and consubstantial with what might be termed the paradisiacal monomyth, comprising seven features: importance of setting, separation from others, social harmony, freedom from encumbrances of civilization, special significance of home, absence of death and sexuality, and overall innocence (21). Nikolajeva's discussion of Soviet utopias here is particularly engaging and supports the position that Arcadian literature en toto stifles personal development. Nikolajeva concludes this section with a discussion of "one of the most painful themes in chil-

Children's Literature 30, ed. Elizabeth Lennox Keyser and Julie Pfeiffer (Yale University Press, © 2002 Hollins University).

dren's fiction: the child who is reluctant to grow up" (87). Regardless of whether one agrees with her scholarly assessments of *Winnie the Pooh, Peter Pan, Tom's Midnight Garden,* and *Tuck Everlasting,* they clearly help to demonstrate the vast scope and variety of the Arcadian myth.

The next section looks at texts portraying an interruption in Arcadian time, a "picnic in the unknown" (passim). This section continues the broadly comparativist approach, moving freely between realism and fantasy, reviewing stories of time travel, secondary world fantasies, and female initiation. Carnival texts include such well-known novels as *Tom Sawyer, The Chronicles of Narnia,* and *Bridge to Terabithia.* Whatever befalls the characters in these novels and stories, they are assured of returning home, none the worse for wear. Having discussed food in her first section and asserted that in children's literature, it "corresponds to sexuality in the mainstream" (11), Nikolajeva returns to the discussion here. One can appreciate that in a book of encyclopedic scope (her index lists more than two hundred children's books), it would be impossible to fully pursue this comparison, though one wishes for greater specificity and definition. Certainly one cannot usefully infer a single set of meanings from "sexuality in the mainstream" literature; and the assurance that "food and sexuality are interchangeable in myth" (131) seems more revelatory than definitive.

Nikolajeva concedes the differences between Carnival, or "thereand-back" stories, and "there" (Collapse) stories are "subtle," for which I think readers confused about the placement of certain texts will be grateful. Nikolajeva relies upon the question of whether the protagonist—or something she calls "the collective protagonist"—experiences personal development to guide her understanding of temporal structure. In Arcadian literature, personal development is inconceivable; in Carnival literature, it becomes a tantalizing possibility; and in Collapse, it figures as the preeminent element, the purpose or consolation of suffering. Nevertheless, the overriding values of categories are heuristic and catalytic. Certainly readers can and should arrive at different conclusions about particular texts or, perhaps even short of a conclusion, without casting doubt on the means of decision making.

The last chapters of *From Mythic to Linear* look at texts that represent "linearity," or a collapse of "cyclical time" into temporality, such as YA novels, travel instructions and—an ingenious insertion—the Moomin tales. Here the characters tend to be drawn realistically, possess greater psychological complexity and color, and wrestle with damaging and even lethal conflicts. Nikolajeva's critiques work best when her considerable powers of empathy are engaged, as they are with YA novels. Her analyses of Peter Pohl's *Johnny, My Friend,* Katarina Mazetti's *It Is All Over Between God and Myself,* and Gunnel Beckman's *Admission to the Feast* are all pedagogically skillful. In her elucidation of Pohl's polished narrative techniques, she demonstrates a wonderful sensitivity to his complex representation of the autodiegetic narrator Chris's reliability on the subject of whether he realized or not that his friend, Johnny, had been a girl passing as a boy. "Chris the narrator can pretend that Chris the character does not know that Johnny is a girl; it is however impossible for the reader to decide whether this is an objective fact (the narrator states that the character did not know), a subjective memory (the narrator believes, a year later, that the character probably did not know), a self-deceit (the narrator does not realize that the character knew) or a deliberate lie (the narrator wants us to believe that the character did not know)" (215).

On another level, Nikolajeva perceives the mythic act inscribed in recounting the story as a "restaging . . . which leads [according to her own Jungian interpretation] to the novice's initiation" (215). Nikolajeva's concluding observation, however, is puzzling. "Chris has realized that time is irreversible. His childhood time, the mythical circular time has turned into the linear time of adulthood, the time which has a beginning and an end, which goes from birth through painful growing and aging toward inevitable death" (215). I am unconvinced that Pohl shares this understanding, as such, in part because Nikolajeva gives no explanation for why the determining narrative structure should remain collapsed. Even Chris's statement "was just a child until a hour ago" (215) suggests a *recursus ad rerum,* a process of symbolic return to the primordial state traditionally culminating in a figurative rebirth. Chris's adolescent solecism implies that perhaps he has not fully matured, that his self-assessment, to the extent that it invokes linearity, is, in part, still unreliable, and similar stories or imaginative "restagings" await him.

Nikolajeva's analyses are original and provocative, the texts she discusses are diverse and interesting, and her schematic generally compelling. If *From Mythic to Linear* proposed only to show that children's literature can be schematized according to deep temporal structures, or that temporality is a determining component of meaning in children's literature, I think it would have been a better, or at least a more fully successful book. But, it also proposes to demonstrate that "the central theme in children's fiction . . . is the irreversibility of time

224

MICHAEL JOSEPH

and the high price any individual who defies it must pay" (259). According to this hypothesis, Arcadian (timeless) literature attempts to
keep children dumb—"innocent: sexually, intellectually, socially, and
politically" (28)—while linear (time-full) literature is more honest and
conducive to growth. This ulterior argument seems vulnerable on several counts: Nikolajeva's uneven handling of myth, her lack of clarity
about the concept of linearity, and her too loose interpretations of the
seminal ideas from her source material.

Nikolajeva adopts her notion of mythic time from Mircea Eliade
(1907–86), citing him as her "main source" (5). In order to argue
that children's literature first represents and then virtuously abandons
mythic time, Nikolajeva must demonstrate precisely what that is, or
what Eliade meant by it. But there are several points at which Nikolajeva's interpretations misleadingly diverge from Eliade: in her fusion
of the concepts of "mythic time" and "cyclical time," in ascribing "cyclical time" to seasonal circularity, and in the exclusive identification of
"cyclical [or mythic] time" with the bliss and perfection of early childhood. These errors of interpretation superficially strengthen Nikolajeva's progressivist view of children's literature, but they ultimately
confuse it.

In describing *The Wind in the Willows*, Nikolajeva writes, "time is circular, mythical, expandable" (32). Again, about *Winnie the Pooh:* "the
mythical time has started to turn into linear, when changes occur"
(103), and *The Little Prince*, "Time on the tiny planet, childhood time,
regulated by recurrent sunsets, was circular, mythic, eternal, sacred"
(119). Thus, mythic and cyclical time seem to be synonymous, a sort
of Neverland where individuals perform actions over and over again:
"the circular merry-go-round of childhood." (206). Eliade intends the
two terms differently: mythic time refers to The Beginning, the imagined turf of the ancestors or gods. Cyclical time describes a temporal
notion held by archaic humanity, Eliade's metonymy for its cognitive
ability to shift from the profane or linear time of history into the sacred
time of The Beginning. Thus, by repetition (repeating the *originary* actions of exemplary beings), archaic humanity could cyclically return
to The Beginning. By melding these concepts, Nikolajeva loses sight of
the *otherness* of the paradigmatic and the powerful utility and accessibility of what is a transforming act of the creative imagination. So, her
grasp of Janosch's *The Trip to Panama* denies the intrinsic power of The
Beginning and sacred, originary acts become merely boring routine,

like commuting to work or housekeeping. "And so the stories go on, page after page, book after book. The two friends may venture on little harmless excursions, much like Mole, but they always return home, which is waiting for them, where they can live 'for ever and ever'" (52).

Nikolajeva also collapses Eliade's notion of cyclical time into the natural circularity of the seasons. So, for example, she writes: "Aslan's death and resurrection . . . restores the cyclical time. Spring comes, as it always has come after winter, as it always will come. The idyllic setting is recovered" (128). The equation of cyclicality and seasonal circularity also figures into her discussion of *The Wind in the Willows.* "Seasonal changes" are elided to "cyclical time [as it] is associated with the notion of home, and the inevitable return home" (32); in *The Secret Garden,* "Season changes . . . symbolize the return to paradise" (32). The implication is if they are not synonymous, then one is an analog of the other: that the myth of return is ultimately about the great round of nature. In *The Myth of the Eternal Return,* Eliade specifically refutes this assumption: "Nature recovers only itself, whereas archaic man recovers the possibility of definitively transcending time and living in eternity" (158).

The tendency of *From Mythic to Linear* to frame myth in terms of a naturally recurrent pattern constellated by a not fully human mind is undoubtedly the inheritance of the nineteenth-century definition of mythology as a body of prescientific explanations of natural phenomena. This misconception dovetails with an assumption all too frequently seen in children's literature and education that myths are simply one kind of traditional tale. This perspective fails to see myth's functionality as "pre-reflective positive valorizations," an important dynamic in Eliade and in Eliade studies, and necessarily short-circuits any attempt to interrogate myths in the contemporary (i.e., adult) world. Interestingly, while Nikolajeva relies on Jungian analysis to highlight archetypal patterns, even in YA novels, she neglects to concatenate these with the archetypal patterns in Arcadian literature. Thus while assuming the legitimacy of Jungian archetypes, she rejects Platonic archetypes as they are constellated by children's fiction, reading them instead as immature representations or precipitous regression.

"Children's literature maintains a myth of a happy and innocent childhood, apparently based on adult writers' nostalgic memories and bitter insights about the impossibility of returning to the childhood idyll" (4), she writes in a remarkably polemical passage. Similarly, the following passage from *The Mouse and The Child* becomes definitive of "a perfect philosophy of mythic existence":

> This mud being like other mud, we may assume that other mud is like this mud, which is to say that one place is all places and all places are one. Thus by staying here we are at the same time everywhere, and there is obviously no place to go. Winding, therefore, is futile. (qtd. in Nikolajeva 177)

Nikolajeva's remark seems intended to imply that mythic existence is illusory, a self-deception. She makes this point over and over again.

On *The Secret Garden*, she writes, "Mary Lennox [was] creating her own private paradise in the garden and thus conserving herself in the state of eternal childhood" (25). Arcadian "characters . . . are [forever] conserved in this stage and have neither wish nor possibility of evolving. Therefore, there is no growing up, no maturation, no aging and subsequently no death." (27–28). The close of *Wind in the Willows* suggests to her a "regression into childhood, almost infancy, the total reluctance to accept growing up" (33). The feeling of well-being and acceptance Colin's father achieves at the end of *The Secret Garden* signifies merely his "regressing into perpetual happiness" (39). Yet again, at the end of *The Nutcracker,* Marie and the Nutcracker "regress back into childhood" (54). In *The Kingdom by the Sea,* Harry's "peaceful homecoming is a regression into the security of childhood" (145). Finally and most resoundingly: "A child who does not grow up is conserved in his or her childhood, while a grown-up who goes back to the innocence of childhood is undoubtedly regressing, mentally and morally" (262). While she does concede that Arcadian literature introduces children to "the sacred," she rigorously consigns this sacred to the category of the unreal, the illusory, the lie. (Hence, apparently, the "moral" lapse in a writer who would divert children with sacred stories, or cyclical time.)

A reductive notion of myth as a simplistic representation of early childhood prefigures what seems to me to be an inadequate understanding of linearity. True linearity, if I understand it correctly to represent history or modern thought regarding being in the world, repudiates any and all transhistorical models. Any view of the human condition that posits the existence of exemplary figures, archetypal patterns, or even allows some guiding purpose to history, is, by definition, mythical (or religious, which is the same from the point of view of philosophy). According to a mythic view, death can be a renewal, a transformation, a sacrifice for the common good, a shift of personal awareness into a truer reality; it can lead to resurrection or rebirth, it can be copied and repeated, it possesses meaning. In a historicist view, death is an unforeseen event, with no significance, that happens once. In discussing linearity, Nikolajeva moves back and forth between the two worldviews. In her discussion of Hector Malot's *The Foundling*, we read, "The straight, irreversible linear development from beginning to end, from child to man, is nothing like the circular movement of *The Lion, the Witch and the Wardrobe*" (227). But further on Nikolajeva claims to have shown the possibilities of analyzing the novel using a Jungian model, in which Remi "has met his Shadow and his Anima, and has reached his Self in the center of his mandala, the ancestral home. He has, in other words, successfully accomplished the process" (227). If one insists on this as linear—and perhaps even the term "process" is then inappropriate—one cannot resort to a Jungian model for analysis, since the Shadow and Anima figures are transhistorical or mythic. They are predicated on or imbued with a culturally constructed belief in some order of universal stability, of constancy, of an overall purpose in individual life, and of return. History admits of no teleological interventions, no Shadows, no Anima figures; it simply is "a succession of events that are irreversible, unforeseeable, possessed of autonomous value" (*Myth* 89). The purposes of personal development, of growing up, of the very existence of a real world, which Nikolajeva ascribes to "linearity," are inextricably part of myth, which is an attempt to escape linearity by valorizing it. In *Myths, Dreams and Mysteries,* Eliade writes, "It seems unlikely that any society could completely dispense with myths, for, of what is essential in mythical behaviour—the exemplary pattern, the repetition, the break with profane duration and integration into primordial time—the first two at least are consubstantial with every human condition" (31–32). Eliade's discourse might therefore reasonably be considered as a basis for more open explorations of all of children's literature as a body of myths and mythographic tendencies in their broadest and richest sense. Such would bring children's literary studies into an ongoing discussion with other humanist thinkers, including literary scholars, anthropologists, theologians, religion historians, and philosophers about issues surrounding representation and being or the real as a distinct topic of analysis.

Nikolajeva approaches such a consideration in her observation on storytelling, which, she tells us, "is a ritual act, a reenacting of *recur-*

rent mythical events" [italics mine] (33). In *No Souvenirs,* Eliade notes that "the novel must tell something, because narrative (that is, literary invention) enriches the world no more and no less than history, although on another level" (205). It would seem that, while attempting to "demonstrate . . . the irreversibility of time" (259), Nikolajeva has not completely worked out the problem of this pertinacity of literature to engage the creative imagination, that the form of the novel, or the mind within the creative space of the novel, is itself recursive. Surprisingly, she claims a philosophical valorization of an existentialist position in the fiction of James Joyce, which she finds exemplary: "The modern novel describes a never-ending quest that is doomed to fail. Therefore motifs and characters such as Faust, the Wandering Jew, Ulysses are so attractive for contemporary adult readers. . . . Existential problems that torment modern protagonists do not leave any room for positive answers" (230). In considering narrative art, Eliade wrote: "More strongly than any of the other arts, we feel in literature a revolt against historical time, the desire to attain to other temporal rhythms than that in which we are condemned to live and work. One wonders whether the day will come when this desire to transcend one's own time—personal, historical time—and be submerged in a 'strange' time, whether ecstatic or imaginary, will be completely rooted out. As long as it persists, we can say that modern man preserves at least some residues of 'mythological behavior'" (*Myths and Reality* 192). In a sense, he anticipates Nikolajeva, and his argument—in accepting "linearity," one must renounce such stuff as dreams are made on—is persuasive.

Works Cited

Eliade, Mircea. *Myths, Dreams and Mysteries: The Encounter Between Contemporary Faiths and Archaic Realities.* Trans. Philip Mairet. New York: Harper & Brothers, 1960.
———. *The Myth of the Eternal Return, or, Cosmos and History.* Trans. Willard R. Trask. Princeton: Princeton University Press, 1971 [1954].
———. *No Souvenirs. Journal II, 1957–1969.* Trans. Fred H. Johnson, Jr. Chicago: University of Chicago Press, 1989, [1977].

Identity Crises

Valerie Krips

Transcending Boundaries: Writing for a Dual Audience of Children and Adults, edited by Sandra Beckett (New York: Garland, 1999).

Text, Culture, and National Identity in Children's Literature, edited by Jean Webb (Helsinki: Nordofino, 2000).

The question that has been put to me most often in the last few months by people with an interest in children's literature is: what do you think of the Harry Potter phenomenon? It's a question that has returned to me repeatedly as I read *Transcending Boundaries: Writing for a Dual Audience of Children and Adults* and *Text, Culture and National Identity in Children's Literature.* At first glance, it might seem that Harry Potter is irrelevant if not beside the point, since neither text refers to him. And they are none the worse for that, of course. Instead they offer insights about and analysis of works from many cultures and subgenres, and the conditions under which literary work for children is produced. To the extent that the range of works they discuss constitutes a boundary that is operative both for the genre and the child addressee and, importantly, the child portrayed in and by the books, they also deal in questions of identity. The literary works through which they examine this theme range from picture books to recent novels, many of the latter existing on (or sustaining—the question remains open) the boundary between fiction for children and fiction for adults. These books frame, delineate, and affirm identity; whether they question it, or are in fact capable of such questioning, is another matter. Do the Harry Potter books do so? These collections have helped me to think carefully about that, whether they meant to or not.

Both collections assume to a greater or lesser extent that children's literature exists. Of its existence per se there can be little doubt, but its relationship to literature—whatever we decide that is—and children— whatever we decide they are—poses perennial problems. Writing for a dual audience or "cross-writing child and adult," a term Beckett, in *Transcending Boundaries,* attributes to U. C. Knoepflmacher, assumes

Children's Literature 30, ed. Elizabeth Lennox Keyser and Julie Pfeiffer (Yale University Press, © 2002 Hollins University).

that we can make some distinction between child and adult, however difficult that may be nowadays. A literature for children only makes sense in terms of that distinction, of course, and in producing books for children and young adults we materialize our concepts of childhood. That this is our, adult, concept Zohar Shavit affirms in her contribution to Beckett's volume. She goes so far as to ask us to consider whether "children's literature is not reaching a point where the child-reader is not being abused in favor of the child's parents" (Beckett 95). There are many texts (many more than was once the case, she implies) that address adults over the shoulder of children. Importantly, it seems that many of these are addressed to the very young. Some of the books she thinks of in this way, "rife with pseudophilosophical and pseudopsychological statements, which adults allegedly like to find in books for children" are written by Maurice Sendak and Shel Silverstein (Beckett 94). Books such as these writers produce appeal to adults, in her view, because they "repeatedly try to recall the illusion of experiencing childhood time and time again" (Beckett 95). Writers, readers, and critics use the "cultural differences" between adults and children strategically, and do so at the expense of the child, she argues. In brief, she argues that even though childhood today is different in many ways from that of in earlier periods, a book for children will not "stand a chance" of being evaluated as "good" if "only" children like it or find it a "good book"; to this end, it always needs to be authorized by adults (Beckett 95).

No matter how we argue otherwise, this is surely as true now as it has ever been; perhaps more so in the age of simultaneous, or near simultaneous publication of books for children, particularly of picture books, in many places. But what would a book for children that did not "abuse" them look like? Carole Scott, writing about picture books, helps the reader think this through. In her chapter on Colin Thompson, Tord Nygren, and Maurice Sendak, Scott suggests that books such as theirs offer a "unique opportunity for . . . a collaborative relationship between children and adults, for picturebooks empower children and adults much more equally" (Beckett 101). Of the three writers discussed by Scott, Thompson turns out to offer the most "collaborative" text, *Looking for Atlantis*. Neither of the other authors manage so well: in Nygren's *The Red Thread*, adults "control, entertain, instruct and mesmerize children," Scott writes, while Sendak "sets child and adult against each other so that the reading experience becomes rather a separate than a joint one" (Beckett 106, 109). She refers to Sendak's

We Are All in the Dumps with Jack and Guy, which has proved a fascinating and problematic text for many critics. Scott's point is that the political message in Sendak's book is accessible only to the adult reader, who takes the book seriously, whereas children (and she quotes a reader response survey to make her point) find humor in it and tend to think the ending happy—ignoring, or simply not seeing, other pointers (such as the newspaper subtext).

To add to the conundrum, John Stephens, quoting the historian Agnes Heller, reminds us that "modern men and women are contingent" (Stephens, "Maintaining Distinctions: Realism, Voice, and Subject Positions in Australian Young Adult Fiction," in Beckett 195). Stephens's largely narratological account examines what subjectivity is implied in Australian fiction for young adults, suggesting that while such fictions "presuppose some version of a self that is unique and essential" that self nevertheless has much in common with "neo-humanistic accounts of subjectivity as contingent and heterogeneous" (Beckett 194). Implying that "social apparatuses are radically meaningless, and significance is grounded . . . in the everydayness of interpersonal relationships," Australian novels for young adults occupy a "middle ground between literature for children and literature for adults," in Stephens's view (Beckett 196). This presupposes, of course, a distinction between child and adult that is, in fact, difficult to make, given that the child or young adult represented in the fiction discussed is the construct of an adult; the questions raised by Shavit and Scott are as valid for young adult fiction as they are for picture books, and perhaps even more so since the relationship of adult writer to less-than-adult reader is usually effaced in young adult fiction.

Other contributors to Beckett's volume take the reader through the complex webs of censorship and canonicity and into the arena of modernism and postmodernism, all with cross-writing in view. In Beckett's words, the genre has become "a field of innovation and experimentation, challenging the conventions, codes, and norms that traditionally governed" it (Beckett xvii). The collection will form an important addition to the library of those who want to think, teach, and write about children's books, and in particular to those who are concerned to understand the problems of the genre's audience. Who is the child for whom children's literature is written, published, taught? Who is the child imagined by "cross-writing"?

Webb's collection helps the reader to think about these questions from the perspective of national identity and culture. If not subthemes, national identity and culture are thought to be the political unconscious, to use Fredric Jameson's term, of the books discussed. In looking at the ways in which national identity is produced and described in books intended for children, Webb's text reminds the reader of the extent to which the description of landscape, the representation of speech patterns, history, gender, and stereotypes play their part in making a book Finnish or Greek or Czech. Webb's collection ranges over many national formations and is interesting for its insights into publishing for children both nationally and internationally. What it indicates is not so much that nation, and being of a particular nationality, is important in books for children, either as a theme in itself or as a subtext, but that books represent a picture of the world that is responsive to a criticism which interrogates them in such a way.

This is not to suggest that the contributors do not pay close attention to difference. In "A Room of One's Own: The Advantage and Dilemma of Finno-Swedish Children's Literature" Maria Nikolajeva and Janina Orlov discuss the "self-definition of Finno-Swedish literature for young people, separate from both the metropolitan Swedish and the Finnish literature" (Webb 77). To readers more used to thinking in terms of varieties of English, this chapter is thought-provoking as it outlines the difficulties faced by Finnish, which only emerged as a literary language in the late nineteenth century, as the authors point out. Finnish writers need both to distinguish themselves linguistically and to meet Swedish norms if they want to find a wider audience. This is a difficult but, according to the authors, not impossible task that an interesting literature, including the well-known Moomin books, tackles.

If language is one of the markers of identity thought of in national terms, so too is landscape, according to Anna Heidi Pálsdóttir. Her "Rolling Hills and Rocky Crags: The Role of Landscape in English and Icelandic Literature for Children" is an account of the "connections between landscape and a common heritage and what it means for the individual to share the national landscape with bygone generations" (Webb 65). This encompassing phrase, however, indicates some of the difficulties that beset a number of chapters in this book, including Pálsdóttir's own. Writing about national identity is a touchy business, not least because the term is, in itself, open to so many critical interpretations. How is nation to be defined; how is identity to be defined? Does it reside in the eye of the beholder, so to speak, or is it a self-identity? What is a "common heritage"? Whose "heritage" is at issue? And how can we share with the dead?

The writers in Webb's collection can scarcely be taken to task for failing to settle questions such as these, but they nevertheless remind us of a troubling aspect of writing about books for children. This is that while the audience for children's books themselves is somewhat problematic, so too is the audience for criticism. With what theory and criticism can the writer expect her reader to be familiar? This surely depends upon where the reader comes from in the increasingly large and diverse audience for children's literature criticism. At a conference the audience tends to self-select; when those conferences proceedings are reproduced in a book, as is the case in Webb's collection, slightly different assumptions may rule. We tend to expect that books that deal with nation, identity, and culture might enlighten us about those terms, but this is not necessarily the purpose of the paper-givers, who are responding to the given of the conference title. In Pálsdóttir's very interesting chapter about landscape and nation, for example, which depends heavily upon the unexamined concept of a "common heritage," some vital clues are missing. This is scarcely surprising in a ten-page paper that covers both English and Icelandic literature for children. This is a paper that could, and perhaps should, have been greatly extended to allow the writer to ground her reader more securely in the kinds of thinking and theorizing that supports her own, far from insignificant, criticism.

The purpose of this extension would have been, in part, to acknowledge that many of the book's potential readers are those who are training as professionals in the fields that have an interest in children's literature. It is as important to provide students with good reading as it is to ensure that the profession itself contributes to, and benefits from, a strong and healthily self-critical criticism. Both the books discussed here offer valuable insights, but Beckett's is by far the most appropriate for the beginning scholar, insofar as it provides examples of writing and thinking in depth. Webb's should be handled with some care: it is interesting and thought-provoking, but it bears unnecessary scarring from an insufficient revision and extension of otherwise good, but necessarily limited, conference papers.

For the student of identity, however, both books offer much of interest. Is it appropriate to think in terms of a particularly French or African or, come to that, American childhood today? Can we register appropriate concern for the starving children of another nation if we do so? Is the apparent rise of nationalism a response to multinationals, its inevitable and necessary concomitant, or is it merely multinationalism in another guise? We can't expect these volumes to answer questions such as these, but they can be thought about when reading them. As it can when we are reading and thinking about Harry Potter.

In some ways the Harry Potter books are quintessentially British, and yet they aren't. It might be nice to suggest that these novels have broken the barrier that seems to have been erected between British and American novels for children, for example, at least so far as the penetration of British books for children in the American market since around 1950 or so is concerned. Of that I am not sanguine, however. It seems instead that Rowling's mix of fairly standard, if not formulaic, plot and characterization, fits all, nationality aside. Perhaps most important, the novels confirm the fairy and folktale concept of the omnipotent child who, mistaken for an ordinary mortal, brought up among uncomprehending adults, finally betters them. That this is no merely "national" conceit is clear to the reader of Webb's collection.

Children seem to like the Harry Potter books. Whether they want them, or need them, is a different matter. With Jacqueline Rose, I tend to think that it is seldom a question of "what the child wants, but of what the adult desires" (2). The Harry Potter books suggest that what the adult desires is the child as victor, all-powerful, capable of much more than any adult. This is an old story, beloved as much by Walter Benjamin as it was by Jean-Jacques Rousseau. And by us all, perhaps. The collections under consideration in this review do nothing to dispel the myth, but they do make us think about it, and think hard.

Work Cited

Rose, Jacqueline. *The Case of Peter Pan or The Impossibility of Children's Fiction*. London: Macmillan, 1984.

"Bad Boys" in Translation

Klaus Phillips

Klassiker der Jugendliteratur in Übersetzungen: Struwwelpeter, Max und
Moritz, Pinocchio *im deutsch-italienischen Dialog,* by Sonia Marx. Pub-
blicazioni de Dipartimento di Lingue e Letterature Anglogerma-
niche dell'Università di Padova 8. Padua: Unipress, 1997. 220 pp.

Dr. Heinrich Hoffmann's *Der Struwwelpeter* (1845), Wilhelm Busch's
Max und Moritz (1865), and Carlo Collodi's *Pinocchio* (1881), three internationally known literary classics about ill-behaved children, have
been the most popular children's books in their respective countries
of origin for well over one hundred years. There is hardly a language
into which the works have not been translated. In many languages
more than one translation appeared. In Germany the verses by Hoffmann and Busch exist in various dialect incarnations, and the perhaps best-known English *Struwwelpeter* was translated by none other
than Mark Twain. *Pinocchio,* available in the former Soviet Union in
24 versions and in more than 220 translations worldwide, remains the
most translated Italian book and, after the Bible, the most widely read.
Clearly, the impact of these steady sellers has been extraordinary, extending far beyond their geographic boundaries and the confines of
the printed page.

Sonia Marx's richly illustrated study, essentially a collection of seven
previously published essays with slight revisions, examines how the
three works burst out of the cultural contexts within which they appeared, and how effectively, and with what modifications, the memo-
rable literary figures inhabiting these narratives have managed to
survive in translations from Italian to German or German to Italian.
Readers suspecting a forbiddingly narrow focus in a study arguably intended for those who can read Italian as well as German will discover
that Marx's methodology could guide them toward developing valid
analogies to more recent popular culture phenomena such as *Beavis
and Butthead* or *South Park.*

The controversy inherent in these television programs pales in comparison with the notorious picture book "for children three to six years

Children's Literature 30, ed. Elizabeth Lennox Keyser and Julie Pfeiffer (Yale University
Press, © 2002 Hollins University).

of age." According to Hoffmann, a Frankfurt neurologist, who wrote and illustrated *Struwwelpeter* when he could not find a suitable book to give to his son at Christmas, children needed to be taught from the start how to behave properly. Most readers today would argue that the misbehavior scarcely warrants the severity of punishment in Hoffmann's tales, such as the particularly grisly episode in which a thumb-sucking boy's thumbs are cut off with enormous scissors. Although Marx finds some justification for such a harsh deterrent in the fact that unsanitary conditions in mid-nineteenth-century Germany probably made thumb-sucking a much less innocuous activity than it is today, her study largely eschews the exploration of sociological reasons for a work's popularity and, instead, champions the power of linguistic and visual imagery.

She concludes that a comparison of Hoffmann and Busch not only shows text and image to be on an equal artistic plane in *Max und Moritz*, but that biting social satire has replaced didacticism. The tale's two protagonists are "bad boys," to be sure, but the adults populating their world, mostly stereotypical representations of teachers, tailors, and bakers, tend to be pedantic, scheming, and nasty as well. Perhaps it should not be surprising, then, that *Max und Moritz* was banned in parts of Austria until 1929.

Busch's drawings seem to anticipate the comic strip and the movie cartoon. The images resemble storyboards and illustrate an array of movie-making techniques (slow motion, perspective shift, simultaneity, shot/countershot). Even while standing still, the figures of Max and Moritz suggest aggressive dynamics, predators preparing to pounce. The texts accompanying the drawings complement and reinforce the fast pace of the "seven tricks" that comprise the misdeeds of the mischief makers. Here Busch assaults his readers with inventive noun and adjective compounds, neologisms, intentionally incorrect grammar and syntax, occasional French phrases, dialect, and outrageous rhymes.

How different translators have managed to capture the meaning of the source material as well as retain any flavor of the original language and of the authors' style is one of the central concerns in Marx's study. Does Collodi's long-nosed wooden puppet lose something in German translation? Could it possibly gain something? It has been argued, after all, that Agatha Christie's mysteries are more suspenseful in German because German dependent clause word order dictates that the reader must wait until the very end of the sentence to discover what it actually was that the butler might have done with the pliers. Marx convincingly argues that these translations resonate with a life of their own and that a close analysis of the translations greatly enhances our understanding of the original work.

Minor quibbles with Marx's study include an occasional random umlaut ("Ānfäng," p. 46, and "Schnitzerhändwerkzeug," p. 212), inconsistent bibliography formats, and repetitions common in collections of essays previously published as separate entities. On the whole, however, these small faults do not diminish the high quality of Marx's scholarship.

Children's Literature Criticism: The Old and the New

Ian Wojcik-Andrews

Understanding Children's Literature, ed. Peter Hunt. New York: Routledge, 1999.

Understanding Children's Literature sets itself up as an introductory collection of essays about the relationship between literary theory and children's literature. The essays are by well-known, highly respected critics, such as Karin Lesnik-Oberstein, Tony Watkins, John Stephens, Perry Nodelman, Hamida Bosmajain, Lissa Paul, and Hugh Crago. These and other critics in the book focus their theoretical lens, as it were, on such important issues in children's literature as definition, history, culture, ideology, linguistics, picture books, psychoanalysis, feminism, intertextuality, and literacy. Placed under the microscope are a wide range of old and new children's texts. *The Wind in the Willows, The Secret Garden, The Hobbit, Low Tide, Where the Wild Things Are, Mr Gumpy's Outing,* and *Higglety Pigglety Pop!* are just some of the closely examined books that give students an understanding of how literary theory might be used to dissect children's literature. The opening essay, "Introduction: The World of Children's Literature Studies," is by Peter Hunt, a critic who as well as anybody can see the complexities that inform an understanding of children's literature.

Understanding Children's Literature has been the central theoretical text in my undergraduate theory class this semester, along with Rebecca Lukens's *A Critical Handbook of Children's Literature.* I chose Hunt's book because I was reviewing it (what better way to know a book than to teach it). I chose Lukens's book because I didn't want my students to think that the ideas and concepts about children's literature criticism in Hunt's book, indeed the whole concept of children's literature studies, appeared out of nowhere. Quite the contrary. I wanted them to understand the history of children's literary theory, the theories themselves, and the direction in which children's literature criticism seems to be heading today, i.e., toward a much more interdisciplinary mode of interpretation. By reading back and forth between the two quite different approaches to children's literature of which Lukens and

Children's Literature 30, ed. Elizabeth Lennox Keyser and Julie Pfeiffer (Yale University Press, © 2002 Hollins University).

Hunt are generally representative, my students, mostly language arts majors though not exclusively so, were able to see precisely how far children's literature criticism has come since the 1970s, when Lukens's book was first published.

In this regard, an important issue both books tackle at the outset is that of definition. Lesnik-Oberstein's "Essentials: What Is Children's Literature? What Is Childhood?," the second chapter in Hunt's book, scrutinizes closely that which Lukens glosses over. Lukens, writing within the Anglo-American, New Criticism tradition of Richards, Eliot, Leavis, and others argues that touchstone literature and children's literature texts— *Charlotte's Web,* for example—provide readers with fundamental insights into the nature of the human condition, in the case of *Charlotte's Web* the transformative and transcendent power of love, friendship, and language. Children's literature rewards us with an understanding of what it is and who we are and, by definition, children's literature and the child reader exist. Lesnik-Oberstein, writing from within a poststructuralist tradition, deconstructs these commonsense assumptions. Reiterating the kind of question previously asked by such critics as John Rowe Townsend and Michele Landsberg, Lesnik-Oberstein asks: "But is a children's book a book written by children, or for children? And, crucially, what does it mean to write a book 'for' children. . . . What of 'adult' books read also by children—are they 'children's literature'"? (15). Once the children's literature theorist sharpens the focus on these questions, others come clearly into view. Indeed, Lesnik-Oberstein goes on to address other equally important issues that Lukens ignores. Discussing the work of historians such as Philippe Aries and anthropologists such as Margaret Mead and Martha Wolfenstein, Lesnik-Oberstein points out that if the definition of what constitutes children's literature is uncertain, so logically must the definition of what constitutes a child and childhood. Indeed, according to Lesnik-Oberstein, drawing on the work of "British theorist Jacqueline Rose" (17), the "'child' is a construction invented for the needs of the children's literature authors and critics, and not an 'observable,' 'objective,' 'scientific,' 'entity'" (17). Consequently children's literature, as Rose pointed out in 1984 and Lesnik-Oberstein now repeats, is an impossible fiction.

Academic critics and literature students familiar with the history of literary theory and the concomitant developments in children's literature criticism represented by the differences between Lukens (1970s) and Lesnik-Oberstein (1990s) will likely accept the latter's argument, that defining children's literature is a complex, theoretical process. Language arts majors, on the other hand, coming from a completely different theoretical, that is to say pedagogical orientation and meeting children's literature criticism for the first time, might be rather more skeptical. Certainly many of my students, reading about these issues at the beginning of the semester, had to work really hard (not that that's a bad thing) to understand the idea that children's literature is not "kiddie lite," that the dominant images of the child and the child reader in today's society are aesthetic and social constructions built by powerful interest groups, and that subsequently a range of critical theories, from formalism to feminism, from history to new historicism, from linguistics to literacy is required to understand children's literature (talk about a learning curve!). As we moved through the semester, returning on occasion to the simplicity of *A Critical Handbook* before heading out again for the complexity of *Understanding Children's Literature,* the value of the latter text became increasingly apparent. *A Critical Handbook* is where one might wish to begin a journey into children's lit criticism. *Understanding Children's Literature* is where one might wish the journey to end.

To illustrate, another important development in children's literature criticism worth considering is that of setting. For Lukens, setting is "the time and place in which the action occurs" (298). To show that this is a useful but relatively narrow definition of setting, I had students read chapter 3 of *Understanding Children's Literature,* the essay by Tony Watkins called "The Setting of Children's Literature: History and Culture."

Essentially, Lukens discusses the settings *within* texts. Watkins discusses the settings *of* texts, in particular those of history and culture. Watkins distinguishes between old and new versions of history, a familiar enough distinction for students acquainted with literary theory. The older, more traditional form of literary history, whereby history remains ultimately separate from literature, is espoused by children's literature historians, such as John Rowe Townsend. The newer, less traditional form of literary history, whereby history and literature are intimately linked, is espoused by theorists, such as Michel Foucault, Raymond Williams, and Edward Said, and children's literature critics, such as Mitzi Myers, whose work on Maria Edgeworth Watkins cites. In the remainder of his essay, Watkins draws upon H. Aram Veeser's oft-cited introduction to *The New Historicism* for a discussion of the basic ideas of new historicism, of which Myers and Vallone are prime examples, and upon the work of H. Felperin, Lawrence Grossberg, Raymond Williams, and the University of Birmingham's Centre for Contemporary Cultural Studies for a discussion of how children's literature might be set not just in history but also culture.

In England, government regulations require beginning drivers—learners—to stick an "L-plate" on their car until they pass a stringent driving test: in terms of reading criticism, Lukens is for learners and Hunt is for those who have passed the test, in this case the children's literature criticism test, but who still want to know more! Reading Lukens on setting, students can learn how to shift gears between, say, setting that clarifies conflict and setting that illuminates character. Given that children's literature itself is being neither questioned or redefined, the ride will always be smooth, the test easily passed, and the road ahead an open highway. Reading Watkins on setting is another matter entirely. Watkins creates a critical map, as it were, full of signs absolutely necessary for a full understanding of how children's literature itself is a setting. His map shows how old literary history was replaced by new historicism, which itself then took two different paths, cultural poetics (in the United States) and cultural materialism (in the United Kingdom). He then also shows how "The same crises in the humanities which resulted in radical questioning of the nature of history and the emergence of . . . literary New Historicism . . . also brought forth cultural studies" (33). Watkins lays out in detail six basic arguments that underpin cultural studies and then concludes by citing Fred Inglis, Karin Lesnik-Oberstein, Jacqueline Rose, and Jack Zipes as examples of cultural studies oriented children's literature critics.

It's a long and winding critical road students, education majors or otherwise, must take if they want to be on the information highway: understanding the way children's literature is set in history is to understand the direction in which children's literature criticism is heading. While it is possible to understand, say, *Harry Potter and the Sorcerer's Stone* in terms of its various textual settings, to make sense of the book's social, economic, and religious impact requires an understanding of more than just the elements of children's literature: plot, character, setting, theme, tone, and point of view. Understanding the settings *inside* children's literature requires understanding the settings *outside* children's literature.

Understanding Children's Literature contains many informative and useful essays about the relation between literary theory and children's literature. There is Perry Nodelman on picture books, Michael Benton on reader-response theory, Lissa Paul on feminism, Christine Wilkie on intertextuality, Geoffrey Williams on reading and literacy, and Hugh Crago on bibliotherapy, for example. Of these, the work of Nodelman and Benton are particularly worth mentioning.

The differences between Lukens and Nodelman on picture books is the difference between black-and-white and color! Lukens points out, quite rightly, that picture books can be read, as it were, using the traditional elements of literature: character, plot, theme, point of view, and so forth. This assumes, of course, that the young reader has learnt the codes and conventions that allow him or her to read a picture book, precisely the assumption Nodelman critiques. Nodelman, in "Illustration and Picture Books," argues convincingly that young readers must have a "knowledge of pictorial conventions" (71) before they can read or see picture books. Indeed, Nodelman goes on to argue that picture books work "by surprisingly complex means, and communicate only within a network of conventions and assumptions, about visual and verbal representations and about the real objects they represent" (72). Nodelman's essay (and Robyn McCallum's "Very Advanced Texts: Metafictions and Experimental Works") was most useful as we looked at David Macauley's *Black and White,* a picture book that seems to defy the very category to which it appears to belong.

If this weren't interesting enough, Nodelman then situates the picture book in the contexts of film theory and psychoanalysis. In relation to the former, Nodelman draws attention to the way in which picture books and films, both of which contain text and images, imply "subject positions" (75), one for the reader and one for the viewer. By subject positions, Nodelman suggests that it is the text (literary or filmic) that creates the subject (reader or viewer) not the other way round. In relation to the latter, psychoanalysis, Nodelman is in fact talking about how some visual objects in picture books are "weightier" (77) than others. These objects demand more of the reader's attention than other visual objects. They resonate more deeply within our minds. Accordingly, picture books can be legitimately interpreted from the point of view of "Freudian or Jungian psychoanalytic theory" (78).

All the essays in *Understanding Children's Literature* are thoroughly researched. Part of what is useful about Nodelman's essay on picture books or Michael Benton's essay "Readers, Texts, Contexts: Reader Response Criticism" is that they provide contemporary examples of scholars working in the field. Benton provides a clear sense of how reader-response theory emerged in the post–World War II era in a section of his essay called "A Shift in Critical Perspective." Acknowledging that reader-response theory is "difficult to map because of its diversity" (82), Benton nonetheless shows how in the 1940s and 1950s "the reader was hidden from view" (83) and remained so until the 1970s when the work of such critics as Norman Holland, Stanley Fish, Jonathan Culler, and Wolfgang Iser (83) highlighted the reader's role in the construction of a text's meaning. Benton's essay gives a good sense not just of what reader-response theory does—it asks who the implied reader is and how actual children respond during the reading process (81)—but also the history of reader-response theory; neither of these are provided by Lukens.

Understanding Children's Literature addresses the important issues in children's literature criticism today—definition, history, and culture, for example—and does so in detail. For some students, reading this book might involve a journey into the proverbial heart of critical darkness. For others, it will shed important light on how far children's literature has come since the 1970s.

Dissertations of Note

Compiled by Rachel Fordyce

Bade, Faith Polk. "Emergent Readers and Access to Books: An Investigation into the Benefits of Checking out Books to Young Children." Ph.D. diss. Claremont Graduate University, 2000. 179 pp. DAI 61: 1271A.

Bade is concerned about literacy development among children who are just beginning to read, how to increase the time they spend with books, and how to improve their attitudes toward reading. She found that "the checkout process [at libraries] as well as choosing books provides young children with experiences that contribute to [their] motivation to develop into active, engaged or lifelong readers."

Bardsley, Doreen Olive. "Boys and Reading: What Reading Fiction Means to Sixth-Grade Boys." Ph.D. diss. Arizona State University, 1999. 211 pp. DAI 60: 653A.

Having asked what fiction reading means to middle school boys, Bardsley finds that students view reading as an important ingredient of their being students. Unfortunately, what she also finds is that "school district policies, teachers' preferences, grading practices and outside commitments" all limited and put constraints on students' ability to read what they wanted to read, as well as when and how much.

Bereska, Tami Marie. "The Construction of Masculinity in Young Adult Novels for Boys, 1940–1997." Ph.D. diss. University of Alberta, 1999. 175 pp. DAI 61: 1166A.

Bereska asks whether or not there is a "crisis in masculinity" in contemporary young adult literature, and determines that the structure of books for adolescent males has not changed in the past fifty years. Its components, "emotional expression, aggression, collectivity, adventure, athleticism, morality, hierarchy, and competition—as well as the conditions within which masculinity is realized (embodiment, heterosexuality, and No Sissy Stuff), are stable in the novels" from 1940 to 1997.

Brock-Servais, Rhonda. "Constructing Childhood through the Victorian Fairy Tale." Ph.D. diss. University of South Carolina, 1999. 197 pp. DAI 60: 2501A.

In a dissertation that deals with Christina Rossetti, Jean Ingelow, Lewis Carroll, Charlotte Brontë, and Charles Dickens, Brock-Servais takes issue with some of the "commonplaces" of Romantic literature in which childhood is seen as a "haven from the anxieties and appetites of adulthood." She believes that Victorians "only overtly" celebrated the potential freedoms of childhood in literature for adults. Her writers "all found ways of commenting on and sympathizing with the constraint of the impossible idealization of the child, and displaced the resulting complexities with the fairy realm."

Bunnell, Gloria Delores Currier. "Stylistic Analysis of the Contemporary Retold Folktale." Ph.D. diss. Mississippi State University, 1999. 115 pp. DAI 61: 114A.

Bunnell analyzes seven contemporary retellings of traditional folk tales in an effort to determine what stylistic and dictional choices authors make to create good literature. Her ultimate goal is "to guide teachers and others who share folk literature with children to identify quality folkloric material for use in the classroom and elsewhere."

Chance, Rosemary S. "A Portrait of Popularity: An Analysis of Characteristics of Novels from Young Adults' Choices for 1997." Ph.D. diss. Texas Woman's University, 1999. 209 pp. DAI 60: 3306A.

Children's Literature 30, ed. Elizabeth Lennox Keyser and Julie Pfeiffer (Yale University Press, © 2002 Hollins University).

Using Lukens's and Cline's *A Critical Handbook of Literature for Young Adults* as a
model for evaluating plot, character, setting, point of view, style, tone, and theme,
Chance asks, "What are the literary characteristics of young adult novels chosen
and read by young adults?" She finds that "becoming self-aware and responsible"
is the most common theme in young adult novels; that humor is present in more
than half of them; that most novels are "character-driven;" that the majority have
a serious tone; and that "the focus on character matches Carlsen's developmental
stages as outlined in *Books and the Teenage Reader,* 2d edition."

Churchill, Sue. "Taken Seriously: American Modernist Children's Poetry." Ph.D. diss.
Auburn University, 1999. 292 pp. DAI 60: 2490A.

Churchill examines the work that modernist and "crossover" writers Elizabeth
Madox Roberts, Vachel Lindsay, Carl Sandburg, Langston Hughes, Gertrude Stein,
and T. S. Eliot did for children "in the context of nineteenth- and twentieth-century
children's poetry and against the background of their writing for adults." Among
other things, she found that "Robert's traditional pastoral, Eliot's mock heroic, and
Stein's radical experimentation all reveal the modernist feminization of pastoral
song and masculinization of nonsense."

DeMarcus, Cynthia Lynn. "Reawakening Sleeping Beauty: Fairy-Tale Revision and the
Mid-Victorian Metaphysical Crisis." Ph.D. diss. Louisiana State University and Agri-
cultural and Mechanical College, 1999. 192 pp. DAI 61: 617A.

DeMarcus is concerned with "subversive social and political content in Victorian fairy tales" and looks at three revisions of *The Sleeping Beauty,* dating from the
early 1860s, "as pointed efforts to enter the intensified religious debate following
the publication of Charles Darwin's *Origin of the Species.*" Specifically she discusses
Great Expectations, Christina Rossetti's "Goblin Market," and George MacDonald's
"The Light Princess." She believes that the authors collectively argue that the fairy
tale "has become a false societal emblem of material advancement and domestic
security" and that they "indict Victorian society for smugness, superficiality, obses-
sion and delusion."

Dudley, Katherine Lynne. "Corporate Broadway: Disney and the Theatre of Reassurance." Ph.D. diss. University of Nebraska–Lincoln, 1999. 303 pp. DAI 60: 2741A.

Dudley looks at the Disney involvement with revitalizing Broadway, between
1994 and 1999, and focuses on productions of *Beauty and the Beast, Kind David, The
Lion King,* and *Elaborate Lives/Aida,* as well as on the renovation of the New Amsterdam Theatre. She believes that her investigation "provides a unique opportunity
to examine both the corporatization of the American commercial theatre and the
shared American cultural values the popular theatre reflects;" and she concentrates
on the critical reception of the Disney production, the "aesthetic choices/changes"
that the corporation may have effected, how cultural myths are portrayed, and corporate and marketing practices.

Dutro, Elizabeth Marie. "Reading Gender/Gendered Readers: Girls, Boys and Popular
Fiction." Ph.D. diss. University of Michigan, 2000. 304 pp. DAI 61: 534A.

Dutro notes that more than 500 million copies of popular series books have
been sold in this country since 1990 while she focuses on four of them: the American Girl series, Goosebumps, the Baby-Sitters Club, and the Christopher's sports
series. Her intent is to identify what visions of girlhood and boyhood the books
portray and to what extent the books influence children's understanding of these
portrayals.

Estridge, Patricia Gaskins. "Changing Attitudes and Behaviors Toward Reading Using
Children's Literature." Ph.D. diss. Union Institute, 2000. 153 pp. DAI 61: 918A.

Estridge observes that most adults in this country are aliterate in that they have
access to books, but they chose not to do serious reading; and this observation is
supported by evidence from a course in children's literature that she teaches for

adults. Sustained reading of children's literature, however, did increase a positive attitude toward reading, slightly, and her class did read more at the end of the class than when they began the class.

Granahan, Louise Margaret. "The Selection and Use of Multicultural Children's Literature." Ph.D. diss. University of Toronto, 1999. 275 pp. DAI 60: 3620A.

Granahan determines that three factors influence the selection of multicultural literature and how the literature is used. She finds that selection and rejection are affected "by content, illustrations, and familiarity with the book or author, while the illustrations played a major role in the rejection of literature." She also found that teachers generally use multicultural literature as an add-on in their classrooms.

Hock, Beverly Vaughn. "The Labyrinth of Story: Narrative as Creative Construction: A Participatory Study." Ed.D. diss. University of San Francisco, 1999. 259 pp. DAI 60: 2015A.

Hock looks at the literature of fifteen writers for children to determine "the effect of a defining story upon the lives of authors" and, consequently, their writing. The authors are Jack Zipes, Gianni Rodari, Betsy Hearne, Alan Dundes, Marina Warner, Carl Jung, Joseph Campbell, Alma Flor Ada, Lauren Artress, and Iona and Peter Opie. She also engaged in dialogue with Nancy Farmer, Thacher Hurd, John Langstaff, and Virginia Euwer Wolff. She found the latter were "intrigued by the connection" they found between a defining narrative and "their lifelong creative processes."

Hua, Ivy Lyn. "The Theme of Prejudice in Selected Plays from American Children's Theatre, 1956–1995." Ph.D. diss. New York University, 1999. 285 pp. DAI 60: 25A.

Hua explored the potential and ability of ten plays to enlighten children about hate crimes and the prejudices and stereotypes that often accompany them. The plays are *The Diary of Anne Frank, The Ice World, To Kill a Mockingbird, Steal Away Home, Circus Home, Three Girls and Clorox, Dragonwings, Jim Thorpe, All American,* and *Kimchi Kid, Mother Hicks.* She is most concerned with "the potential of drama and play production [to break] down prejudice and promoting tolerance," although her findings are inconclusive.

Hurley, Frances Kay. "In the Words of Girls: The Reading of Adolescent Romance Fiction." Ed.D. diss. Harvard University, 1999. 266 pp. DAI 60: 1946A.

Hurley bases her study on the Sweet Valley High series of romances for girls while testing Brown's and Gilligan's 1992 hypothesis that "adolescent psychological distress in white, middle-class culture in the United State [is associated with] adolescent aspiration toward and capitulation to an ideal of female perfection." She finds that most readers are influenced by, imitate, or emulate the character who is most "perfect," even if perfection appears to be passive, selfless, and thin. She also discusses the "carefully crafted marketing campaign" that makes the series so popular and so widely read.

Hurst, Linda Kay Whittington. "A Content Analysis of Reading and Writing Episodes in Selected Teacher Recommended Children's Tradebooks Compared to Commercially Successful Tradebooks." Ed.D. diss. Texas A&M University—Commerce, 1999. 192 pp. DAI 60: 3909A.

Using content analysis, Hurst "investigate[s] examples of literacy in children's trade books to identify characters engaged in episodes of reading and writing." Her work is based on the eleven books from the 1998 Teachers' Choice Awards, and sixteen of the trade books for children on the *Publishers Weekly* children's bestsellers list. Interestingly, she finds that "males were more often found performing literary actions than females" and that the acts themselves were in the text, not in pictures.

Jackson, David Harold. "Robert Louis Stevenson and the Romance of Boyhood." Ph.D. diss. Columbia University, 1981. 196 pp. DAI 42: 2685.

Jackson's premise is that Stevenson's four classic children's adventure books—

Treasure Island, The Black Arrow, Kidnapped, and *Catriona*—are "a four-part romance in which an immature hero quests, literally and metaphorically, towards a goal of bourgeois adult identity." He also argues that "the romance of boyhood" is "the essential paradigm" of Stevenson's fiction. He discusses "The Ebb-Tide" and "Weir of Hermiston" as "continuations of the hero of the adventure tales."

Johnson, Judith Ann. "Passive Perfection: Images of Women in Nineteenth Century English Art and Children's Book Illustration." Ph.D. diss. University of Minnesota, 1999. 201 pp. DAI 60: 1808A.

Johnson notes that women in Victorian art and children's book illustrations are "frequently depicted" as passive and submissive. She seeks reasons for this type of depiction and questions whether the illustrations represent reality. Her emphasis is on the Pre-Raphaelites and the illustrations of Kate Greenaway and Walter Crane. In fact, she finds that images of passivity and submission are "pervasive and remarkably similar;" that they probably are due to "the convergence of cultural norms" as much as to changing workplace attitudes, and the influence of Ruskin and William Morris who found women the "weaker other" within a "separate sphere."

Judd, JudithAnn T. "Intercultural Children's Literature: A Critical Analysis of Picture Books Published between 1983 and 1998." Ed.D. diss. University of San Francisco, 1999. 103 pp. DAI 60: 1551A.

Judd notes that most children's picture books fall into three categories: those that are "culturally specific, focusing on individual cultures;" those that "promote global understanding;" and those that illustrate cultures interacting, that are "intercultural." Of the 500 books she originally considered, because they were cited in reviews as being multicultural, only forty-four fit her criteria for promoting cultural understanding; only one dealt with conflict resolution.

Kaser, Sandra E. "Exploring Identity through Responses to Literature." Ph.D. diss. University of Arizona, 1999. 347 pp. DAI 60: 1019A.

Kaser concludes that it is evident that "the power of literature," particularly dramatic literature discussion, written response, and the analysis of visual images in writing, allows young people to develop or construct their own identity while exploring the identity of literary characters. She bases her study on a group of multiage fourth and fifth graders.

Kim, Keumhee. "The Portrayal of the Child in Korean Folk Stories Written in English for Children." Ph.D. diss. Texas A&M University, 1999. 108 pp. DAI 60: 1947A.

Kim's purpose in analyzing 206 child characters in 141 Korean folk stories, written in English and published both in Korea and the United States, "was to describe how the child characters are portrayed," particularly in terms of character, values, and pictorial images. She finds that illustrations of child characters are not authentic and most characters are portrayed as model, filial children in a traditional Korean setting.

Kim, Yun-Tae. "History of Children's Theatre in Korea: From the Beginning to the Present Time, 1920–1998." Ph.D. diss. New York University, 1999. 257 pp. DAI 60: 1835A.

Korean children's theatre has its origins in the early twentieth-century imports of Western culture and, particularly, in Protestant church drama based on Bible stories. Early Westernized plays were intended to enlighten children about this "new culture," to encourage nationalism, and to discourage Japanese colonization. Not until the 1950s did children's theatre turn from propaganda and colonial thinking. Professional playwrights emerged in the 1960s and "stagnated" in the 1970s with the inception of television. "Today commercial productions and educational ones are paralleled in children's theatre of Korea," and children's theatre reflects the social changes in Korea in the past eighty years.

Lee, Jennifer Serena. "Ethnic Identity Development and the Influence of Multicultural

Children's Literature." Ph.D. diss. University of California–Davis, 2000. 185 pp. DAI 61: 564B.

Lee studies 192 Asian American and European American children in fourth through seventh grades to determine the "effects of reading multicultural children's literature have on ethnic identity, personal self-esteem, collective self-esteem, and knowledge and attitudes about an ethnic group." The study produced moderately beneficial results, although "attitudes toward diversity and Chinese Americans [the subject of the study] did not change over time."

Lin, Yi-Chun. "Becoming Illustrious: A Study of Illustrated Chinese American Children's Literature Featuring Female Protagonists from 1963 to 1997." Ph.D. diss. University of Wisconsin–Madison, 1999. 222 pp. DAI 61: 480A.

The purpose of Lin's study "was to examine the gender-role ideology in illustrated Chinese American children's literature featuring female protagonists" and published in the United States. Since Confucianism "stresses a society with a gender-role division of labor," it is significant to note that the literature she studied changed a bit over time in that not all books "present a sexist view toward women." But the number of these books is few.

Lockhart, Andrea Fern. "Perceived Influence of a Disney Fairy Tale on Beliefs About Romantic Love and Marriage." Ph.D. diss. California School of Professional Psychology–Berkeley/Alameda, 2000. 218 pp. DAI 61: 1698B.

Lockhart worked with twenty-four men and women ages twenty-two to twenty-nine to determine the influence of the 1959 film *Cinderella* on their perceptions of romantic love and marriage. She found that all but two perceived that the messages in *Cinderella* "had had a profound impact on [their] beliefs and expectations of love relationships" and that the influence of Disney was "pervasive."

Magnanini, Suzanne Marie. "Between Fact and Fiction: The Representation of Monsters and Monstrous Births in the Fairy Tales of Gianfrancesco Straparola and Giambattista Basile." Ph.D. diss. University of Chicago, 2000. 234 pp. DAI 61: 1009A.

Noting that stories about the marvelous and monstrous "circulated in both scientific treatises and in . . . Italian fairy tales" between 1550 and 1650, Magnanini argues that "Straparola and Basile participated in a rewriting of the category of the monstrous with their fairy-tale depictions of monsters and monstrous births that blend literary conventions and scientific discourse." She bases her study on a reading of Straparola's *Le piacevoli notti* (1550–53) and Basile's *Lo cunto de li cunti* (1634–36).

McColskey, Mary Kathryn. "Spiritual Concepts in Children's 1994 Contemporary Realistic Fiction." Ph.D. diss. University of South Carolina, 1999. 257 pp. DAI 60: 2378A.

McColskey cites 1,179 instances of "spiritual belief in a power greater than self and a belief in an existence after death" that occur in 145 realistic books for children written in 1994. Some observations and conclusion include: "Female characters more often express beliefs and participate in acts involving spiritual concepts than male characters" and the "Jewish faith [is] discussed with more detail and passion than the Christian faith."

Mello, Robin Ann. "Narrating Gender: Children's Responses to Gender Roles Depicted in Orally Told Folk Tales and Other Traditional Stories." Ph.D. diss. Lesley College, 1999. 331 pp. DAI 60: 1947A.

Mello finds "that storytelling had a profound impact on students' perceptions of their own gender roles and that stories told aloud caused participants to build meaningful relationships to both the text and the teller." Boys had far less trouble identifying with the traditional folktale roles of "aggression, strength, and warrior status;" girls had trouble equating themselves with warrior heroines who contradict "the more socially acceptable roles of housekeeper and caretaker."

Mitchell, Deirdre Ruth. "Reading Character in the Caldecotts: Adult and Child Perceptions of Character Traits in Children's Picture Books." Ph.D. diss. Ohio University, 1999. 220 pp. DAI 60: 1500A.

Mitchell evaluates sixty-two Caldecott books "for character traits as perceived by adults and children," specifically, respect, compassion, justice, discipline, courage, loyalty, responsibility, and forgiveness. She finds child readers more visually oriented than adults and they "often perceived character trait instances which were bypassed by adults." She concludes that "character trait analysis of picture books is a flexible framework to assist children to discern and discuss perceived messages in texts and illustrations; it may also help adults to better understand how children construct meaning in books."

Mullen, Paul J. "The Grinch, Lorax, Yertle the Turtle and Others as Advocates in a Literature-Based Collaborative Group Approach to Social Skills Building in a Therapeutic Day School: A New Use for Seuss." Psy.D. diss. Chicago School of Professional Psychology, 1999. 89 pp. DAI 60: 1012B.

In a dissertation that relies on the techniques of "collaborative bibliotherapy," Mullen analyzes *Horton Hears a Who! How the Grinch Stole Christmas! Yertle the Turtle, The Sneetches, The Lorax,* and *The Butter Battle Book* to achieve an intervention that facilitates the development of social skills. He does not find that working with literary works, rather than those expressly designed to produce a social effect, is more beneficial or effective.

Nelson, Claudia B. "From Androgyne to Androgen? Ideals of Gender and the Gender of Ideals in Novels for Boys, 1857–1917." Ph.D. diss. Indiana University, 1989. 289 pp. DAI 51: 867A.

Nelson "examines the changes in the complex value systems offered to adolescent boys within the major categories of middle-class boys' fiction" such as school stories, adventure novels, historical tales, and fantasies. She documents an "increased tendency of authors to reject overtly 'feminine' behavior from about the 1880s" on, even though early "novels for boys typically seek to inculcate many of the same values and virtues as novels for girls." Eventually the Victorian admiration for the angelic feminine ideal gives way to Darwinian ideas that discourage the "effeminate" in favor of the manly.

O'Kelly, James B. "Children's Learning of Science through Literature." Ed.D. diss. Rutgers The State University of New Jersey–New Brunswick, 1999. 172 pp. DAI 60: 694A.

O'Kelly studied the effect of modern fantasy, fiction, and nonfiction picture books on sixty-one K–2 students to evaluate the amount of learning generated by the three different genre. He found that "nonfiction had its strongest impact on the learning of science when children have a relatively small fund of knowledge about a topic."

Olich, Jacqueline Marie. "Competing Ideologies and Children's Books: The Making of a Soviet Children's Literature, 1918–1935." Ph.D. diss. University of North Carolina at Chapel Hill, 2000. 380 pp. DAI 61: 1566A.

Ultimately Olich's dissertation "draws on children's literature to view how and why powerful actors attempted to establish cultural uniformity, how the process was contested, and how it failed." She shows that children's literature, after the 1917 revolution, was a ground highly contested by "pedagogues, political figures, bureaucrats, authors, and book illustrators" who disagreed widely about what "form a Soviet children's literature should assume."

O'Malley, Andrew Sean. "The Creation of the Modern Child Subject: Children's Literature, Pedagogy, Pediatrics, and the Politics of Class in Late Eighteenth-Century England." Ph.D. diss. University of Alberta, 1999. 250 pp. DAI 61: 1001A.

O'Malley asserts that the eighteenth-century middle class, the emerging bourgeoisie, "recognized that their bid to reform a corrupted and archaic social and class structure" rested on their ability to inculcate "their class ideology to the rising generation." "Countless stories depicting the various vices of the upper and lower classes, the proper uses of charity, and rational diversions were designed" to train children to become responsible adults; and tracts also taught parents and guardians how "to instill discipline [and] manage . . . physical and psychological health."

Onofrey, Karen Ann. "Laughing through Adolescent Literature: Middle School Students' Use of Humor as a Vehicle for Understanding." Ph.D. diss. University of Arizona, 1999. 297 pp. DAI 61: 116A.

This qualitative case study explores how middle school children use the humor in young adult literature "as a vehicle for understanding according to Louise Rosenblatt's transactional reading theory." Onofrey finds the children are wary of "superiority humor," where the targeted character is a victim, and slow to embrace humor that is "closely related to their world of understanding"—accepting it "only after careful deliberation." However, if "characters presented themselves as resilient and unaffected by the humor, then the students were willing to laugh at the characters."

Patterson, Deborah Elizabeth. "Identifying Theoretical Foundations for the Integration of Children's Literature and Mathematics: Two Case Studies." Ed.D. diss. University of Massachusetts–Amherst, 1999. 106 pp. DAI 60: 3889A.

Patterson notes that integrating literature into the study of mathematics is a "popular strategy" but she regrets that "an articulated theoretical grounding for this strategy [is] largely absent in current literature." Using two case studies, she explores the history and theory behind this teaching strategy.

Perini, Rebecca L. "Teacher Use of African-American Children's Literature." Ph.D. diss. University of Virginia, 1999. 244 pp. DAI 60: 3609A.

Perini's thesis is that "African American children's books have the potential to inform children," to raise consciousness and cultural issues, and to heighten perspectives "that largely have been ignored in the schools." Unfortunately, it is not clear that teachers use the literature in this manner. Her observations of three first-grade teachers' classrooms suggest that "teachers tended to ignore or interrupt discussions." In effect, their method created a "barrier." The dissertation has implications for teachers as well as publishers of children's literature.

Phillips, Lelia Louise. "Manners and Morals: Social Class and Morality in Children's Fiction, 1860–1910." Ph.D. diss. Vanderbilt University, 1998. 183 pp. DAI 59: 4437A.

Phillips explores "the ways in which British and American children's fiction uses social class as a way of promoting moral codes." She examined etiquette manuals to determine to what extent their standards are observed or criticized in children's fiction between 1860 and 1910. One chapter "analyzes the ways in which working-class characters are used to promote and sometimes critique the gentry ideal, as objects of charity, as good servants, and as ambivalent examples of working-class imperfections."

Raynard, Sophie Gabrielle. "Preciosity and Representations of the Feminine in Fairy Tales from Charles Perrault to Mme Leprince de Beaumont." Ph.D. diss. Columbia University, 1999. 619 pp. DAI 60: 1589A.

Raynard contends that female writers of fairy tales in the seventeenth century and first part of the eighteenth century, such as Mme d'Aulnoy, Mlle L'Héritier, Mlle Bernard, Mlle de La Force, Mme de Murat, Mme Durand, Mme d'Auneuil, Mme L'Evêque, Mlle de Lubert, Mme de Lintot, Mme de Villeneuve, Mme Leprince de Beaumont, and Mlle de Scudéry, "have their place alongside the canonical *précieux* authors." She believes that "they wrote from a 'feminocentric' point of view, which can be viewed as feminist, because they used the marvelous to emphasize, to an even greater degree than the [*précieux*] novel, feminine heroism."

Reddish, Barbara Smith. "A Postmodern Critique of the 'Little Red Riding Hood' Tale." Ed.D. diss. University of Massachusetts, 1999. 206 pp. DAI 60: 3940A.

Reddish believes that the Little Red Riding Hood tale "is a classic example of a stereotypically sexist depiction of the protagonist, whose traditional portrayal ranges from polite and naïve, to carnal and seductive." She divides the many tellings of the tale into traditional, modern, and postmodern categories to evaluate changes in the telling, both progressive and regressive. She is forced to conclude that "while little Red Riding Hood's outward appearance changes (clothing, landscape) sometimes dramatically . . . her inner personality characteristics with which we are familiar, the naïve/cute, unwavering politeness, and pleasant demeanor, often remain constant and serve to define her as the quintessential victim."

Rosa, Kathy Susanne. "Gendered Technologies: Gender in Electronic Children's Literature." Ed.D. diss. University of Houston, 1999. 90 pp. DAI 60: 1523A.

Rosa deals with the issue of gender imbalance and inequity in Electronic Children's Literature (ECL), explores its "negative effect on girls' self-esteem and role identify," and wonders if gender bias in schools and the literatures used there are responsible for the fact that girls are less likely "to pursue the fields of math, science, and technology." She believes that "the overall pattern of gender bias found in schools and curricular materials is also being perpetuated in ECL."

Sammond, Nicholas Stowell. "The Uses of Childhood: The Making of Walt Disney and the Generic American Child, 1930–1960." Ph.D. diss. University of California–San Diego, 1999. 609 pp. DAI 61: 17A.

Sammond compares professional and popular concepts about childhood in the mid-twentieth century as they relate to Walt Disney Productions, while he traces "significant shifts in social and cultural meanings assigned to childhood." He concludes with "a discussion of how arguments about child-rearing reveal the culture's working through of contradictions in its social and material relations, describing the child as a homunculus for future adult relations, the means by which American society may defer solutions for contemporary social and political problems from one generation to another."

Sarrocco, Clara Anna. "Phenomenological Influences in the Writings of C. S. Lewis." D.A. diss. St. John's University (New York), 2000. 193 pp. DAI 60: 4022A.

Sarrocco finds that C.S. Lewis's unfulfilled aspiration to teach philosophy led him to become a prolific writer, one who examined "lived experience." Thus his writing can be viewed as phenomenologically based; and it joins "him to a major twentieth-century European value-based philosophical movement."

Schacker-Mill, Jennifer. "National Dreams: Folktale Collections and the English Mass Reading Public, 1820–1860." Ph.D. diss. Indiana University, 1999. 235 pp. DAI 60: 3074A.

Schacker-Mill "addresses the intersection of folkloristics and popular publishing" as she examines the first English edition of the Grimms' fairy tales; *German Popular Stories,* edited by Edgar Taylor; T. Crofton Croker's *Fairy Legends and Traditions of the South of Ireland* ("and the complexities of represent[ing] . . . oral traditions on paper in a politically charged environment"); Edward W. Lane's *Arabian Nights;* and George W. Dasent's *Popular Tales from the Norse.* She believes that all five authors "discovered the tremendous imaginative appeal of folklore's scholarly processes and the rhetorical efficacy of traditional motifs, [that blurred] the boundaries between fantasy and science, the popular and the learned," thus establishing the "precedents for the entextualization, organization, and interpretation of fairy tales."

Searsmith, Kelly Lin. "Imaginary Forces: The Reformist Poetics of Victorian Fairyland." Ph.D. diss. University of Illinois at Urbana-Champaign, 1999. 253 pp. DAI 60: 4022A.

Searsmith "identifies the liberal, recursive mid-Victorian literary fairy tale as a specifically reformist institution, rather than . . . the subversive or reifying genre it is frequently claimed to be." She analyzes George MacDonald's theory concerning fairy tales and his *Phantastes,* as well as Charles Kingsley's *The Water-Babies,* Jean Ingelow's *Mopsa the Fairy,* and Lewis Carroll's *Alice's Adventures in Wonderland.*

Self, Rebecca Lynn. "Mickey and Minnie Aren't Married? Disney, Family Values and Corporate America." Ph.D. diss. University of Colorado at Boulder, 1999. 197 pp. DAI 60: 4237A.

Self explores "varied and contradictory responses to Disney" by using "qualitative field data [and] culturalist media studies" to determine how media, audience, and content interact. She asserts that "the controversies surrounding Disney today tell us more about large cultural fissures and preoccupations, about larger discourses or metanarratives (specifically about family and corporate power) than they do about the corporation itself, its practices or its products."

Silver, Anna Krugovoy. "Waisted Women: The Anorexic Logic of Victorian Literature." Ph.D. diss. Emory University, 1997. 207 pp. DAI 58:888A.

Silver "argues that Victorian literature employs the physical signs of the female body—hunger, appetite, fat and slenderness—to construct cultural ideals of womanhood and girlhood." She analyzes the poetry, prose, and novels of Charlotte Brontë, Christina Rossetti, Lewis Carroll, Kate Greenaway, John Ruskin, and Charles Dickson while exploring how anorexia nervosa "functions figuratively in Victorian literature."

Small, Mary DeMaris. "Elementary Teachers' Resources for Learning About, Reasons for Reading, and Responses to Children's Literature." Ph.D. diss. University of Minnesota, 2000. 201 pp. DAI 61: 117A.

The purpose of Small's dissertation is to evaluate elementary teachers' knowledge of and responses to children's literature; to find out what resources they use to teach children's literature; why they read children's literature; and their responses to "self-selected works." She discovered, among other things, that teachers rely on other teachers, libraries, and librarians for their knowledge of children's literature, and that teachers believe that an "aesthetic response [does] have a place in the classroom, but most teachers do not approach children's literature from an aesthetic stance."

Stallcup, Jacklyn Edna. "'What a Capital Place the World Would Be!': Child-Rearing Theories and Louisa May Alcott's Domestic Utopian Vision." Ph.D. diss. University of California–Riverside, 1999. 308 pp. DAI 61: 614A.

Stallcup believes that "through writing 'scientific' child-care manuals, men sought to control and direct the power exerted by women over children, while women produced texts for young adults and children which attempt to reestablish the domestic sphere as a utopian space ruled by powerful women." She believes this tension, exhibited in literature from the early nineteenth through the early twentieth centuries, is manifest in the novels of Louisa May Alcott, and "juxtaposing these manuals with Alcott's texts allows [Stallcup] to demonstrate how the body of the child becomes the site of struggles for control of the future."

Starkenburg, Edward L. "Social Class Depiction in Selected Award-Winning Children's Narrative Fiction." Ed.D. diss. University of Northern Iowa, 1999. 189 pp. DAI 60: 4352A.

Starkenburg analyzes *Mrs. Frisby and the Rats of NIMH; Ramona and Her Father; The Great Gilly Hopkins; Maniac Magee; The Giver; I, Juan de Pareja; The Sign of the Beaver; Sarah, Plain and Tall; Park's Quest;* and *Torado* through the lens of eleven social class concepts: "appearance, authority, capacity for making choices, career, housing, knowledge, language, social mobility, money, possessions, and status." His object is to heighten the "awareness of the depiction of social class in children's literature" and, more poignantly, its lack of depiction. He believes many authors are "silent . . . on the issue of social class."

Stevenson, Deborah Jane. "For All Our Children's Fate: Children's Literature and Contemporary Culture." Ph.D. diss. University of Chicago, 1999. 236 pp. DAI 60: 2023A.

Drawing on "research and practice in library science, education, history, sociology, and art," Stevenson looks at texts for children and, more significantly, "looks at us looking at . . . texts," while she examines "the basis of the establishment of children's literature criticism and situat[es] it in the larger cultural debate as well as in overall literary discourse." Works she studies include Jon Scieszka's *The Stinky Cheese Man and Other Fairly Stupid Tales*, Maurice Sendak's *Where the Wild Things Are*, and Beverly Cleary's first six Ramona stories.

Sundmark, Bjorn Nils Olof. "Alice in the Oral-Literary Continuum." Ph.D. diss. Lunds Universitet (Sweden), 1999. 224 pp. DAI 60: 0683C.

Sundmark's dissertation "points to the perpetual cross-breeding between oral and literary genres—in this case between the traditional folktale and the Victorian literary fairy tale—and discusses the nature of the oral-literary continuum, and what media transposition do to a story." He focuses his study on *Alice Under Ground, Alice in Wonderland, Through the Looking-Glass,* and *The Nursery Alice.*

Tedesco, Laureen Ann. "A Nostalgia for Home: Daring and Domesticity in Girl Scouting and Girls' Fiction, 1913–1933." Ph.D. diss. Texas A&M University, 1999. 182 pp. DAI 60: 3172A.

To define "the Girl Scout style of femininity" Tedesco combines "cultural studies and historicist methods, rhetorical analysis, and literary analysis of girls' fiction" from 1913 to 1933 "to gain an understanding of the cultural values that girl readers brought to the" Girl Scout manuals. The girls' fiction she uses as models include Alcott's *Eight Cousins,* Margaret Sidney's *Five Little Peppers* books, and Anna Chapin Ray's *Teddy* and *Sidney* sequences.

Tumanov, Larissa Jean Klein. "Between Literary Systems: Authors of Literature for Adults Write for Children." Ph.D. diss. University of Alberta, 1999. 222 pp. DAI 61: 978A.

Tumanov focuses on crossover writers Kornei Chukovskii, Mikhail Zoshchenko, Danill Kharms, Eugene Ionèsco, and Michel Tournier and likens them to nineteenth-and early-twentieth-century authors like George MacDonald, A. A. Milne, and Antoine de Saint-Exupéry, "whose turn to the field of children's literature has likewise resulted in the creation of ambivalent works."

Vey, Shauna. A. "Protecting Childhood: The Campaign to Bar Children from Performing Professionally in New York City, 1874–1919." Ph.D. diss, City University of New York, 1998. pp. DAI 59: 3292A

Vey discusses the history of children on the stage from ancient times until 1874 when attitudes toward child labor changed and when the Society for the Prevention of Cruelty to Children took a major role in trying to ban children from performing professionally. She argues "that class bias, fueled by the fear and distaste of the native-born Protestant elite for the immigrant population, contributed to the passage and continued enforcement of the anti-exhibition law." She also discusses conflicts in the goals of educating stage children—educational vs. vocational—and the ultimate "laissez-faire position of Actors Equity . . . toward stage children."

Also of Note

Acosta-Alzuru, Maria Carolina. "The American Girl Dolls: Constructing American Girlhood through Representation, Identity, and Consumption." Ph.D. diss. University of Georgia, 1999. 197 pp. DAI 60: 1377A.

Focusing on the Pleasant Company and the 48 million books for children and 4 million dolls it has sold, Acosta-Alzuru uses feminist cultural studies "to understand cultural artifacts as mass media."

Adams, Katherine Ann. "Publicizing Privacy: The Subject of Citizenship in American Life Writing, 1840–1870." Ph.D. diss. University of Wisconsin–Madison, 1999. 289 pp. DAI 61: 606A.

Among others, Adams looks at the lives and works of Bronson and Louisa May Alcott "to show how literary treatments of private life through identity function as critiques and contestations of prevailing political conditions."

Arend, Mary Kate. "The 'Full Bloom of Rosy Health': Fitness and Feminism in Nineteenth-Century American Fiction." Ph.D. diss. University of Illinois at Urbana-Champaign, 1999. 452 pp. DAI 60: 738A.

Arend challenges the notion that nineteenth-century literature, in general, promoted the idea of women as invalids, through the "Cult of True Women." Her research is widespread, across authors and genre, and one of her major areas of research is "post–Civil War children's literature."

Bade, Thomas Arthur. "From Boyhood to Maturity: The Hero's Journey." Ph.D. diss. Saybrook Institute, 1983. 258 pp. DAI 44: 3213B.

Based on Joseph Campbell's mythic theme of the hero's journey.

Barrow, Isabel Hansford. "The Reciprocal Nature of Children's Negotiation of Gender Roles and Literacy Acquisition: How Do Children Negotiate through Literacy Acquisition and How Does This Negotiation Impact Literacy Learning?" Ph.D. diss. University of Virginia, 1999. 226 pp. DAI 60: 1485A.

Bianchi, Lisa Lenz. "Finding a Voice: Poetry and Performance with First Graders." Ph.D. University of New Hampshire, 1999. 304 pp. DAI 60: 993A

Bianchi's research is based on a "study of a ten-week immersion unit in reading, writing, and performance of poetry."

Boufis, Christina M. "Where Womanhood and Childhood Meet: Female Adolescence in Victorian Fiction and Culture." Ph.D. diss. City University of New York, 1994. 255 pp. DAI 55: 3518A.

Boufis's dissertation "examines female adolescence—what the Victorians labeled girlhood—during the years 1830 through 1870 as a 'site of cultural contestation' in which there were many cultural and literary changes."

Boyd, Anne E. "From 'Scribblers' to Artists: The Emergence of Women Writers as Artists in America." Ph.D. diss. Purdue University, 1999. 304 pp. DAI 60: 4007A.

Boyd looks at the lives and work of the "first generation" of American women writers who tried to be recognized as professionals (among them Alcott) and concludes that "the American literary canon that was formed in the early twentieth century had no room for them."

Byrne, Elena Maria. "Effect of Food Messages in Children's Books on Preschool Children's Vegetable Acceptance." Ph.D. diss. University of Wisconsin–Madison, 2000. 143 pp. DAI 61: 788B.

While 73 percent of the books Byrne sampled contained food references, only 7 percent referred to vegetables. Despite aspirations, she found that "positive messages [about vegetables] did not measurably increase the proportion of children" who chose vegetables over snacks after they had read about healthy foods.

Cassar, Anna Maria. "Fairytales, Child Development and Psychotherapy: A Study Documenting Parents' Perspectives on the Use and Function of Fairytales with Children in Malta." Psy.D. diss. University of Hartford, 2000. 158 pp. DAI 61: 1108B.

Chesner, Geralyn A. "Invitations for Interpretation and Appreciation: How Five-Year-Olds Construct Meaning through Response to Picture Book Illustration and Design." Ph.D. diss. University of Wisconsin–Milwaukee, 2000. 239 pp. DAI 61: 863A.

Chesner studied "verbal, movement, dramatization, and expressive" modes in children's responses to book design, composition, and artwork. She determined that kindergarten children "have the ability to detect and discuss art and book design elements."

Conover, Robin St. John. "Growing Up in Glass Town: An Investigation of Charlotte Brontë's Individuation through Her Juvenilia." Ph.D. diss. University of Victoria, 1999. 254 pp. DAI 60: 2036A.

Conover is concerned with the Brontë's "psychic maturation, both as a writer and as a young woman."

Davidis, Maria M. "The Romance of Empire: Gender and Fantasies of Youth in Imperial Narratives, 1890–1930." Ph.D. diss. Princeton University, 1996. 224 pp. DAI 57: 1629A.

Davidis deals with the work of Joseph Conrad, E. M. Forster, and Virginia Woolf.

Davis, Brook Marie. "Constance D'Arcy Mackay: Playwright, Director, and Educator. Inspiring Women, Children, and Communities through Amateur Theatre." Ph.D. diss. University of Maryland College Park, 1999. 297 pp. DAI 60: 941A.

Davis's dissertation is a history and analysis of the "books, articles, plays and pageants" of the early-twentieth-century champion of amateur theatre and children's theatre, Constance D'Arcy Mackay.

DeLuzio, Crista Jean. "'New Girls for Old': Female Adolescence in American Scientific Thought, 1870–1930." Ph.D. diss. Brown University, 1999. 308 pp. DAI 60: 1631A.

DeLuzio focuses on the disciplines of medicine, psychology, education, and anthropology.

Diehl, David Christopher. "Emergent Literacy and Parent-Child Reading in Head Start Families: The Implementation and Evaluation of a Multigenerational Reading Program." Ph.D. diss. Cornell University, 2000. 338 pp. DAI 60: 6396B.

Diehl's dissertation analyzes "a multigenerational reading program," which he designed.

Dollard, Catherine Leota. "The Female Surplus: Constructing the Unmarried Woman in Imperial Germany, 1871–1914." Ph.D. diss. University of North Carolina at Chapel Hill, 2000. 329 pp. DAI 61: 1564A.

Fairy tales are among the literary formats that Dollard uses to determine "the plight of the single women," or old maids, and the Germanic literary "notion of a demographic crisis called the *Frauenuberschuss*."

Doty, Deborah E. "CD-ROM Storybooks and Reading Comprehension of Young Readers." Ph.D. diss. Ball State University, 1999. 85 pp. DAI 60: 2429A.

The purpose of Doty's study "was to determine if there was a difference in the level of reading comprehension of young readers [exposed to] an interactive CD-ROM story book" and a control group that was not. She concludes that the CD-ROM effect may be beneficial.

Eilers, Ulinda J. "A Content Analysis of Literature Written in South Midland Dialect; and a Study of the Knowledge, Attitudes, and Practices of Middle School Language Arts and Secondary English Teachers Related to Dialect in Literature and in the Classroom." Ed.D. diss. University of Northern Colorado, 1999. 516 pp. DAI 60: 2429A.

Eilers studied four young adult books, Twain's *The Adventures of Huckleberry Finn*, Forrest Carter's *The Education of Little Tree*, and Phyllis Reynolds' *Shiloh* and *Shiloh Season*, then analyzes the "knowledge, attitudes, and practices of educator's concerning literature written about sociocultural groups."

Fizzano, William J., Jr. "The Impact of Story Drama on the Reading Comprehension, Oral Language Complexity, and the Attitudes of Third Graders." Ed.D. diss. Rutgers The State University of New Jersey–New Brunswick, 1999. 159 pp. DAI 60: 3908A.

Fizzano found that story drama "significantly impacted the literacy achievement and attitudes of third graders" while they acted out and responded to various characters in folktales.

Fordham, Nancy Williams. "The Effect of Visiting Authors of Multicultural Literature on Elementary Teachers' Classroom Literature Choices." Ph.D. diss. University of Toledo, 1999. 239 pp. DAI 60: 2863A.

Fordham investigated the impact on classroom teachers' literary choices of a two-week institute focusing on multicultural literature. She found that the teachers were not significantly affected and that "the older the teacher, the less positive" the reaction.

Fromm, Katherine Barber. "Images of Women in Eighteenth-Century English Chapbooks, from Banal Bickering to Fragile Females." Ph.D. diss. Iowa State University, 2000. 620 pp. DAI 61: 731A.

Fromm notes that chapbooks in the early decades of the eighteenth century "retold traditional fairy tales and legends" which illustrate "a recurring strand of bickering and humorous exchanges between men and women." Later in that century chapbooks employ a theme of "fragile and dependent females" that is also reflected in early novels.

Ginsberg, Lesley Ellen. "The Romance of Dependency: Childhood and the Ideology of Love in American Literature, 1825–1970." Stanford University, 1998. 357 pp DAI 59: 2023A.

Ginsberg addresses the works of Poe, Hawthorne, Beecher Stowe, and Alcott.

Haegert, Sheila Ann. "How Does Love Grow? Attachment Processes in Older Adoptees and Foster Children as Illustrated by Fictional Stories." Ph.D. diss. University of Victoria, 1999. 269 pp. DAI 60: 1903A.

Haegert evaluates fictional works, based on her experience as a psychotherapist, and analyzes how literature can be constructed to teach attachment.

Han, Eunhae. "Vocabulary Learning from Storybooks: Effects of a Teacher's Reading Strategy on Korean Preschoolers with Different Prior Word Knowledge." Ed.D. diss. Boston University, 2000. 198 pp. DAI 61: 1284A.

Hatfield, Charles William. "Graphic Interventions: Form and Argument in Contemporary Comics." Ph.D. diss. University of Connecticut, 2000. 456 pp. DAI 61: 1386A.

Hatfield observes that by "mingling pictures and text, comic art represents a vast fund of examples that can illuminate the entire field of word and image studies." He focuses on the history and form of comics, "with emphasis on recent book-length narratives."

Hemenway, Elizabeth Jones. "Telling Stories: Russian Political Culture and Narratives of Revolution, 1917–1921." Ph.D. diss. University of North Carolina at Chapel Hill, 1999. 364 pp. DAI 60: 2639A.

Hemenway looks at how the story of the Russian Revolution is told and focuses on revolutionary *skazki*, or fairy tales, to demonstrate how "socialists rewrote Russian history as a story of oppression."

Hollander, Elizabeth. "Fiction's Likeness: Portraits in English and American Novels from *Frankenstein* to *Middlemarch*." Ph.D. diss. City University of New York, 1999. 231 pp. DAI 60: 3354A.

In chapter 4 of her dissertation Hollander looks at realism and iconography in the works of Louisa May Alcott.

Hult, Marte Hvam. "Framing a National Narrative: P. Chr. Asbjoornsen's *Norske Nuldeeventyr og Folkesagn*." Ph.D. diss. University of Minnesota, 1999. 229 pp. DAI 60: 2510A.

Hult's thesis is that "the modern Norwegian's difficulties in search for a unique Norwegian national identity can be linked to a literary canon which does not admit plurality." She believes that Asbjoornsen's work and, by extension, that of Jorgen Moe, merits "increased scholarly attention."

Ings, Katharine Nicholson. "Illegal Fictions: White Women Writers and the Miscegenated Imagination, 1859–1867." Ph.D. diss. Indiana University, 2000. 232 pp. DAI 61: 986A.

Among others, Ings looks at Louisa May Alcott and her treatment of interracial issues—in her work and her life.

Kirk, Elizabeth W. "Dictation and Dramatization of Children's Own Stories: The Effects of Frequency on Children's Writing Activity and Development of Children's Print Awareness." Ed.D. diss. Ball State University, 1999. 147 pp. DAI 60: 3897A.

For the most part Kirk's effects were positive.

Lewis, Janene Gabrielle Burnum. "'Coming to Terms with Identity': Social Commentary on Race, Gender, and Work in the Domestic Fiction of Louisa May Alcott and Jessie Redmon Fauset." Ph.D. diss. Texas Christian University, 1999. 219 pp. DAI 60: 2925A.

Lewis believes that Alcott's work promotes "equality between the sexes and among . . . races and classes."

Lin, Shu-Min. "The Effects of Creative Drama on Story Comprehension for Children in Taiwan." Ed.D. diss. Arizona State University, 1999. 174 pp. DAI 60: 3265A.

Lin demonstrates the value of repeated literature experiences and shows that "the creative drama strategy did enhance story comprehension."

Lunning, Nancy French. "Comic Books: Sex and Death at the Edge of Modernity." Ph.D. diss. University of Minnesota, 2000. 211 pp. DAI 60: 4225A.

Lunning asks what codes and conventions related to sex, death, and transcendence are evidenced in comic books, and how they "suggest identity in the superhero narrative in comic books," particularly regarding young males.

Marsh, Prudence. "The Role of Children's Literature in the Family Context: In-Depth Interviews with Parents." Ed.D. diss. University of Massachusetts, 1999. 233 pp. DAI 60: 1486A.

Marsh concludes that more study, focusing on children's experiences with literature in a family context, are necessary as are more interpretations of recent scholarship on the subject become available.

Mazow, Lauren Alyse. "Fantasy in the Service of Reality: An Ego Psychological Perspective on Fairy Tales and Child Development." Ph.D. diss. George Washington University, 2000. 212 pp. DAI 60: 6374B.

Mazow's dissertation in clinical psychology "investigated whether children respond differently to fairy tales than to more realistic stories." She found a number of different responses among children but, broadly speaking, "children responded to stories of both genres in individualized ways, suggesting that they adapted the fictional material to meet their own psychological needs."

McCoy, Patricia Ann. "The Beauties and Beasts of Nineteenth-Century French Fiction." Ph.D. diss. 1999. 254 pp. DAI 61: 629A.

McCoy studied major and minor nineteenth-century French fiction and "applied ethnographic research methodology to ascertain how the patriarchy reappropriated the Beauty and the Beast motif after the French Revolution as a tool of subversion and introspection."

McDonnell, Susan Marty. "Patterns of Change in Maternal/Child Discourse Behaviors across Repeated Storybook Reading." Ph.D. diss. University of Texas at Dallas, 2000. 126 pp. DAI 61: 1112B.

McDonnell applies a developmental psychology methodology to the reading of storybooks.

McEnery, Patricia Ann. "The Role of Context in Comprehension of Narrative Text in First Graders." Ph.D. diss. University of Houston, 1999. 180 pp. DAI 60: 2430A.

McEnery's study "examined the effect of context on the comprehension of first graders reading short narrative passages taken from authentic text."

Mitchell, Kathleen Ann. "The Problem of the Girl: Reading for a Transitional Age." Ph.D. diss. University of California–Los Angeles, 1999. 198 pp. DAI 60: 2270A.

Mitchell "proposes that books of enduring popularity share a set of themes or concepts" and she develops a "Girl's Special Books Model."

Nayar, Sunita. "'Santa in Fairy Tales? Let's Talk About It': From Talking About It, to Thinking About It, to Writing It." Ed.D. diss. University of Cincinnati, 1999. 136 pp. DAI 60: 3322A.

Nayar worked with hard-of-hearing and deaf children while they read and discussed fairy tales "in preparation for writing their own."

O'Day, Shannon Alicia. "Creative Drama as a Literacy Strategy: Teachers' Use of a Scaffold." Ph.D. diss. Georgia State University, 2000. 226 pp. DAI 61: 919A.

Offerle, Frank Anthony. "The Fairy Tale Operas of Richard Faith." D.A. diss. University of Northern Colorado, 1999. 266 pp. DAI 60: 2283A.

Offerle analyzes Faith's unpublished operas: "Sleeping Beauty," "The Little Match Girl," and "Beauty and the Beast."

Pache, Corinne Ondine. "Baby and Child Heroes in Ancient Greece." Ph.D. diss. Harvard University, 1999. 319 pp. DAI 60: 3996A.

Pache believes it is "possible to reconstruct both Greek attitudes toward child heroes and the rituals" surrounding them by exploring the anxieties of parents expressed in Greek narrative. She relies on "literary, iconographical, and archaeological evidence."

Phillips, Laurelle Bell. "Effect of Group Size on Two-Year-Old Children's Interactions during Story Time and Voluntary Reading during Freeplay." Ph.D. diss. University of Tennessee, 1999. 71 pp. DAI 61: 489A.

Phillips finds that children respond better to literature if they are read to in small groups or on a one-to-one basis; and that children should be permitted and encouraged to physical and verbally participate in the reading.

Putzi, Jennifer. "Identifying Marks: The Marked Body in Nineteenth-Century American Literature." Ph.D. diss. University of Nebraska–Lincoln, 2000. 309 pp. DAI 61: 1407A.

Among others, Putzi investigates Alcott regarding "the ideological work of race, gender, and genre."

Raczynski, Cheryl Ann. "Narrative Analysis of a Fairy Tale in Application to Relational Psychotherapy: A Critical Review." Psy.D. diss. United States International University, 2000. 198 pp. DAI 60: 5232B.

This dissertation in psychology examines *The Wizard of Oz, Alice in Wonderland, The Velveteen Rabbit,* and *Charlotte's Web* using the premise that "significant mythical narratives . . . articulate [the] social and psychological challenges" that confront people who seek psychotherapy.

Ranta, Judith Alice. "Women and Children of the Mills: An Annotated Guide to Nineteenth-Century American Textile Factory Literature." Ph.D. diss. City University of New York, 1999. 673 pp. DAI 60: 1135A.

Ranta's annotated list of texts includes short fiction, poetry, novels, drama, narratives, and children's literature.

Roberts, Catherine Elizabeth. "Telling 'Truth Truly': The Startling Self of Adolescent Girls in Nineteenth-Century New England Diaries." Ed.D. diss. Harvard University, 1999. 262 pp. DAI 60: 1944A.

Roberts looks at the youthful diaries of three girls from prosperous New England families, one of whom is Louisa May Alcott, and finds that "the diaries are rich, sustained texts which cover at least six years of adolescence." Moreover she demonstrates that all three adolescent girls "strove heartfully to become educated good women in the years between the American Revolution and the Civil War."

Rolz, Eckhard. "Genderless Childhood: Narrative Literature and the Case Study in Eighteenth-Century Germany." Ph.D. diss. University of North Carolina at Chapel Hill, 2000. 187 pp. DAI 61: 1429A.

Rolz discovers "a persistent picture of a childhood in which family constellations produce children who lack a fixed gender identity, a clear notion of sexuality, and find their identity in fantasy worlds" as he looks at autobiographical novels and case studies in eighteenth-century German literature.

Ryan, Susan M. "The Grammar of Good Intentions: Benevolence and Racial Identity in Antebellum American Literature." Ph.D. diss. University of North Carolina at Chapel Hill, 1999. 337 pp. DAI 60: 2495A.

Ryan finds that antebellum Americans "used the terms *benevolence* and *benevolent* with astonishing frequency" and, to demonstrate to what purpose, she "put canonical literary works (back) into dialogue with a variety of cultural materials, including charity society reports, African American newspapers, children's literature, and religious tracts."

Sili, Surya. "An Exploration of the Implementation of Literature-Based Instruction in Three Fourth-Grade Indonesian Classrooms: Promises and Challenges." Ph.D. diss. Ohio State University, 1999. 236 pp. DAI 60: 369A.

Sitz, Shirley Ann Ellis. "Children and Childhood in Hawthorne's Fiction." Ph.D. diss. University of North Texas, 1999. 194 pp. DAI 60: 3366A.

Sitz believes that "the child and childhood are keys to a better understanding of Hawthorne's fiction." She studies both his works about and for children. "In the children's works, Hawthorne uses authorial intrusion more, but he uses less ambiguity" although he uses "many of the same characterization devices, techniques and symbols in both genres."

Spadorcia, Stephanie Andrea. "Analyzing the Word-Level, Sentence-Level, and Passage-Level Demands in Easy Books of Interest to Adolescent Readers." Ph.D. diss. University of North Carolina at Chapel Hill, 2000. 103 pp. DAI 61: 1342A.

Sofer, Naomi Ziva. "Rites of Authorship: Gender and Religion in the American Literary Imagination." Ph.D. diss. Boston University, 2000. 398 pp. DAI 61: 991A.

Sofer looks at the works of Alcott, among others.

Suratinah. "An Exploration of Fourth- and Fifth-Grade Students' Learning Activities in Social Studies Using Children's Nonfiction Trade Books." Ph.D. diss. Ohio State University, 1999. 226 pp. DAI 60: 2808A.

Suratinah explores how teachers organize their instructional materials related to social sciences; what "learning activities students engage in;" and what students learned. He then shows the implication for instruction in the United States and Indonesia.

Sychterz, Teresa A. "The Voices of Children: First Graders' Responses to Selected Picturebooks of Maurice Sendak." Ph.D. diss. Pennsylvania State University, 1999. 215 pp. DAI 60: 2414A.

Sychterz believes that Sendak's works frame "the political question that children face daily—to be themselves or who they are expected to be."

Vactor, Vanita Marian. "A History of the Chicago Federal Theatre Project Negro Unit: 1935–1939." Ph.D. diss. New York University, 1999. 244 pp. DAI 60: 26A.

Significant to Vactor's study are "the theatrical activities accomplished by the African-American participants in the areas of playwriting, children's theatre, directing and choreography" within the Chicago Federal Theatre Project.

Williams, Jeffery Littleton. "Culture, Theory, and Graphic Fiction." Ph.D. diss. Texas Tech University, 1999. 239 pp. DAI 60: 1538A.

Each chapter of Williams' dissertation "focuses on a specific historical/cultural aspect of the [treatment of comics] and a contemporary literary theory."

Willner, Elizabeth Harden. "A Descriptive Study of Factors Related to Preservice Teachers' Written Responses to Children's Literature with Geometric Content." Ed.D. diss. Oklahoma State University, 1999. 117 pp. DAI 60: 3626A.

Willner uses "content analysis, t-tests, and regression analysis . . . to describe" teacher responses "and the relationship of the responses to the van Hiele Test and the Literary Response Questionnaire."

Contributors and Editors

RUTH B. BOTTIGHEIMER teaches in the Department of Comparative Literature at the State University of New York at Stony Brook. She has published *Fairy Tales and Society* (1986), *Grimms' Bad Girls and Bold Boys* (1987), *The Bible for Children* (1996), *Folklore and Gender* (1999), and is currently working on a study of the fairy tales of Giovanfrancesco Straparola.

KAREN COATS is an assistant professor of English at Illinois State University, where she teaches children's and adolescent literature. Her publications on children's literature have appeared in *Children's Literature, Children's Literature Association Quarterly, JPCS: Journal for the Psychoanalysis of Culture and Society, Pedagogy, Bookbird*, and *Paradoxa*.

R. H. W. DILLARD, editor-in-chief of *Children's Literature* and professor of English at Hollins University, is the longtime chair of the Hollins Creative Writing Program and is adviser to the director of the Hollins Graduate Program in Children's Literature. A novelist and poet, he is also the author of two critical monographs, *Horror Films* and *Understanding George Garrett*, as well as articles on Ellen Glasgow, Vladimir Nabokov, Federico Fellini, Robert Coover, Fred Chappell, and others.

ELLEN BUTLER DONOVAN is an associate professor at Middle Tennessee State University where she teaches courses in children's and adolescent literature. Her research centers on the ways in which texts allow or encourage reader participation.

CHRISTINE DOYLE is an associate professor of English at Central Connecticut State University, where she teaches children's literature, storytelling, American literature, and courses on women writers. She is the author of *Louisa May Alcott and Charlotte Brontë: Transatlantic Translations*.

CHRISTOPHER A. FAHY is an assistant professor of humanities and rhetoric at the College of General Studies, Boston University. He has published entries on "Domestic Life," "Religion," and "A Pair of Eyes" in *The Louisa May Alcott Encyclopedia* and an article entitled "Dark Mirrorings: The Influence of Fuller on Alcott's 'A Pair of Eyes'" in *ESQ*.

RICHARD FLYNN is professor of English at Georgia Southern University, specializing in children's literature and contemporary poetry. His work on childhood and postmodern poetry has appeared in James McGavran's *Literature and the Child* and in *African American Review*, and he is completing a book-length study titled "Postmodern Poetries, Postmodern Childhoods."

RACHEL FORDYCE recently retired as the vice chancellor for academic affairs at the University of Hawai'i, Hilo, and is former executive secretary of the Children's Literature Association. She is the author of five books — on late Renaissance literature, children's theater and creative dramatics, and Lewis Carroll. She is currently working on an anthology of early American children's literature.

MARAH GUBAR is a graduate student at Princeton University. She is currently completing a dissertation entitled "Collaborative Efforts: British Children's Fiction, 1860–1911." Her most recent publication, an essay about the *Anne of Green Gables* series, appeared in the January 2001 issue of *The Lion and the Unicorn*.

MICHAEL JOSEPH is a librarian at Rutgers University, where he also teaches graduate and undergraduate classes in children's literature. He is currently working on a book about the reflexive dynamic between nineteenth-century wood engraving and the emerging American picture book.

ELIZABETH LENNOX KEYSER is professor of English at Hollins University, where she teaches children's literature and American literature. She is the author of *Whispers in the Dark: The Fiction of Louisa May Alcott* (1993) and *Little Women: A Family Romance* (1999) as well as the editor of *The Portable Louisa May Alcott* (2000).

VALERIE KRIPS is an associate professor of English at the University of Pittsburgh, where she is director of the Children's Literature Program in the Faculty of Arts and Sciences. Her book, *The Presence of the Past: Memory, Heritage and Childhood in Postwar Britain*, was published by Garland in November 2000. She is currently writing a book on the representation of the Viking past in the Jorvik Museum in York, England, together with Richard Kemp, the museum's director.

MICHELLE H. MARTIN is an assistant professor of English at Clemson University in Clemson, South Carolina, where she teaches children's and young adult literature, women's studies, and laptop composition. She has published articles in *ChLAQ*, *The Lion and the Unicorn*, *The Five Owls*, and on CNN.com.

JAMES HOLT MCGAVRAN is professor of English at the University of North Carolina at Charlotte, where he is also serving as interim chair of the Department of Dance and Theatre. He has published two edited collections of essays, *Romanticism and Children's Literature in Nineteenth-Century England* (Georgia, 1991), and *Literature and the Child: Romantic Continuations, Postmodern Contestations* (Iowa, 1999). He has also published numerous critical essays in the fields of Romanticism and gender studies.

JULIE PFEIFFER is an assistant professor at Hollins University, where she teaches children's literature, British literature, and women's studies and coedits *Children's Literature*. She is currently writing on gender and girls' fiction.

ANNE K. PHILLIPS is an associate professor of English at Kansas State University. She is the coeditor, with Gregory Eiselein, of *The Louisa May Alcott Encyclopedia* (Greenwood, 2001) and the forthcoming Norton Critical Edition of *Little Women*. She is currently pursuing an interest in WW II-era American literature for children and young adults.

KLAUS PHILLIPS (Ph.D., University of Texas at Austin), who first read *Struwwelpeter*, *Max und Moritz*, and *Pinocchio* in German as he grew up in Munich, is professor of German and films at Hollins University, where he directs the graduate program in screenwriting and film studies. His principal research and teaching interests are German films, motion picture censorship, women in films, and children's films.

JACKIE E. STALLCUP is an assistant professor in the Department of English at California State University, Northridge, where she specializes in children's and adolescent literatures. She is currently working on a project exploring intersections of surveillance and power in children's texts.

MICHELLE PAGNI STEWART is an assistant professor of English at Mt. San Jacinto College, where she teaches courses in children's literature, Native American literature, fiction, and composition. She has published articles on Native American literature and Native American versions of Cinderella and has an article forthcoming from *MELUS* about ethnic children's literature.

C. ANITA TARR is an associate professor of English at Illinois State University. Her publications include essays on Esther Forbes, Scott O'Dell, Marjorie Kinnan Rawlings, James Barrie, Virginia Woolf, and children's poetry.

ERIC L. TRIBUNELLA is a doctoral student in English at the City University of New York Graduate School and University Center.

IAN WOJCIK-ANDREWS is professor of English at Eastern Michigan University where he teaches children's literature and literary theory. He has published articles in *Children's Literature* and *The Lion and the Unicorn* and presented papers at numerous national and international conferences. Book publications include *Margaret Drabble's Female Bildungsroman: Gender and Genre* (Lang, 1993) and, most recently, *Children's Films: History, Ideology, Poedagogy, and Theory* (Routledge, 2000).

Award Applications

The Children's Literature Association (ChLA) is a nonprofit organization devoted to promoting serious scholarship and high standards of criticism in children's literature. To encourage these goals, the Association offers various awards and fellowships annually.

ChLA Research Fellowships and Scholarships have a combined maximum fund of $1,000 per year, and individual awards may range from $250 to $1,000, based on the number and needs of the winning applicants. The fellowships are awarded for proposals dealing with criticism or original scholarship with the expectation that the undertaking will lead to publication and make a significant contribution to the field of children's literature in the area of scholarship or criticism. In honor of the achievement and dedication of Dr. Margaret P. Esmonde, proposals that deal with critical or original work in the areas of fantasy or science fiction for children or adolescents will be awarded the Margaret P. Esmonde Memorial Scholarship. Applications will be evaluated based upon the quality of the proposal and the potential of the project to enhance or advance children's literature studies. Funds may be used for—but are not restricted to—research-related expenses, such as travel to special collections or purchasing materials and supplies. The awards may not be used for obtaining advanced degrees, for researching or writing a thesis or dissertation, for textbook writing, or for pedagogical projects. Winners must either be members of the Children's Literature Association or join the association before they receive any funds. Winners should acknowledge ChLA in any publication resulting from the award.

The ChLA Beiter Scholarships were established to honor the memory of Dr. Hannah Beiter, a longtime supporter of student participation in the ChLA. The Beiter Scholarships have a combined maximum fund of $1,000 per year, and individual awards may range from $250 to $1,000, based on the number and the needs of the winning applicants. The scholarships are awarded for proposals of original scholarship with the expectation that the undertaking will lead to publication or a conference presentation and contribute to the field of children's literature criticism. Beiter Scholarship funds are not intended as income to assist in the completion of a graduate degree, but as support for research that may be related to the dissertation or master's thesis. The grant may be used to purchase supplies and materials (e.g., books, videos, equipment), as research support (photocopying, etc.), or to underwrite travel to special collections or libraries. Winners must either be members of the Children's Literature Association or join the association before they receive any funds. Winners should acknowledge ChLA in any publication resulting from the award.

The annual deadline for applying for either the Research Fellowship or the Beiter Scholarship is February 1. For further information and application guidelines, contact the Scholarship Chair (see address below).

In addition to fellowships and scholarships, ChLA recognizes outstanding works in children's literature annually through the following awards. The ChLA Article Award is presented for an article deemed the most noteworthy literary criticism article published in English on the topic of children's literature within a given year. The ChLA Book Award is presented for the most outstanding book of criticism, history, or scholarship in the field of children's literature in a given year.

The Phoenix Award is given to the author, or estate of the author, of a book for children published twenty years earlier that did not win a major award at the time of pub-

lication but that, from the perspective of time, is deemed worthy of special recognition
for its high literary quality.

The Carol Gay Award is presented for the best undergraduate paper written about
some aspect of children's literature. The annual deadline for applications is January 20.

For further information, or to send nominations for any of the awards, contact the
Children's Literature Association, P. O. Box 138, Battle Creek, MI 49016–0138, phone
616 965–8180; fax 616 965–3568; or by e-mail chla@mlc.lib.mi.us. This information is
also at our Web site, address www.childlitassn.org.

Order Form   Yale University Press
P.O. Box 209040, New Haven, CT 06520-9040
Phone orders 1-800-YUP-READ (U.S. and Canada)

Customers in the United States and Canada may photocopy this form and use it for ordering all volumes of **Children's Literature** available from Yale University Press. Individuals are asked to pay in advance. All payments must be made in U.S. dollars. We honor both MasterCard and VISA. Checks should be made payable to Yale University Press.

Prices given are 2002 list prices for the United States and are subject to change without notice. A shipping charge of $3.50 for the U.S. and $5.00 for Canada is to be added to each order, and Connecticut residents must pay a sales tax of 6 percent.

Qty.	Volume	Price	Total amount	Qty.	Volume	Price	Total amount
___	10 (cloth)	$45.00	___	___	23 (paper)	$19.00	___
___	11 (cloth)	$45.00	___	___	24 (cloth)	$45.00	___
___	12 (cloth)	$45.00	___	___	24 (paper)	$19.00	___
___	13 (cloth)	$45.00	___	___	25 (cloth)	$45.00	___
___	14 (cloth)	$45.00	___	___	25 (paper)	$19.00	___
___	15 (cloth)	$45.00	___	___	26 (cloth)	$45.00	___
___	15 (paper)	$19.00	___	___	26 (paper)	$19.00	___
___	16 (paper)	$19.00	___	___	27 (cloth)	$50.00	___
___	17 (cloth)	$45.00	___	___	27 (paper)	$18.00	___
___	17 (paper)	$19.00	___	___	28 (cloth)	$50.00	___
___	20 (cloth)	$50.00	___	___	28 (paper)	$18.00	___
___	21 (cloth)	$45.00	___	___	29 (cloth)	$49.00	___
___	22 (paper)	$19.00	___	___	29 (paper)	$19.00	___
___	23 (cloth)	$45.00	___	___	30 (cloth)	$45.00	___
			___	___	30 (paper)	$20.00	___

Payment of $_____is enclosed (including sales tax if applicable).

MasterCard no._____

4-digit bank no._____ Expiration date_____

VISA no._____ Expiration date_____

Signature_____

SHIP TO:_____

_____

_____

See the next page for ordering issues from Yale University Press, London. Volumes out of stock in New Haven may be available from the London office.

Volumes 1–7 of **Children's Literature** can be obtained directly from Susan Wandell, The Children's Literature Foundation, P.O. Box 94, Windham Center, Conn. 06280.

Order Form   Yale University Press, 23 Pond Street, Hampstead, London NW3
2PN, England

Customers in the United Kingdom, Europe, and the British Commonwealth may photocopy this form and use it for ordering all volumes of **Children's Literature** available from
Yale University Press. Individuals are asked to pay in advance. We honour Access, VISA,
and American Express accounts. Cheques should be made payable to Yale University
Press.

The prices given are 2002 list prices for the United Kingdom and are subject to change.
A post and packing charge of £1.95 is to be added to each order.

Qty.	Volume	Price	Total amount	Qty.	Volume	Price	Total amount
____	8 (cloth)	£40.00	_____	____	17 (paper)	£14.95	_____
____	8 (paper)	£14.95	_____	____	22 (paper)	£14.95	_____
____	9 (cloth)	£40.00	_____	____	23 (cloth)	£40.00	_____
____	9 (paper)	£14.95	_____	____	23 (paper)	£14.95	_____
____	10 (cloth)	£40.00	_____	____	24 (cloth)	£40.00	_____
____	11 (cloth)	£40.00	_____	____	24 (paper)	£14.95	_____
____	11 (paper)	£14.95	_____	____	25 (cloth)	£40.00	_____
____	12 (cloth)	£40.00	_____	____	25 (paper)	£14.95	_____
____	12 (paper)	£14.95	_____	____	26 (cloth)	£40.00	_____
____	13 (cloth)	£40.00	_____	____	26 (paper)	£14.95	_____
____	13 (paper)	£14.95	_____	____	27 (cloth)	£40.00	_____
____	14 (cloth)	£40.00	_____	____	27 (paper)	£14.95	_____
____	14 (paper)	£14.95	_____	____	28 (cloth)	£40.00	_____
____	15 (cloth)	£40.00	_____	____	28 (paper)	£14.95	_____
____	15 (paper)	£14.95	_____	____	29 (cloth)	£35.00	_____
____	16 (paper)	£14.95	_____	____	29 (paper)	£14.95	_____
____	17 (cloth)	£40.00	_____	____	30 (cloth)	£35.00	_____
				____	30 (paper)	£14.00	_____

Payment of £_____is enclosed.

Please debit my Access/VISA/American Express account no._____

Expiry date_____

Signature_____ Name_____

Address_____

See the previous page for ordering issues from Yale University Press, New Haven.

Volumes 1–7 of **Children's Literature** can be obtained directly from Susan Wandell, The
Children's Literature Foundation, Box 94, Windham Center, Conn. 06280.